"Please put down the gun, Miss Olwen," Stephen said.

To his surprise she lowered the rifle, leaned it against the wall.

He moved forward, took her by the arms and pulled her to him. She gasped and struggled, but he did not let her go. He brought his mouth down upon hers, and a volcanic urge possessed him; he started to force her backward against the wall. Then suddenly, snapping to his senses, he released her.

Doña's eyes gleamed with anger. "So," she said, her voice low, furious, "you have come to . . . take me."

"I have come to ask you to marry me."

Doña stared at him in disbelief. Marry the man she had vowed to hate? Never!

But before the new moon she would be his bride. . . .

TRAITOR IN MY ARMS

a novel by

Vivian Lord

FAWCETT GOLD MEDAL • NEW YORK

TRAITOR IN MY ARMS

© 1979 Vivian Lord
   All rights reserved

Published by Fawcett Gold Medal Books, a unit of CBS Publications, the Consumer Publishing Division of CBS Inc.

ISBN 0-449-14130-6

Printed in the United States of America

10 9 8 7 6 5 4 3 2 1

For
FRAN GLASGOW, with love;

For
LOUIS KNOX and YOLA

ACKNOWLEDGMENTS

I am particularly indebted to the authors of these fine books:

Fabulous Chicago by Emmett Dedmon (Random House, 1953)

Treasure Rooms of America's Mansions, Manors and Houses by Rita Reif (Coward-McCann, Inc., 1970)

Stagecoaching on El Camino Real by Charles Outland (Arthur H. Clark Co., 1973)

1

The Deer of Fire

Chapter One

When Stephen Raike first looked into her dark and burning eyes, she was pointing a Colt .44 at his heart.

Only those lustrous eyes were visible; the rest of her delicate face was covered by a shining handkerchief of brightest blue, a mocking note that matched her insolent stance.

Raike had been an instant late to draw: it had all happened swiftly—a shout somewhere ahead from the engine of the almost-empty train, then silence, and the woman's entry, soundless on soft-booted feet like an Indian's. Two men followed her, guns drawn.

Stephen Raike had handled guns too long not to know how heavily the weapon must weigh in her slender, gloved hands. He saw that she held the Colt in both hands, but did so with a kind of practiced ease that drew his unwilling admiration.

The woman was clad in dusty leather, as her companions were. But though the men's garb was a motley of dun buckskin and sweaty flannel, the woman's had a raffish elegance. She was dressed from head to foot in sooty black. Her vest and trousers had the dullish glow of calf.

Even to Raike, who was a lean six feet four, the woman appeared tall: his glance flicked over her body, perceiving its pride and grace, the slender softness which her heavy vest and shirt could not conceal, and which the fitted trousers emphasized. Her slender, sun-touched neck showed through the open collar of her black shirt. Under the shadow of a black slouch hat her dark and strangely hostile eyes stared straight into his slate-gray ones.

In seconds Raike's quick brain recorded this, while his darting wits, honed by years of riding shotgun on stages, gauged his present chance. Then his hard, astonished body burned with sudden heat; he felt the pounding of his blood. There was a challenge, which he swore to meet, in the woman's very stance. Raike stared coolly at the three dark barrels trained upon him.

The woman had not said a word. Suddenly she indicated, with the slightest motion of the Colt, the golden chain on Raike's waistcoat.

One of her companions barked in a rough, accented voice, "We don't have time. There is enough."

The woman ignored him, continuing to stare with that peculiar anger at the impassive, fine-boned face of Stephen Raike, with the nose arrogant, the mouth firm below a thick light-brown mustache. The slate-gray eyes met her stare head-on.

Finally the man with the rough voice growled to Raike, "Give the lady your watch." Something like a smile reached the woman's smoldering eyes. She extended one narrow, long-fingered hand.

"Go to hell." Stephen Raike sounded calmer than he felt; he was buoyed by a mighty anger. The watch had been his mother's gift to his father, Daniel Raike.

The other man hesitated and looked to the woman. His action seemed strange to Raike: could the woman be the leader?

The woman nodded and her companion leveled his Smith & Wesson.

"Don't be a fool," the man said to Raike. "Take off the watch and throw it to me."

Raike began to unfasten the watch and chain: he threw them then with stunning force straight at the face of the other man, who jerked with surprise. The Smith & Wesson in the robber's hand discharged itself into the air an inch from Raike's ear. Raike's skin stung with the hot impact and there was a sharp whistling in his head, but he had already leaped forward, tackling his assailant. The

9

man crashed to the floor of the car as the third bandit moved in, knocking Raike back on his haunches.

The woman, lithe as a puma, snatched up the watch and chain. Raike felt the explosion of a .44: there was a searing pain in his right arm.

Then, quickly as they had come, the three train-robbers were gone. Through the fog of his throbbing pain, Raike heard the nicker of expectant horses. He lunged for his fallen Colt, got to his feet, and aimed the gun through the half-open window. He fired in the failing light at the dim form of a mounted man: now there were two more. The woman and one of her companions mounted their horses with ease and galloped off, each hanging from only one stirrup hidden on the far sides of their mounts, Comanche-fashion.

Then they were gone, over a ragged rise, their horses' hoofdrums fading in the dusty emptiness of the Texas plain where the autumn dusk was falling.

Stephen Raike's head swam with a hundred angry questions, for the moment blotting out his urgent pain: how in the devil had they taken the Short Line by surprise like that? Where the hell were the others all this time? And worst of all, how could Stephen Raike be bested by two scruffy hired guns, and a woman?

A woman. Raike felt an overpowering weakness in his long, tough-sinewed legs. But he soon realized that it was not the thought of her—though that would be enough —that had brought on the wave of dizziness. It was the loss of his own blood, seeping through the broadcloth of his gray tailored coat.

Thrusting his gun back into its holster, Raike cursed, and clutched his right arm with his left hand. He could shoot with his left, but he'd be damned if he could bandage up a wound with it. What was the name of that shotgun in the cab? Luke. Luke Allen.

On unsteady feet, Raike lurched ahead toward the engine of the train. He could hear the low murmur of voices somewhere in the next car as he approached it.

A small, thin man with graying hair, dressed as Raike

himself was in the garments of the East, consoled a woman who might be his wife—a smartly attired woman whose hair was also gray. Even her face looked gray with fear, and she shrieked at the sight of Raike with his bleeding arm.

"It's all right," Stephen Raike told them quietly. "They're gone."

"But you're hurt!" the woman cried out, the plumes in her hat trembling, though the air of the carriage was still.

"Not much." Raike saw Luke Allen, then, staggering into the car with a strange and sheepish expression, his weathered hand rubbing his hatless head.

"How you doing, Mr. Raike?" Allen called out, his gaze fixed on the bleeding arm.

Raike nodded curtly in the direction of the frightened couple, and said, "In the cab."

Luke Allen turned and Raike followed him toward the engine. "Shut the door," Raike ordered curtly.

Allen complied. Once they were in the engine cab, the older man urged Raike, "Let me take a look at that."

With practiced hands, Luke Allen whipped off the gray broadcloth coat and rolled up Raike's shirt sleeve. Raike's firm mouth tightened, repressing an outcry of pain; his jaw muscles rippled with the clenching of his white, even teeth.

"Just a snakebite, after all," Raike said to Luke Allen in a taut voice.

"All the same—" Allen ripped at Raike's left shirt sleeve, and wound it tourniquet-fashion around the bleeding arm. "Won't be long now," Allen added, "till we get to Berwick Bay."

Another question flashed into Raike's mind: it was only a flesh wound, but she knew how to shoot. Why hadn't she finished him then?

But he put the question aside and asked Luke Allen, "What happened? How could they get the jump on us?"

The other's eyes held that strange expression Raike had noticed before. The look dropped, just for a split

11

second, but long enough for Stephen Raike to know that there was something very peculiar about it all.

"There were three of you in the cab," Raike said. "Two others in the caboose. What happened, Allen?".

Luke Allen shook his grizzled head and drawled, "Got the drop on us, Mr. Raike. They always operate like that."

"What do you mean, always?"

"This ain't the first time, won't be the last."

Raike, trying to ignore the throbbing of his wounded flesh, snapped, "A woman—and four men? Against an armed train? It won't wash, Luke. It makes no sense. They got the payload, I take it."

Allen nodded, an angry redness flooding his swarthy, pocked face. "They stopped you, too," he blurted. But then he seemed to want to bite back the impulsive words, for the red of his face deepened.

Raike fought down his anger and managed to say, with a dry, one-sided smile, "You've got me there, Luke. We'll talk about it again, at Berwick Bay. Right now—"

Relieved, Luke Allen said quickly, "You better take it easy now, Mr. Raike. Maybe you better sit down."

Raike nodded grimly. "See if those folks are all right." He motioned over his left shoulder.

"Right, Mr. Raike."

Back in his own car, Raike sank down with a sigh of relief on the dusty seat of maroon plush and lay his head against its prickly shoulder. His body tensed as he felt the starting chug of the train's engine, but he soon relaxed again.

As the Opelousas Short Line jounced toward Berwick Bay, Raike felt his eyelids grow leaden. He closed his eyes, thinking not about the stolen payload and the shifty eyes of his father's employee, Luke Allen. Instead, the image of the slender woman in black, with the bluebird handkerchief on her narrow face, appeared before him.

Stephen had been glad from the trip's start that there were so few travelers, and he had a car to himself; now more than ever it was welcome.

We have a score to settle, he reflected hazily. She needs

to be taught some manners. But first, before I tan her on her backside, I'll take back my father's watch.

The Raikes had owned their land above the bay for nearly forty years, a long time, by the reckoning of the raw, new Texas nation. Stephen's father, Daniel Raike, had arrived in December of 1821 with his young, high-born Southern wife, fifty wagons and a hundred slaves, as part of the "Old Three Hundred" of Stephen Fuller Austin's colony. By the terms of the law that governed the colony's establishment, each family who raised stock was to receive a square league of land, or more than four thousand acres. As the owner of many slaves, Daniel Raike received ten times that number and his rich plantation lands extended farther than a man could ride in two suns' rising and setting.

Owning so much land was the culmination of ruthless Daniel's long, fevered dream, and the end to his forebears' humiliation. Daniel Raike's antecedents had been English convicts shipped to the muddy jungles of the state of Georgia to work out the terms of their sentences. There Daniel Raike had been born in want and need, and there he also acquired a lifelong hatred of the copper-skinned Indians.

The old wars of the Choctaws and Chickasaws were done, and the Indians had become, for the most part, peaceable people. Some even wore white men's clothes, cultivating their own land and raising stock. But Daniel Raike could not forget the old people's stories of what the Indians had done long before—burning the white men's houses, stealing away their children, scalping their hated enemies.

Even after all those years, some of the Indians still carried red-painted scalps as souvenirs dangling from the waistbands of their loincloths, or from the belts of their trousers. And Daniel recoiled from them in fear, hating the peculiar scent of their coppery skin and greased hair.

Then something happened that confirmed all he had feared, igniting his undying hate. Late one night while all the family was asleep, Daniel heard a soft knocking

13

on the door of their rude wooden house. The knock was a light rap, such as a woman who had come to call might make.

Daniel got up and went to the door. His father, holding a musket, was already standing there. "Don't answer," his father said. "The Indians knock like that; it's a trick."

And, peering from the window, Daniel and his father saw three big Chickasaw men, by the light of the moon. The Indians were drunk, obviously, for they were standing on unsteady feet.

"That damned trader sold them whiskey," Daniel's father said. "They're up to mischief, you can bet."

The soft knock came again. In a moment they heard another sound: one of the Indians was beating with a stick on the wall of the house.

Daniel's father cursed. "Tryin' to scare your ma and the girls." Then he ordered Daniel, "Open the door."

"What?" The boy was dumbfounded.

"Do what I tell you. Open the door, then get out of the way."

Daniel obeyed, trembling with terror.

His father fired the musket through the half-open door, and Daniel heard the Indian fall. Then, amazed and thankful, Daniel heard one of the others cry out. Peeping through the window, Daniel saw the third Indian running away.

Daniel's father slammed the door. He, too, was shaking with fear and anger. "Red bastards!"

It was a long time before Daniel's frightened mother and sisters could be soothed enough to fall asleep. "Don't let them go outside in the morning, until I've had time to—"

Daniel shuddered, knowing his father was referring to the removal of the dead Indian's body. Finally the boy went back to bed, praying it was over.

But he was to awaken again, when it was nearly dawn, to the smell of burning wood. One of the Indians had set fire to the house. By the time they put out the fire, the whole house was gutted.

And to their surprise, the Indian they had thought dead had disappeared.

But Daniel Raike did not forget. His animosity was to spread to the Indians of Texas, his adopted land. His animosity for the Georgia Creeks and Cherokees was to extend to the Kiowas and Wacos, the Comanches and Tawakoni of the West.

Daniel Raike was hardly more than a child when he first heard from a traveling medicine man of the splendors farther west—the city of New Orleans and the burgeoning plantations of Mississippi and Louisiana, along the winding brown river where the steamboats from the north were beginning to nose out the river barges and canoes.

At the age of fifteen Daniel stole away. He took with him his father's small store of hard-won coins, a musket and some food. He had no affection for his family: they bore the marks of the hardship and servitude which he had resolved to put aside. He never saw them again, nor did he mourn his loss; it was often said of him later that he had been born without the need to love.

Daniel made his laborious way west, where the broad, treacherous river of swirling waters ran. In the years that followed, he kept himself alive in any way he could. Sometimes he found work, but discovered soon that the robbing of unwary travelers was the swiftest way to gain.

At last Daniel Raike had property enough to buy himself a berth on a Mississippi steamboat. He was only in his early twenties, but was already as tough and worldly-wise as any sharper traveling the snaking river's muddy path. He gambled, cheated and won.

He had just turned twenty-five when he first heard of Stephen Fuller Austin's projected colony in the vast area called Texas, to the west. Austin, pursuing his father's plan of establishing an Anglo-American settlement in the wide, western country, was even then negotiating with Governor Antonio de Martinez in San Antonio the final settlement of the plan.

Daniel Raike wondered how he would fit in with the high and mighty families who would be colonizing Texas: Kuykendall and Boatright, Gilliland and Bell, families

15

(they said) of property and spotless pasts. There was even a nobleman involved—the Baron de Bastrop, a friend of the Austin family.

But who am I, Daniel Raike asked himself bitterly? Stephen Austin might grant to those men of long probity many *sitios*—massive land grants of thousands of acres—but not to the unmarried son of felons, not to a man whose activities during the past years could not bear too close a scrutiny. Moreover, the settlers, according to the colony's laws, had to declare their affiliation with the Catholic faith. And Daniel Raike had no faith at all, except for his belief in his own ruthless effort.

Then, one fateful night in the city of New Orleans, the answer came, like a blinding flash, to Daniel Raike. On the first night of Mardi Gras as Raike was proceeding with his flashily dressed companions to one of the public balls, he caught sight of a frail and beautiful young woman, in a passing carriage. The pale, dark-eyed young woman, whose aspect was both proud and shy, was accompanied by a stern, older woman dressed in black.

When Daniel Raike exclaimed upon the young woman's beauty, one of his tipsy companions muttered, "Oh, don't bother lookin' at her. She's one of them high and mighty Gerards."

Raike did not reply, but continued staring after the departing carriage. In the days that followed, he made it his business to learn all he could about the "high and mighty Gerards." The name of the lovely girl was Louise Gerard, and she was betrothed to the son of the governor of Louisiana. A devout Roman Catholic, Louise went daily, Raike learned, to mass at the cathedral church.

Louise Gerard was, Raike decided, his passport to the Texas acres, to his dream of building an empire. Someday, he would be an *empresario,* as they said in the West, and men would take off their hats to Daniel Raike as he rode by.

Every day during the season of Lent, Daniel Raike, dressed in his quietest clothes, made it his business to appear in the church where Louise Gerard worshipped with her grim-faced aunt in attendance.

At last, when his patience was almost at an end, he caught the eye of Louise Gerard: she met his bold, slate-gray look with a brief stare of shy admiration. He lifted his costly hat and bowed. The frail girl lowered her eyes, then, and colored painfully at a sharp comment from the suspicious dragon at her side.

Thus it was that Daniel Raike, in his slow, relentless manner, finally made the acquaintance of Louise Gerard. One morning she appeared alone, and Raike persuaded her to accompany him to a nearby café. Terrified but thrilled at her own daring, Louise Gerard confessed to the lean, hard-muscled stranger that in the forty days of the Lenten season she had come to love him. Louise Gerard imagined Raike as a hero from a romantic novel. He reminded her, Louise told him, of the adventuresome men in the books of Mr. James Fenimore Cooper, whose novel *The Spy* had just been published. Daniel hardly paid attention; his mind was on the *sitios* granted to slave-owners in Texas.

Louise Gerard's romantic heart responded to Daniel's idea of elopement. It took some doing to evade her watchful aunt, but they managed it when the old woman was abed with a migraine headache and the other relatives at the opera. All the way to St. Louis, Daniel Raike avoided every stranger on the boat; he feared that Gerard would send someone after them. But no one appeared. They had covered their tracks with skill and were able to marry in St. Louis. In succeeding months Daniel acquired slaves and supplies for the journey West.

In December, 1821, Daniel and his bride entered the state of Texas. Except to impress Austin, they kept her maiden name quiet, for fear of discovery. But with the respectability of his married state, fifty wagons and a hundred slaves, Daniel was granted not one, but ten *sitios,* or 44,280 acres.

Louise soon learned that Daniel was not the lover of her dreams, but a man as rough as the land they settled. Used to bayou moisture, she withered in the dry, blazing air of Texas. Accustomed to mannerly, soft-tongued ways,

17

she withdrew into herself. Over the next ten years she bore in silent agony six stillborn children.

Finally in 1832, despite the warnings of the Raike physician, Louise Raike bore another child, a living son, only to die before the child had given its first protesting wail.

Primed with brandy, the bitter Daniel regarded the crying infant. This small weeping bundle, then, was all Louise had been able to give him, he reflected sourly.

"What will you name him, Master?" asked the slave woman who was to be the babe's wet nurse.

"I will name him Stephen Austin, for the Father of Texas," Raike replied.

For the first time in his life Daniel began to feel something akin to love—not for the infant in the black woman's arms, but for the broad acres of his Texas land; land his son would inherit in his very name.

Now at last, men raised their hats as he passed by, from the sombreros of the grandees to the battered felts of his field-hands, black and Mexican. There were no Indian workers on Raike lands; sometimes the peaceable Pueblos, skilled at farming, would hire themselves out to other ranchers. But Daniel Raike could not forget his ancient fear and hatred, his childhood terror of the red-skinned Creeks and Cherokees.

Someday they would all be driven out, reflected Daniel Raike, driven from the Texas that was his kingdom and his pride.

Indian raids were not the colonists' only concern. Stephen Austin Raike had almost reached young manhood before there was at last a measure of peace. Nearly every year was marked by another crisis in the turbulent expansion of the Texas nation-state.

The colonists had long been at odds with Mexico, which was trying to prohibit the further immigration of Anglo-Americans into the territory. In October, 1832, a month after Stephen's birth, Stephen Fuller Austin was named president of a constitutional convention called by the colonists.

Mexico's president, Santa Ana, frowned upon the colonists' act, for he saw in it the germ of rebellion and the birth of a republic. Unintimidated, the Texans held another convention the following spring; the spirit engendered there led to the Texas Revolution in 1835.

Stephen was little more than three years old and to his father's delight, learning to ride a small pony, when Stephen Fuller Austin was named head of the "Army of the People," and the cry arose, "On to San Antonio!"

Daniel Raike, feeling a wave of passionate patriotism that sprang from his possessive love of the land, fought in the Revolution, and in 1836 received an almost mortal wound at San Jacinto; a bone was removed from his leg, leaving him with a permanent limp, and scars that made his weather-toughened face as rough as buckskin and saddle-hard.

At San Jacinto, Daniel fought side by side with a steel-eyed young immigrant from Wales by the name of Hugh Olwen. The Welshman gained Raike's reluctant respect by declaring openly that he was fighting to gain land—for those who served a year under the Revolutionary forces would be granted more than a thousand acres of Texas soil.

Raike considered Olwen an ignorant fool: the man had no conception of the Indian problem, for instance. But if there was one passion Daniel Raike could understand, it was the passion for possessing land that seemed to ignite Hugh Olwen with a heat equal to Raike's own.

Daniel Raike had had enough of fighting; he did not serve with his fellow colonists in the Mexican War, which followed almost a decade later.

He watched the growth of his son as he watched the growth of his crops and cattle; one of Raike's proudest possessions was the boy. At first Daniel looked askance on Stephen's fine-boned looks, for along with Daniel Raike's arrogant features and fair coloring, the boy Stephen had inherited his mother's air of narrow delicacy. Daniel Raike was irritated by that air, and determined that his son would grow into a tough, strong man.

He need not have felt such uneasiness, for Stephen

Raike, by the time he reached sixteen, was tough as leather, burned by the raging sun, possessing a whipcord leanness. Stephen learned to ride bareback with casual ease, and already had the power to rope and break the wildest *milos* as the men called the most intractable cattle and horses.

There was one thing in which Stephen displeased his bitter father. Daniel Raike had accepted, as an inherited weakness, the boy's interest in his mother's books, but Stephen's attitude toward Indians was what really upset the elder Raike.

This conflict came to a head when young Stephen rode away one morning and still had not returned by late night. Daniel Raike questioned his foreman, Varden Williams.

The foreman laughed his easy laugh and replied, "Boy probably rode into Galveston. He's just about a man, you know, and maybe it's time—"

Daniel Raike smiled a little tightly; his own occasional visits to the port city for female company came to his mind. "Maybe so, Vard. Maybe so." But Raike suspected otherwise.

It was after midnight when Daniel Raike awoke to the sound of approaching hooves. Shaking his head to clear it of sleep, he got up and stumbled down the stairs. Before he reached the verandah, the front door parted and he encountered his dusty, sweating son.

"Where in hell were you?"

The boy stared back at him from slate-gray eyes so like his own; the two were almost level, for Stephen in the past year had shot up to nearly six feet in height.

"At the Comanche camp," Stephen replied in a challenging tone.

"What did you say?"

Coolly the boy repeated his statement.

Daniel Raike's hard-bitten face was flooded with a sudden, ugly red. "Why, you—you damned—" Fairly mad with rage, Daniel Raike whirled around and grabbed a bullwhip from a corner. He raised it and fetched his son a stinging blow across the face. Then he raised the whip and brought it down, again and again, on Stephen's back and shoulders.

"No son of mine," he said, taking deep, sobbing breaths, "will run wild with Indians. You damned young fool, they'll kill you the next time you go."

Stubbornly, Stephen Raike replied, "They will never kill me. They are my friends."

Daniel Raike stared for a long moment at his rebellious son. "Well, you won't be friends much longer," he retorted at last, his voice cold. "I'm getting you into the Point."

"The Point!"

"That's right, boy. West Point. It took some doing! If it's good enough for Captain Robert E. Lee, it's good enough for a Raike," Daniel said, mentioning the name of the hero of the Mexican War. "You need the discipline. It'll make a man out of you."

The day of Stephen's departure, Daniel Raike, with a tardy gesture of paternal feeling, placed in his son's hand the gold watch and chain he had worn since 1821. "Your mother gave me this; before you were born, she told me to give it to our son someday. I'm giving it to you now."

In miserable silence Stephen took the watch and left the room.

Stephen Raike learned nothing at the Point, for he never got there. He saw an advertisement in a California newspaper that someone had left behind on the riverboat. It read: *WANTED—Strong boys under 18—Expert riders—willing to risk death daily—Orphans preferred—$35 weekly. Wells Fargo Company.*

The wages seemed a fortune. He'd show Daniel Raike who was a man! Stephen applied and was accepted.

He set out from St. Joseph, Missouri, and crossed the desert and mountain country, passing the strange salt lake in Utah Territory, arriving after an endless time in Sacramento, California.

There he succumbed to the madness around him, and joined the trail to gold. In nine nightmare days, shooting it out with older men who tried to jump his claim,

21

Stephen panned forty thousand dollars' worth of gold. On the tenth day he buried the gold and lay down nearly dead with exhaustion.

He made it, but not before an attacking grizzly bear had almost torn his ear from his head. The ear hung like a loose button hangs from a shirt. A friendly trapper sewed the ear back on with cotton thread. Miraculously it grew right again, leaving only a thick scar. Stephen knew then that he would endure.

With the gold he bought his own stage line and rode shotgun beside his men. Finally he ended in Chicago, where his business genius was bringing him wealth akin to his father's.

Now, an older Stephen jerked awake as the Short Line stopped at the Berwick depot. His visit had begun.

Chapter Two

The moon was on the rise before Mrs. Idalou Mundey, who owned—with Mr. Hiram Mundey—the Baytown Inn, heard her coming back. Idalou sniffed; she just knew it was *her,* didn't have to look.

With consternation, Hiram Mundey heard his wife's particular sniff: it was a signal he had known for forty years, the sign that his helpmeet was about to spout forth her special venom.

And the beautiful young lady on the second floor—she was a lady, no matter what Idalou said—was the latest target of Mrs. Mundey's jealous wrath.

"Knew it was her, I did," said Idalou in her querulous, piercing voice, "comin' back like the Queen of Sheba after dark. I tell you, it ain't decent! I'd like you to tell me, Hiram Mundey, where that woman goes, all by herself, out ridin' in the moonlight. There's a man in it, you mark my word. A married man, if you ask me."

Hiram Mundey hadn't asked; he sighed. Indeed, it was never necessary to ask Idalou anything at all. She would volunteer her opinion quick enough.

But now, gathering his courage, Hiram retorted with as much severity as he dared, "Hush, Idalou! She's comin' in, and she'll hear you."

Mrs. Mundey, reflecting that their mysterious guest had always paid on time, and paid in gold, subsided. She busied herself at the desk of the Baytown Inn. Always knew when *she* was coming, Idalou Mundey thought sourly; that stable boy don't move so quick to take anybody else's horse. No, sir, but he moved like greased lightnin' for that woman's roan!

The subject of the Mundeys' discussion entered the lobby, dressed as always in her sweeping habit of purple cloth; the tight basque, open in front, revealed a crisp cambric pleated shirt of pale gray, and the fit of the jacket pointed up the tall young woman's incredibly narrow waist. The sleeves were plaited snugly on the upper arms, and belled at the elbow into a slight, graceful fullness; were plaited again back from the wrists over the cuffs of her cambric shirt. The cuffs, above her gray-gloved hands, matched her collar, which *Godey's Lady's Book* called "Charles the Fifth"; Mrs. Idalou Mundey seethed with envy every time she beheld the ensemble.

On the young woman's glossy, flame-colored hair, smooth at the ears and abundant in back, perched the chapeau that further ignited Mrs. Mundey's covetous ire —a rakish straw, shaped like a small fedora, of lavender-gray, with lilac ribbons cascading behind.

The young woman moved like a queen, with an easy, upright posture and soundless, fluid motion. Just like a redskin, thought Idalou. For most women of fashion, at least those Idalou Mundey had seen in pictures, were much fairer of face. And this young hussy was almost as coppery as a Comanche.

Hiram Mundey's wizened face took on a foolish look —like a dying calf, Idalou decided—as he said ingratiatingly, "Good evenin', miss. You had a nice long ride today."

Idalou sniffed loudly; she could just *kill* Hiram when he simpered like that! Nevertheless, Mrs. Mundey managed a stingy smile for the prompt-paying guest, who had replied to Mr. Mundey's pleasantry by smiling. Her wide, childlike smile lit up her high-boned, austere face; the teeth were dazzling white, of perfect evenness.

But there was in the young woman's dark eyes always a veiled look—the look that so infuriated Idalou and enchanted Hiram Mundey.

Without a word, the willowy young woman extended

her gloved hand, and Hiram Mundey placed on her palm the key to her room on the second floor.

Both the Mundeys watched, fascinated, as the guest ascended the rather creaky stairs, her fiery hair, an abundant glory, gathered into neat and shining loops under the brim of her riding hat.

When she heard the upper door shut, Idalou Mundey exploded, "Well!"

Hiram turned away, embarrassed, to shuffle the papers on the desk.

"Hiram Mundey," said Idalou, "you didn't ask her!"

"Ask her what, Idalou?"

Exasperated, Mrs. Mundey mocked, "Ask her *what?* Ask her *what?* You know right well what, you foolish old turkey-cock! Ask her how long she aims to take up that *room,* that's what, and you *know* it. You *promised!*"

"What difference does it make?" Hiram asked defensively. "We don't need the room. She pays her board right prompt, she don't make no racket. She don't entertain no gentlemen! Why *should* I ask her? Listen here, Idalou, her money's been a good thing. Now that you got to admit."

"Maybe so." Idalou Mundey stared up at the white, closed door, as if it could tell her the secret of the strange young woman. "But I don't like it, all the same. I don't like it at all. You know right well we're an inn, not a—a summer resort like them places up East, where the rich folks come to spend the summer."

"She ain't been here that long."

"Two months ain't long? What does she *want* here, way out here between Galveston and nowhere? Where does she go on that roan, leavin' early in the morning, comin' back at nightfall without a speck o' dust on her? It ain't *natural,* I say. If you don't ask her tomorrow, I will."

Maybe, Hiram Mundey thought, she suffered a disappointment in love, like that Cathy in *Wuthering Heights.* Mr. Mundey had been fascinated with the Brontë novel, left behind by an Eastern traveler.

"All right, honey, whatever you say." Hiram said

aloud. He was quick to back down for the sake of peace. He'd read the book again just last night; when that Cathy went to see her rich friends, he bet she wore an outfit just like the upstairs lady's. Except that Cathy never had such wonderful red hair as the woman in the purple gown.

But still Hiram kept thinking of how that stable boy in the book kept calling her "My wild, sweet Cathy." And that was the thing most like the lady upstairs, with her big, sad, dark eyes.

No, the red-haired woman thought, this place is certainly not the Winedale Inn! She had once visited the famous inn near Round Top, a relay station for passengers on the line from San Antonio. But the Baytown Inn imitated, as well as it could, the trim, two-storied spaciousness of the Winedale, with its cropped lawn, its picket fence and great shade trees that reminded more than one wayfarer of New England.

The woman with the fiery hair took out two hatpins and tossed the hat on the bureau. She sighed with relief and exhaustion, throwing herself full-length on the white-covered bed, carelessly creasing the purple habit. Soon she must take off her boots: her eyelids closed, feeling heavy.

And soon she would have to leave the inn, she thought. They were getting suspicious—just as Tahre warned her they would. But for a time it had to be this way—the way her mother had wanted it. In the very giving of her name, the name that meant "Lady of a Great House," her mother had declared these things for her.

Yes, she had had to buy the purple dress, the hat, brush her hair shining; lie in a soft bed, these weeks, instead of on the strong-smelling bed of buffalo hide. Had to, the woman repeated silently, to rest from the dust and the anger, the fear of the hard-riding days in the blazing sun and sometimes, the hot dark.

The woman rose from the bed and began to undress, hanging the pretty garments with care in the scarred chifforobe against the wall. She sat down then in her undergarments on the edge of the white bed and un-buttoned the small gray boots, exhaling with pleasure as her feet were released from their confinement.

She padded on her stockinged feet to the dresser and poured water into the basin to wash herself. This done, she unpinned her hair; it fell almost to her knees, vivid, shimmering, as if she were wearing a shawl of fire. Taking up her worn hairbrush, the woman began to brush its luxuriant waves with crackling strokes.

How tired her arms were—aching with tension, sore from the weight of the gun. She studied herself in the glass: all at once a mischievous, childlike smile creased her tawny face.

With renewed vitality, she hurried to the chifforobe and took from it the little reticule that she had hung on a hook. She opened it and took out a heavy golden watch and chain. Sitting on the bed again, she opened the back of the watch; engraved inside were the words in flowing script: "From L.G.R. to her beloved D.R., June, 1821." The red-haired woman's grin widened. Here was a souvenir, indeed!

Laughing softly, she shut the watch and fastened the other end of its chain, slipping it over her head; the satiny weight of gold felt rich and warm between her breasts.

As she reached for her nightgown, she heard the un-expected sound—a wild waving of tree-branches beside the upper verandah, just outside her window. She leaped to her feet: there was no wind, it was a still, calm night. What could it be? Her heart thudded. She was transfixed, listening again for the peculiar sound through the half-open window.

"Isse!" she heard then. "Isse-Loa!"

Tahre. By all the gods of wind and water, it was Tahre, in that very tree, whispering out her Indian name, the name he always called her. Isse-Loa, for Fire-Deer.

Oh, ye gods! she thought, in panic. What if Hiram Mundey heard, or worse, Mrs. Mundey?

She hurried to the window and leaned on the sill. "Tahre!" she cried in an urgent whisper. "Come in, quickly. Quickly!"

Silently, a lean red man stepped from the tree onto the verandah; his buckskin moccasins made his movements soundless as a cat's. He climbed into the window, grinning.

The red-haired woman, who had hastily donned a full white wrapper, stood glaring by the chifforobe.

"What do you mean by this madness?" she demanded in a trembling whisper. "You know you will be shot if they find you here."

But it was impossible to keep affection out of her voice as she looked at the tall young man with the noble face, her childhood companion.

Tahre's grin widened. He stood before her in mock-sheepishness, lean and comely in his fringed buckskin shirt and trousers. He wore his straight black hair in two long, leather-wound plaits that depended over his chest, and the laughing look relieved his coppery face of its accustomed severity. When Tahre was unsmiling, his face struck fear into the heart, with its beaklike nose, its full lips compressed into an angry line, the black eyes gleaming over his prominent cheekbones.

"It is a good joke," he said, still smiling. He spoke now in the tongue of the Comanches. *"Wahkane,* isn't it?"

"A good joke, I must say," the woman retorted in English, "if the Mundeys catch you."

Tahre laughed softly, and squatted down on the faded carpet. "The old squaw is more of a brave than he is."

The woman could not help laughing at Tahre's incorrigible, mocking humor.

"What are you doing here?" she demanded in a sterner voice.

The flat black eyes of Tahre glinted: he had seen the gold watch-chain around her neck. He shook his head, and the long braids bobbed. "Isse," he said softly in his hoarse, rough whisper. "Isse-Loa, Deer of Fire. Hishshe-Loa, Fire-Hair."

"Why have you come?" she repeated.

"You should not have taken the watch," he said, ignoring her question. "I have told you before; I have told you that word came from our Shoshoni cousins to the north that he is a man not to be ridiculed. He spoke to my cousin in the Shoshoni tongue when he was riding to the great West, many years ago, when he was but a boy. We were lucky to get away alive; I tell you he is not to be mocked. And you have mocked him by taking the watch."

The beautiful young woman's face grew cold and hard, and her soft mouth tightened. "He is the son of a murderer," she retorted, "and I will wear this golden scalp with pride."

"You will have us all hanged," he countered, "if you wear it in the streets of Galveston." She was silent. "Isse," he said in a gentler way, "my Isse-Loa. Come back to the village tomorrow. Give this up. We will die if we do not cease this way. *Il-let min-te,* death is coming."

"You are free to do as you please," she said. Her voice had the crack of a small leather whip, and Tahre winced as if she had struck him. She stood up then, tall and proud, looking down at the handsome Comanche squatting at her feet.

He rose, too, towering above her. The easy smile was gone, and again he wore the face that so many men had learned to fear: his flat eyes glittered with anger and wounded pride. His full mouth was drawn down at the corners.

"Do you think, my Fire-Deer, I would leave you alone in this enterprise? With only those white scoundrels to guard you?"

The woman saw that she had gone too far. "I beg your pardon, Tahre," she whispered meekly. "But I will not come back to the village. I am going to the house tomorrow."

"The house? The house of your father?"

She nodded. "The time has come. I have the money now to hire workmen to rebuild it. I want to reclaim my parents' house. That is what I have been working for."

Tahre shook his head and sighed. "I fear this will lead to trouble."

"I must, Tahre, my dear cousin. You know I must." He stared at her an instant, then nodded with resignation.

"And you," she added, "must go. Please, oh, please be careful."

He grinned at her, his good humor restored. "I came like the wind in the leaves; I will go like the cat of the mountain, on feet so silent that the great brave, Mrs. Mundey, will never know."

And with that he climbed delicately through the window, his footfall imperceptible upon the verandah. Only someone with Comanche blood, the woman thought, would realize that the rustling on the grass, coming a moment later, was not a startled rabbit, but an Indian passing.

The woman with the flaming hair lay down to sleep, feeling the weight of the heavy gold between her breasts, and smiling. What a warmth it had!

As warm as the sweet hatred that had sustained her these five years, years in which she had grown to nineteen, the age of a woman. Yet something gnawed at her triumph: she could not forget the slate-gray eyes of the tall man, the son of the murderer. There was something in his strength and leanness, a shadow on his face, that reminded her oddly of Tahre, and her father.

In the sultry air she shivered; the familiar hatred did not warm her limbs somehow as it had in the past.

Varden Williams, foreman to Daniel Raike, studied the strapping young man riding beside him in the smart new trap.

Stephen, who was driving, inhaled with sensuous pleasure the fresh night air of the plain. The boy was sure no dude, Varden Williams judged, even in them fancy clothes.

"Steve, boy," Vard said, and Stephen started: he had evidently lost himself in his own thoughts.

"Well, boy," Vard said uneasiy, for the tall young stranger beside him was so self-possessed and grim that Vard could hardly believe he was only twenty-five. Vard Williams felt obscurely intimidated at the side of this new Stephen Raike. Nevertheless, he went on, "Doc Fitch was mighty glad to see you." The older man chuckled. "I reckon he's patched you up a hundred times since you got that pony."

For the first time since their meeting at the depot, Stephen Raike seemed to relax. He smiled broadly, and Vard could see again a trace of the boy he had known.

"How's the wing?" Vard Williams inquired.

"Fine, Vard. It's not much. What ails my father?"

The white-haired man at Raike's side studied his companion with keen blue eyes. Bound and determined, he thought, not to talk about the thing that happened on the train! "Well," Vard drawled in a considering way, "he's just wore out, if you want my opinion. But as Doc told you, your father had a mild stroke. That's why he wrote and asked you to come home."

"He's not that old."

"Old's not it, Steve. Your pa's lived hard. And now this fight with Pease's men—it'll sure do him a power of good if Runnels gets in. And I reckon he will. Pease was all hellfire against the slaves, you know."

Stephen nodded. He had read of Texas' coming gubernatorial election; the present governor Pease was an ardent Unionist. The Democratic party and Runnels, it was judged, would look with less disfavor on the owning of slaves. And Daniel Raike now owned nearly two hundred.

"But he'll be mighty glad to see you, boy."

Stephen Raike made a skeptical sound.

"No, I swear to God, he's changed, Steve, changed a lot in these last nine years. Ever since the Olwen—"

Vard Williams stopped abruptly.

"The Olwen what? What about the Olwens?" Stephen asked. He remembered vaguely their distant neighbor, Hugh Olwen, who had fought with his father at San Jacinto. Olwen, a Welshman from the East, had earned his thousand acres fighting for the Revolution, won the respect of his neighbors through his industry and determination.

Then, Stephen recalled, the man had scandalized the country by marrying a Comanche woman. And there had been a child. A boy, or girl? Stephen could not remember; somewhere in the back of his mind there was the dim picture of a small child dressed in a fringed shirt and buckskin trousers, playing with Indian children. It was all so long ago. Just a kid with sandy hair, whom he had seen once in passing.

"Oh, well," Vard Williams said uncomfortably, "I guess you wouldn't know about that. Happened about five years ago."

Eager to change the subject—a fact that did not escape the sharp ear of Stephen Raike—Vard blurted, "What'll we tell your pa about the payload?"

"Nothing."

"Nothing?" Vard stared at the younger man in amazement. "How can we keep it from him?"

"Leave it to me. He's laid up; I'll see he gets the news only from you and me."

"But why in the name of Tophet do you want to keep it still? Sweet Jesus, boy, what do you think you're doin'?"

Stephen Raike smiled grimly. "Leave it to me," he repeated. "I think there's a little more here than an ordinary robbery, and I want to find out what it is. Dad still do business with the McKinney & Williams Bank in Galveston?"

Puzzled, Vard answered, "Sure. Two others now, besides. Your pa's a rich man now, Steve. Ever since the tracks were laid, across the Olwen—" Vard stopped abruptly. In haste, he said, "Yeah. Mills, too, and Ball-Hutchings."

There it is again, thought Stephen. The Olwens. But he put the thought aside and asked, "You deal with the banks for Dad, don't you, Vard? You did in the old days. Who do you talk to in Galveston?"

"Yep, I still do. You might call me a kind of manager now." Vard said with pride. "I talk to D.G. Mills, most times."

"Fine. I'll write my bank in Chicago tonight, and give you a letter for Mills. They'll transfer enough from my account to cover this payload. Stall off the men a few days, until Mills can issue another payroll."

32

"But, boy, this is crazy! In the first place, where would you get the money?"

Stephen grinned. "I've done all right, Vard." He told the old man then of his Western ventures and his Chicago business. Land deals and city coaches had brought him almost on a par with Daniel Raike.

"Jehosophat!" Vard expelled his breath. " 'All right' is puttin' it kind of mild." Then he sobered and demanded, "What's behind this, Steve? Why do you want it done this way? These folks always rob Raike property —Raike money, Raike trains and coaches. Always Raike holdings, yet you're keepin' quiet."

"I'll look like an almighty fool if this Short Line thing gets out." Vard doubted that: Stephen's cool self-confidence was so strong he knew the boy didn't give a damn for anybody's opinion. But he kept his peace as Stephen resumed speaking. "And I don't want any more talk about Raike losses. There's been enough. All right?"

"All right." Vard was grudging. "I'll talk to Mills tomorrow. Give me the letter. Though what you can say to him, it's beyond me, way beyond me."

"Why, Vard, it's as easy as rolling off a log." Stephen grinned his broad white grin once more. "It's a gift for my father, the repayment of a loan he made me, in cash. That's all."

Vard laughed. "Well, you're a apple off the ol' tree, Steve Raike."

They were on the long, winding road that led to the Raike house. The bright moon made clear the structure's awkwardness. What his mother must have thought of the house, Stephen reflected, he couldn't imagine. But it must have jarred her Eastern sensibilities, used as she was to the grace of the lacy houses in New Orleans.

The Raike house was an eyesore: Daniel Raike had once seen a house in Savannah, Georgia, which had struck his fancy. Here in the baked plains he had had the house duplicated as far as he was able. In the East its lines would have been softened by surrounding trees; here in the sands it rose grotesquely stark and tall, three

33

stories, embellished with cast-iron ornament and fences on the first- and second-story balconies.

Stephen thought with compassion that it must have represented his father's attempt to capture the splendor he had so deeply desired. And it probably reminded Daniel of the lacy balconies of New Orleans; in a way he might have been trying to atone to Louise Gerard for all she'd given up.

As they entered the familiar hall, and Stephen saw the bullwhip in the corner, he wondered if it were the same one his father had used that midnight nine years ago. He followed Vard upstairs; when they looked in on his father, the old man was fast asleep.

"Don't wake him up," Stephen ordered. "I'll see him in the morning."

And when he was lying in his own bed, Stephen felt all his ancient animosity and anger melt away.

Yet as the moments passed he was restless in the warm September night, accustomed as he was to the brisk winds of Chicago that blew in from the lake. However, it was not the languor of the air, or the sad forgiveness he felt for the old man sleeping, which kept Stephen's drowsiness at bay.

His arm hurt. And a hot sweat of desire ran down his muscled chest and back, tickled his long legs. The image of the woman on the train teased Stephen. He had told Varden Williams there were five bandits, omitting mention of the fact that one was an Indian and one a woman. The reason for his omission had not been clear to Stephen before.

But when Stephen dropped into a kind of throbbing black that was an uneasy sleep, he dreamed the dark-eyed woman stood before him.

She placed her long hands on either side of his excited face, lifting her arrogant mouth for his caress. She was skittish and narrow as a deer, but the softness of her was quite incredible; the softness of a cloud of thistle-down wherein blinded, lost, enclosed, Stephen drifted, sinking, sinking.

Chapter Three

Stephen slept heavily at last, exhausted by his loss of blood and the potion Doc Fitch had given him against infection. So the sun was high when he strode down the hall toward his father's room the next day.

Surprised, he saw Vard Williams standing at the half-open door, surrounded by a knot of frightened-looking servants, black and Mexican. Then Stephen caught sight of Cyrus Fitch, hurrying up the stairs.

"What is it?"

Vard came toward him. "He's had another stroke."

"Why didn't you call me?" Stephen demanded. The servants fell back as Stephen shouldered his way behind Doc Fitch into his father's room.

"Just happened little while ago," Vard mumbled. "There was nothing you could do, Steve. Lucky the doc was right down the road. We caught him just in time."

Stephen nodded, watching the doctor examine the rigid old man on the bed, a man he hardly recognized. Nine years ago this man had been alive with a ferocious life blazing from his every gesture. Now Daniel Raike, his coarse hair wholly white, lay with staring eyes, his swarthy face suffused with an unhealthy redness, the powerful hands rigid and pathetic at his sides.

Stephen was assailed with guilt and pity: this was all that was left of his father's power!

The doctor straightened from his scrutiny of the old man and said to Stephen, "Come with me," gesturing toward the other end of the large room. Stephen followed the doctor to the windows; glancing back, he thought he saw a flicker of sense in the old man's slate-gray eyes, the eyes so like his own.

"It doesn't look good, Steve." Fitch's voice was low-pitched and somber. He put his thin hand on Stephen's shoulder. "We'll just have to watch, and wait. I'm sending out another man from Galveston. And you'll need nurses."

"Whatever he needs," Stephen said impatiently. "But what happened? What's made him like this, Doc?"

"Stephen, I warned him. I warned him five years ago, when the Olwens—" The doctor paused, as Vard Williams always did, after uttering the name. Stephen resolved that he would get to the bottom of it, once and for all. But there was no time to linger on it now, for the doctor was continuing, "He drove himself too hard, took things too hard. Wouldn't cut out the whiskey. Got all riled up over this Pease and Runnels thing, but you know about that. I guess Vard told you."

Stephen nodded. "Will he—pull through?"

"I don't know, Steve. I just don't know right now." Cyrus Fitch smiled sadly up at the tall, anxious man beside him. "Meanwhile, it's a blessing you're here. You might have to take hold, sooner than we think. I won't lie to you, Steve, I never have."

"No, you haven't, Doc. I thank you for that."

"Well." Fitch placed his hand on Stephen's muscled arm again in an awkward gesture of comfort. "I'll be getting on. His condition's stabilized now. The nurses should be coming tonight, tomorrow at the latest. Vard sent a rider in already."

"We'll stay close by until then."

"Good. Get yourself something to eat, boy. You look a little peaked."

Stephen made a casual gesture of dismissal. "I'm all right. Talk to Vard, will you, Doc? He's like—"

"Your other pa?" Fitch asked, smiling. "Of course."

Stephen Raike sat down in a chair by his father's bed. When the others had left the room, he leaned forward and said softly, "Dad?"

But the man on the bed neither moved nor turned his

insensate gaze toward his son. The flicker of awareness that Stephen had seen before was gone, and Daniel Raike stared straight ahead, lost in some world beyond their reaching.

Daniel Raike's condition was unchanged in the two days following; he was neither worse nor better. And on the third day after his father had been stricken, Stephen, who had spent most of the time in the sick man's room, felt that he would explode if he could not get out and away. There were a hundred things he had to do: a multitude of tasks confronted him. Most of all, his unexercised body fairly itched for a saddle, for the air.

The mystery of the Olwens teased his brain, and in his tense half-sleep, at night when a part of his mind was alert, fearing a call from the evening nurse, Stephen dreamed again of the woman on the train, woke sweating in his strange, resentful desire before he dropped off again.

"You'd better get out for a while," Vard said at the breakfast table on that third morning. "You're as white as a sheet."

Stephen smiled and nodded, without replying. His mind was busy, already into the day ahead. Vard Williams had completed the banking business in Galveston, but that was only the start. He had returned to Stephen with papers to sign, giving him his father's power of attorney in case of need. But gnawing still were the unfinished matters of the robbery, and the woman who'd robbed the train.

By God, she had tried to make an almighty fool of him! Stephen thought savagely. He'd find her and pay her back. And he'd find out, too, why the name of Olwen brought that look of dismay to Varden Williams and Dr. Fitch.

"All right, Vard. I won't go into Galveston yet; it's too long a ride. But I'll take a little trip into Berwick today."

Vard Williams drained his coffee cup and examined

the man across the table. Stephen could see him wondering.

"I'm going to have a word with the sheriff," Stephen explained, smiling.

The village Stephen had known nine years ago had changed. A Yankee visitor, entering the town of Berwick Bay, had asked once, "Where's the town?"

He'd know now, Stephen decided, as he cantered down the main street on his tall gray stallion, delighted to feel again the horse's solid rhythm under him.

There was a new hotel, an additional saloon. Wells Fargo had set up an office and down the way he saw a dressmaker's sign. In the window of her establishment was a headless form dressed in a bright blue gown full of flounces—the exact shade of blue as the handkerchief the woman on the train had worn. The curved shape of the form reminded Stephen of the woman's body; the sweat broke out along his broad back despite the coolness of the autumn air.

He muttered a silent curse. He had wanted to get even with her; now he wanted something else entirely. Stephen reined in before the county sheriff's office.

Inside he found a young fellow he did not know, a man with bright, inquisitive eyes and a nervous manner.

"Afternoon," Stephen said. "Sheriff Briscoe around?"

"Briscoe! You're new in town."

"Hardly." Stephen pushed back his broad-brimmed hat and wiped away the sweat from his tanned forehead. "Been away. What happened to Mr. Briscoe?"

He had a funny look, Stephen decided, but the fellow answered with a fair amount of steadiness, "He died four years ago. Now it's Sheriff Lamb."

Stephen, judging that the new sheriff's name was an unfortunate one for a lawman, smiled a little, and replied, "Thanks. Is he here?"

"Well, what's—who—"

"Stephen Raike."

The young man with the nervous manner repeated, "Raike! Well, now, you must be Mr. Daniel Raike's son that's been in Chicago, I hear tell."

"Aways been a lot of hearing and telling in Berwick Bay," Stephen returned dryly.

"Well, the sheriff ain't here now. I'm his depitty. Name's Charlie Scurry." Scurry held out his hand.

Stephen shook it. No wonder the thieves get away, he thought. Lamb and Scurry. A rabbit and a sheep. Sounds like they couldn't catch their breaths.

Charlie Scurry looked a little puzzled at the twinkle in Raike's cool eyes, but he said dutifully, "Maybe I can help."

"Well, now, Charlie, that's neighborly of you, but I think maybe I'll wait for Sheriff Lamb."

"Oh, he won't be back for a while," Scurry protested. "Something you want to talk to him about, I reckon?"

Stephen repressed a desire to laugh. "That's the idea. Do you reckon he'll be back this afternoon?"

Charlie Scurry seemed abashed. "Well, now I guess you could find him down the street. Not much goin' on here lately," he added defensively.

Not much! Stephen thought. But with great patience, he inquired, "Just where down the street, Charlie?"

Young Scurry's thin face flushed a deep brick red and his adam's apple bobbled as he swallowed. "Reckon you might run across him in the Golden Girl Saloon, right down from the hotel."

So that was the way the land lay. Stephen pulled his hat over his brow and smiled at Deputy Charlie Scurry. "Thanks, Charlie," he said and strode toward the smudgy glass door.

When he turned to close it, he glanced back: the nervous young deputy was staring after him, and Scurry looked as frightened as the running rabbit which his name suggested.

Now that is very interesting, Stephen decided. That is very interesting indeed.

The Golden Girl Saloon was only fifty paces down the road; on the way Raike passed again the blue-clad, headless form in the dressmaker's window. He paused before the glass, indulgently studying the bright blue dress, and the picture of the woman with the gun was so sharp in his inner vision that he felt as if someone had punched him in the groin.

A coarse laugh behind him, startling and loud, made him whirl. A sweaty, unshaven cowboy who, Stephen judged from his swaying stance, had spent some time in the Golden Girl, was pointing at the dress-clad form.

"Hey, bub," the cowboy called thickly, "things can't be that bad. Go on down t' the Golden Girl. Plenny o' li'l ladies there."

Stephen Raike burned with a quick, irrational anger: without thinking, he reached for the Colt that hung in the holster at his narrow hip. Then he stopped, appalled.

The cowboy's face was slack with fear, and he mumbled, "Hold on, pal. Hold on! I didn't mean t' rile you. I was funnin' with you, that's all." Stephen looked at the quaking man, and his sanity returned.

"No harm done," Stephen said with forced calm, and walked away toward the Golden Girl.

The woman in faded calico surveyed the smoke-blackened walls of the quiet house, rubbing away a cobweb with the back of her slender hand. The damage was not as terrible as she had feared; the fire had not destroyed the roof or walls, or eaten away at the foundation. The Indians had been quick to put it out.

She blew at the cobweb on her hand, then brushed it off against the folds of the ugly dress, so often washed that its original rich brown had faded to the color of dusty tumbleweed.

"It will not take me long to make it right," she said aloud, and the sound of her rich, husky voice echoed in the deserted room where the few pieces of handsome furniture still stood. Across the table, in the dust, she saw the pawprints of a tiny creature, and birds had nested in the dark fireplace.

In the center of the table a Pueblo vase still held the dry stems of long-vanished prairie flowers: it was that sight, more than any other, that made the woman's throat ache with unshed tears. But with a gesture of defiance, she drew a rag of faded red from a bundle she had brought, and dusted the table. Then she took up the vase and moved with it toward the front door, her footing uncertain where some boards were missing. She would set a fresh bunch of flowers in the vase before she began to sweep the leaves and debris of five years from the porch.

Then she heard steps at the other end of the ruined verandah: an echoing, hard step like that of a hoofed creature. A creature, surely, for now four separate steps sounded.

The woman put down the vase on the floor and peered from the window. A hesitant doe was moving along the porch; she raised her soft muzzle and fearfully, curiously sniffed the air. Noiseless on her moccasined feet, the woman stole through the half-open door and for a moment, where a hole in the roof of the verandah admitted the full sun, the woman's unbound hair burned like a pillar of fire in the brightness.

She faced the doe, which had paused, quivering. The creature looked straight into the woman's eyes, terror-gaze gleaming, transfixed. As the two great pairs of dark eyes met, the doe sniffed the woman's scent.

And the woman knew that the creature would lose its fear, for the man-musk of the dreaded hunter was not on her tawny flesh; she had seen deer come to women in the village, and to female children, none of whose bodies bore the odor of the bringers of death.

The red-haired woman stood still as a tree in a windless noon, delighting in the picture of the wild, buff-colored thing standing on the ruined porch, examining her with its melting eyes.

The animal took a tentative step forward; the woman did not speak, but only smiled, still not moving, aware that waves of friendliness were emerging from her own body toward the deer, slowly calming its distrust.

All of a sudden, there was a fantastic cry of a whip-poor-will in the brightness. A whip-poor-will, that night-bird, crying in the afternoon! The woman almost laughed aloud, but forbore to frighten away the deer. That could only be Tahre. Only the wild humor of Tahre could produce a night cry in the sunny afternoon.

But the doe, scenting man, pricked up its ears and leaped with precipitate grace from the ruined verandah, fleeing into a thicket. From the thicket's edge Tahre emerged, grinning at the woman on the verandah.

"Isse-Loa," he called, walking silent as a cloud across the beaten grass, his flat black eyes were fixed on the woman. "Here is the *qualee-qualoo,* the night bird."

He was up the broken stairs in a single bound—very much, the woman thought, like the bounding deer—saying in his strangely hoarse Comanche, "So you are bound to do this thing, as you were bound to do the other." There was a rueful affection in his greeting.

The woman's smile of welcome faded. "I am."

"Isse, Isse-Loa," he said reproachfully, touching a strand of her glorious hair, still burning in the path of the late sun, "you should not show yourself here. Already they speak of it in the town."

"I had to come," she said simply, and turned back into the house, where she retrieved the Pueblo vase. "Come with me to the stream."

He nodded, and followed her down the steps and over the beaten yard into the thicket, towering tall beside her, moving as smoothly as water. His stern, coppery face relaxed into a smile when he looked at her. She pulled the sere twigs from the vase and threw them into the stream, stooping to wash the long accumulation of dust from the vase.

He watched in silence as she set the clean vase on the bank of the stream, and looked about for flowering weeds. Breaking some stalks of yellow blossom, she said matter-of-factly to Tahre, "Would you get the buckets behind the house? I will need some water for scrubbing."

Tahre rose from his squatting position and laughed.

"What are you laughing at?"

"The lady with the gun, getting down to scrub the floor." He turned then and moved off in the direction of the house.

Still kneeling on the bank, she watched him. She loved to watch her cousin move, recalling how the Indians walked in spring—softly, more lightly than ever, on bare feet, reluctant to bruise the pregnant earth, even removing the shoes of horses, so the mother, earth, would not be wounded. Quick tears came to her eyes; then she turned with renewed energy to the arrangement of the yellow flowers.

When she had carried the vase back to the house, and set it in the center of the dusted table, Tahre entered with two buckets of water.

He set them by the door, and asked, "You are still bound to do the other thing?"

"Yes, Tahre. This one last thing for a while. There may be a great deal of gold on the stage."

He shook his proud head, without further comment. Then he said in his wry and humorous fashion, "I will leave you now to your tipi. I will ride with you, and shoot; your scrubbing you must do alone. *Ake-rooka,* I will shoot. That ends it."

The woman laughed merrily and waved him away.

The Golden Girl Saloon boasted few customers at this hour of the afternoon. Only three pairs of spurred boots rested on the brass rail around the bar, and two ancient men, with no drinks before them, were playing a two-handed game of cards at a far table.

A beefy man with a large handlebar mustache leaned against the sink behind the counter watching as a sleepy-looking, portly woman in a spangled satin dress descended the stairs. Seeing Stephen, she smiled and put a plump hand to her spurious golden hair.

The other six took instant notice as Raike strode toward the bar; the two old men put down their cards and frankly stared. The three men removed their right feet from the rail and straightened. Stephen smiled a one-sided smile; he had seen that phenomenon a thousand times before, in the rougher towns that he had known—that snapping to alertness, preparing for whatever might come.

Genially, he nodded to the three men, and said to the man behind the bar, "Afternoon."

The man returned his greeting and asked with professional amiability, "What'll it be?"

"Bourbon, please." Stephen, leaning one elbow on the bar, looked around the room with his cool gray eyes. The three men had taken note of the "please," and were examining him from dove-gray Stetson to handmade boots, with practiced covertness that Raike recognized.

"Nice day," he said calmly to the nearest man, a paunchy man with close-set, weasel eyes and a hat that seemed too big for him. A metal star gleamed on the weasely fellow's chest.

The man with the star nodded at Raike. "It is, all right." Stephen heard a slurring in the words, and took in the red-veined nose and watery-eyed appearance.

"You Sheriff Lamb?" he asked quietly.

"That's me," the man replied, and the other two snickered as the barkeep set Stephen's glass before him.

"Thanks." Stephen put a gold piece on the bar. Lamb's close-set gaze flicked to the coin as quickly as a hopping flea, a minute thing, but it did not escape Stephen's sharp eye.

"And who might you be, mister?" Lamb inquired.

"The name is Stephen Raike." A cautious expression crept over the flushed face of the paunchy sheriff.

"Well, now," he began with the same nervous geniality Raike had seen in Charlie Scurry, "you must be Mr. Daniel Raike's son. Been living East, I hear tell."

Stephen had a feeling he was going to become very tired of that particular expression, but managed a friendly nod. "Like to have a word with you, Sheriff, if you have no objection."

Lamb's ill-hidden consternation filled Stephen with elation: he was on the right track, after all.

"Why, sure," Lamb said uneasily. "Sure."

"Can I buy you a drink?"

Lamb looked down at his empty glass. "Why, yeah, Mr. Raike. I call that mighty friendly."

Raike raised a casual finger to the man behind the bar. "Why don't you bring the bottle, friend?" he suggested.

Lamb's flushed face brightened. "Well, now, that is *mighty* fine, Mr. Raike."

Stephen saw the other two men at the bar exchange a weary look. He placed another gold piece on the bar and, picking up the bottle and his glass, gestured with his head toward a corner table. Lamb followed, shambling a little in his worn boots.

When the men were seated, the plump woman, who had been listening intently from the stairs, came flouncing over to Stephen's table. The barkeep and the two old men watched; the two men at the bar turned to see.

Leaning over Stephen, the woman said softly, "I haven't seen anything so handsome for a long, long time. You feel like a little relaxing?"

Stephen Raike looked up into her bovine eyes, set wide apart in her powdered, doughy face. The paint was greasy on her tired lips. He shook his head and answered with the gentle courtesy he used with all women. "No, thank you, ma'am. Not right now. Some other time I sure will come to see you." He smiled his dazzling smile.

The plump woman in the spangled dress inhaled with surprise; she straightened, and there was a certain pride in her posture. "You do that, Mr. Raike," she breathed, her rouged cheeks burning. She squeezed his muscled arm with her plump ringed hand. Stephen turned and called in the direction of the bar, "Give the lady a drink, would you?"

The barkeep drew a beer with an impassive face, and the two men at the bar snickered at this evidence of gallantry. But their laughter died when Stephen Raike turned his hard, slate-gray look on them.

He turned back to Lamb and said casually, "Wanted to have a little talk about that payload, Sheriff Lamb."

Lamb stuttered, "Wha—wha—what d'you mean, a talk, Mr. Raike?" He laughed an uneasy little laugh. "You been a good while in comin'. We couldn't find those bastards anywhere. Never can. Figure they don't come from around here. Thought you'd kind of—chalked it off."

Stephen stared at Lamb. "My father's had another

stroke. I couldn't get in to see you before. What I wanted to say, Sheriff, was this: next time maybe I can give you a little help."

Lamb seemed at a loss. Stephen laughed. "Guess you wonder how I could be of help when I let them get away this last time. I was asleep," he added frankly. "They crept right up and got me by the short hairs."

"Well, I wasn't goin' to say . . ." the sheriff stopped, embarrassed. "My God, you *seen* 'em up close! Mr. Raike! Did you know 'em? What was they like?"

It seemed to Stephen that Lamb's query held an undertone of fear, not the cool interrogating tone of a lawman.

"Had bandannas over their faces," Stephen said. "Five men." Lamb's puzzlement, now, was comic.

"What kind of men?" he asked, recovering.

"Just ordinary men, nothing special about them." Nothing special, Stephen thought wryly, except that two of them were a woman and an Indian with something wrong with his vocal cords! "They caught me napping then, but I don't want it to happen again. I'd like to go along with the posse, next time around."

"It coulda happened to anybody," Lamb remarked with generosity, pouring another bourbon. "I heard you're quite a fellow with a gun, Mr. Raike. But do you want to mix in this?"

"Well, it's not exactly mixing, Sheriff," Stephen said mildly. "The Short Line is a Raike enterprise." He gave a sardonic smile. "Maybe some of our boys can help you out, next time."

"How do you know there'll be a next time?" Lamb demanded.

"That's what Luke Allen said, Sheriff." This time Stephen was sure, dead sure; the mention of Allen's name brought an odd expression to Lamb's flabby face.

So Allen's in it, too. Who else? Stephen questioned in silence as he studied Lamb. He rose, then, and said quietly, "I'd best be going along. Be seeing you, Sheriff, I'm sure."

He nodded to the others in the saloon and moved with

his long, loose stride toward the swing-door. When he turned back, he saw with satisfaction that Lamb was looking after him, dismayed, just as Scurry had.

The other women were beginning to come downstairs for the day. One, a small brunette in pink, with a fresher face than the others, was smiling an invitation to Stephen. He touched his brim and pushed open the swing-door without another backward look. The crazy heat and pounding of his body earlier had stilled, and he had decided coldly that the woman on the train had become the only one who could ease his passion. The conclusion disturbed him not a little.

Chapter Four

That evening, after dinner, in a somber, restless mood, Stephen wandered into his father's study. He poured himself a glass of brandy and sat down before the old man's huge, untidy rolltop desk. Vard would be in soon to familiarize him with the accounts.

The study, like the rest of the house, was unmistakably a man's room, a room in a house where women had little part. A certain feeling of oppression came over Stephen Raike in the now-sultry air of the room. It felt as if a storm were brewing.

Stephen got up and walked around, wishing irritably that he could settle down to the books, stop wool-gathering. The single-minded discipline that had brought him such success in Chicago seemed to have deserted him.

He studied the room again. There were no pictures on the walls, none of the doodads women generally managed; he could hardly have said what those doodads were, but he noticed their absence.

"A house without women," he whispered. Then he cursed himself and sat down again before the desk. Bad enough that Vard knew his blunder on the train; it wouldn't do at all to be found dreaming here. Reluctantly he picked up one of the heavy ledgers, covered in brown pebbled leather, and opened it, feeling the nervous sweat stain his clean, crisp, light-brown hair. His mustache itched him.

He unbuttoned the rest of the buttons on his shirt; the perspiration trickled down his hard brown chest and clung to the hairs of his belly.

"A house without women." Well, not exactly without: there was Mrs. Parmer, the housekeeper, with her pepper-and-salt hair screwed back into a hard, neat knob, her dresses the washed-out colors of the dust and sage. Did she count? Stephen smiled grimly. Probably not. The painfully refined presence of the widowed Mrs. Parmer had never warmed Stephen as a boy; she had been, always, an unobtrusive and almost silent machine, superintending the emotional blacks and Mexicans whom she ruled with a fair but iron hand. He supposed the house had always been like this—clean and fairly ordered, with the desolate smell and look of an institution.

Of course Daniel Raike would never notice such a thing, but Stephen noticed it now, for the first time. Curious, he decided to look around the hall. He walked through the open door and surveyed it: with a sense of seeing it through different eyes, as if he were a stranger, Stephen noticed a vase of flowers, stiffly arranged, on a table by the wall.

The flowers reminded him so much of Mrs. Parmer that they seemed worse than nothing at all. He turned back to the study.

Face it, he ordered himself in silence, it's that wench with the Colt, and the big black hat. That wild woman as slim as a reed, but with breasts that—it's that one who has you thinking like this.

And Stephen had a sudden, insane impulse to saddle up Sam and ride out into the sultry night to find her. Christ, what a damned fool he was. Where would he look? What would he do when he did find her? *If* he did.

But the itch, the desolation persisted, even as he heard Vard Williams' stolid footfall on the stair.

"How is he, Vard?"

The older man looked exhausted. "No change, Steve. Same as when you seen him before supper."

"Sit down, Vard, take a load off your feet. Want a drink?"

Varden Williams' reply was fervent. "I could sure use one. What're you drinkin'?"

"Brandy."

"Don't give me none of that Frenchy stuff. Taste o' bourbon'd go down smooth."

Stephen poured the drink and brought it to Vard.

"Thanks." Vard Williams swigged, made a face, exhaled, and said, "Ah! That's good liquor, boy." He set down his glass and inquired, "Been over the books yet?"

"Not much yet. Listen, Vard, there's something you've got to tell me, and tell me now."

"What's that?" Stephen's grim tone made him sit up.

"About what happened to the Olwens. Every time their name is mentioned, ever since I got back—you, Doc Fitch, clam up like a redskin brave. What's behind it, Vard? I've got to know."

Vard was silent. Then he said in a somber voice, "Well, I guess you do. You're entitled, because the Raike name is all tangled up in it. Now I've said from the first, and I'll say it again to you, I don't think your pappy was at fault."

"What do you mean?"

"They said he was—behind it. But I won't believe it; I can't believe that, boy, of your pa."

"I think you'd better go back to the beginning."

"Yeah. Maybe you better get yourself another drink," Vard said with bitter humor.

Stephen seldom drank much, but at this moment he felt like taking Vard's advice. He poured himself a little more brandy and sat down again in the squeaking leather chair before his father's desk and swiveled to face the older man. "All right. What's it all about?"

"Five years ago," Vard began, "was when it happened, the fire and the—but I'll get to that. You remember the Olwens, remember them some, don't you, Steve? You recall how Hugh Olwen and your pappy met at San Jacinto. Then after the fighting was over, and Sam Houston was givin' away land, Hugh got his.

"Wasn't much, as Raike land-measure goes—a thousand and some acres, and part of it fell on Raike land, down there on the southeast hundred. Well, they'd made some kind of mistake, surveyin'. And your pappy, he was in a generous kind o' mood. What the hell, he had forty times as much land as Hugh Olwen, so he said 'Let it go.' Olwen was proud as Lucifer, tried to pay 'im for it, but you know how your pa can get sometimes, like a king or somethin' givin' gifts to the plain folks." He stopped and flushed.

Steve nodded and said, "It's all right. Go on."

"Well, finally Olwen accepted the land, but said he'd pay back the Raikes some day. And everything seemed to go fine for a while. Olwen was a worker, a good man, a real tough fella, and he built up his thousand acres pretty good, had some sheep and cattle, all that."

"Then he married the Comanche woman."

"I remember that now," said Stephen. "Yes, I remember."

"Yeah, the way it happened was just like a story, like the story the redskins tell about that thing a hundred years or more ago, in Oklahoma, when the hostile tribe stole one of their gals, and were about to use her as a sacrifice, when the brave rode in and took her away. Happened just like that with Olwen and this pretty squaw. This woman," he amended quickly, remembering Stephen's peculiar kinship with the Indians.

"Yes, sir, them Apaches stole that gal, don't recall her name now, after all this time. Was gonna cut her heart right out, and Hugh Olwen rode in ahead of her brothers and snatched her right off thr⁴ tree—they said her arms and legs had rope-burns for a month after— and he took 'er right away. I guess you could call it that love at first sight," Vard said with awkward sentiment.

Stephen Raike thought of the woman in black, but he did not speak.

"The Comanches took it kind that Olwen had saved their gal, so when he asked for her, they gave her to him, white as he was. The neighbors didn't take too kindly to it, though. The women were always down on Olwen after that. You know how these cacklin' hens can be. And your pappy took it worst of all. I don't have to tell you how he feels about Indians."

Stephen nodded again, and his handsome mouth tightened with annoyance under his full mustache.

"They had a child, a daughter, funny little sandy-haired thing, dressed all the time like a boy, and ran around with the Indians. As far as your pa was concerned, their friendship was just about over. Then five years ago, while you was away, they had to lay track on the southeast hundred. And by then your pappy was feelin' no kindness for Olwen and his red wife and the halfbreed kid. He rode down there and told Olwen he was ready to reclaim his land. Olwen offered to buy it from him, the way he did before, but your pa just laughed in his face. Well, after all, nothin' Olwen could pay would have come up to the value of rail-land. We all know that.

"Olwen got mad as hell, and shouted at your pappy about 'honor' and all, but your pappy said he was reclaiming his land, and Olwen said 'Over my dead body it will be.' You recall that funny, foreign way he used to talk. Come from Wales, you know, and worked in the mines and then on the railroads before he got his fightin' land. A mighty tough man, Olwen.

"And your pappy said, 'Dead body it'll be, if I don't get my land.'" Vard paused and took another sip of his whiskey. He said apologetically to Stephen, "Now I don't think he meant it at all. Your pa has his ways, has a high temper, you know, but that's the way he always was. I coulda talked sense in him, if I'd had the chance. But I'd busted my danged leg in the roundup and was laid up there for a long time. Well, your pappy just rode away, fumin' about Hugh Olwen and his halfbreed child. The boys told me all this later, when they came back to the ranch.

"And the next day—" Vard swallowed, but went on doggedly, "some strangers, fellows nobody around here knew, set fire to Olwen's house. Killed him and his Indian wife."

Stephen felt his sweating body chill.

"It was a bad thing," Vard said quietly. "There stood the kid. She was growin' up into a pretty girl by that time, with that bright red hair, like Olwen's, and them black eyes like her ma's. A little ol' fourteen-year-old girl. She raised up her fist at the men, spunky little devil, wasn't afraid of nothin'. And she said, 'It's the Raikes, the Raikes did it. And I'll never rest until the Raikes have paid.' Of course the men just laughed and rode away. A couple of our boys got there in time to hear all this, and help the Indians put out the fire.

"People said your pa had paid the men to do it, but I don't believe that, Steve. If I believed that, I couldna stayed here all these years." Vard looked at Stephen earnestly from his clear blue eyes.

"I believe you, Vard," Stephen answered with gentle ambiguity, but his feelings were in turmoil. He forced calm to his tone, and inquired, "What happened to the girl?" Some sixth sense was working: he recalled the young girl's vengeful feelings against the Raikes—and that the Short Line was a Raike property. And there was the matter of the watch. Was it possible?

Vard was saying, "The Indians, I guess."

"What's that?" The old man, looking puzzled at Stephen's sudden inattention, repeated, "I said we always thought she'd gone off to the Indians. Nobody's seen hide nor hair of her for the last five years. But now, that you mention it, Steve, there's something kind of funny going on."

"Funny? How?"

"Well, Juan and Henry was in Berwick the other day, gettin' some stuff for the spread, you know, and they told me a young gal had been around. Real young, not more'n twenty, I guess, asking for some hands to do some work. Out on the Olwen place, she said."

"Then you think it's the Olwen girl?" Stephen asked, and something in his tone made Vard prick up his ears.

"Could be," Vard said casually, studying Stephen.

"What was her name?"

"The Olwen gal? Lord, I don't know. Lemme see if I recall. Why, I do. It was Doña, you know, Spanish for 'lady.' " Vard pronounced the name in Spanish fashion, "Doanyah." He chuckled. "Her Indian ma was awful set on makin' her a lady, I hear. But she sure ran around like a wild Comanche in them days, that gal did."

Like a wild Comanche, Stephen repeated silently. His

conviction was strengthening; he saw again the fine-boned face of the woman with the Colt, her tawny coloring and high, shadowed cheeks; her lithe stance and arrogant grace.

A loud voice coming from the hall interrupted them. A man's hurrying, heavy tread, and the jingle of spurs.

"What in tarnation is that?" Vard rose and went to the door.

Juan, the boss of the *vaqueros*, came rushing in. His dark eyes snapped with excitement. "Mr. Raike! They hit us agin. The stage was robbed!"

Stephen rose to his full lean height; his impassive face showed nothing as he asked quietly, "Where?"

"Between the Baytown Inn and Berwick. The sheriff's getting up a posse now."

Stephen looked at Vard. "What do you say we go for a ride, partner? "

Vard grinned. "Bet your life."

As the two men followed Juan from the study, they scooped up their wide-brimmed hats from the hooks by the door, and all three headed toward the stables.

The ringed moon was dim above them when Stephen, Vard and Juan, accompanied by four Raike *vaqueros*, reined in before the sheriff's office in Berwick Bay.

There were already twenty other men, widely assorted riders, in every manner of gear, from the faded denim and flannel of the cowpoke to the costlier buckskin of the merchant. Stephen heard someone mutter, "Don't know why he didn't pull us out for the Short Line haul."

Then there was an abrupt silence. The speaker had caught sight of him and was embarrassed.

Sheriff's a damn' slow starter, too, Raike judged wryly. The thieves could be in San Antone by now. Nevertheless he kept silent and listened to the fumbling directions of Lamb, who was addressing the posse from the porch. Might as well play out the farce, Stephen thought, wondering how much Raike money had been on the stage.

When they started to ride away, Stephen brought his gray stallion, Sam, abreast of Vard's old paint, Abilene, and said quietly, "I'll ride with you as far as the fork.

54

Then I'll head south. I have a feeling, Vard, and I want to check it out."

"South?"

"If anybody asks, tell 'em the dude has got cold feet."

Vard laughed. "Nobody gonna swallow that, boy. You could shoot off their whiskers without burnin' their mouth. But I'll go along, Steve."

"Thanks."

At the fork, Stephen raised his lean right hand to Varden Williams, and took the darkening road toward the Baytown Inn and the southeast hundred.

He felt it in his very innards, that certainty as to where he would find her. He would hide her from the others, if need be. For he doubted very much if all of the posse were being paid; they couldn't have taken that much if they'd robbed every stage and train between Berwick and Santa Fe.

Why the hell he was set on covering for her, Stephen couldn't figure out. Sure, she had gotten to him. One look into those deep, black eyes had done it. But all the same, he vowed. What he wanted most was to pay her back for what she had done to him, and to take back his most precious possession, that watch his mother had given to his father.

Then Stephen reined in his startled horse and began to laugh; the gray stallion laid back its sensitive ears and turned its head a trifle, as if to see what ailed the man upon its back.

"I'm a fool twice, Sam," Stephen said softly, and patted the stallion's neck. Revenge was not in his mind, no matter what he tried to tell himself. He wanted to see her again, it was as simple as that. He wanted to touch her and look into those wonderful, angry eyes and kiss her mouth, her neck, her breasts—he wanted—

"Jesus!" Raike swore, and looked up at the storm-moon over the shaggy hills. Yes, he wanted that, and had, from the first moment he saw her.

And he had wanted most of all to ride through the night alone, to think of her and what he planned to do. Even if she—liked him, what the hell would he do then?

He was the son of the man she considered her parents' murderer. For he knew in his bones now that the woman on the train was Doña Olwen. It all fit in, fit in too well. Doña Olwen.

As he rode through the oppressive dark, Stephen heard the mutter of thunder over the far hills; a light rain was beginning to fall. Sam didn't seem to mind; he shook his great head and whinnied with a peculiar sound like pleasure, for the air was cooling, and the stallion had worked up a sweat in the heavy, electric air. Raike himself liked the feel of the soft drizzle on his hard hands, misting against his chest, half-bare in his unbuttoned shirt. The small rain was like the caress of a woman's hand.

Doña Olwen, he said to himself again, the daughter of a Comanche and a Welshman.

A long-buried memory came to Stephen, a memory of an afternoon when he was only eight years old. Aching with a peculiar loneliness, fired with curiosity about his dead mother, of whom he had heard the servants talking, the boy Stephen had come to the hushed place, the room that was like no other in the house.

It did not occur to him to question why the room was kept as if someone still slept there—and he was not to know in the years that followed, for Daniel Raike maintained a mysterious silence on the subject of his wife—or whether it was someone's sentiment or indifference that kept it so.

But he had found it a magical place, with the most wonderful bed he had ever seen, a bed whose footboard was as high as its head, and painted with a scene of castles and towers looming up above a dark wood. The curtains were thin and white and clean, stirring in a spooky way when he came in. By the window a little curly chair stood, with the same castles painted on it that he saw on the bed. The rug beneath his feet was all full of leaves and flowers, in pretty colors; it was like walking on a garden, and he tried not to step on the roses.

There was a sweet smell in the room that did not seem to come from the vase of flowers on the table by the curly chair. The boy wondered where all these things had come from—there was nothing like them in Galveston—and what the sweet smell was.

He crept to the tallboy and opened its doors; there were shiny dresses inside, and when he handled them, they whispered.

Then he saw the books. They were not like the books downstairs in his father's office; those books were brown and gray. The brown ones felt like tapioca, which Stephen hated, and the gray ones were rough to the fingers. These books in the strange room, he noticed, examining them with wonder, were funny-feeling and full of golden, curly designs on the outside.

He opened one of them, and began to read laboriously the small print on the yellowed page; he could not understand what it meant at all, but something in its phrases struck his heart: "Now when the man and maid, Tristan and Isolde, had drunk the potion, suddenly that prime disturber of tranquility was there—love, the highwayman of hearts. . . . "

"Love, the highwayman of hearts," Stephen repeated aloud, in the rhythm of Sam's cantering hooves. My God! He'd remembered that after all these years, remembered how he'd taken that book, and the rest of his mother's books, to his own room, turned them face down, hidden them whenever his father or Mrs. Farmer or Vard Williams came in.

Suddenly Stephen realized why he had remembered the book. Isolde of Cornwall, in the country of Wales. Though the book had called her dark-haired with a face as white as the foam of the sea, and Vard had told him Doña Olwen's hair was red. And her skin wasn't white at all, but smooth and tanned. The feeling that had come over him was like the feeling described in that book, strong and wild and compelling, as if his want were a bucking mustang out of control.

Stephen shook himself out of the peculiar dream: he tried to figure how far he had to go. The bend in the road ahead looked familiar. He was near the Baytown Inn, he was sure. There ahead in the dimness he recognized its picket fence. He could swear he had heard the hooves of stealthy horses.

Sam nickered, perhaps protesting the heavier fall of rain. Stephen ordered softly, "Quiet, boy, quiet. Steady, fella." He touched the stallion's neck and the animal ceased his faint whinnying.

The inn was in sight now and Stephen could make out the forms of two riders. One looked like a woman. They were cantering quietly down the road past the inn. And suddenly they were lost in a wooded area, apparently heading south.

Stephen came up behind and, riding to the edge of the wood, dismounted. He spoke a few more soothing words to the stallion, who waited, tetherless and patient, at the edge of the thicket.

Stephen crept forward; it was raining harder now, and he was glad, for the sound would cover the sound of his steps, although he avoided stepping on the thicker twigs, Indian fashion.

Where had they gone? The riders had disappeared, as if by Indian magic. Then Stephen saw the horses, in a clearing ahead; he heard an owl hoot, wagering it was not an owl at all. The horses were riderless but, all of a sudden, they galloped away. On the rim of the clearing was a huge, hollow tree. Stephen went to it, seeing a gleam of brightest blue in its yawning hollow. So sure was he of what the blue gleam was that he did not even raise an eyebrow as he withdrew the blue scarf from the hollow tree, and after it, a folded black shirt, small enough for a woman; a leather vest and slender leather trousers. The garments were still warm from her body's heat.

He put the shirt to his face and inhaled its scent; her scent was in it, like some unnamed flower, and the shirt still bore the shape of her breasts.

Stephen replaced three of the items in the tree and trudged back through the wood to the place where Sam was waiting. Better get him back to the ranch, he reflected, and rub him down. The rain was getting cold. Currying Sam was a task Stephen never left to the hands;

Vard had told him long ago that a horse trusted the man who saw to all its needs.

Tomorrow, Stephen said to himself, I will go to the Olwen ranch. It is we who have stolen from her; she has taken nothing. And we have taken everything.

He could almost feel the warm leather, still, between his fingers, as he took the long road back through Berwick Bay. The blue scarf was in his pocket.

Chapter Five

By morning the storm was spent, and the day dawned clear and bright. Stephen had slept little; nevertheless he rose at five, the same hour as the hands, and went to the big kitchen, asking the surprised Mexican presiding there to bring a pot of coffee to his father's study.

Stephen went with eagerness to his father's desk, despite the sleepiness that blurred his eyes. He had to know the truth about the Olwens, and he thought he might find it there, among the heavy ledgers and the untidy papers.

The day was dry again, and cool: he felt the return of his usual driving energy, that singleness of thrust that always enabled him to do a day's work while other men were still sleeping.

He received the coffee with indifferent courtesy, grateful for its first black jolt of stimulation. Years ago Louise Gerard Raike had set the precedent of serving New Orleans coffee—"black as night, strong as the devil, hot as hell"—and Stephen welcomed it doubly now.

For an irresolute moment Stephen hoped he would not find what he was looking for; then he concluded that even if what he learned was not pretty, at least it would be the truth. Somewhere in these books there had to be a clue to his father's part in the tragedy of the Olwens.

It was nearly eight o'clock before he found it: there was a smaller, separate, leather-covered book with notations unrelated to the main accounts. In this he saw the mysterious abbreviations that gave him the dark information he sought.

Recorded, in his father's familiar hand, were various

figures, cash amounts with names beside them. Names of men who were not employed on the estate, for Stephen had compared them painstakingly with the long, alphabetical roll of names kept by Varden Williams. And the date of disbursement was April 2, 1852, a week after the incident at the Olwens'.

Stephen let the book fall shut and laid it with trembling hands on the desk. He rubbed his reddened eyes and poured another cup of black, sweet coffee. Daniel Raike had paid the five strangers to kill Hugh Olwen and his wife, to fire their house and drive their sheep and cattle from the land he needed for the Short Line train.

Stephen's empty stomach rumbled and rebelled. He had eaten nothing since the early evening before, and the quantities of black coffee, and two thin cigars, on top of the ugly fact he had swallowed a moment before, were making him dizzy. He was almost weak with anger.

Vard Williams' voice assailed him from the door. "You're at it mighty early, aren't you, boy?"

Stephen turned and surveyed the smiling Vard.

"What in tarnation's eating you?" the older man cried out, seeing Stephen's pale face and odd expression.

"Come in, Vard. Sit down. I have something to tell you." He got up to pour coffee into his cup, and handed it to Vard.

Then he related what he had found.

Vard replaced the cup in its saucer with a rattle. "I don't believe it, Steve. No, I just don't believe it."

"Look for yourself." Stephen tossed the small black book to Vard and leaned back tiredly in the squeaky wooden chair. He put his hand over his sleep-reddened eyes.

There was a long silence as Vard examined the mysterious account.

"Those men never worked for the Raike estate. Isn't that right, Vard?"

The older man shook his head reluctantly. "No. No, they didn't. All the same, Steve, it could be something else. It could be anything."

"A week after the Olwens' house was burned?" Stephen Raike asked skeptically. "Come, now, Vard."

Vard looked up, still holding the book absently in his weathered hands. "What do you aim to do, boy?"

"First I'm going to see Miss Olwen. And I'm going to make her some compensation."

"Your pa's going to raise hell, when he's up and around again."

"*If* he's up and around again," Stephen retorted practically. "He's a very sick man, Vard. In any case, it's up to me now. If necessary I'll use the funds that are due to me, or my own. That part doesn't matter. What matters is the Raikes owe Doña Olwen, and I aim to pay."

"But you don't *know,* Steve."

"I know enough, Vard. And I'm going to—"

"Señor Stephen!" The woman's excited voice cut into Stephen's sentence.

"What is it, Consuela?" Stephen asked the plump little maid who was standing at the door, her black eyes snapping with excitement.

"It's Señor Daniel!" she cried. "The Dr. Fitch says that he is seeing again, and moving, and speaking!"

The two men got to their feet and rushed past Consuela into the hall. Stephen took the winding stairs in a few bounds of his long, lean legs, Varden close behind him.

Doc Fitch, who was emerging from Daniel Raike's room, smiled at Stephen. "He can use his right arm again, Steve. It's like a miracle. And his right leg has feeling. He can even say a few words. He'll know you now. But take it easy. He's still not well, you know."

Stephen Raike nodded and started into the room. But Vard Williams took him by the arm, and said, "Be careful, Steve."

"Of course I'll be careful, Vard. You know I can't say anything to him now, not yet."

Vard watched as Daniel Raike's gray eyes registered their recognition of his tall son. He smiled a one-sided smile and said almost inaudibly, trying hard to pronounce the words, "Hello, son. Welcome home."

The sun was straight above the plains when Stephen left his father's room; the old man had fallen asleep again while Stephen sat looking at him, his mind in turmoil. Daniel Raike, said Dr. Fitch, had survived a stroke that would have killed any other man.

"He's a fine man, Steve," Fitch had said to Stephen.

A fine man—or a murderer, Stephen thought now, guiding the stallion toward the south.

Stephen had gotten his second wind, at least, and the sun felt good on his back through his thin blue shirt and the light vest of tan buckskin; the clear air was good to breathe.

And Stephen put away for a time dark thoughts of the man he had left behind, heading for the house of Doña Olwen.

The house was set on a high, wooded hill, where cooler winds could blow; a likely spot judged Stephen, for the man from Wales. The burning flatness of the plains would have smothered him; then, too, the high vantage point gave a man a seeing edge that worked to his advantage in a country where strangers could not always be trusted.

Stephen made good time: he spied the wooded rise that must be Olwen's homesite, for the Short Line tracks crossed the land not far away.

Sam took the climb with spirit. They rounded the last bend, and Stephen could see the house. The place was small and plain by Raike standards. Stephen had seen an ancient Indian house in Illinois that looked much like this one, squat and square, of weathered frame, with a comical central chimney that gave it a look of surprise, and few and narrow windows. The porch was low, near the ground, and covered by a slight projecting roof in which there was a gaping hole.

Three Indian women were in the yard, digging in the

ground, and on the porch, in a path of sun, was the most beautiful woman Stephen had ever seen.

She had not yet seen him, evidently, for the chatter of the women and a loud sound of hammering within the house must have covered the sound of Sam's soft-drumming hooves in the dust of the road. Stephen reined in and stared: she was smiling at one of the Indian women, and by her side was a tall tame doe.

The Olwen woman wore a simple, bright yellow dress, and in her hair, over one ear, she'd fastened a cluster of yellow wild flowers. She was tall for a woman, and very slender; from a distance Stephen could not clearly see her eyes, but he could tell that they were full and dark, and her skin was tawny and sun-touched. Her face proud and narrow.

But it was the hair that made Stephen draw in his breath: loose, it flowed over her shoulders and arms like a shawl of silken fire, and it was the color of flame. The sun fairly spoke when it touched her flaming hair, and the hair's vivid hue, coupled with the yellow of the dress and the flowers, made him blink in the brightness of the noon.

And he knew then, for sure, that this was the woman on the train, the slender woman with the Colt, whose dark and smoldering eyes had regarded him in angry challenge.

All those stinging thoughts flashed through Stephen's mind before Doña Olwen saw him.

The deer, scenting man when the wind moved toward the house, looked up in fear and leaped from the porch, bounding into the thicket.

Doña Olwen cried out something to the Indian women, and they ran into the house. It had been a long time since Stephen had heard Comanche, but he thought he recognized some words of Doña's cry.

For one long moment Doña stared at Stephen, suspicious as the deer had been. Then she, too, disappeared inside the house.

Stephen's heart hammered against his ribs; his hands were sweaty on the reins. Now that he was here, he wondered what the hell he was going to say. He wished he hadn't come.

It was easier to drive a six-mule team—or rope a calf —than reason with an angry woman.

But suddenly she was back, standing on the porch, a rifle held in her slender hands. She cocked it and fired. Dismayed, Raike heard its loud, singing *whang* above his brow, and his wide-brimmed blue-gray Stetson fell into the dust. His Colt fired the moment it cleared the holster, and the cluster of yellow flowers fell from her hair, the shattered petals floating to the porch. Confident that his bullet had not even singed the glorious hair around the yellow flowers, Stephen dismounted and began to move forward, holding up his long hand in a gesture of entreaty.

The woman in the yellow dress seemed stunned: irresolute, she lowered the rifle. But as he drew near Stephen could see she was trembling, not with fear but with a strong, overpowering anger, for her eyes were bright. And her beautiful mouth was compressed into a furious line.

She raised the rifle again as he came forward, but he did not slacken his pace. If she fired, then she would fire; but he had to walk to her now. The nearer he came, the lovelier she appeared.

Apparently impressed by the recklessness of his courage, the woman lowered the rifle again. But she did not move from her rigid, challenging stance as Stephen reached the low steps that led to the ruined porch.

He found his voice. "Good afternoon, Miss Olwen." She was silent, staring. "I regret that I cannot take off my hat to you, but you have done that for me already."

"You could have killed me," she answered at last, in a rich, husky voice.

"If I had meant to," he answered coolly, "you would be dead now. I don't kill women. Look at your hair."

"What do you mean?" Some of her poise had deserted her, he noted with satisfaction, and in those full, dark eyes, he saw uncertainty.

"Look at your hair, where the flowers were," he said in the same easy voice. "Is it burned?"

With reluctance, then, she took up a strand of the fiery, glittering hair and scrutinized it. "No, not a hair." She looked up at him with grudging respect.

At that moment he saw a glint of gold, half-hidden under the modest V of her yellow dress. "I'll take my father's watch," he said casually, mounting the stairs toward her.

Her tawny cheeks flushed red as he held out a lean, brown hand, waiting for the watch.

With an angry gesture, she unfastened the chain and slapped the heavy golden watch into his palm. The smooth, worn gold was warm from its shelter between her breasts, and the feel of it made his legs weak all of a sudden.

But Stephen held onto his control, and smiled. "Thank you, Miss Olwen. Now, do you mind if we talk?"

She had recaptured some of her earlier calm. "What about?" she inquired in that husky voice. The advantage was with her again; he sensed she knew it, for she smiled. And her smile was as enchanting as the rest of her— warm and wide, mingling the sweetness of a woman with the sweetness of a mischievous child.

"What has a Raike to say to me?" The name was pronounced with a contempt that jarred. "Am I arrested?"

"I've come to tell you that I want to make amends."

"Amends?" She was genuinely surprised, and Stephen felt again the triumph of control.

"For the death of your father and mother, and the losses you have had."

Doña Olwen was stricken silent in astonishment.

"Please," Stephen said gently, "I want to talk with you about it." He repressed an overwhelming desire to take her in his arms.

She still did not reply, but moved past him and sat down on the top step.

He sat down beside her, alive to the warm softness so close to him. As he drew in his breath, he inhaled her fresh, sweet scent of soap and flowers. His restless elbow brushed her shoulder; she drew away.

"What did you mean?" She shot the question out all of a sudden. "Just what do you mean to do?"

"I want to make it up to you," he began slowly. "Make up to you—in some small way—for all you've lost. There must be some—financial compensation that—"

She turned on him, fuming. "You mean you'll buy my parents back? Will your money bring them back from the dead? Is that what you mean, Mr. Raike?"

Doña got up abruptly and stood on the stair, looking down at him. Unprepared for this attack, and feeling a little drunk at her closeness, Stephen Raike gazed up at Doña Olwen. For a moment he was unable to frame a reply.

Then he rose awkwardly, saying, "I have come to help you." His gaze dropped to her mouth, like a dark rose against her gold-tan skin. It was trembling.

The sound of a whip-poor-will came to Stephen. A whip-poor-will at noon. No, he silently protested, and his hand dropped to his holster. His keen ear detected the signal of an Indian. But what kind of Indian would make a night sound in the bright, sunny noon? The humorous aspect of it came to Stephen, even as the cautious watcher in him kept his hand upon the leather.

His gesture had not escaped the woman beside him. "It is my cousin, Tahre, Mr. Raike," she said coldly. "Will you add a new murder to your family's record? Tahre goes unarmed today without a *nakke,* a single arrow."

"Tahre!" Stephen repeated. And at Doña Olwen's look, he answered, "I have known Tahre for nearly twenty years."

Her anger seemed to be at war with another, more veiled emotion. The dark eyes softened almost imperceptibly, and Doña Olwen looked at Stephen in an altered fashion.

Then Stephen saw the Indian coming from the trees; the copper-skinned boy he had known had changed beyond the ordinary changes that turned a boy into a man.

The tall Indian approaching them now exhibited the stern pride of the highest chieftain. At first glance, the lithe and handsome Indian had stiffened to behold the white face of the other man. But as he came nearer, seeing the relative ease with which the white man and his cousin stood together, Tahre's hard mouth relaxed a little.

"Isse-Loa," he said, and Stephen recognized the strangely hoarse voice of the man on the train. What had happened to him, Stephen Raike wondered, that made his voice come out in such a croak?

Stephen came down the stairs, holding out his hand. "Tahre," he said. "I am Stephen Raike. Stephen. Do you remember?" He could feel the woman's dark gaze on them, suspenseful, waiting.

"Stephen Raike." Tahre did not take the proffered hand, but something gleamed far back in his flat, black eyes. He almost smiled. "Have you come to lose a race to me again, or to arrest us?" His dark glance flicked to the watch that Stephen still held in his hand.

"Mr. Raike," said Doña Olwen coldly, "has come to give me money for my mother and my father." Stephen turned and looked at her; the full, dark eyes were hot with anger again. "I have persuaded him not to kill you, Tahre."

Indignantly, Stephen Raike opened his mouth to speak.

But Doña Olwen rushed on. "Why don't you get off my land, now, Mr. Raike? That is your portion there." She gestured down the hill and across the meadow, where the tracks of the Short Line gleamed in the bright, bitter sun.

"Isse-Loa—" Tahre began.

"Get off my land, Mr. Raike," Doña Olwen repeated, and her voice had the lash of a narrow whip of leather. "You cannot give me back my mother and father, and you cannot give Tahre his voice again."

"What do you mean?" Stephen asked.

"Not only did your father's men kill my parents, and burn down our hourse, and drive our sheep and cows away. They put a knife into Tahre's throat. It left him to speak as he does today."

Stephen could find no further words. Then, after a long look at Tahre and at Doña Olwen, he said, "I'm going, Miss Olwen. But I will be back again."

Stephen turned and walked down the dusty road to the fence where Sam was tethered. As he mounted his horse, there came again the loud, singing *whang* of a rifle bullet; it almost grazed his leg. The wire fence behind him shuddered with its impact, singing.

The sun was sinking again when Stephen rode into Berwick Bay and tethered Sam on one of the hitching posts before the Golden Girl. He needed a drink, and needed it badly.

Nothing in his life had prepared him for Doña Olwen and the tangle of trouble surrounding her. From the moment that her parting shot had grazed his jeans, Stephen had hardly known whether to curse or to laugh.

He could handle anything that was simple and clear—he had ridden through Indian-haunted woods with a sack of gold when he was seventeen; shot it out with granite-faced men from California to Illinois. He had used his fists and strength and brains to get to where he was, and none of it had troubled him. But this, he decided, was like tangling with a cobweb that clung no matter how he flailed.

The mustachioed, beefy man behind the bar of the Golden Girl greeted him now like a friend, and as Stephen sipped his whiskey, soothed by its bite against his tongue, Raike recalled what Vard had said.

Maybe he was a hundred kinds of fool; maybe Vard was right. The cash amounts in the separate book could have been for anything. Yet he had gone off, half-cocked, assuming right off the bat that his father had had the Olwens killed, riding off like Don Quixote to make love to a halfbreed bandit woman.

The magical aura surrounding Doña Olwen on the wooded hill was fading a little now in the matter-of-fact light of the day, he thought wryly in his injured pride.

And yet the heat she had ignited could not be denied. Stephen saw the dark-haired whore in pink coming down the stairs from an upper floor, and he caught the eye of the beefy man behind the bar and nodded. The barman gestured the girl upstairs again; she smiled and obeyed.

She had, Stephen Raike could see, a freshness he had not often known in women of her kind. And she looked very young, as young as Doña Olwen.

"Damn her!" he muttered, turning embarrassed from the barman's curious, half-smiling face. He put a gold piece on the bar and followed the girl up the stairs.

She went into a room at the end of the hall. He waited for a while, then tapped softly on the door.

The door parted slowly, and he stood on the threshhold, looking at the girl.

She was wearing some kind of loose, white garment, and he could see her full young body through it. Her skin was very white, and up close, he could see that her long dark lashes were spiky with a stuff of black, her round, rather foolish mouth oiled with a bright pinkness. A strong scent of roses emanated from her skin.

"Come in," she smiled, and her voice was flat and a little thin. Stephen Raike stepped into the room and closed the door, remembering the rich, husky tone of Doña Olwen.

He placed his hat on the bureau and moved toward the girl, testing with his hard, lean hands the smooth skin of her neck. Holding her, he ran his hands down either side of her young body; it had a spongy softness that held no delight for him. And he thought of the lithe, slender softness of Doña Olwen with her skin the color of red gold.

Stephen felt an instant draining of desire.

The girl, on the other hand, was looking up at him with expectation, breathing with a quickened breath, a look almost of worship in her dark eyes.

Stephen Raike's gray look met hers an instant, then he removed his hands from her waist. Without a word, he picked up his hat from the bureau and placed there in its stead two pieces of gold.

An older, more experienced woman might have jested

coarsely; the girl in white merely looked at Stephen with black, bewildered eyes as he left the room.

In a rage of shame, Stephen moved quickly down the stairs and past the curious barman.

He untied the stallion, mounted and galloped away on the road leading north to his father's house. Nothing like that had ever happened to him before, and he began to ache now, ache with anger and confusion and the pain of wanting unfulfilled.

She had him now, by God, that wild and crazy vixen. And he would be driven past enduring until he had Doña Olwen—had her, or forgot her. Either way, it made no difference to Stephen. Because she had robbed him for sure, in a way that he had not foreseen.

Worst of all was the way the watch had felt in his hand, when she had first removed it from the shelter of her breasts; so warm, and tantalizing.

Chapter Six

Stephen was soothed by the rasp of the currycomb on Sam's sleek hide. The stables were pleasant at that hour of the morning, still early enough to be cool, but late enough for quiet reflection since the work horses were gone with the hands. Vard was out with Abilene, Stephen noticed.

As he applied the comb, Stephen's thoughts lightened for a time. But his flesh still ached for Doña Olwen.

The rhythmic beat of hooves, a snort and jingle, announced the approach of another horse.

The stallion snuffled at the air and pricked his ears, but calmly, for it was a horse and man whose smell he knew. Vard was guiding Abilene, the old paint, into another stall.

Vard called a greeting from over the stall and Stephen heard him mumble with rough affection to the paint while he was unsaddling and rubbing it down.

"That horse is gettin' old, poor bastard," Vard said as he came into Sam's cubicle.

Stephen tossed the comb in a wooden box nailed to the boards of the stall and patted the stallion on the rump.

"Somethin' about a horse's outside that's good for a man's inside." Vard leaned against the stall, watching Stephen.

It was an old saying, a saying that Vard liked to repeat, and Stephen hardly heard him. But he looked up with surprise when the old man shot out a question:

"When would you calculate I was born, Steve?"

Stephen stared at him. "Well, I don't remember your birthday, Vard. What do you mean, what are you getting at?"

"What I'm getting at, boy, is this. I wasn't born last Tuesday, or the week before. I was born a long time ago, and I seen a lot o' things. And I know you're up to somethin'."

Stephen looked steadily at Vard Williams; Stephen's slate-gray eyes and impassive face were cool, giving away nothing.

Vard explained, "You been runnin' around like a jack-rabbit, goin' here and there and never tellin' me nothin'. First you say you're ridin' south, the night we was with the posse, and you came back tight-mouthed as an Indian. Then yesterday you made a trip over to the Olwens' and came back lookin' like you ate a cactus. Didn't tell me doodlum-squat what happened.

"Now, boy, I'd have to be crippled, deaf, dumb and blind not to reckon them things has some connection. The Short Line robbery—that ride you made south, when you found nothin'—and this Olwen gal, are all tied up together some way. Am I right?"

Stephen was silent for a long instant. Then he said, "All right, Vard, you are. I've got to trust somebody. I've got to tell somebody, or bust with it."

And Vard squatted down to listen as Stephen told him about seeing Doña Olwen.

When Stephen finished, Vard unfolded his wiry legs and, grunting, stood. "Sweet Jesus, boy, you got yourself a lot of trouble. There's talk of sendin' to Galveston for the federal marshal. Lamb and Scurry ain't worth a damn, and everybody knows it. Gettin' sick of 'em in Berwick."

Vard chuckled, adding, "Lord, those two couldn't find their pecker in their flies to pee."

Stephen laughed, a deep, loud laugh that was the first sound of mirth Vard had heard from him in many days.

"That's better now," the old man said. "What do you aim to do, Steve? When they bring the marshal in, they've got to find out about the Indian and the Olwen gal."

"I know that. I want to marry her, Vard. Marry her and take her away, get her out of it."

"Marry her! Jesus, kid, your pappy won't accept no halfbreed daughter. And an *Olwen!*"

"I want to marry her," Stephen repeated stubbornly. When Vard saw the mulelike obduracy—a mark of the Raikes—in the set of his mouth, he knew there was no point in arguing.

"What you need is a little recreation," Vard said, grinning.

Stephen looked at him. Then he took a deep breath and told Vard what had happened at the Golden Girl.

"That Olwen gal's got you by the horns."

Stephen agreed in silence, but did not answer.

"Say," Vard said in a brighter voice, "what do you say to a little bulldoggin', down to Berwick? Can you still handle that, or have you got all softened up, livin' East?"

Stung, Stephen said, "I could always handle that, and you know it damn well. I'd like it fine. Let's go."

Vard laughed. "All *right*. You just saddle up that stallion, an' I'll take one of your pappy's horses. That old paint is winded."

As they rode from the stables toward the Berwick Bay road, Stephen felt foolish—foolish but relieved, glad he had told everything to Vard.

There was so little recreation in the Berwick Bay of 1857 that the Saturday event, in which the local men roped calves and wrestled longhorn steer, drew quite a crowd of watchers. As Vard Williams and Stephen Raike sat on the split-rail fence surrounding the crude corral, the dust behind them was already thick with farmers and their wives; a couple of ostentatiously dressed women from the Golden Girl, their faces strangely naked-looking and white in the unaccustomed brightness; cowhands and merchants, laborers and *vaqueros*.

"There they go," cried Vard, his old blue eyes snapping with excitement. A dancing, half-grown calf came bounding out of the chute at the corral's other end. At the shout of "Go!" a skinny young cowman rode into the corral at a gallop and went after the calf whirling his rope above his head.

Once the calf was roped, the horse stopped dead, backing to keep the lariat taut, while the rider jumped off, threw the calf expertly and tied three of its feet together.

"Pretty good," Vard commented, "but he wasn't as fast as you used to be."

Stephen smiled, and remarked, "You're having a high time, partner. Do you come here every Saturday?"

"Lord, no, boy! But after thirty years I guess I rate a day off."

Vard looked around and then exclaimed, involuntarily, "Oh-oh. Lordy-lord."

"What's the matter?" Raike followed the direction of Vard's stare. Then his heart began to hammer like a drum.

Doña Olwen, on a shining roan, sat poised and cool a little apart from the milling crowd. In defiance of tradition, she was mounted astride her horse; but her grace was such that the posture detracted not a jot from her beauty. Her narrow hips were covered by the fringe of a doe-colored, sleeveless jacket of buckskin, which matched her trousers.

She wore no boots or spurs, but her small feet in the stirrups were moccasined. On her head she wore a tan sombrero with a wide, sweeping brim. Her glorious hair was hidden, gathered up under the hat, but the ripe mouth and the heavy-lidded dark eyes, sleepy now with a kind of arrogant amusement, were not.

Vard Williams shook his head. "So, you're goin' to break your neck for this halfbreed filly to see?"

Stephen's tanned face darkened with anger, and he balled his fists. "Don't talk like that about her, Vard."

The old man fell silent and shook his head again, shifting a wad of tobacco to his other cheek. "What're you goin' in for, Steve?"

"All of it. The cutting, too." Yes, thought Stephen, I'm going in for all of it.

Stephen put up his name for the bulldogging contest and the cutting.

He mounted Sam, glad that Doña Olwen would see what he could do in a rodeo. At the starting shout, he galloped with the hazer into the corral, just as the dangerous longhorn came tearing out from the chute.

The hazer, a *vaquero* of the Raikes, rode alongside the steer, which was snorting wildly and rolling its furious, red-veined eyes; the hazer stayed on the steer's off side to keep it from turning away. Stephen came up on the near side and with a mighty lunge, grabbed the huge animal by the horns, swung out of the saddle and twisted the galloping steer's great head to throw him on his side.

The steer weighed eight hundred pounds, but the strength of Stephen's arms and body were immense, his horsemanship superb.

He wrestled with the titanic steer for a few seconds, then released him with a skilled and lightning motion, jumping from the range of the perilous horns. There was a burst of applause and shouting from the crowd.

"Hi, hi, hi!" bellowed the *vaquero,* and two other mounted men galloped into the corral to herd the baffled steer back into the chute. Stephen Raike raised his gray hat to the crowd and grinned.

When he'd remounted, he joined Vard at the fence. Doña Olwen had not moved from her position; she stared through the surrounding knot of admiring men as if they were invisible. Stephen touched his hat, with a mocking gesture at the bullet-hole she had decorated it with the day before.

She neither smiled nor gave any other form of recognition, but triumphantly he saw a touch of admiration in her eyes, the same look they had had when yesterday she examined her undamaged hair.

"That was mighty fine, Steve, mighty fine," Vard said. "Why don't you give the cuttin' a miss? You've done enough for one day."

Stephen, still breathing hard, retorted, "I've just begun."

The object of the "cutting" was to separate a lively

calf from the middle of the longhorns; the horse was required to do the task with no help from its rider, who was supposed to use neither legs nor rein to guide the mount. Stephen, however, used both, so cleverly that others could not detect it.

When Stephen went in, Vard muttered anxiously to himself, "These danged longhorns, scariest animal in creation."

Since Sam was not a cutting horse, Stephen rode into the corral on a fast little mustang that reminded Vard of a sheepdog, stalking the calf almost the way a dog did a sheep, knowing ahead of time the calf's every move, spinning until Vard thought Stephen must be giddy.

"That little ol' horse can turn on a dime," Vard said nervously to himself. He turned a second to glance at Doña Olwen; it seemed to him that stony-faced gal was breathing a little quicker.

Stephen's inside stirrup almost scraped the dust, and Vard breathed in nervous gulps. That boy hadn't lost his cow-sense, for all the time he had spent in the East!

There was an awful moment when Vard Williams thought the longhorns with their razor points would slice both the mustang and Stephen's leg. But with an unbelievable grace and speed, Stephen drove the calf from the midst of the longhorns and into the other chute.

Stephen was soaked with sweat when he got off the mustang and strode across the surrounding yard toward Vard.

"Lord, Steve, you had me going there!"

Stephen took off his hat and wiped his head and face with a handkerchief. For the first time Vard Williams saw the bullet hole, saw Stephen Raike staring again after Doña Olwen, who had turned her shining roan and was riding off.

"Looks like you didn't tell it all," Vard said ironically to Stephen.

Stephen, with the sweat blinding his eyes and soaking his body, swore to himself that from now on he would leave her alone.

His resolve was firm at sunset, in the evening, and it held as he went wearily to bed. But he could not fall asleep. He could see the high, round moon of late September from his open window, the moon that the Indians called the "Moon of the Changing Season."

Tomorrow their new year would begin as the moon turned full, and the final weeks of Indian summer would follow.

"Isse-Loa," Stephen whispered. Isse-Loa, Tahre called her. "Deer of Fire." And Stephen remembered her fleeting look of unwilling admiration, her mouth that was like a hurt child's—when she smiled, like a small girl planning new mischief. Stephen felt a tautness in his middle when he thought of her.

He threw back the covers and swung his long legs to the floor, sitting on the edge of the bed with his head in his hands.

I'm tied, he reflected darkly, tied like the calf in its noose, with three legs together. And Vard had said there was talk of calling in the marshal from Galveston. He must warn Doña Olwen. For Stephen was sure now; he loved her. There was no running from it anymore.

He rose and dressed, stole from the house to the stables and saddled his father's mare. Sam had had enough today, Stephen judged.

The ride in the moonlight did not seem long, for Stephen's mind was busy with remembering. He recalled the race he'd once had with Tahre. The high, wooded hill, dark in the moon, where the Olwen house stood came into view. A wind was rising.

She was still being carried in her mother's arms when Tahre and I raced our ponies that afternoon.

He smiled, recalling how ignominiously he, skilled rider that he was, had fallen when the Comanche boy had tried to teach him Indian riding—hanging from one stirrup, on the far side of his pony.

Then as he took the winding road up the hill, Stephen sobered. Doña Olwen had been hurt, hurt so very much. And a feeling of hot tenderness swept over him. He decided that he would make it right, no matter what she said or did.

Suddenly it occurred to him how late it was. He would be taken for a wandering prowler, and she would surely bring out her rifle again. Stephen grinned as he dismounted and tethered the mare to the fence. Better give himself a fighting chance, before she heard him.

He stole forward, treading carefully on the path, avoiding the dry twigs that might snap loudly and advertise his presence.

One dim light shone in the Olwen house, and someone's horse browsed in the sweet grass near the porch. Doña Olwen had a visitor; one who rode a rather swaybacked mare of a darker color.

The door of the Olwen house opened quietly, and he could see Doña Olwen talking to a thin, young man with a small pouch in his hand. The faint murmur of their voices reached Stephen. He stepped behind a tree.

Who was the bastard? Stephen wanted to confront the man, to feel his own hands around the intruder's throat. There could only be one reason for such a late visit. Stephen Raike grew hot, then cold.

But the man and woman in the dim path of light from the door did not embrace. The man turned, and the lamplight gave Stephen a clearer view of his face. Charlie Scurry! Stephen flattened himself against the tree.

His sharp ear caught the sound of a dull chink from the bag in Scurry's hand. Money! She had given him money: the payoff for silence about the stagecoach raid.

Even in his consternation, Stephen could have laughed aloud with relief. Doña Olwen had not received a lover; she was paying off a henchman. Stephen knew, as he watched Charlie Scurry mount his swaybacked mare and head away toward the descending road, that the right thing to do was to confront the deputy.

But he knew even more surely that he would not. For the only thing that mattered now was to warn Doña Olwen, to protect her. Slowly Stephen moved around the tree as Charlie Scurry rode past, hoping against hope that his father's mare would be still. She was tethered in the shadows; it was possible that Scurry would ride by without seeing her.

Stephen held his breath: Scurry came nearer. Quiet, Molly, quiet! Stephen begged in silence.

The tractable mare, bless her, made no noise at all. And the young deputy rode off and down the hill.

Stephen exhaled, taking his tense hand from his holster. He had had no desire to shoot a damn fool kid.

The door of the Olwen house was shut, and now as he moved cautiously forward, Stephen saw the lamplight dim. He stepped quietly onto the porch; she must have heard, for the door was open, and she stood there with her rifle in her hands.

"Charlie? Is that you?" The rich, husky voice held a note of fear.

"Don't be frightened, Miss Olwen. It's Stephen Raike." He took a tentative step forward. "Didn't anyone ever tell you a rifle is no good at this range?"

Her dark eyes hardened. "What do you want?"

"Please let me come in. I must talk to you."

She stepped backward, setting the rifle to her shoulder. "What have you come for, at this time of night?" she asked suspiciously. "To take advantage of the fact that I live alone?"

"You shouldn't be living here alone," he replied calmly. "It isn't safe, you know."

She still held the rifle pointed at him. "I can see that," she retorted coldly.

"Please," he said again. "Put down the gun, Miss Olwen. I have not come to—hurt you. I saw what you gave Charlie Scurry. He went right past me as he rode away. I've got to talk to you, I tell you. They may be sending for the marshal, from Galveston. He's a smart man, Miss Olwen, and a hard-headed man, as hardheaded as they come."

Without changing her stance, the red-haired woman demanded, "Why are you telling me this?"

Stephen thought, How beautiful she is, even now with the hardness in her eyes, and dressed in an old, dust-colored dress. Her hair was tied back in a leather thong, and her high-cheeked face naked and spare without its shelter of tresses. "I want to help," he answered simply.

Something in his tone must have struck her, for to his surprise she lowered the rifle and leaned it against the wall.

"Why?" she inquired bluntly, still standing with her back pressed to the wall.

"Because I love you," he said roughly and, moving forward, took her by the arms. He pulled her to him, holding her about her supple waist. She gasped and struggled, but he did not let her go.

He held her still with one powerful hand, the fingers of the other stroking her satiny red hair, then softly taking her chin, raising her reluctant face to his. He took the other hand from her narrow waist, and held her face between both hands, bending to place his deep, starved kisses on her startled mouth.

For a timeless, dizzy interval, the soft mouth, as she made a murmuring sound of protest, answered the pressure of his, and Stephen drew her closer, yet closer, marveling in the downy softness of her body. He could not believe how soft she was: the body that looked so slim and taut had its roundness and its hollow secrets.

He felt her tremble, heard her continuing to make that small, sound of half-protest, and a volcanic urge began to possess him; his grasp upon her tightened, and he started to force her backward against the wall.

She was struggling again and moaning; in the sounds he heard a kind of terror. Snapping to his senses, Stephen released her mouth, and let her go, breathing heavily. Somewhere in his shuddering body he felt a deep, triumphant joy, for that little time when Doña Olwen had answered his caress with a savage pressure of her own sweet mouth.

But now, he saw she had lost her fear, and her dark eyes gleamed with the anger he knew so well, the stubborn courage that made him treasure her.

"So you have come to—take me," she said in a low voice, furious.

"I have come to ask you to marry me," he said, hearing his own impetuous words with astonishment.

He smiled at her surprise. "Marry you?" she repeated, in a wondering voice.

"Yes."

"*Marry* you!" she cried then, slipping out from under his detaining arms and flouncing to the door. She opened it, and ordered, "Get out. Get out of my house! Marry a *Raike?*"

He winced at the way she said his name, with such utter loathing.

"Get out."

Grinning, he retrieved his hat from a little table by the door, where there was a Pueblo vase full of yellow flowers.

"All right, Doña Olwen. But I'll be back. You liked it when I kissed you, almost as much as I did."

Her face of rosy tan grew dark with anger, and she shook her head, releasing the fiery shawl of hair from its thong. "Liked it! Why, you—you—get out of here!"

He grinned again and made no answer, bending to kiss her slim hand.

"Raike."

At the sound of his name, Stephen whirled, his hand on his Colt.

The Indian Tahre stood on the threshold, glowering. Stephen recalled in a flash of memory: *Tahre* was the Indian word for "stone." And Doña Olwen's Indian cousin looked like a stone at this moment—stone-hard, immovable, enduring. A quick glance told Stephen the Indian was unarmed, but there was an ugly gleam in his flat, black eyes, and his mouth was drawn into a thin line, so tightly it had almost disappeared.

Tahre flexed his strong hands, but Stephen's gray eyes met Tahre's coolly. "Good evening, Tahre," he said in an easy tone.

"Have you done harm to Isse-Loa?" Tahre thundered.

"No. I've asked her to marry me."

A look of momentary surprise—and something else, Raike judged—came into the Indian's angry stare.

"Is this true, Isse-Loa?" he demanded, turning to the flame-haired woman.

"Yes. He had the—nerve to ask me to marry a *Raike*."

"I am thinking that a man does not do evil, to the one *he* asks to wed," Tahre said, considering Stephen.

"That is true." Stephen was encouraged by Tahre's words. "I have come to tell her—and you—that I wish to save you from that evil." Sensing his advantage, he went on, "Tahre, you are her *anggona,* her friend. You must listen."

Tahre's coppery face relaxed a trifle at the sound of the Indian word, but he said, "She cried out. I heard her cry out like a frightened *easooba*."

Stephen flushed, and as the Indian looked at him, he saw that Tahre understood. "I haven't done her any harm; I would never harm her. I wish her only good. You must listen to me, both of you. In town, there's talk about sending for the marshal; he will learn the names of those who robbed the stage—and the train." He was speaking eagerly and fast, but in the stately measures of the Indian tongue.

To Stephen's amazement, Tahre addressed Doña sternly: *"Che-a-sa-ah,* Isse-Loa, I am displeased with you. Stephen Raike has come to warn us and you turn him away in anger."

But Doña cried, "I will not listen to a Raike! Tahre, how can you be such a fool? How can you trust him? Get out, both of you! Oh, God, how can men be such fools? Is there no one left to understand me?"

The two tall men stood staring at her, uneasy in the presence of an emotional woman. They were united, for the moment, in their discomfort.

Then Stephen said quietly, "Yes, Doña, there is someone." He looked at her with yearning, and she returned the look, confused.

He touched his hat and followed Tahre onto the porch. "I trust you, Stephen Raike," the Indian said in a low voice.

"Thank you."

As they walked down the path together, Stephen asked quietly, "Do you love her, too?"

"I have always loved her. But you will win her, not I."

Stephen gave the Indian a sidelong look, speechless with sudden hope.

"You mean her well," Tahre added. "You can give her the soft beds and pretty dresses she has always craved. You will care for her."

"Yes, by God, I would care for her."

Tahre gave a sudden chuckle. "She is a little angry at all men, sometimes even at me. But she will listen to my mother, Patche. I will ask Patche to plead your cause."

"Why are you doing this?"

"Because I want what is good for her, Stephen Raike." Stephen held out his hand, and Tahre grasped it strongly.

Then Tahre said, "I know now why she cried out." He smiled. "In great feeling the most quiet man is sometimes a wolf, a *nassooba*."

Stephen's face darkened in the moonlight. "She should not be living here alone. I don't like it; she's not safe."

"Oh, she is safe enough, Stephen Raike. Tahre watches."

Raike mounted his father's horse and rode down the hill, consoled by the Indian's words, "Tahre watches"; his heart was high, thinking of tomorrow.

Chapter Seven

On a flat, dusty, treeless plain circled by protecting hills, there were rows of crude, cone-shaped structures, like great duncecaps. The structures were made of the skins of buffalo; through their open points protruded, like broomstraws, the ends of the thin poles supporting the cones. Tipis in a Comanche village.

A group of women worked together at one end of the row of tipis, in the waning sun. Several were young, one heavy with child; almost to a woman, the group of workers wore sleeveless dresses of buckskin, their arrow-straight black hair divided into two long braids, one on either side of their faces.

But one of the women, although dressed like the others, wore her hair loose around her shoulders, and the hair was a vivid glory in the sun. A little boy, half-naked, ran to the woman with the bright hair and touched it gingerly.

"Hasse believes your hair will burn, Isse-Loa," said the plump, smiling Indian woman who was stretching a buffalo skin over a wooden frame.

"Let me help you with that, Patche." Doña Olwen rose from her kneeling position.

"No, no, Isse-Loa, the work is hard and hurts the hands. And you have never liked doing this," Patche protested.

It was so; Doña had always disliked the smell of the newly skinned hides, preferring other tasks.

"Why don't you help Amma mend the leggings?" Patche suggested. She inclined her head toward the pregnant woman, sitting by a small fire where a pot of water was coming to the boil. "Or look to the *soot-te,* there; you can put the leaves in for tea."

Doña went to the pot; the water was not ready. She knelt down next to Amma and taking up one of the pairs of leggings, began to work on it.

"You need not work at all, Isse-Loa," said Patche. "The joy of your visit is enough, *wahkane,* is it not so, Easooba?"

Patche addressed a third woman, who was stretching out a buffalo skin on the ground, using sharp wooden stakes. Easooba made a sound of assent, and Doña studied them, one after the other, with affection.

Patche was Comanche for pigeon, and Tahre's mother was well-named, with her plump breast and domestic ways, the soft, round intonations of her voice. *Easooba,* on the other hand meant "dove," and the gentleness of the woman stretching the skin had doubtless occasioned her naming.

Doña worked for a time in silence, marveling, as she often did, that her cousin Tahre was so much more worldly and intelligent than these simple women. His musical way of speaking reminded her of their relatives, the Shoshoni to the north. The Shoshoni had elected to stay when the wandering and warlike Comanches had come south in pursuit of the Spanish horses. The Comanches never planted anything, never stayed anywhere for long: they were hunters and warriors, excellent riders. But Tahre had always seemed to have something of the ways of the Shoshoni. Doña recalled a poem he had taught her long ago, a word-song made by his northern kinsman: *Wacoba, Wacoba, calling, come to the willows! You have heard my blood whispering through the grasses, Wacoba, Wacoba, you have heard my blood by the wild rose under the willows.*

"You are very silent, Isse-Loa," Patche remarked.

"I was thinking of the song old Kora made, in the North."

The women Amma and Easooba looked at Doña with tolerant incomprehension.

"Where are Anowa and the others?" Doña asked, to

distract them from their contemplation of her. Anowa was Patche's husband, the leader of the village. "In council?"

"Ai! They still stay a moon in council," Patche replied sourly. "In council, and smoking their pipes on their backsides, while we bring them food and sew up the tears in their leggings. Once they have killed enough buffalo, you know how it is, there is not much left for them to do. And now that there is a peace with the *u-nehka,* the white animals."

Patche stopped, dismayed. She remembered that Doña's father was a white man.

The compassionate Amma, to cover Patche's embarrassment, began to chatter, "Ai! Ai! They brought in three great *yanas-O!* The buffalo meat will last us many, many weeks. They will be able to sit in council, smoking, until the very Moon When the Deer Shed Antlers!"

That was the next star-month, Doña knew, which began near the end of October.

Patche commented wisely, "Every buffalo Anowa brings in is a great buffalo, never a *yanasa,* always a *yanas-O!*" It was a statement of rueful affection.

Doña thought, At least I know where Tahre gets his sense of humor.

Glancing at Doña, Patche remarked, "The sun is almost dead, *chu?*"

Looking into the woman's wise black eyes, Doña's intuition, bequeathed by her Celtic father, and the sharp hearing of the Indian in her blood, told her that Patche was leading up to something.

"It is not far away," Patche added, "the Moon of Wait Until I Come." The Indian woman smiled slyly. The Indians, Doña knew, had several names for their moons, and the moon to which Patche just referred was the same moon of late October.

"What are you waiting for, Isse-Loa, in your house upon the hill, all alone?" Patche asked softly.

Doña's cheeks turned to a golden rose as she remembered Stephen's kiss.

"The old man has his cub again, they are saying in

the town." Patche handed Doña a small handleless cup of clay filled with the steaming tea Easooba had prepared.

Doña nodded her thanks, taking the cup. "Yes." She wondered if Tahre had said something to his mother. What did it mean?

"He played as a boy with Tahre," Patche went on in a quiet voice that did not reach the ears of the other women. She had abandoned her task and moved near to Doña. "He is good, Isse-Loa, and has none of the evil of his father. You have sworn revenge. What sweeter food is there to the tongue of your hate than to take the old bear's only cub?"

Startled by the idea, Doña stared at the cackling Patche. The Indian's wily question echoed in her brain.

"When that ol' quack comes here tonight, you tell him I've got to get out of this bed."

Stephen shook his head, grinning at his father, who sat propped up against his pillows. The old man's color was returning, his voice was almost as strong as it had ever been, and he could even speak more easily.

"Not so fast," Stephen said calmly, looking at his father. It was possible, Stephen thought, that he would be on his feet again, and soon. He remembered what Doc Fitch had said, that Daniel Raike had survived a stroke that would have killed a lesser man.

Stephen, for all his dark suspicions of his father, could not help admiring the determined old tyrant; and Daniel's near brush with death had aroused in his son a kind of grudging affection that began to warm him as he sat again by his father's bed.

"Vard tells me you been actin' up in the corral at Berwick," Daniel said, a twinkle in his hard gray eyes.

"Vard talks too much. And so do you," Stephen added. "Doc Fitch says you've got to be still a while longer."

"Still!" Daniel exclaimed, and muttered an obscenity. "I been lying here like a damned corpse all these days and nights. What am I going to do with myself? I'm not a book reader like you. And when are you going to bring me those accounts, so we can go over them together?"

At the mention of accounts, Stephen recalled the little leather book, with the strangers' names and the mysterious amounts of listed cash disbursements. A shadow fell across his face.

"What's the matter?" his father demanded. "Something wrong? Vard told me you'd taken hold pretty well. Must be all that business you're doing in the East. You've done damn well, Steve. I'm proud of you."

Stephen could see that his father's pride in him was great.

"Vard told me a lot of things," the old man said. "About the prospecting, and the bear that got you. That's some story!" He chuckled.

Stephen smiled, feeling confused. His father had committed wrongs he could never stomach, yet Stephen could not help being touched by his father's approval.

Stephen rose and wandered to the window; his father's room overlooked the long, winding road to the house. Beyond it were the vast, sweeping plains with their shaggy ridges; the wooded ridges that reminded Stephen of the hill where the Olwen house stood among the scrubby pines and cooler breezes.

"You figuring on settling here now, Steve?" Stephen, in spite of himself, was touched by the tentative, almost beseeching quality of the question.

Still not turning, he replied, "I don't know yet, Dad. I just don't know. There's an awful lot to take me back to Chicago."

Aware of his father's silence, he turned to meet the old man's questioning look. "Don't let's worry about it now," he said, smiling.

"Don't talk to me like I'm a blasted invalid!" Daniel cried out, and the color in his weathered face deepened.

Stephen walked back to the bed and sat down again in the chair beside it. "Simmer down, now, Dad. You know damn well that Fitch said if you get all het up again, you'll never get out of that bed."

Daniel sighed. "I know it. I know. You're right. But there's something we've got to talk about."

"What's that?"

"I heard that Olwen girl is back in town, that she's trying to rebuild the house. And I heard you've been to see her. What was that about?"

Stephen's lean face flushed with annoyance. "How in the name of hell did you hear about that?"

Daniel laughed softly, and his shrewd eyes studied his son. "So you been keeping a few things from your old man?" There was triumph in the question. "I still hear things, you know."

"Yes. All right, I went to see her."

"What for?"

"I wanted to see if there was anything I could—do," Stephen said uncomfortably.

"Why? What do you owe the Olwens?"

Owe, his son thought.

Stephen hesitated, burning to tell the old man what he had seen in the book, pour out all his suspicion and dismay. But to do that might be to precipitate another seizure. So Stephen answered, very carefully, "It's not a matter of—owing. Hugh Olwen was your friend, wasn't he?"

The old man's gaze dropped before the piercing gray look of his son. "Not exactly a friend," he answered uneasily. "Are you courting the girl?" Daniel asked abruptly.

"Yes." Stephen's steady gaze met his father's; the cool eyes, meeting, were very like. So like, Stephen decided with a cold feeling, that it was almost like looking into a mirror.

In an instant he regretted having spoken, for the old man's face completely lost its specious calm, and the cheeks were suddenly livid with anger. Daniel trembled, and said in a shaking voice, "You are courting that half-breed woman! You damned young fool, her mother was a red Indian! And her father was—was nothing! He came crawling out of the mines of Pennsylvania—like a damned —lizard—came crawling to Texas with his hat in his hand, and got the land that I—"

Daniel stopped, choking. His angry words were cut off in an instant, chopped off to a strangled wordlessness. In his paroxysm of rage, he kept making those terrible, choking sounds, and his eyes rolled back in his head.

Stephen leaped to his feet, sending the chair crashing behind him, and ran from the room. "Juana!" he cried out in the hall. "Consuela! Where in hell are you?"

When the women appeared, with frightened faces, Stephen shouted, "Send one of the boys for the doctor—pronto. Pronto, woman!"

Juana scurried off to obey.

Stephen cursed himself for a loose-mouthed fool. Whatever his father had done, he was a sick old man. Stephen would have to keep his mouth shut about Doña Olwen, at least for now.

As Doña Olwen drifted toward sleep, she mused: When I marry, if I do, it will be goodbye then to fear—but also to the other.

Also to the exhilaration, and that wild, sweet triumph she had known that afternoon in summer. Drifting, Doña let herself remember; half-dreaming, half in memory.

She felt again the bruising weight of the ammunition belt that slanted from her waist down over her right hip; it felt heavy and present even through the layers of cambric underclothes and the denim of the Levis cut for boys. Her small feet were sweating in their constricting boots; her head hurt a little from the tightness of the hat over her much-pinned hair. For that was vital—once seen, her hair would never be forgotten, and she must look like a boy. She was sure the loose shirt and generous trousers would hide her figure sufficiently.

Her reputation as a sure shot, as a woman of cool, uncharacteristic nerve, had won the men who joined her. They had smiled when she refused to use a running rabbit as her target; their smiles had disappeared when, galloping on her horse, she brought her gun up and fired two quick shots: the top and second wires of a fence snapped and sang, lopped clean, halfway between two posts. She had done the trick three times in succession, when the men Tahre had brought to her said they would join the band to rob Raike.

The town they chose was forty miles away: they hid fifteen miles away, for from there it was an open valley, and settled. They had hired a buggy the night before to transport rifles across the settled range without attracting attention. They started then, that night, planning how to make the fifteen miles in three hours.

She and Tahre rode in the buggy, leading the horses. The others—there were six of them then—rode two by two, about a mile apart. As they came near the town, they closed up, to reach a back street all at the same time. The arrangement was that two men were to take their rifles from the buggy as soon as they dismounted; the others were to handle the hitching. One would stay with the team while two others covered the ground between the bank and the horses.

Tahre led the way at a stiff dogtrot, and as the bank door parted, he jumped into it from the street with Doña and the third man at his heels.

"Hands up and silence!" Tahre ordered in his rough voice; he and Doña and their companion took the cash. But they had not been there moments before the shooting started across the square: two men from under cover were trying to pepper them with rifles. They returned the fire, without result.

While Tahre was in the vault, their companion was shot in the leg; the customers in the bank had dropped to the floor, the horrified employees crouching down behind their cages.

Somehow they made it back to the horses—another bullet grazed Doña's arm. Tahre carried the bag with over twenty thousand dollars in his hand. He and Doña were the first ones to ride out of the valley, heading at a breakneck pace for the deep ravine they had chosen for their refuge.

They rode on part of the night and the next day in the sun burning on the plains, finally, they came to the ravine. Three large oak trees grew on the site; it was a perfect place for defensive action.

The third day, in the afternoon, they saw sixteen riders a couple of miles away, who were evidently following their trail. There was time enough to get away; the horses had rested for many hours, but the horses of the posse were lathered, winded. The bandits had the ravine with its three great trees, and shelter, while the posse had to approach them from the open.

From their vantage point, with their cartridges spread on blankets, the six fugitives could have killed them all.

"No, Tahre," Doña said. "They have not seen us."

"You're crazy," said the man with the wounded leg, raising his rifle.

"No." Tahre put his coppery hand on the rifle butt. The other lowered the rifle. The sixteen men rode on upriver.

The peril, the hot excitement, the high exhilaration! Doña Olwen burrowed into her pillow. Frank, the man with the wounded leg, had died of the infection, she recalled somberly. But Tahre, blessed Tahre, had treated the flesh wound on her arm with skill; the Indian remedy had made her whole again.

Yes, it would be goodbye to all of that, she mused in the darkness. From outside there came to her the lonely whisper of the wind-filled pines, the ghostly hooting of an owl—then something else. The soft drumming of hooves, down the road toward the house.

Doña sat up and, taking the Colt from under her pillow, leaped from the bed. She hurried to the window.

There along the path, in the light of the moon that had already begun its waning, came a man on a tall gray stallion, a man whose garments matched the coat of the animal, a pale cloud-gray that seemed to shine in the whiteness.

He rode with the ease of a man born to the saddle, the lines of his lean body seeming almost to flow into the body of the animal. The man was straight and tall, and his hands were easy on the reins.

It was Stephen Raike.

As Doña watched him approach, something stiff and hard inside her body seemed to melt, moving with the rhythm of a strong, warm river. Despite his hated name, and all that had happened to her, Doña's flesh recalled his touch. She remembered with excitement the feel of his hard hands upon her face, the contours of his narrow, muscled form.

Her heart began to hammer with a strange feeling, with an emotion she had not yet known in her crowded days.

Hesitant, she stood staring; he had tethered his mount and was striding, in his loose-limbed but flat-footed and determined way, in the direction of the house.

Doña replaced the Colt under the pillow and pulled on a cream-colored robe. She heard his knock.

She knew the answer now. That sharp, unfamiliar feeling was not desire; it was still a kind of hate, hate with its comforting familiarity. Coolly Doña told herself that to accept Stephen Raike was the subtlest kind of revenge. To take the old bear's single cub, as Patche said—to have like a dangling scalp, the name, the property of Raike.

Doña laughed softly and moved toward the door. Stephen would have his answer. He would have it tonight.

Chapter Eight

Dr. Cyrus Fitch sipped the aged bourbon and leaned back with a sigh in the old leather chair opposite Stephen. "I'll say it again, Steve: that old man up there is made of iron and leather. How he pulled through this last one, I'll never know. But the next time—" Fitch's pause was significant.

Stephen faced him from the wooden swivel chair at his father's desk. "There won't be a next time, Doc."

Fitch peered at the young man over the top of his wire-rimmed spectacles. He had never seen Stephen in a state of such buoyance; the boy appeared to be in the grip of some strong excitement, his gray eyes huge with it, and glowing, his color high. "You're looking chipper, anyway," Doc Fitch commented, smiling.

Stephen was still so elated by Doña's acceptance that he could not conceal his joy. The news about his father's recovery was an added blessing. But no one must know about Doña; he could not risk his father finding out. They might have to go away, Stephen thought. He said to the doctor, "I'm relieved about Dad, of course."

Finch studied him a moment more, then grunted, his curiosity unsatisfied. "Well, like I said, I think Daniel's going to make it." He set down his glass and hauled himself from the chair. "Getting old myself," he commented. "Guess I'll be getting along."

Stephen rose and walked with him to the hall. "Thanks, Doc. I'll try to keep him out of trouble."

When they reached the wide verandah that circled the facade of the awkward house, they saw a rider approaching, a tall, stern-looking man of middle age. He was wearing a dark coat and hat and twill trousers tucked into decent, shining boots, and he did not smile as he rode toward the men on the verandah.

A stableboy ran out to take the stranger's horse. The man tossed the reins to the small, dark child and touched his hat.

"I'm looking for Stephen Raike," he said. "Name's Bonner, Marshal Will Bonner, from Galveston."

"Well, now," said Fitch, glancing sidelong at Stephen.

"I'm Stephen Raike, Marshal. Come on in the house." His voice was steady and cool, but Stephen felt a faint twinge of apprehension.

Itching with curiosity, the old doctor drawled, "I'll be going, then." He seemed to want to linger, awaiting an invitation to stay. When it was not forthcoming, he started down the stairs. "Dr. Fitch, Marshal," said Stephen.

Will Bonner touched his black, wide-brimmed hat again. "Doctor."

"Good day to you, Stephen. Marshal." Fitch glanced back once more as he got into his buggy.

While the doctor was driving away, Stephen Raike took Bonner's measure; he was almost of a height with Stephen, and out of his calm, hard-bitten face, his piercing brown eyes gleamed with a shrewd intelligence.

"Come in," Stephen said again, leading the way into the entrance hall and through the open door of the large stiff parlor.

The parlor, more than any other room, bore the oppressive touch of Mrs. Parmer. Not a speck of dust was allowed to remain: the parlor was scoured daily by the harried maids, no matter how few others ever entered. It was a gloomy receptacle for horsehair furniture, rigid bouquets of flowers, steel engravings of morbid subjects, and a dark, mahogany-manteled fireplace.

"Sit down, Marshal. Drink?"

"No, thanks." Bonner sat down gingerly on a horse-hair sofa. He did not remove his hat, but only pushed it back a little on his head. He ran an eagle eye over the room. "Handsome house," he said.

Stephen made a noncommittal sound and sat down in a high-backed chair.

"Since I was passing through to Galveston, thought I'd save you a ride into Berwick; wanted to ask you a few questions."

"I take· that kindly, Marshal." Stephen crossed one long leg over the other and put a hand on his extended knee. His voice was calm but his every sense was wary. He waited for Bonner to continue; to speak first would be to put himself at a disadvantage.

When Bonner saw that Stephen would not break the silence, he grew abrupt. "What do you think of Sheriff Lamb?"

"You're asking the wrong man, Marshal. I'm new in town. Been away for nine years. East, other places."

"But you talked with him about the Raike train robbery. And rode with his posse after the stage was raided, I hear." Bonner looked at Stephen, then continued, "When I talked to Lamb, and that foolish young varmint —what's his name?"

"Charlie Scurry." Stephen smiled.

"Scurry. I didn't think much of them, either of them. That Scurry looks scared out of the woods."

The description of the rabbitlike Scurry was so apt that Stephen laughed loudly. Bonner's sharp black eyes bored into him. "Glad you think all this is funny, Mr. Raike," he said oppressively. "Seems to me a man that lost as much as you might take it a little serious. But then I was never such a rich man myself. Maybe I just don't understand."

Bonner's resentful envy was plain. He glanced again around the shining, ugly parlor.

"Sorry, Marshal. I was never a man to cry over spilt milk." Bonner turned back to him, measuring him.

"But you're not a man to let somebody knock the pitcher out of your hand, either, Mr. Raike. Even though it might not have been much milk by Raike standards." He smiled sourly. "Lamb tells me you saw the people on the train, and that when you rode with the posse, nobody turned up a thing."

Stephen noticed that he had said "people," not "men." He felt an itch of unease at the back of his neck. And also: "When *you* rode with the posse." The man was wily as an Indian.

"Well?"

"Seems funny to me, Mr. Raike, that you haven't sent for me before."

"Why should I, Marshal? I told you I don't know the lawmen here anymore. Thought they could handle it."

"Hogwash, Mr. Raike. A man like you wouldn't let Lamb get the drop on him. I've heard about you, in the town. You're no ordinary man. Doing the things you done takes more than ordinary strength. Driving a stage, for instance."

That was true enough: it was no easy job to drive a six-horse team over narrow trails that cut into the sides of mountains; on bumpy corduroy roads or over mud where the coach could sink to its hub, and through the worst of weather, one eye always out for Indians and other marauders.

"That may be," Stephen replied coolly, "but what are you getting at, Marshal?"

"Don't take me wrong, Mr. Raike. Have to look at all sides of everything. Friends of Governor Pease are all riled up about Lamb and Scurry. What I'm trying to say is, maybe a man like you don't care to leave it to fools like them. Maybe you've let it be because you're figurin' on some kind of private war. I don't know, Mr. Raike. What I do know is this: we've got laws and I aim to uphold them. If you got some kind of war in mind, well, Mr. Raike, I hope you'll forget it. There's quite an army here, on your lands, and it could get messy." Bonner smiled grimly.

"You're—" Stephen paused, about to say, "You're off the track." But what the hell. He considered. Let him think it. Maybe it was a way out for Doña and Tahre. That it was also a way out for that bastard Lamb, too, was unavoidable.

"You've got a point there, Marshal."

"Glad you agree, Mr. Raike." Bonner pulled his hat down over his forehead and rose. "Meanwhile I'm keeping an eye on Scurry. There's something about that varmint—"

As Stephen followed him to the verandah, Bonner said, "Lamb tells me you saw four men."

"Yes."

"Could you give me a description?"

"Sure." Stephen described a vague, fictitious picture of the four men.

"Thanks, Mr. Raike. I'll be in touch, when we find something."

As Bonner mounted his horse, he turned and said, "Funny thing. I've heard there was a woman along on some of the robberies. A woman and an Indian."

"It's news to me."

Bonner gave Stephen Raike another long, ironic look. When he rode away, Stephen again took the measure of his ramrod posture in the saddle. He had the look of a man who did not give up. Bonner had not believed him, that was certain; and he knew there had been an Indian, and a woman.

I've got to get Doña away from here, thought Stephen. Soon!

The women hired to care for him were on duty again in Daniel Raike's room, and all was quiet again for the moment.

That afternoon after Bonner left, Stephen went back into his father's study and opened the safe.

He took out a locked wooden box and set it on the desk. The box contained his mother's jewelry. According to his father's will, with which Vard had acquainted Stephen, the jewels belonged to Stephen, to give to his "promised wife."

Doña Olwen had given him her promise: at the thought of her, his body felt its now-familiar aching. He was acting like a sick calf!

"Get hold of yourself," Stephen said aloud, smiling.

He sat down and opened the combination on the box, began to take out the jewels from their velvet bed.

Stephen had learned something of the jeweler's art, which, for some reason, had caught his interest. Many of the things he had seen in the shops of New Orleans and New York, and in Cincinnati, the new "Athens of the West," were eyesores to him for all their costliness.

But his mother's things, relics of the proud Gerards, were simple and beautiful, austere as the face of Doña Olwen. Stephen examined a necklace of heavy gold, much like one of great price he had seen in New York—a copy of an ancient Etruscan piece, a weblike collar of criss-cross chains. Hanging in the openings of the webbed gold were many small acorns and leaves, and small, savage faces. The necklace had been wrought with infinite care.

Stephen could not imagine it on the delicate throat of the woman who had been his mother. But on the tawny neck of Doña Olwen it would indeed look like the ornament of a primitive queen. It would suit her as it would never suit another woman.

He put the necklace aside and opened a small velvet box: it contained a ring bearing a magnificent Australian opal, set simply in swirling copper gold. Called the "black opal," the stone was in reality a burning blue-green, with great points of fiery orange and yellow in it, flickers of fire like Doña Olwen's hair. The stone was reputed to have magical powers, Stephen recalled. The ring seemed a size to fit her slender finger. He put its companion ring in his vest pocket.

Yes, he would take the opal ring and necklace to her now, this afternoon, and give her the other things later. Replacing the rest of the jewelry, he locked the box, and stowed it back in the safe.

Going into the hall where his saddlebag was hanging, he took up his hat, put the jewels in the saddlebag, and headed for the stables.

A "private game of cards" was the reason the three men gave for taking the room above the bar at the Golden Girl. The skeptical proprietor did not comment, concluding privately that Lamb and Scurry, and the deep-eyed Luke Allen, were up to something more.

He was right. The three men in the room were not playing cards. An uncut deck lay before them on the table.

Luke Allen growled, "I think it's a damn fool notion, Lamb, the kind of no-good, damn fool thing that's got the marshal sniffin' around right now."

"I tell you, Luke, she'll talk," Lamb protested. "A woman always talks, but we can keep our mouths shut when the time comes."

Allen scoffed, "And Charlie here? Our brave boy, Charlie Scurry?" He turned his sly look on the uncomfortable deputy. The boy squirmed under Allen's stare.

"You didn't make such a good showin', did you, Charlie boy?" Luke Allen twitted. "When the marshal was questionin' you, you looked like a sheep-killin' dog, didn't you now?"

Charlie Scurry flushed and Lamb said, "Lay off Charlie, Luke. That don't do no good now. What I'm sayin' is, we've got to get rid of the girl."

"And what about young Raike?"

"He's only one man, ain't he? Didn't he let 'em walk away with the payroll on the train?" Lamb argued.

"Raike's only one man, all right, but he ain't no dude, for all the way he looks," Allen retorted. "You danged ol' fool, he let 'em walk away because of the girl. He's sweet on her. And I wouldn't want to be the man he catches if something happens to the Olwen gal."

"He'll think his pappy done it," Lamb grinned unpleasantly. "His pappy downright enjoys killin' Olwens. But you'd know all about that, wouldn't you, Luke?"

Allen shot Lamb an angry look. "Watch your mouth. Raike's pappy, you say?" he concluded in a tone of speculation.

"Daniel Raike'd be grateful to us if somethin' happened to the Olwen gal," said Charlie Scurry.

"What you gabbin' about?" growled Lamb. "The old man's half dead, can't hardly see or hear, I been told."

"You been told wrong," said Allen.

"What in tarnation are you gettin' at, Luke? How come you know so much?"

"Got a Mex there in my pay," Allen boasted. "Right in the house. Peso here and there, Mex'd sell his mother," Allen said nastily. "I heard plenty and one thing I heard was that the old man yelled his head off at his youngun about courtin' Doña Olwen."

"Daniel Raike'd be grateful," Charlie Scurry repeated.

The others turned to him. "You know, Charlie," said Luke Allen, "you ain't half as dumb as you look. He might at that."

"Let's do it, Luke," Lamb said, in a rush of enthusiasm. "Let's do it, and then we'll see ol' Raike."

"What good is that? He had no part in it; why should he give us anything?" Allen demanded.

"Because you're goin' to tell him, Luke, that the word'll get around. He's got to thank you for keepin' quiet about the Olwen thing."

Allen studied Lamb. "You do beat all for meanness." He cackled. "But if the word got around about Raike, it'd get around about me, too. That won't wash."

"How'd he pay you?"

"Well, it wasn't by check," Allen cackled again. "Wasn't by check," he repeated.

"So who can prove anything?"

"Yeah, but who could prove it against Raike, either?" Luke Allen argued.

"Don't need to," said Lamb. "It'll get to his *son*. Do you get me now?"

"Yeah. Yeah. I get you. When are we goin'? I say make it this afternoon."

There was a gesture of protest from Charlie Scurry.

"What's ailin' you?" Lamb asked his deputy.

Scurry recalled how Doña Olwen always treated him—kindly, not laughing at him as the others always did.

"I dunno," he said miserably.

"Buck up, kid." Allen laughed, and the laugh had a hard, unpleasant sound in Scurry's ears. "I don't think you got any choice."

"All right. All right," Charlie mumbled.

But he was far from reassured as he followed the others from the room and down the stairs of the Golden Girl. He had always been grateful to Doña Olwen. He prayed he wouldn't be the one who had to do it.

Doña and Tahre raced along the meadow at the foot of the hill that held the Olwen house. The woman with her free-blowing hair rode her spirited and gentle roan; the horse almost matched the color of her tresses. Doña, who rode Indian-style, with a blanket, not a saddle, wore moccasins and the buckskin jacket and trousers that were her favorite clothes.

She liked to feel the horse's sleek, solid body more closely beneath her than a saddle allowed. Tahre also used a blanket on his swift mustang, the hardy animal which he had tamed himself. The mustangs thrived on the brief, crunchy buffalo grass of the prairies, nourishing, and nut-sweet to the horse's tongue, but the beasts were shorter than their ancestors, the Spanish war horses captured long ago by the Indians. They made wonderful hunting ponies, when trained by the Comanches to gallop at incredible speed after the lumbering buffalo.

Doña laughed at the sight of the tall Comanche on the small, docile mustang pony; Tahre's long legs almost hung to the ground. And yet he was a spectacular rider: mounted, he seemed to borrow the grace of a bird. At a gallop, as he was riding now, Tahre leaned forward, his long thighs gripping the pony's sides like a vise.

The horses cleared the Short Line tracks in one flying bound; still laughing, Doña drew in her horse's reins just short of the trees, inches ahead of little mustang's muzzle.

"You have won, Isse-Loa," said Tahre with mock dismay. "Let them rest now, a little." He slid with ease from the back of the mustang, sending him with a light pat on the rump out to the meadow to graze. Doña followed suit; the roan trotted off to nibble at the crisp, browning grass at the mustang's side.

"Play the hand game with me, Tahre, the game of Why the Bear Waddles When He Walks!"

She dropped negligently to the grass, stretching her

long legs in their fringed buckskin, to take the afternoon sun.

Tahre laughed and looked at his cousin with teasing affection. "What a child you are, still, Isse-Loa! You know well we cannot play a hand game while the snakes are still out. Why do you joke with me? All afternoon I have known you are keeping something from me."

He lounged beside her, pulling up a handful of the sweet grass to chew. She lay back with half-closed eyes, the sun glittering on her vivid hair.

When she did not reply to his questioning comment, Tahre said softly, "Hishshe-Loa, Hishshe-Loa, Fire-Hair. There are other things I would rather say to you than Why the Bear Waddles When He Walks. I would rather say to you another word-song of my kinsman Kora: 'Do not come unto my song, with its soft breath upon you, or from out of my singing, my heart will leap upon you.' "

Doña shaded her full, dark eyes and looked up at Tahre. She was stricken by the look of sadness on his coppery face.

"No, Tahre. Don't say those things. Tahre," she added abruptly, "I am going to marry Stephen Raike."

The Indian turned and lay face-down then in the grass.

"It has come then, at last," he said in a muffled voice. She stared at him in silence.

He turned over and sat up with a sudden, graceful movement, his arms crossed over his bended knees. After another long moment, Tahre said quietly, "He is a good man, Isse-Loa. He has none of the evil of his father. You will be safe, you will have comfort." With a chuckle, he asked, "Did my mother, Patche, say these things to you?"

Doña studied her cousin. "It *was* you, then! You put those ideas in her head."

"What ideas?" he asked innocently.

"You know very well—the idea that to steal the single cub of the old bear Raike would be the best revenge of all!"

Tahre turned to her, staring. "I had no such idea, Isse-Loa. You have no cause to take vengeance on the

104

younger Raike. He had no part in his father's doings. No," he said, sadly smiling, "Patche's idea is her own, some devilment of women I do not understand."

Doña smiled, and they sat for a while in companionable silence. "When will you marry?" Tahre asked.

"He wants it to be soon."

The Indian was silent; he put his head upon his knees, closing his eyes.

"Tahre." Doña leaned to him and touched his knee. He drew away, as if stung.

"What is it, what's the matter?" she asked, dismayed.

"Please do not touch me thus, my cousin," he said sternly. And at once she understood.

"Tahre, oh, Tahre," she whispered. "Forgive me. But I must go on with it; I must follow the course I set myself when they—they killed my mother and father that day, five years ago."

"It is not for vengeance only that you marry Stephen Raike," Tahre remarked.

"Why, what do you mean? What other reason could I have?" she cried.

"Isse-Loa, I saw the way you looked at him, when I came into your house the night you cried out like a dove frightened. No, it is not just for revenge you have consented to marry."

She did not answer but looked away over the long, sweet meadow stained by the sunset's crimson, where the mustang and the roan were peacefully grazing. "You are wrong, Tahre," she said at last in a firmer voice.

"I think, Isse-Loa, that your greatest argument is with yourself," Tahre declared, rising. "I must return to the village; I will be wanted in council."

"In council!" Doña exclaimed, mocking. "Again?" She was glad of the reprieve.

Tahre laughed good-naturedly at her twitting. "Again, and still," he admitted.

When they were riding up the hill, he said, "Will Stephen Raike be coming here tonight? Will I be safe leaving him to guard you?"

"He is coming," said Doña, "but surely I need no one to guard me, after all we've come through together. Don't you think I can look after myself?"

"I am not sure, Isse-Loa," Tahre replied in a serious tone. "I wish you had never confided in those men, that Lamb and Scurry. I have never trusted them."

"But, Tahre, none of it would have been possible without them, you know that."

"And have you said goodbye to all that now—at last, as I have asked you to for so long."

"Yes. Yes, I suppose I have, Tahre." And there was a peculiar regret in her rich, husky voice as she answered.

"Then I will bid you good-bye for now, Hishshe-Loa."

"Goodbye for now, Tahre." With a casual wave, Doña Olwen turned the roan onto the path that led to the house.

How foolish Tahre was, she thought, to believe that she needed protection. She, Doña Olwen, who could handle a gun like a man, and outride any Comanche!

But when she had a clear view of the house, and saw the three mounted men waiting in the shadows of the gathering dusk, Doña Olwen felt a deep unease, in spite of the fact that the men were men she knew.

Allen, Lamb and Charlie Scurry. But somehow they did not look the same as they had before; there was a peculiar expression on their faces. And all of them had their hands on the holsters at their sides.

Doña Olwen wheeled her horse, so swiftly that the men were transfixed an instant with surprise. And she galloped off wildly in the other direction, letting out a high, wild scream for Tahre.

Chapter Nine

Tahre had made good time, so he was a good distance when his sharp ears caught Doña's desperate cry. He jerked the mustang about and took off at a breakneck gallop in the direction of the cry.

Another man heard and he was nearer.

Doña doubled back, heading for the thicket, and for an instant confounded the three pursuers. Allen was the first to rally; he saw Lamb raise his gun. "Don't shoot, you danged crazy fool!" he shouted. "There's another way."

Lamb sheathed his gun.

They overtook her, at a hard gallop, in the woods, and Luke Allen bellowed, "Hold on! Rein up, or I'll cut you down."

The woman obeyed, sitting the roan proudly despite her terror.

Allen dismounted, grinning; the others followed suit. "Get down off that horse."

She hesitated, glaring at them. But when Allen brandished his Colt, she complied, angry with herself for getting caught totally unarmed. Her guns were in the house; she did not even have a whip, for she never used one on a horse; she was too skilled with hand and knee to need such a device. But she wished angrily that she had a whip now.

Facing the men, Doña raised her head in an arrogant gesture to feign courage she did not feel.

Suddenly, the sound of a heavy stallion's hooves crushing drying leaves in the thicket froze the men. Stephen Raike rode into the woods on his huge gray mount; when he caught sight of the three men, the fury on his lean face was terrible. Before anyone could draw, Raike moved in on Allen and Lamb, who were standing a little behind the other man. With a savage kick of his boot, Stephen sent Luke Allen sprawling backward. Allen's weight knocked the lighter Lamb to the ground beneath him.

Before Doña knew what was happening, Tahre had galloped into the woods. Charlie Scurry, who had been stupidly staring, began to draw his Smith & Wesson, but Tahre, with a mighty lunge leaped from the mustang onto Scurry, throwing him to the ground.

Allen got to his knees, and Lamb still knelt dazed on the ground, shaking his head. Stephen jumped off his stallion and waded into Allen, smashing a fist against his jaw. Allen reeled back, but Lamb moved forward. Stephen's fist crashed the sheriff's jaw, knocking him unconscious, and wheeling, he delivered another blow to Allen. The heavier man was hard to down, but Stephen smashed away, again and again, at Allen's jaw, taking two hard punches in his turn. At last Luke Allen went down, sinking first to his knees; then his knees buckled under and he crumpled to the ground.

All at once Scurry wriggled from Tahre's grasp and snatched up Lamb's gun from the ground. Wrestling with him for the gun, the Indian was unpleasantly surprised at Scurry's wiry strength. Stephen, leaning back for a second against a tree, breathing hoarsely, saw the struggle between the Indian and Scurry, and leaped into the fray again, kicking the gun from Charlie Scurry's hand. The gun discharged and caught Tahre in the shoulder.

Tahre cried out in pain, recoiling for a moment. Lamb stirring again, crawled for the gun, but Stephen stamped on Lamb's reaching hand, and gave him a savage kick on the jaw. Lamb groaned and fell face forward on the ground. He was very still.

Stephen reached down to feel the pulse below Lamb's ear, then straightened with an impassive face.

"He is dead?" Tahre gasped.

"No." Stephen smiled. "I know how to deliver that kick just right. How are you? Is it bad?"

Doña rushed to Tahre to examine his wound. She looked up at Stephen; her eyes were soft and melting. "You saved me, you have saved us—again."

He asked, "Are you all right?"

She nodded.

"Do something for me, then. Quickly. Get some rope from the house, please."

She was off at once, on her roan, without pausing to question. In no time at all she was back with the rope. And a knife to cut it. Stephen blessed her quick common sense.

"Thanks. Now, can you help me cut the rope to tie them?" he asked. "I think Tahre's arm is a little out of commission."

"I'll help," Tahre protested, taking a knife from his own belt.

In a short time the three men's hands were tied behind them; their feet were bound.

Stephen began to lift Lamb to his horse and lash him to the saddle; Tahre, over Stephen's protests, helped.

When the tying was done, Stephen hit the sheriff's horse smartly on the flank, and the animal took off in the direction of Berwick. He repeated the process with Scurry and Allen.

Doña started to laugh. "What fools they'll look in town!" she gasped.

Stephen grinned. "They may not want to stay there long."

"It was well done," Tahre said, holding his shoulder.

"Come to the house, at once," said Doña to the Indian. "I must see to your wound."

The three companions led their horses from the thicket, past the narrow stream where Doña Olwen had gathered her yellow flowers, toward the Olwen house.

A faint chill came into the air with dusk. Tahre, his wound cleaned and bandaged, had dismissed his pain with a casual reference to Patche's remedies, and had ridden

109

away. When they were alone, Stephen sensed a sudden shyness in Doña.

She stood before him in the airy room, outlined before the fire he had built in the hearth. As Stephen looked at her, he felt the overpowering thud of his heart against his throat. He resisted the desire to take her in his arms, for there was a distance in her shyness, an uncertainty he was hesitant to probe. Her dark eyes were shadowed now with a strange confusion. More than ever she reminded him of a deer from the plains, wanting to trust yet still trapped in its fear.

He got up, moving without knowing he moved, and walked toward her like someone in a dream. She waited, still gazing at him with that look of peculiar entreaty and puzzlement.

"You have not changed your mind?" he asked softly. "You will marry me, Doña?"

She hesitated for so long that he almost ceased to breathe.

Then at last she nodded, and said "Yes" in a tone of resignation, which tore at him.

Stephen, moving to her, touched the flaming hair. And as he held her nearer, there was nothing else in his sight except her dark eyes into whose depths a warmth had crept. He looked into the eyes and felt himself drown.

With gentleness and caution he took her narrow face in his hard hands, not wanting to frighten her. Suddenly, Doña drew in her breath, and her slender body trembled slightly. But she did not move away, and Stephen felt again that rush of fire ignite at the point of their touching, spreading from the throbbing center of his body into his head and legs and arms.

Finally she said, "Let me give you some tea."

Stephen imagined that he heard in the simple words something more profound, a kind of greater offering.

As he sat down on the rough bench before the hearth, he reflected there was something in Doña so wild and free, so full of the tembling tautness of passion leashed, that she was like no other woman he had ever known.

Doña handed him a cup, saying softly, "You did not kill them."

He set his cup on the floor, and answered as quietly as she had spoken. "I've killed enough. I don't like it. I never kill if there is any other way."

She sat down beside him and he studied her fine profile. When she turned, her wonderful eyes were warm again, and some of the confusion seemed to clear. It was as if she had said without speaking: You are not like your father; you are a different man.

He took her hand.

"They have not finished with us, you know," she said.

"I know. Maybe I was a fool not to finish them. Maybe I've endangered you," he said bitterly. "But I have killed enough."

"I am glad."

"Doña." She was looking ahead into the flickering fire, but Stephen knew she was examining him out of the corners of her eyes, in her wily, Indianlike fashion.

"Doña," he said again, "we will have to go away."

It seemed to him that she made a small, leaning motion away from him, and he gripped her hand tighter.

"Doña, listen. The marshal knows there was a woman involved in the robberies; those three will be after us now. And you cannot—" He hesitated, hating to mention the thing he tried to avoid. "You cannot live this close to—my father's land."

He felt her stiffen. "Tell me," he said firmly, "tell me now, once and for all, can you marry the son of Daniel Raike?"

Her mouth quivered in the orange light.

"Tell me."

After another long, heart-stopping pause, Doña turned to him and said with something of the resignation that had been in her voice before, "Yes. Yes, I can marry you, Stephen Raike."

At the emphasis on his own name, Stephen drew her to him and kissed her hard, his heart pounding so now that he could hear it drumming in his ears.

"You *will* go away with me?" he asked, when he could speak again.

"From my father's house?" she asked sadly. "From this house?"

"I will build you the finest house you have ever seen," he said jubilantly. "The finest house in Chicago."

"Chicago," she repeated.

"Please," he said, "you cannot change your mind now."

"I will not go back on my word." Once more, the peculiar sadness of her words rubbed something raw in him, but the triumph of his victory was louder inside him than the doubts she had planted.

"What will happen to my father's house?" she asked reluctantly.

"I will have my father's—I will have my friend, Vard Williams, see that everything is taken care of," he promised, urging. "I swear to you that nothing will be lost, or harmed. And you can send for whatever you need, later, when we are settled in the East."

She said with changeable softness, "I—I have never known anyone like you. You do everything a man could do, and you do it better than anyone. And still you are very gentle."

Feeling a hot, languid melting inside, he bent his head to hers and hungrily took her mouth. The brief softness of her lips seemed to respond, and for a timeless time they clung together, nearer and nearer still until a small cry from her asked him for her release.

She leaned her fiery head upon his chest and he kissed the wonderful hair again and again, letting its long wavy flames play over his hand.

He said, against her hair, "We should leave soon."

She answered, surprised, "Now?"

"Yes. I am not going to leave you alone again. I'm not going to let you out of my sight." To lighten the shadow of the threatened danger implicit in his words, Stephen laughed, and said, "Not until we are safely married. I don't trust you."

She raised her bright head from his shoulder and looked at him, answering his smile.

"All right." She stood up and he gazed at her, admiring her cool, slender loveliness, and the calm with which she consented to leave her present life behind. "I had better pack a few things, and change my clothes."

Stephen held her about the waist and leaned his head against her narrow body, feeling her pressing against him. Again he marveled at that softness in a form so slender and taut.

"I love you," he said, "I love you so very much."

She touched his hair lightly, but did not answer in kind. Nevertheless, his elation could not be dampened. "I have something for you," he said.

He released her and, reaching into his pocket, took out the necklace and the little velvet box which he had withdrawn from his saddlebag before they came into the house. He opened the box and slid the wonderful opal ring on the fourth finger of her left hand. It was a perfect fit.

She gasped, admiring its blue-green brilliance by the light of the fire. Then she looked at him again with that odd, dualistic expression he found so hard to read. "Thank you," she said. "It is beautiful."

"And this," he smiled, handing her the heavy golden necklace with its crisscross webs of golden chains. "An engagement present."

Doña Olwen held the beautiful thing in her hands, its gleaming, tawny gold akin to the color of her sun-touched flesh. "I have never had anything like this," she said with childlike pleasure. "Never in all my life. Put it on my neck."

He rose and clasped the necklace about the slender, tanned column of her neck and stepped back a little to admire it against the smoothness of her skin.

"I think it was made for you," he said, and kissed her again, lingering on her compliant mouth.

"I must get ready," she said after a time. He watched her move toward the stairs, lithe and noiseless in her small Indian shoes.

To Stephen's delight she returned more quickly than he had expected, carrying only one small, soft, leather bag. And she returned another woman: she was wearing a tight-jacketed suit of dull, dark green cloth that looked like a riding habit. Stephen knew almost nothing of women's clothes, but he thought Doña had a fashionable look, from her rakish gray felt hat with its green plumes to her gray-gloved hands below the turned-back cuffs of the jacket.

There was only a glimpse now of the wonderful hair, smoothed back into a heavy coil below the brim of the narrow hat.

He rose, smiling, and took the bag from her hand. "You travel light," he commented admiringly. "That's good. We will buy everything you need in New Orleans, and in the East."

"New Orleans!" she repeated, and her dark eyes sparkled with excitement. "I have never been there. I've never been anywhere," she admitted, "beyond Galveston."

"We will go to many places," he assured her, with his arm about her waist. "When my business is squared away, we'll—" he paused and took out his watch. "But we've got to hurry."

She nodded, without further comment, and followed him from the house. Again he was overcome with admiration for her coolness, and he could see how she had enlisted men to ride with her to attack the stages and the train.

He helped her onto the roan and hanging her bag from his saddle, mounted the stallion. Suddenly she asked, "What about the horses, Stephen? After we have ridden into Berwick?"

"We are not riding into Berwick," he replied.

"What do you mean?"

"Come. Follow me down the hill, and I'll show you."

Puzzled, she rode behind him down the hill from the Olwen house toward the Short Line tracks that crossed the meadow.

Stephen dismounted, smiling up at her. Hesitantly she sat for a moment upon the roan, then followed his example.

"I'm going to flag down the train," he said, grinning.

"I've done it before. They always stop for a Rai—for me."

"But the horses," she protested.

"Look." He detached her bag from his saddle, though his own saddlebag remained on his horse. Tying the reins of the two animals together, he said gently to the stallion, "Home, Sam, home. Take your friend with you." He slapped the gray horse on its rump, and Sam took off toward the road that led to the Raike estate, matching his gait to that of the roan.

"Sam will go right into the stables, at the house," Stephen explained to Doña. "He is trained just like a dog." He stared after the animals with affection. "And he and the roan will be taken good care of, you can be sure. Vard and the boys will see to them. While you were upstairs, changing, I wrote directions to Vard; they are in my saddlebag, which he is sure to open. Everything is squared away now—he'll get the right people to stay in your house, until he hears from us."

"Do you always do things like this?" she asked him, smiling. "All at once, to the last detail?"

"Yes. I even knew that you would not be sad over the roan, as I am over Sam."

"How? How do you know so many things about people?"

"It is my business to know." Indeed, he was sure that Doña would have the Indian matter-of-factness about her horse; the Comanches were never sentimental about the beasts. It was only whites, like himself, who treated their mounts like pet dogs. He was amused and pleased by the admiration in her eyes.

She watched him with consternation as he stepped onto the tracks. "The train slows down here, you know," he reminded her. She nodded, but uncertainly.

When they heard the approaching engine, she made a nervous gesture. He laughed and stayed where he was, raising both arms to seesaw a signal to the engineer.

They saw him: the Short Line crew and, with screaming wheels and gears, the train drew up and paused about twenty feet before him.

"Come," he said to Doña, picking up her bag. As he helped her onto the train, she looked back once, swiftly, at the Olwen house.

Then she went ahead into the train, feeling as if she were stepping from the old life, the old world, into the new.

As the Short Line train pulled away from Berwick and headed for Galveston, Stephen said, "I thought you might not want to go with me to the house; that's why we are traveling this way, direct. Besides, it wouldn't do to linger after what happened to Allen and the others." He gave her a wry smile.

"You are very kind to me," she said, looking up at him with searching eyes. He was seated next to her, on the prickly upholstery of the train, and he touched her gently.

She looked down at the gleaming blue-green fire of the opal on her hand, and added, "No, I did not want to go to the house."

To change the subject, he said lightly, "We'll be getting in late tonight. I'll get us rooms at the new hotel. It's not the Menger in San Antone, but it's not bad."

Doña Olwen had already begun to feel the power of Raike money; only rich people and professional travelers patronized hotels, others put up at wagonyards. The new hotel in Galveston seemed very fine to her indeed.

"And then tomorrow," he said in a solemn voice, "after I have taken care of some business at the bank, we will be married." Stephen looked down at her with great tenderness, and she felt herself softening again in the enveloping warmth of his gaze.

But this, she thought, returning his smile, is the son of the man who killed my mother and father. No matter how good he is, I must never forget.

His gray eyes seemed to read her thoughts. Doña turned and looked out the window of the train into the gathering darkness.

Early the next morning Stephen Raike, in his cleaned, refurbished clothes, cashed a substantial check on his

Chicago bank account, and another on his Galveston account for good measure. The amount was far more than they would need for their journey, but he intended to show Doña every delight of the city of New Orleans, to buy for her anything that caught her fancy. There was not enough he could ever do, Stephen reflected, to atone for the loss of her parents, but he needed to repay in some small measure the happiness she had already given him with the promise to be his wife.

Stephen bought fresh linens and cravats and went to a barber for a haircut and shave. Roaming the streets of Galveston, he searched in vain for a gift to take her, wishing for the wonderful shops and flower vendors of the city of New Orleans.

At last, among the gaudy wares of a jewelry store, he came upon a narrow gold bracelet, a simple cuff, heavy and gleaming, that seemed presentable. He bought the bracelet and put it in his pocket.

Stephen had left orders at the hotel that Doña not be disturbed until the late morning, for she had seemed exhausted on their arrival the night before.

He sent word upstairs that he had returned, and he stood in the lobby, eagerly waiting for her to descend, and within minutes she came down with a look bright as morning. She had contrived, with the mysterious skill of women, to look quite fresh and new. He had left a quantity of money with her the night before, suggesting she send out for anything she needed.

There was something different-looking about the blouse she wore under her trim, dark green jacket; the ruffles and lace had disappeared and on the plain neckline his mother's necklace glowed.

He gave her one long yearning look and without speaking, led her to the hired buggy outside. When he had settled her into the buggy, he took the bracelet from his pocket and clasped it around her wrist.

Doña admired the bracelet and then looked up at him, smiling. "You do—too much," she said softly, almost uneasily.

"Nonsense," he laughed and kissed her gloved hands, one after the other.

They were married by a justice of the peace, a little way outside of town.

When they rode away, the official and his wife stood staring after the departing buggy.

"Proud-looking people," said the justice of the peace. "Did you see how much he gave me?"

The woman nodded. "A very unusual bride," she remarked.

"An unusual groom, too, if you ask me," the official retorted with a faint chuckle. "Most times it's the ladies, no matter how they simper and look so danged modest, that are anxious. Afraid the men'll get away." He laughed.

Nettled, his wife said, "That's a fine thing for you to say."

"Yessirree, it's so. Generally the ladies are the eager ones, but not this one. Cool as a cucumber, she was, almost hesitatin'. But *him*—crazy about her. Looked like a dyin' calf in a thunderstorm."

"Well, *I* think it's mighty nice for a man to be devoted. There's some could take lessons from him!"

"Come on, now, Mary Ruth. Well, she'll lead him a merry chase, that one will. You mark my word."

Sighing, the justice's wife followed him into the house, thinking how nice it would be to be young again, and have a man that handsome be looking at you that way.

Stephen Raike was hard put to keep his eyes on the road ahead. Again and again he looked down at Doña, staring at the band of gold above the opal on her left hand, which, still gloveless, was lying gracefully on her lap.

He blessed the chance that had let him bring his mother's wedding band in the pocket of his vest. Then, suddenly, he was conscious of the long, slender thighs below the dark green of Doña's soft skirts, the secret roundnesses and wonders of her body pressed close to his.

"Doña," he said urgently, and stopped the buggy. He

118

took her in his arms with roughness, kissed her so hard she cried out for breath.

"Oh, my God, Doña," he said again, holding her with bruising tightness. Her dark eyes looked up into his with an anxious uncertainty.

I must go slowly, he thought desperately, I cannot frighten her. It may ruin everything.

He released her and said in a light, friendly voice, "Are you hungry? Maybe they will give us something good in the dining room of the hotel."

She seemed reassured at the mention of the dining room; he saw happily that she was beginning to relax.

"Let's go, then," he said easily. "I don't know what entertainment a place like Galveston can afford this afternoon, but I'll do my best."

She leaned back then against the cushions of the buggy, her long, lovely hands placid in her green lap, and Stephen congratulated himself on his restraint.

But when they were driving up to the entrance of the hotel, he saw a familiar figure at the hitching post.

It was Marshal Bonner.

Chapter Ten

The marshal caught sight of the buggy. Stephen could see the gleam of the man's dark, piercing eyes in the shadow of his broad hat.

"Well, well," Bonner drawled, "if it isn't Mr. Raike." He strolled toward the buggy.

With a carefully expressionless face, Stephen said, "Hello, Marshal."

He turned back to Doña and smiled at her reassuringly, proud to see that her face was blank as his own felt.

"Mr. Raike. Miss." Bonner touched his brim to Doña, and there was frank admiration in his sharp eyes.

"My wife, Marshal."

Will Bonner swept off his hat with a courtly gesture. "I'm honored, ma'am. Why, I didn't know you were a married man, Raike."

"We were married this afternoon."

"Congratulations," Bonner said heartily. Looking at Doña again, taking in the lustrous eyes, ripe mouth and tawny face, the blaze of her smooth hair under its shelter of felt, Bonner repeated in a fervent voice, "Congratulations, Mr. Raike. You are a very lucky man."

Doña acknowledged the tribute with the slightest nod of her lovely head and a cool half-smile.

Stephen was almost bursting with pride.

"Could I have a word with you, Mr. Raike? We needn't bother Miss—your wife."

Stephen excused himself to Doña, saying, "I won't be a moment."

She gave him a brief but dazzling smile in answer; it

warmed him even more than the brilliant sun. He followed Bonner a few paces, and said coolly, "Yes? What is it?"

"Thought you might not have heard the news, being away from Berwick. When did you get to Galveston, by the way?"

Stephen knew there was more than appeared in the casual question. "Yesterday," he lied.

"Um, yesterday. Well. There's been a bit of trouble in Berwick Bay."

"Trouble?" Stephen asked.

"Seems five or six fellows, some gang, attacked Sheriff Lamb and his deputy, and a fellow named Luke Allen."

"Oh?" Stephen glanced back at the buggy.

Bonner laughed indulgently. "Don't want to hold you, Mr. Raike, new-married man and all. Yeah, some gang attacked the three of 'em, sent 'em back to town trussed up like turkeys on their horses. Looks like the ones who robbed the stage and the train are acting up again. We'll be looking for them." He studied Stephen. "Guess you'll be too busy to ride in a posse the next few days." He laughed again, suggestively.

Stephen gave him a level look, unsmiling. "We're leaving town tomorrow. We'll be going back East."

"That's right smart of you, Mr. Raike."

"Smart?"

"Well, you know as well as I do, a wife can't testify against her husband, nor a husband against his wife."

"I don't follow you, Marshal." Stephen's gray eyes blankly met Bonner's. "Now, if you'll excuse me."

"Sure, Mr. Raike. Good luck to you. Good luck to you both." Will Bonner strode away.

As Stephen helped Doña from the buggy, she asked softly, "What happened?"

"Come inside," said Stephen, grinning, "and I'll tell you all about it."

Even Galveston's newest hotel was not accustomed to serving champagne at lunch, but the determined charm of Stephen Raike—and money changing hands—procured it for them.

And as he told Doña of Lamb's face-saving invention, the story and the bubbly wine, at that unusual and early hour, made their lunch a merry one. Stephen was jubilant, referring whenever he could to Doña as "my wife."

"Please bring my wife some more wine. My wife would like these fruits," he said repeatedly, and could feel her relaxing more and more, her sun-touched face flushed faintly with the laughter and champagne.

"I don't think we will have to worry any more about Marshal Bonner," he remarked. Doña's dark eyes sparkled at him above the rim of her glass.

Later, they took a boat across the bay to see a horse race advertised in a poster at the hotel, and dined at an inn that Doña fancied.

As Stephen plied her with more wine, she said lightly, "You will make me quite drunk if you are not careful."

"I would like to see you a little drunk. How do you feel?"

She smiled, and Stephen could not look away from her full, silken mouth, with its hint of wildness. Her eyes were brighter than he had ever seen them. Stephen realized that he had never seen such eyes: they were deeper and more alive than the eyes of any woman he had ever known.

His mouth burned to taste her silken petallike flesh and he felt a more aching desire than before. It seemed to him she could read his yearning, for her face sobered and her glance dropped before his.

"I feel—" she said slowly, at last, "so strange. Stranger than I ever felt in all my life."

He took her hand to his mouth and kissed it. Then lightly again, playing his difficult part, he asked, "Shall we go to the lyceum tonight and see the play?"

She studied him for an instant, puzzled, and triumphantly he knew he had aroused her wonder, teased her interest.

"Why, yes," she began hesitantly. "Yes," she said more firmly, and her smile was wide. "I've never seen a play."

He was so touched by this evidence of her bare, deprived existence, that he kissed her hand again with lingering kisses. When his lips moved from her palm to her narrow wrist, he felt a strong and dancing beat from the blue-veined skin. His triumphant feeling grew.

Sitting in the lyceum, Stephen heard nothing of the play, a foolish, melodramatic piece, but glanced again and again at the woman beside him. He was conscious that she drew the eyes of other men, like a magnet, and took an almost boyish delight in the knowledge.

Doña attended the foolish play with the closest interest, like a child; again Stephen felt a tender pity, a protectiveness so overpowering he found it difficult not to press her in his arms, in the sight of all the others.

Suddenly he remembered the little *milo,* as the hands called an intractable horse or calf, in the corral at home— again and again he would catch it with his rope. But just when he thought he had it, the *milo* would slip away. In a moment of resignation he had let it go and the pony ran off, bucking and snorting. And suddenly it had paused, looking back at him with a mischievous eye. Then the pony, for no reason at all, had trotted to him, obedient as a pet, taking the bit of apple he had in his hand.

Stephen smiled in the semi-darkness. Doña was so much like the *milo,* like the wild deer, too, that he had known upon the plain. When he was a child, and the killer's musk was not so strong upon his flesh, sometimes the curious deer had come to him as he waited, still and with feigned indifference.

Doña turned at that moment to look at him, questioning his enjoyment of the play. He gave her a smile, but could not have told her a word that had been uttered upon the crude stage. Stephen could see nothing but Doña's eyes and mouth and hair, hear nothing but the rustle of her clothes as she turned back to her contemplation of the foolish play. He waited for it to be done.

Finally when the heroine fell into the hero's arms, the curtain closed and the lights went up, Stephen and Doña rose. He said, his voice thick with excitement, "Let us go."

None of Stephen's expectations had readied him for that moment, when he opened the door to the bedroom, and saw her.

Doña was standing by the hearth, where a fire had been lit to drive away the chill; through the thin, floating gown she wore, he could see her young body in its rounded slenderness. The fiery shawl of her silken hair, loose and gleaming, almost reached her knees. The hair was a burning cloud, a flickering pillar of light in contrast to the tawny face, the dark, deep, sleepy-lidded eyes.

He said nothing as he closed the door and moved toward her, seeing now that her ripe mouth trembled and that in the dark, waiting eyes was a strange questioning look.

She spoke, and there was a new note of submission in her very question: "Do I—please you?" Her rich, husky voice was like hands upon his skin.

"Please me!" His own voice was so thick and harsh the words grated in his throat, and he came to her, enfolding her, kissing her mouth and hair, her cheeks and brow and chin, lingering again upon her mouth and last, her closing eyes, driven beyond endurance now by the touch of her nearly naked body. She warmed to him, making small, incoherent sounds, and fitting her body to his with a sensuous dancelike motion that drove him mad with wanting.

He ran his lean, hard hands over her, stroking her breasts, and the fragile cloth slid on the smoothness of skin. All at once her satiny breasts were free to his fingers; he bent his head and his tongue sought her warm flesh, tasting its sweet, fruit taste; smelling the perfumed web of her sun-flavored hair that gleamed on her bare shoulders and naked arms.

The gown floated away soundless in a faint whisper to the floor. And he felt an even more urgent craving at the sound and sight, at the scent of this Doña; he held her so close the secrets and hollows of her loins were almost his as their limbs entwined.

Grasping her slender thighs he drew her closer and

closer as his burning mouth opened, devouring her full, sweet mouth.

Dizzily he lifted her and carried her to the bed. He stood over her, saying again and again, "Let me look at you, let me look at you."

Her long, tawny body with its curving slenderness, seemed ripened by the sun, golden-rose against the bed's stark whiteness; her hair fanned out on either side of her body, as if she lay in a nest of fire. Standing above her, undressing, he imagined in his frenzy that her skin was molten, that her flesh would burn. His own skin felt livid and hot, as it did in fever, and when once more his mouth touched the skin of her arms and breasts and belly, he could not believe how soft she was.

She made a small, wondering sound when he savored the flesh of her secret body; it had for him the softness of coursing waters, the feel of her thighs like a new-petaled flower, small heights and shallows, trembling thistledown.

His mouth kept to its firm, caressing course, and he heard with pleasure her joyous cry. Her scent, a dazzlement of clove and cedar, sent him, ever more wild and drunken, to fresh inventions, new abandonments until at some unknown and savage time in his red, loud drumming blindness, they were together in the final nearness, his ultimate discovery of her baffling core.

Doña, through heavy, half-closed lids, could see the orange-lit room, dim on the edges of her sleep.

So this is what it is! she thought in a hazy way, this flowing and burning, this strange not-quite-aching, so good, so pleasurable. The women had always said there must be pain; they were wrong. There had been no pain at all. No pain!

Doña could hardly contain her wonderment, and tried to convey it to the man at her side, but she was overcome with sleepiness. Vaguely she felt his stroking hands, slower now, far gentler, on her drowsy shoulder.

All of her felt drowsy, all her body. She closed her eyes.

When he had bestowed upon her that shocking, startling caress, it had started all the peculiar melting, that melting fire when through her closed eyes she had seen a brightness in her lids' dark; no pain at all, only the widening rings of joyous pleasure spreading throughout her astonished body. She supposed the women had never known a man like this one, this lean, hard man at her side who could also be so tender, so knowing of a woman's flesh.

And this man was her sworn enemy!

Her next fuzzy thought, on the very rim of sleep, was a wondering one as well—she had sometimes felt almost like this after the robberies, when they were riding away with the gold, laughing at those they had stolen from. How strange. It was all so strange.

Most of all, she wondered that this man with his arm about her, caressing her sleepy flesh, was the one she had sworn to hate, to visit with her vengeance.

How could she carry out her plan, keep alive her ancient hate for this son of her parents' murderer? This strong man with the fine, impassive face, whose thick hair smelled like the wind in the pines, and who knew how to bring her such joy!

Doña gave it up and drifted into sleep.

Stephen, for a measureless time, was past all thinking. He lay holding her, breathing her musky fragrance, listening to the gradual slowing of his heart's loud beat.

It had never been like this, with any of the others. He had known so many! Now he could not picture their faces, remember their names.

Stephen turned his head, looking down at his wife, feeling in astonishment another stir of quick desire. His flesh was aching again for her, this woman in his arms, and he buried his face in her hair.

Doña was deeply asleep, lying on her side, facing him, her silken body lit by the dim brightness of the dying fire.

Very lightly Stephen brushed aside the veil of hair and, leaning toward her, studied the sleeping face. He bright, long lashes shone against her tawny cheeks, and her full, impulsive mouth was relaxed and vulnerable. She looked like a small girl again, half-smiling; her long hand curled into a soft fist folded into her neck.

Leaning on his elbow, he continued to look at her, going over in his mind all that happened in these past weeks. It had been only weeks, he realized with amazement. And the whole course of his aimless life had changed, the women and the wandering behind him, the past canceled out.

He would have liked to say goodbye to his father, but he had had no choice. Perhaps his father would be calmer, get well sooner without his son to upset him. Stephen stared at Doña, resolving that he would wipe out from her mind all the hate and horror of the past.

He lay back again, still wakeful, shifting her head gently on his shoulder. He held her close, and she murmured.

"Doña," he whispered, nuzzling the hollow below her ear.

Half-awake, she did not open her eyes, but there was a sweet compliance in her body as she submitted to his many kisses on her head and face, on her languorous arms and bare, sleep-heavy flesh.

"Doña," he said again, pressing her to him. She opened her eyes.

Doña saw the slate-gray eyes, hot and hard now with an almost impersonal lust, staring into hers. And from the depths of farthest memory she heard again a voice she had all but forgotten—her mother's voice, saying, "I fear the man Raike, with those cold gray eyes. He looks the way an eagle looks as it falls to take the hare."

And now looking into her husband's eyes, Doña could see the eyes of the hated Daniel Raike. She made a faintly protesting sound, and struggled in her husband's arms, but his grasp was bruising tight; and she realized that nothing could deter him now, his gray eyes were blank with desire.

Again he was enslaving her body with his skilled caress, and she felt the gradual loosening of her very will, its whirling dissolution as his mouth took her, ungently this time. Yet something in her ignited to meet his new savagery; their meeting bodies seemed almost desperate in their haste, his hoarse breath deafening Doña to the ghostly voice, to all except the moment.

The very desperation of his need endowed this meeting with an agonizing edge of excitement she had not known before.

Her quickening body answered his, her wakened senses leaped, feeling a bladed pleasure she could hardly believe; an almost unendurable joy, narrowing to a sweet, heightened frenzy, a sharpness so acute she could not contain the high, helpless cry that escaped from her.

Gazing up at him, she saw him tighten, heard him cry out with an abandoned pleasure that seemed to exceed even hers. For a silent instant they were together in their forgetting.

Stephen whispered, after a moment, the same word again and again. Raising her limp hand, he pressed it to his mouth.

Doña lay helpless in his grasp, recognizing the slow, drugged-sounding repetition of her own name.

"Isse-Loa," he whispered.

The name of her youth and her blood, thought Doña. The name of the blood of her mother!

And all at once, even as Doña accepted her delight, she was struck by a new, alien knowledge: coldly it jarred. With his wily knowledge, he had taken possession of her body. She was no longer free, free and wild as she had always been upon the vast plains and on the windy, wooded hill, not so long as his touch could bring her to this hot, enslaved forgetting.

All the while, her newly tutored senses, that deep contentment answered, What does it matter now? You are a child no longer.

But something even deeper answered that it did matter, it mattered still.

When Doña's eyes met Stephen's again, as he bent over her to kiss her mouth, he saw by the last light of the fire that old look of hers, that confounding distance in it.

As soon as Stephen returned to sense, he perceived the far-away look in her eyes, still heavy-lidded with satiety, and he was bewildered by it. Her moods seemed to change, quick as a weathervane.

He said, "Doña?" in a questioning way.

She touched his face, half-smiling, but the dark depth of her eyes was still unreadable.

Stephen felt a new greed awaken in him—her bodily submission, sweet as it was, infinitely sweet, was no longer enough.

A deeper pride had been offended; the moment left an odd hunger in his core. He had conquered her flesh. Now he must do battle for her heart.

Well, he had never turned away from a battle yet, nor lost one. This was no exception. If he had to play the game, he would maneuver her with all the skill and power at his command.

Wakeful, he held her against him, listening to her soft, even breath. He was challenged by the new goal that confronted him.

It was long before he fell asleep, so long that a pale light had already begun to creep through the curtains of the window.

When he next awoke, the dawn had not yet come, but he felt, with an amazement of pleasure and an ever-eager freshness of sensation, Doña's fragile touch upon his body, her gesture of invitation.

Again triumphant, Stephen watched her turn to him with a new, willing grace, already with a more practiced motion.

I will never understand her, never, was his fleeting thought before his body took command. But I will have her heart before it ends.

2

The Golden Chain

Chapter Eleven

"Ah, madame, we have just *begun!* Your pro—" Madame Leonide Gautier, the famous New Orleans dressmaker, glanced quickly at Doña Raike's left hand. She had been about to say "protector." Madame Gautier finished, "Proud 'usband is very generous. He has instructed me not to economize on your selections."

Doña, smiling agreeably, nodded, and Madame Gautier's eyes gleamed with greed and delight. The dressmaker raised her fat, beringed hand and called out, "Josette! Bring the brown velvet now, the one with the tight jacket that goes *so.*" Madame Gautier indicated the jacket's cut by a quick outward gesture over her own broad hips.

"You will love this ensemble," she said enthusiastically to Doña. "With it there is a saucy cap, like a man's, just right for your—unusual air."

Madame Gautier congratulated herself on her tact; indeed, she had never seen a rich young woman quite like this one. She was accustomed to dressing the beautiful young women of color who were "protected" by aristocratic New Orleans men. Now as she studied Doña covertly, she thought: There is something about this one, with her dark skin. One would almost think—well, they were an interesting couple, those two. And the husband, *quel homme!* So tall and lean. He knew what he liked, it was certain!

Madame Gautier chuckled, and said to Doña, while she helped the slender young woman into the brown velvet suit, "Your husband is a man of strong ideas. It was a very astute observation he made about the poke bonnets."

Stephen had said that Doña looked like a schoolmarm in the poke bonnets, with their deep brims that almost covered the face.

Doña smiled and examined her reflection in the long pier glass. Madame Gautier was right about the brown velvet suit—Doña loved it. Its tight jacket came to a point at the waist and spread out over her slender hips, above the full skirt, like a great flower petal. The jacket was finished with an elbow-length cape. Madame Gautier carefully placed the saucy cap on Doña's head. The cap was softened by a creamy veil.

"Ah! Now, with this cap," the dressmaker said, "the hair should be brought forward like this," she illustrated, "to hang in two smooth loops, to simulate the short hair of a young boy. You see? And of course a ruffled shirtwaist of ecru, to match the veil, with perhaps a little tie of russet-bronze, to echo your hair? Perfection!"

When Madame Gautier had found the proper cravat, and adjusted it to her satisfaction, she declared, "We must show this to your—'usband."

Doña preceded the dressmaker through the elaborate curtain that separated the dressing rooms from the waiting room where Stephen Raike was sitting. He was lounging negligently, smoking a cigar, his long body dwarfing the delicate chair in which he leaned back.

"Now that's more like it," he drawled. His clear eyes shone with pleasure, admiring Doña. "I like that hat. Try one of these hats, Doña. We've got all the time in the world." Stephen grinned, and Doña was amused to see how strongly he affected the susceptible Madame Gautier. The dressmaker flushed and made a sound that was almost a giggle.

She said coyly, "I believe you want your wife to look like a bandit, m'sieu." Stephen picked up one of the broad-brimmed hats that the dressmaker had shown Doña.

"As a matter of fact, I do." Stephen exchanged a

glance with Doña, and again Madame Gautier was puzzled by the young couple's mysterious air.

"You shall have them," the dressmaker declared, and hurried away to look for more millinery.

"You have impressed her deeply," Doña said to Stephen, laughing.

"You mean my money has," he retorted. He rose and walked to her, placing his muscular hands on her narrow waist. He gave her a lingering kiss; once again Doña felt herself melting, almost unwillingly, half-resentful at his body's power over her own.

But Madame Gautier had returned, and Doña moved out of Stephen's arms, her tawny cheeks glowing with high color.

"Now, see!" cried Madame Gautier. "Are not these wonderful hats?" She displayed a dashing, wide-brimmed hat of cream color, and similar ones in two shades of green, lavender, dark blue and black. "All," Stephen ordered tersely.

"But Stephen—" Doña protested half-heartedly.

"Get them all," Stephen repeated. "Is that everything, now?"

Doña nodded, beaming. She had never dreamed of owning so many dresses at once.

Stephen took out his bank check, and Madame Gautier, with a pleased flutter, indicated a table where he might draw up his check.

She indicated to Doña which dresses could be sent at once to their hotel and which needed further tailoring. Because the day was mild, Doña decided to wear one of her new purchases—a gown of autumn-colored stripes in russet, dark green and cream; with it, she donned the cream-colored hat with its swooping brim, and carried over her arm a cream-colored coat trimmed in dark green with dashing mousquetaire sleeves.

When the handsome pair had gone, Madame Gautier separated the other garments according to which needed work and which were to be sent to the hotel. As she examined the selection once more—a medley of lavender and gray, of brown and bronze and green and a marvelous-bright shade of blue, like the wings of a tropical bird—she thought with satisfaction of how lovely the red-haired woman would be in all the wonderful gowns. Yes, there is something about that one, she thought again. She is no ordinary woman. And he is no ordinary man. The dressmaker's pulses fluttered, remembering the tall, commanding Texan.

Doña Raike realized that Madame Gautier was not the only woman to admire Stephen: all along the river journey and on their arrival in New Orleans, Doña had seen the women's bright glances. She saw their eyes linger on Stephen's lean body and sculptured face, and study his firm yet passionate mouth below the full, light-brown mustache.

The demeanor of other men around Stephen was respectful. They apparently recognized a man who was not to be trifled with—an attitude Doña could understand, for Stephen had told her a little of the adventures that had gone into building his fortune.

Doña Olwen, who had coolly married for revenge, was now puzzled and conflicted as Doña Raike. She remembered what Tahre had said, that her argument was mainly with herself.

Stephen's many extravagant gifts had not brought Doña the triumph she expected. Not only had he bought the complete wardrobe at Madame Gautier's; he insisted she would need more things in the North—furs for the bitter Chicago winter, heavy gowns of wool and other items.

And clothes were not all; from Madame Gautier's, Stephen and Doña had gone to the finest jewelry shops in the old city. There Stephen had bought her a long plaited golden chain, and to wear on it, medallions of tawny topaz and bright Australian opal, as well as an orange Mexican fire opal, a comb decorated with pearls and turquoise beads, heavy gold earrings, and best of all, a remarkable necklace of red, green and yellow gold, of graduating pieces shaped like feathers; it was barbaric and beautiful.

It was all such a puzzle. This was the man she had

vowed to hate, but that was hard to manage. He was so loving, so generous, so appealing. For the time being, Doña put the question aside and gave herself up to enjoyment.

Now as they walked in the mild afternoon, she looked up at New Orleans' pastel houses, tall, mysterious; the shadows of their wrought-iron terrace railings gray on the narrow streets, like giant lace.

Stephen and Doña strolled to the French Market for afternoon coffee. Already she was intoxicated with the city's scents, which were unlike anything she had known before. In the dust of the Texas plains, the wind had brought only odors of pine and dry mesquite, sand and sun and desert creatures.

Doña sniffed delightedly, wrinkling her nose; here was such a bouquet of aromas that her senses were dazzled—sharp fish and harbor smells from the wharves, coffee and flowers, spicy foods and fresh-gathered vegetables, the odor of pungent cigars.

The uneven cobblestones made it a little hard to walk; Doña slowed her pace and Stephen smiled down at her. "All right?" he asked, and she nodded, returning his smile.

His gray eyes lingered on her, taking in the new striped dress and the topaz medallion she wore with it. "You look wonderful," he said. Then she saw again that watchful look she had noticed during their journey. He seemed to be puzzling her out, waiting for something. He put his arm around her waist and pulled her close to his side, indifferent to the staring people around them.

As they approached the famous market, Doña examined its squat, slate roof supported by tapering pillars of masonry. Crowded under the arcade was a great mass of people buying and selling; the place buzzed like a huge cone of bees.

Wagons passed by, creaking under the burden of carrots and cabbages, fat tomatoes shining like carnelians. Men and women lined the curb, bargaining with the sellers. Black women in bright-striped turbans, baskets on their arms, wandered about, buying a bit of this, a bit

136

of that from the stalls. Doña looked at the blacks with excited interest; she had seen few such people, certainly none like these. These people had a gay and colorful air; they were not servile.

Neither Stephen nor Doña saw the large man standing nearby who studied them with great interest. The burly giant was more elaborately dressed than Stephen Raike, and his face, though weather-beaten and hard, was pale —the face of a man who spent much time indoors. He was a clean-shaven man in his forties and had a reckless look about him.

A dark-skinned woman easily bearing on her head a basket of red roses passed Doña and Stephen. Then Doña caught sight of an old Indian woman, wrapped in a blanket, selling baskets striped in red and green.

For a moment Doña's eyes met those of the Indian; in the latter's was a kind of puzzled recognition. The Indian stared curiously at the beautiful redhead in the creamy hat.

Doña said a soft word to the Indian that Stephen recognized as Comanche; the Indian answered in kind, a smile webbing her stern, wrinkled face.

The stranger had moved closer. When Doña spoke to the Indian, the stranger looked surprised, then contemptuous. But his eyes gleamed more brightly as he stared at Doña.

"She knew," Doña said quietly to Stephen as they moved on. For the first time the fact of her mingled blood struck her with force. She began to wonder how she would be received in this wider world, something that had not occurred to her before.

Stephen looked at her, and she felt he was almost reading her thoughts.

"Here we are," he said. He indicated a coffeehouse tucked away between the racks of fruits and vegetables. They sat down on stools, and were served thick black, steaming coffee and cakes flavored with honey, still warm from the oven.

" 'Black as night, strong as the devil, hot as hell,' "

Stephen quoted, grinning. "The kind of coffee my mother brought to Texas."

Doña sipped the coffee with appreciation and bit into one of the cakes again, hungrily. After a moment, she said, "Tell me about your mother."

And Stephen told her what he knew of Louise Gerard.

"The high and mighty Gerards," Doña repeated thoughtfully, after Stephen had used the ironic expression. "They still live here, I suppose."

Stephen laughed. His answer was dry. "There will always be Gerards in New Orleans." Doña realized he had said nothing of visiting them.

"What would they think of me?" she asked him, smiling.

"What anybody would. That you are delightful. I'm the problem, the son of Daniel Raike."

Doña felt an unpleasant coldness in her body at the mention of Daniel Raike's name. But Stephen had apparently not noticed. He went on in a matter-of-fact tone, "I'm sure they never forgave him for stealing my mother away."

The heavy, well-dressed stranger, who had overheard Doña and the Indian, entered the coffeehouse, but as it chanced neither Doña nor Stephen noticed him in the crowded place.

Stephen was looking at Doña at that moment and, noticing her expression, whispered, "What is it, *querida?*" He raised her hand to his lips and kissed the palm.

She remembered this gesture in the inn on their wedding night; again it affected her strongly.

"Nothing, nothing," she answered with unease, half-resenting her pulses' quickening with his caress. "Nothing," she repeated in a firmer voice and managed a smile. How exciting he is! she thought. He has the power to make me forget everything when he touches me. And this realization made her feel helpless again.

Around them the market men were discussing the affairs of the day. Doña heard the rapid trilling of French —Stephen had spoken it to her sometimes at night—and a soft, melodious tongue she did not know, mingling with the drone of the blacks' deep voices. It was all so new and strange that it distracted her from her confused and gloomy thoughts.

The men's voices rose in argument and Doña caught the names of "Brigham Young" and "John D. Lee," the "Mountain Meadows Massacre," and "William Walker."

William Walker's name was pronounced with special heat.

"Who is William Walker?" she asked Stephen. "Is he from around here?"

Stephen laughed. "I hope not. Wherever he shows up there's trouble." And he told her of the notorious adventurer who had set himself up as president of Nicaragua. "There's a rumor that he's looking for men for his private army, though. He could show up here."

The well-dressed stranger with the pale face was staring at Stephen and Doña. He came to attention at Stephen's last statement.

"More coffee?" Stephen asked. Doña assented. When their cups were empty again, they rose and continued on their way through the market. Glancing back, Stephen caught sight of the tall stranger who had been following them, and he stiffened.

"What's the matter?"

"Nothing," Stephen answered carelessly. "Just a man I'm surprised to see, and it's not a pleasant surprise."

"What do you mean?"

"Oh, never mind. A business thing. I don't want to spoil our day with that." Something final in his tone made Doña unwilling to ask him anything further.

He hurried her past the stalls of the butchers and the fish vendors, for her delicate nostrils quivered with distaste.

Stephen laughed. "The crab and shrimp are much more appetizing cooked in gumbo. We'll have some for dinner." He indicated the stalls in front of them. "Here's something nicer."

Doña exclaimed with pleasure, for on the sidewalk in front of them sprawled the flower market, with its hundreds of cut flowers and potted plants; more flowers than she had ever seen in one place. There were roses and ferns, little trees of vivid red peppers, plants and flowers of pink and yellow, lilac and blue, orange and white. Some of the blacks selling the flowers had blossoms behind their ears or in their hats.

"What would you like?"Stephen asked.

"All of them!" Doña laughed, then she said, "Some yellow roses."

Stephen bought her a huge bunch of the dewy roses. "They remind me of you," he said quietly, "so—smooth and sweet." He stared at her tawny face and ripe mouth above the fragrant petals. She felt again that half-unwilling warmth that he was able to arouse in her.

The smiling black who sold them the flowers said in his rich, slow voice, "I thank you, sir. Have a good time while you can."

"Thank you," Stephen answered as they moved away, drawing Doña close to his side again.

"You've walked enough," he declared. "I'll hire us a carriage. Perhaps you would like to—rest awhile before dinner."

His meaningful pause brought color to her face. She had heard before that note of constant desire; once more she reflected that now she belonged to him—belonged to a man named Raike! And the thought was an uneasy one, even as it thrilled her.

Doña remembered what the flower-seller had said, "Have a good time while you can," and wondered why she had read a warning in the light words. Did it have something to do with the stranger they had seen in the coffeehouse?

She looked up at Stephen: her confusion had returned.

"Mon dieu!" Alphonse Tregue whispered to the waiter. "Do not place those near the Gerards, I pray you."

Obediently Georges, the best-known waiter in Tregue's famous restaurant, signaled the handsome pair to a small table as far as possible from the stiff Gerards.

She is a beauty, certainly, thought Tregue, studying the red-haired woman in the simple but dazzling gown the color of a peacock's wing. With the gown the woman wore only one ornament, a vivid blue-green opal on a thick plaited chain. She moves like a queen, reflected Tregue, but she is surely a woman of color. And to seat such a one near the Gerards—the skies would fall! He would lose the patronage of that fine family.

The man, though, he has a look of good blood, Tregue's thoughts ran on. And he doesn't look too happy with the table. Tregue wondered if the man suspected the reason for their summons to the far table.

The restauranteur studied the beautiful woman again, wondering if she were a woman of color, after all. He was used enough to the beautiful quadroons flaunted by young protectors from the city's aristocracy, with their dark, liquid eyes and flawless skin the color of well-creamed coffee. But this woman—Alphonse Tregue ran through the gradings of color—from griffe through metif and sang-mele. She was none of those; that color could surely be only Indian. Mon dieu! Treague said to himself, That is worst of all. A red savage dining at Tregue's! Yet, glancing again at the proud, beautiful woman in the bright blue gown, Alphonse Tregue reflected that she was hardly a "savage."

The woman could not conceal her excitement—this was doubtless her first visit to his famous restaurant—and still she behaved with great correctness, the critical Frenchman judged.

He glanced at the Gerards' table and repressed a smile below his thick black mustache; one of their party, the irrepressible Philippe, who was known throughout the city as a great rake, was staring fixedly at the woman in blue. Philippe's high-nosed mother, dressed in black, had not deigned to glance in the direction of the unusual couple. But her face was stiff with disapproval.

Yes, Tregue thought with amusement, the old Gerard grows impatient with her eldest! With such an eye for the ladies it is no wonder he prefers not to marry.

The exotic menu at Tregue's compensated for its plainness of decor. Stephen Raike, who knew the place well, described its confusing dishes to Doña—the gumbo filé made from the best shrimps and oysters that could be found; pompano and crayfish, soft-shell crabs and oysters.

Doña finally said, "Choose for me."

"All right." Stephen looked up from the large, hand-written menu and studied Doña. "More and more, I realize how beautiful you are. Everyone stares at you."

Doña glanced about her. It was true; several people were staring, one of them a handsome dark man with a reckless look who sat at a large table on the far side of the room. His companions were a noble-looking old man, two timid young women dressed in black, and a stern older woman wearing the same gloomy color.

Stephen followed her glance. "Some of them stare a little too much," he said in an annoyed tone, nodding at the young man. The man returned Stephen's look in a bold way, with a half-smile on his handsome lips.

Doña said, partly to distract her husband, "I think they stare because I look so different." Suddenly she felt a strange uneasiness. "Maybe I don't belong in places like this," she said quietly. "Will it be like this everywhere, even in Chicago?"

"Doña!" Stephen looked concerned and, leaning forward, took her hand. "Men stare at you because you are so lovely; women stare at you because they're jealous. What do you mean, 'Will it always be like this?' "

"I was wondering how it is in other cities. You told me New Orleans was a very—worldly place, where they were used to all kinds of people. What will it be like in Chicago?"

Stephen smiled at her. "Chicago is a very different kind of place. Its very name came from the Indians. And the name Raike means something there."

A stillness had fallen over the restaurant at that moment, and it seemed to Doña that when Stephen pronounced his name, the reckless-looking man at the far table had heard, and was staring at them both now with a new expression.

But Stephen had not noticed, and went on to describe to Doña the character of the booming Northern city. In his enthusiasm, he talked on as they ate the delicious gumbo filé and sipped their wine.

Then he stopped himself, and laughed. "I've been talking your ear off! Here, let me order you a dessert and coffee. What would you like?"

"What would you recommend?"

"Well, the chocolate pudding here is wonderful. Did you know the recipe calls for melting the chocolate in the sun?"

Doña was delighted with the idea, and said, "I must have that, then." She realized that Stephen had forgotten, in his pleasure in the moment, the real meaning of her uneasy question about cities. With an almost maternal feeling, she resolved to put her fearful questions away, so she would not spoil his childlike enjoyment.

At such times, she reflected, it was hard to remember that she had married him from a desire for revenge! And she saw that the eyes of the two timid young women at the table on the other side of the room were returning again and again to the handsome figure and face of Stephen.

Doña saw something else: the heavy stranger they had seen in the French Market was entering Tregue's. Her expression must have alerted Stephen, for he said quickly, "What is it? What's the matter? You look so—strange."

"It's that man," Doña said in a low voice. "The man in the market, the one you said was not a pleasant surprise."

Stephen looked annoyed, but did not turn. Something made Doña glance at the table of black-clad people. The dashing young man who had been staring at her also looked a bit uneasy, yet he gave no sign that he recognized the heavy stranger. Apparently, Doña thought, Stephen was not the only one who felt the stranger was an unpleasant surprise.

The man was approaching their table. He paused beside them and, after a keen glance at Doña, accompanied by a half-bow, the stranger exclaimed in a harsh voice, "Well, Raike! This is a surprise." Doña, with her quick eyes, took in several things at once. She saw her husband's look of irritation as he got to his feet, and at the same time noticed that all the people at the far table were looking in their direction. What did it mean? Doña thought it might have something to do with the stranger's loud pronunciation of the name of "Raike."

But Stephen was saying reluctantly, "May I present my wife? Doña, this is Alfred Torrance, of Chicago."

"Mrs. Raike," Torrance said heavily, and bowed. "This is an honor and a pleasure." Doña nodded in reply. There was something in the man's voice that made her very uncomfortable, indeed. Especially when she looked at Stephen, and saw that his own face, usually so bland, was tight.

"Will you be in the city long?" Torrance asked Stephen.

"A few more days." It was an awkward moment, for it was clear that Stephen was not going to ask Torrance to join them. Sensing this, the big man said, with an unpleasant laugh, "I'm sure we'll run into each other again." With another half-bow to Doña, Torrance strode away and was seated at a small table by himself.

As she preceded Stephen from Tregue's, Doña was hardly conscious of the diners' stares; she was preoccupied with the mystery of the stranger, and Stephen's look of anger.

Chapter Twelve

Doña found it impossible not to be diverted by the spectacle of the theater, where Stephen took her from Tregue's. Dazzled by new sights and sounds, she almost forgot the mystery of Stephen's uneasy reaction to Torrance.

She had never seen anything quite like the St. Charles Theater and its splendid patrons. Looking up at the facade of the wide two-story building, with its high verandah supported by tall columns and its garden blooming with lush shrubs, Doña realized how crude the playhouses of the West were in comparison.

How exciting it was to mingle with the well-dressed women and their elegant escorts, and exciting to realize that she, Doña Raike, was as well-dressed as anyone. She felt an innocent pleasure at the sight of admiring eyes.

Doña had never been much of a reader. Nevertheless she was impressed when Stephen told her they were going to see a play by Shakespeare, something about a "shrew." Turing from her contemplation of a beautiful dark woman in a lavish pink gown, Doña heard Stephen saying, "Edwin Booth."

"Yes?"

"They say he was quite a success in San Francisco. Now he's touring the South. Do you know the play?"

Doña admitted that she did not, and half-regretted that she had never read the big book that her father had read so often when she was a child.

Stephen told her the story of Petruchio and Kate the

intractable. He laughed. "I think you will understand Kate very well."

Doña soon learned what Stephen meant; from the first entrance of Kate, Doña saw something of herself in that impudent character. When she heard Kate say, "What, shall I be appointed hours; as though, belike, I knew not what to take and what to leave. . . ?" Doña sympathized with her at once. In spite of the difficult language, Doña's quick intelligence grasped the meaning of the words. And something within her rebeled when she heard Petruchio declare, "I am he am born to tame you, Kate. And bring you from a wild Kate to a Kate Conformable as other household Kates—"

Certainly the Booth man had a very fine voice and flashing, expressive eyes; his figure was not bad, Doña judged, but he was not nearly as handsome as Stephen.

She whispered this to Stephen, who looked very gratified. But then the declaration of Petruchio recalled itself to Doña, and she wondered uneasily if she herself were going to be made into a "household" Doña. The thought rankled, and she suddenly remembered the things concealed in her trunk, those items she had never let her husband see. Doña began to feel a peculiar restlessness, but imagining Stephen's glance on her, sat still, waiting for the end of the second act.

At the next interval, Stephen smiled at her, and asked, "You do understand Kate, don't you?"

Doña nodded. She saw that look in his eyes again— that affectionate but watchful look, as if he were waiting to see what she would do or say next. What did that look mean? she wondered.

But now Stephen's attention was diverted from her to a pair of men in the crowded lobby. They were Alfred Torrance, the man from Chicago, and the elegant young man who had stared so in Tregue's.

The latter was staring now at Doña, the same mocking smile on his lips that she had seen before. Torrance bowed in their direction.

Smothering an impatient exclamation, Stephen said to

Doña, "Shall we go in?" and led the way back to their seats.

Faced again with the mystery of Torrance, Doña barely heard the rest of the play. She glanced swiftly at her husband and discovered that his fine face in the dim light from the stage was tense, as it had been in the restaurant when Torrance approached them.

At last, Doña realized with disappointment, as she returned her attention to the stage, the independent Kate had indeed been tamed; she was saying, "What is she but a foul contending rebel / And graceless traitor to her loving lord? / I am ashamed that women are so simple / To offer war where they should kneel for peace."

Doña's whole self rebelled at the word "kneel." She remembered, all at once, the old days on the plains. She recalled the surprised faces of Tahre and the other men when her true and steady bullet had split the wires of the fence; what a triumph there had been in that singing sound!

And here was a woman giving in, saying silly words, like "Why are our bodies soft and weak and smooth, / Unapt to toil and trouble in the world?" Did that mean women were weak; that she, Doña Olwen, was weak? It wasn't true, Doña protested in silence. She, Doña Olwen, had ridden and shot as well as any man, better than some! Why, she had robbed this man sitting at her side. Was she expected to "obey" him?

Half-heartedly Doña joined in the applause, after the last line of the play—" 'Tis a wonder, by your leave, she will be tamed so." These foolish people, she thought, were laughing with delight that the shrew had been tamed.

Not I, Doña resolved. Not ever. Then she realized that she had called herself not Doña Raike, but Doña Olwen.

As the crowd of theater-goers moved slowly into the St. Charles lobby, Doña heard a man call out Stephen's name. Turning, she saw Alfred Torrance coming toward them; behind him was the dark, elegant diner from Tregue's.

There was no way to avoid them now without a pointed

cut. Stephen waited with an impassive face while the two men approached.

"I wanted you to make the acquaintance of Philippe Gerard," Torrance said, smiling. Doña glanced up at Stephen; there was a flicker of surprise in his gray look. "Mrs. Raike, may I present Mr. Gerard?"

The slender Gerard, of a height with Stephen, bowed low, taking Doña's hand in his own, and kissing it with a fervor that made her uneasy. She felt her cheeks grow warm. When Gerard straightened, his intense eyes stared into Doña's for a long moment.

"And this is Stephen Raike," said Torrance, sounding amused. "He is a kinsman of yours, I believe."

"Mr. Raike," Gerard said in his insolent drawl. "Louise Gerard was my aunt. We are cousins, then. And obviously the Raikes have an eye for beauty." The intense eyes, twinkling, turned again to Doña.

Doña, who was standing close to Stephen, felt his arm go tense at the challenge in Gerard's tone. However, he said coolly, "How do you do, Mr. Gerard."

"Ah, come! That is a cold greeting for a long-lost cousin." Gerard seemed to be baiting him, Doña thought.

To cover the awkward silence that followed, Gerard added quickly, "We were just going to supper. Perhaps you would join us?"

"I think not," Stephen said curtly. "My wife has had a long day." He emphasized the title.

Doña, though a little annoyed that Stephen had spoken for her without asking her wishes, did not protest. She knew instinctively that Stephen had taken an instant dislike to Philippe Gerard; what the difficulty with Torrance was, she could only imagine.

"Then why don't you join us for a little game later, Raike?" Torrance put in. "You've never done me the honor in Chicago, and I've heard you're quite a man with cards. This is your chance to prove it."

The challenge in Torrance's voice was so open that Doña almost anticipated Stephen's reply. A man like Stephen Raike would never let that go by unanswered, she thought.

"Why not?" Stephen answered casually. "That is, if you don't mind, Doña."

"Of course not," Doña said lightly. "I am a little tired, and surely you deserve an evening with your friends." She said the last word with a mischievous inflection that made Stephen smile.

"Your wife is generous as well as beautiful, my cousin." Gerard gestured toward Doña with his slender hand.

"Then I'll take Doña to the hotel. Where are you staying, Torrance? The game will be in your rooms?"

Torrance named the hotel and gave Stephen the number of his suite.

"I'll see you there. Say a half-hour?" Nodding curtly to the two men, Stephen led Doña to one of the carriages parked before the St. Charles.

"Stephen, who is Alfred Torrance?" she asked as they drove off.

"One of the biggest gamblers in Chicago. And a man with a hand in every enterprise that's questionable," he added dryly. "He and I have locked horns on more than one occasion. I think he's afraid I'll muscle in on his territory. I've already bought out his city stages." Stephen smiled.

"I see. And the little game—what is that?"

"Poker."

"He said you never played with him in Chicago."

Stephen laughed shortly. "Hardly. Every game in his house is rigged. It may be different here."

"May?"

"He could be playing with marked cards, even here," Stephen answered. "I doubt it, though. In New Orleans men have ended up dead for playing with marked cards. Just to be sure, I'll take my own." He laughed again, that short, dry laugh that made him seem a stranger. This hidden side of him excited Doña.

But when he took leave of her in their hotel rooms, kissing her tenderly, she realized he had not said a word about Philippe Gerard. Nevertheless, she had a strong feeling that the Frenchman's challenge, more than that of Alfred Torrance, was the one that Stephen was answering.

I am tired, Doña reflected when the door had closed on Stephen. She wandered to the bedroom and examined herself in the pier glass.

Over her peacock-colored evening gown, Doña was wearing one of the Tunisian shawls recommended by Madame Gautier. The shawls, of silk, were generally of two colors woven together; Doña's was turquoise blue, to match her gown, and dark green. The shades were very striking with her vivid hair and pointed up the mingled colors of the great Australian opal in her medallion.

"I cannot believe this is me," she whispered aloud, staring at the beautiful stranger in the glass. Then, laughing at her own reflection, Doña slipped off the shawl and began to undo her gown.

She would not call a maid; she would undress herself tonight. Having another woman wait on her was still too strange.

As Doña watched the shining gown slide to the carpet, exposing her fragile underthings, she remembered the play. The conclusion taken so lightheartedly by the men and women watching—the taming of Kate, the shrew—still annoyed her, and her preoccupation drove the thought of Gerard and Torrance from her mind.

She took off her petticoats, then her stockings and chemise. How pleasing it was, she reflected, that she did not have to wear the constricting corsets that older women wore; "You are so slender!" Madame Gautier had said enthusiastically. "You do not need to torture yourself with whalebone and wire!"

Doña examined her own naked body in the glass, suddenly very pleased with the body she had always taken for granted—the small but full and shapely breasts, the narrow hips and long, slender legs. It was a pity legs could not be shown! If women wore trousers—with that thought, a wave of homesickness swept over Doña.

She retrieved her clothes from the floor, tossed them over a chair, and lay down on the bed, remembering.

The warm weight of the medallion on her bare flesh

recalled the weight of the stolen watch that she had worn with such triumph.

The watch! Doña's memory of the twilight evening on the train was suddenly very sharp and clear, so clear she could feel the heavy gun in her hands, the snug fit of her leather trousers and the consoling shadow of the black slouch hat. She could smell the silk scent of the blue scarf over the lower part of her face.

Lying naked on the wide bed, Doña closed her eyes and relived that exciting encounter.

Again she was climbing the steps of the Short Line car, vital and unaided by any man's hand, Tahre close behind her. Doña could almost feel the play of her limber muscles as she remembered climbing into the car. . . .

Doña opened her eyes, sighing.

Was it all over, then? Was she never to ride again, wild and free, at Tahre's side, skilled as any man at taking what was really hers?

She sat up in the bed, feeling the weight of the medallion—a shackle now, not an ornament, not even a vengeful proof of Stephen's defeat. A shackle and a bond! She had traded her freedom and the wild winds, she had betrayed her vow, for these golden toys. Now, instead of riding astride her horse, proud and unfettered, she would sit in a carriage, submissive by her husband's side, bound by her voluminous dresses like a bird with a broken wing.

No. No! It was impossible. She could not do it any longer. The vengeance that she had thought would be hers in marrying Stephen would be his, when she became more and more of a "household Doña," like the unfortunate Kate in the play.

Doña sat up with great suddenness and the change of posture made her head swim. She had had too much wine that evening, and now it was making her feel dizzy and her legs and arms heavy as lead.

She sat for an instant on the side of the bed, then determinedly got up and walked to the trunk sitting open near the tall mirror. Burrowing under the gowns that would not be used in New Orleans, she found a small leather bag, the bag she had carried from Texas. She recalled how Stephen had teased her about its heaviness.

Lifting the bag from the trunk, Doña opened it and drew out her Colt. Laying the gun on the carpet, she upended the bag and a stream of golden coins poured onto the thick rug. She counted them with a feeling of satisfaction. Yes, it was enough; there was quite enough of this Raike money for her to go away tonight. She would go home again, where she could be free!

Smiling, Doña replaced the money in the bag, then the Colt, and replaced the bag in the trunk, this time on top of the splendid gowns. She would take nothing, nothing that Stephen Raike had given her!

With renewed energy, Doña started toward the chest where her underthings lay in a deep drawer. But a swift and discouraging thought arrested her in her tracks: how could she go back now? Lamb and Scurry—and the marshal, what was his name? Bonner—would all be after her. And they might take Tahre, too.

Where, then? She would have to think. She would have to plan!

She felt her tiredness returning, sweeping over her in great waves. Why had she drunk so much wine? Doña decided she would take a short nap, then she would determine where to go, what to do. Of one thing she was certain: she could not stay here, chained by this golden chain, by all the golden chains with which Stephen would bind her as time went on. And Doña lay down to rest a moment.

Sleep overcame her, like a wide black wave.

Doña stirred in her sleep, restlessly, feeling a most peculiar sensation: she heard a far, rustling sound and on her bare flesh felt the light impact of something like falling leaves. A strange, tickling sensation. She dreamed, half-waking, that she lay naked under a tall tree that was shaking its leaves upon her, showering her with them. The leaves were almost covering her now.

She opened her eyes slowly, puzzled and confused. Stephen was standing above her, laughing. Stephen,

152

laughing! He sounded a little drunk. Stephen was the tree, then. Doña glanced down at herself and saw that the leaves were bills—many bills of green paper money.

Stephen was still laughing softly, scattering the money over her body.

"Stephen!" she said, not yet fully awake, amazed at his wild behavior. "What—?"

"It's yours, my Doña," he said softly, and she knew from the slurring of his words that Stephen was drunk. He could not stop laughing; she stared at him and then, infected by his drunken laughter, grinned up into his face.

"Oh, Doña! Doña!" he cried, and his voice was changing. "I never saw you—like this." He gazed at her slender nakedness, half-covered by the green bills. She noticed then that he was wearing only a dressing gown. Impatiently he flung it from him and lowered his body to hers, the paper money rustling and crackling as their bodies met.

Now Doña was laughing, too; a deep, wild laughter. "You've won, then," she said softly, gasping a little as her laughter began to subside.

Stephen did not answer, but raised his lean body, and with quick, impatient sweeps of his muscular hand, began to brush the bills way; they fluttered to the carpet and those remaining on the bed were crisp and rough to Doña's tender flesh.

Once again he said her name, very softly, then "Isse-Loa, Isse-Loa," his gray look flickering from her fiery hair to her tawny face with its heavy-lidded, half-asleep dark eyes. His glance descended then to her naked breasts, her arms, her body's secrets now open to him.

He said her name again and again, his eyes taking in the delights of her, one after the other. "I never saw you so—" He seemed powerless to complete the thought. And suddenly, she felt again the command of his lean, muscular body and the skill of his exploring mouth. He knelt on the bed at her feet and took her slender ankles in his hands and bent his lips to her thighs.

Doña was shaken and breathless in the quick grasp of this stranger who was her husband, feeling with wonder almost akin to pain the touch of his lips, thinking hazily in her excruciating pleasure of this bond that held her, almost against her will—the overpowering pull of magic, this lightning touch of his mouth that made her forget all her defiance, her confusion.

Crying out, she heard him exclaim, too, his voice rough with amazement and desiring. He raised himself then, and she felt his body tremble, felt the lifting of her body into his hard, wiry grasp while one of his strong hands explored the satiny expanse of her bare back and traced the sweet outward swelling of her hip before he lowered his face to hers and took her mouth in a starved, demanding kiss.

The prickle of his mustache above her lips aroused in Doña newer, wilder emotion; she felt herself go soft and giving to his hardness and his demanding flesh; he still had not released her from his endless, thrilling caress. All her sense of place and time were gone at once, forgotten in the timelessness of this embrace; she felt almost faint with wanting him.

Laughing a little, so softly the laughter was little more than the sound of excited breath, Doña moved sinuously in his arms.

Again she heard him gasp an incomprehensible word and his hard hands were exploring her wholly, arousing her so that she began to quiver; all at once she became so daring and bold that Stephen cried out in joyous disbelief.

Doña's eyes closed, and she felt herself sinking, sinking: in their coming together, Doña knew nothing but the moment, careless of her earlier resolve, forgetting that a few hours before she had planned to leave him.

For at this moment he alone was the bringer of all delight, and nothing would ever be stronger than this pleasure, this frenzy that was the core of all her longings.

"Stephen," Doña whispered. "Stephen."

He did not stir; he was deeply asleep. She felt a strange, tender pity, contemplating him asleep. In the dim light, his long body sprawled like a tired boy's.

Doña raised herself carefully from the bed and, avoiding the fallen money on the carpet, moved toward the open trunk next to the pier-glass.

Stooping before the trunk, she glanced back over her shoulder: Stephen was very still, and in the quiet of the late night she could hear his even breathing. Quietly she took up the small leather bag and hid it again at the bottom of the trunk. Then, without sound, she closed the trunk's lid and returned to the bed.

Looking at the money scattered on the floor, Doña shook her head and smiled. I will have to pick it up, she thought, before the maids come in the morning. They will think we are insane!

And with great care she began to pick up the bills from the lush carpet, noting by the light of the dying candles that the bills were in small denominations. He must have done that on purpose, she thought, so he would have a great many to dress me in! For some reason the idea was so funny that she had to stifle her laughter, and it filled her with tenderness for his childlike escapade.

Doña bundled the bills together and, seeing Stephen's coat tossed upon a chair, put them into his pocket. The ones on the bed would have to wait until morning, though she wondered how he could sleep on them.

Quietly as she had risen, Doña went back to bed and lay watching the shadows of the candle-flames that danced about the wall. She turned her head and looked at Stephen.

He has done it again, she reflected. He has stilled me with his body. She realized that she would not leave now.

She felt something that was almost resignation. If she left now, she would miss him. Amazed, Doña repeated silently to herself, I would miss him! Whether or not she loved him, she did not know. But she was certain now that she would miss him very much, his hard, lean body and his cool, gray eyes that always seemed to be studying her, the touch of his wily mouth and his long, firm hands.

Somehow it did not seem to matter so much now that in the theater she had assured herself she was still "Doña Olwen."

Chapter Thirteen

The days that followed were so busy that it seemed to Doña no time at all before they were driving to the crowded Mississippi docks to board their northbound boat.

It was a bright, crisp October day, cool for New Orleans. Beside Stephen, in a hired carriage, Doña sat wearing her brown velvet suit with the saucy veiled cap. Thrown over her knees was a rich fur tippet Stephen had insisted she buy for the journey.

"It'll get cold as we go farther north," he said. "When we get to Chicago, you'll have to buy something that covers you all the way," he added. Doña had smiled at this blunt masculine way of referring to a full-length fur. She had never imagined owning such a thing, but he took such purchases very casually.

She learned of Stephen's real winnings from the game with Torrance the day he bought the tippet. When Doña heard the price of the fur scarf, she had raised her brows and looked questioningly at Stephen. Ignoring her, he paid for the tippet in cash. A little later he said easily, "What the hell. I took thirty thousand dollars off old Al that night. It made quite a bundle, didn't it?" He cocked a mischievous eye at her, and she laughed, the color deepening in her cheeks.

To Doña's relief, they had seen nothing of either Gerard or Torrance in the remaining days of their stay. And the feelings of discontent that had assailed Doña at the play were, for the moment, held at bay. After their abandoned lovemaking that night, Stephen's attentions to her redoubled. There did not seem to be enough for him to do for her, and she was swept along on a warm current of grateful affection.

Half-guiltily now, as their carriage drew up among the teeming crowds at the landing, she remembered the leather bag containing her gun and the gold. But her thoughts were interrupted by Stephen's exclamation: "Look! There's my surprise for you!" He was grinning broadly.

"Where?" she asked, shading her eyes against the bright Southern sun, trying to follow the direction of his eyes. He pointed at the nearest steamboat anchored at the landing. The ship was one of many; New Orleans in this year had become the fourth largest port in the world, Stephen had told her.

She could believe it, for the river traffic here was immense. The place was thronged with people and with vehicles; hundreds of black roustabouts were loading cargo onto the boats, shouting and laughing, guided by the colored flags that told them—most could not read signs—where to carry their burdens.

Doña's pulses quickened with the excitement of the scene, and she said, "What is it? Where?"

"There. You see?" Stephen pointed to the nearest steamboat's side. *Princess* was painted there in giant letters. "See what kind of princess she is? Look up there, at the pilot house."

On the pilot house behind the great smokestacks was a statue of an Indian princess.

"Oh!" Doña cried out with delight. She turned to Stephen, grinning. *"That's"* why you were so anxious to get this boat! You think of everything, don't you?"

"When it comes to you, I do," he said, and kissed her gloved hand. Again, she felt that half-unwilling tenderness she experienced so often, part of her wanting to relax and let him command her, let him sweep her along in submissive, unthinking devotion; the other part still hesitant, cautious of capture as the deer that had visited her on the porch of her father's house.

She turned her head away to hide the quick sadness of

remembering. Stephen had done so much; every day, he planned another diversion, another pleasure, and it was stingy not to respond.

So she turned back to him again and, smiling, said, "You are very good to me."

He stared at her a moment, as if waiting for her to say something else. When she did not, and the steamboat's great whistle sounded, he said, "We'd better hurry."

At a gesture of Stephen's, two strong blacks carried their luggage up the ramp to the *Princess,* and Doña's reflections were lost in the bustle of hers and Stephen's boarding. There was too much to see to waste time on useless thoughts: the puzzle of her marriage to Stephen, in any case, would not be solved in a day. Doña gave herself up to the pleasure of her new surroundings.

She could see at a glance that the *Princess* was nothing like the smaller boat that had carried them from Texas to New Orleans. The *Princess* was truly one of the "floating palaces" that had begun to sail the Mississippi in the last few years. Stephen had described them to her with enthusiasm, and the *Princess* lived up to her name: she was huge, and as they walked along the main deck toward their stateroom, Doña glimpsed, through their open doors, luxurious cabins. The cabins were furnished with crystal chandeliers, large mirrors and heavy carpeting; the furniture was ornately carved.

"Why, it's like a hotel!" she said to Stephen. He was pleased at her surprise, and answered, smiling, "Guess what they call the deck up there."

"What?"

"The Texas deck. Texas became a state about the time they started using decks like that. As a matter of fact, that's why they call them staterooms. They used to be named for states. Here we are." He made a sweeping gesture and she entered their stateroom.

"This is *better* than our hotel!"

"It's the honeymoon suite," he said, and turned to direct the men in the placement of their trunks. Handing them coins, Stephen hardly heard the men's thanks; he stared at Doña's silky face behind the creamy veil of her cap. Excitement had brightened her dark eyes, and her ripe mouth was half-parted. When the men had gone, Stephen closed the door firmly. With two long strides, he was near her, gently lifting the creamy veil, kissing her soft mouth at first with tender slowness, then with ever-increasing savagery.

In a dim, drowsy way she realized that he was locking the door, drawing the curtains to shut out the light from the room, which was golden, shadowy in the last of the sun.

They hardly knew when the *Princess* left the landing to begin the journey north.

The great dining saloon of the *Princess* was painted a dazzling white, from corniced wall to vaulted ceiling; at intervals six great chandeliers of polished brass held fixtures of white glass that shed a soft sunlike light on the white-spread tables set for eight.

The waiters' black faces were startling above their immaculate white jackets and against the white wall. Doña as well was dressed in sooty black, relieved only by the plaited gold chain holding its bright blue-green medallion. Her hair, unlike that of the other women about her—dark or white or pale yellow, decorated with flowers, foliage, feathers and gauze—was done simply and unadorned. The hairdo was a style Stephen liked very much, one she had learned in New Orleans; Madame Gautier had told her it was a style they were beginning to wear in the French court, smooth and striking, with a center part and a great heavy loop of hair combed down over the right ear and pinned behind. Doña's sun-touched face and neck were greatly enhanced by the severe black gown.

The waiter handed them each a long, narrow menu that looked like a Valentine, with its curlicues and flowers and gilt. A sketch of the *Princess* decorated the top, and Doña glanced at the amazing variety of dishes offered— soups, two kinds of fish, twenty-five main dishes, a dozen vegetables and more than a dozen pastries, fruits and desserts.

Stephen laughed at her helpless expression. "Take your time," he said. "We have plenty of that." And his sharp glance wandered over the long saloon.

The diners were as varied as the bill of fare. There were Quakers in drab clothes, fine ladies from the South, obvious foreigners, Federal soldiers in full regimentals, modish young Spanish Creoles and sober-looking businessmen. There were as usual the complement of gamblers, and one buck wore an astonishing cravat made of cloth of gold.

Stephen turned to Doña. "Have you decided?"

"Not yet, I'm afraid," she answered, and Stephen returned to his scrutiny of the saloon. This time he noticed two newcomers: Alfred Torrance and Philippe Gerard.

They were approaching Stephen and Doña. At Stephen's annoyed exclamation, Doña looked up and saw the men.

Before they could reach the table, a family party of six entered from a nearer door and were seated at Stephen's and Doña's table.

Doña heard Stephen's sigh of relief. He muttered, "What the hell are they doing here?"

Gerard and Torrance paused, bowing to Doña, who returned their greeting with a cool half-smile. Stephen frowned and nodded to them curtly. Gerard stared at Doña boldly, and with a disappointed look gestured Torrance to a neighboring table.

As the family chattered around them, Doña said mildly, "I suppose it was time for Mr. Torrance to go back to Chicago."

"No, it isn't, as a matter of fact. He told me had some business in New Orleans in November. I have a feeling it has something to do with William Walker, and outfitting his private army. That's the way the rumors go, anyway. But why Gerard?" Stephen was speaking in a low voice audible only to Doña. But the waiter interrupted, and Stephen ordered their dinners.

Waiting until after the waiter had set their soup before them, Doña asked quietly, "Why does Gerard disturb you so?"

"I don't like the way he looks at you," Stephen answered bluntly. "I have a feeling he's going to cause trouble. He and Torrance together, I wonder where they're headed."

Doña took a few spoonfuls of soup, then put her spoon aside to sip her wine. "Is Torrance angry because of the money you won?"

Stephen smiled grimly. "Oh, yes," he said lightly, but there was a dark undertone to his words. "We've been at war for quite a time; it riled him very badly, an amateur taking him for that amount."

"What do you think he'll do?"

"With Torrance you never know. And with Gerard around, I trust him even less. They make a mighty funny pair."

Studying the two men covertly, Doña was forced to agree. Just as she had wondered in the theater, she wondered now at the friendship of the two men so unalike—the thoroughbred Gerard and the dray Torrance!

Then she saw that Gerard was staring back at her; his intense gaze caused her acute discomfort, and she lowered her eyes at once. If Stephen, in his jealousy, misunderstood, she did not like to think of what might happen.

At the end of the long, elaborate meal, Stephen asked her if she would like to hear the orchestra in the main saloon. She assented gladly, thankful for the distraction.

But she saw with fresh dismay, when Stephen seated her in a spindly gilt chair, and took his place behind her, that Torrance and Gerard had entered the saloon, too.

Doña's tension was high: Stephen had told her that serious breaches of riverboat decorum were dealt with harshly. Gamblers caught cheating had actually been thrown in the river; brawling was never tolerated. Offenders would be turned over to the authorities at the nearest port, sometimes were even stranded at the first landing place or on a sandbar in midriver.

And from the feel of Stephen's hand on her shoulder, Doña knew that his anger could reach the boiling point.

If Philippe Gerard was insolent—Stephen never traveled without a gun. She shivered.

Stephen leaned over to her and inquired, "What is it? Are you cold?"

She shook her head. "No, no. It's nothing." She was almost afraid to see his expression, recalling all too vividly how he had dealt with Lamb and Scurry that afternoon, how quickly Gerard had offended him at the play.

But when she heard his cool reply to Gerard's greeting, Doña relaxed.

Torrance bowed to her and she said "Good evening" in a neutral voice; she patiently received Gerard's hand-kissing and intense look, thinking how comical he was with his exaggerated manners.

Stephen and Torrance were speaking calmly to each other, Doña noticed with relief. Gerard drew up a gilt chair and sat down at her side.

"Each time we meet, you are more beautiful," he said in his accented way, as if English were not the language he was accustomed to. She imagined he spoke French a good deal among his own people in New Orleans.

Ignoring this, she parried. "Are you and Mr. Torrance going far?"

Gerard laughed and his dark eyes narrowed. "You are an excellent fencer, madame. I would like to see you with a rapier."

Doña was strongly tempted to say that she was better with a gun, but instead repeated, "Are you going far?" Stephen and Torrance were silent now, and she could feel their interest; they were standing behind her and she could not see their faces.

Gerard glanced up at Torrance, then answered, "We're going to St. Louis. Have you ever been there?"

Doña shook her head and heard Stephen say casually, "I thought you had business in New Orleans, Al. I'm surprised to see you here."

Doña turned in her chair then and looked up at Torrance. His hard face looked annoyed. "That's been—taken care of," he said gruffly.

Gerard said to Stephen, "I am looking forward to this

162

voyage. It will be most interesting to know my kinsman better, and of course, his so-beautiful wife." The dark eyes lingered again on Doña. She saw that Stephen could hardly contain his dislike of Gerard.

Torrance said, with a short, barking laugh, "And I'm looking forward to a return match with you, Raike. I'd like to make good my losses, if I can." The gambler's friendly-sounding words had an undercurrent of anger.

"Sorry, Al. I never play on the boats."

"Now why is that, Mr. Raike?" Gerard asked with mock-innocence.

"I think you know very well, Gerard." Stephen's tone was curt. Doña recalled what he had told her of the river-boat gamblers; the stakes were very high when they played, and they were rarely honest.

"Now what do you mean by that? I do not like your tone." Gerard's silky voice had become very cold. And Doña realized at once what was behind it all: the angry Torrance was using Gerard to bait Stephen, hoping a quarrel would result.

"I think you know what I mean." Stephen's answer was quiet, controlled. "Any friend of Al Torrance's would know. And while we're at it, Gerard, I don't like your attentions to my wife." Doña shivered.

"My attentions, Raike? No civilized man could object to my actions. But then you are not civilized, are you? My family knows that too well—that the Raikes are not civilized men."

Doña waited tensely for Stephen's reply. "If we were not on this boat, Gerard, you would see just how un-civilized a Raike can be." She had never heard him sound so hard, or so calm. "But I am not about to jeopardize my wife's safety, and leave her unprotected, which is ex-actly what would happen if we had a brawl. Because you wouldn't come out alive. And you'd like that, wouldn't you, Al?"

Doña felt her blood run cold. The whole exchange had been conducted with such quiet that no one else in the great saloon knew what was going on. All three men had terrible smiles on their faces.

"Stephen—" she began. He ignored her, staring first at the elegant Gerard, then at the coarse-faced Torrance.

"You're a cool customer, Raike," Torrance said at last, smiling the same unpleasant smile.

"I look forward very much to seeing you again, Gerard," Stephen said with meaning. "Is there any chance you will come to Chicago?"

"There is every chance." Gerard's answer was colder than before.

"I'll count on it, then. Doña, shall we take a turn around the deck?" She was amazed at the even tone of his voice, his smiling face and steady hand as he helped her from the chair.

Without further discussion, he led her to the carpeted stairs, as the band played a light-hearted tune.

When they had reached the deck, she looked up at Stephen and shivered.

"You're cold," he said, putting his arm around her. "You can't stay out here without a wrap."

"I'm frightened," she protested. "What will he do, Stephen? What will *you* do, in Chicago? Will there be a duel? You said that the French always do that."

Stephen laughed and said in a consoling way, "Nothing so high-flown as that. I'll likely knock him down, that's all. I have a feeling he's not too good with his hands."

"Why can't you both forget it?"

"Forget it?" he repeated, studying her with his cool, gray eyes. "That's a strange thing for you to say, Doña. You are not a person who forgets."

He knows, then! she thought. He knows that I still remember the wrongs of Daniel Raike.

And in the moonlight Doña saw the sadness in his look, a sadness that had nothing at all to do with the encounter with Gerard. Even the threat posed by Torrance and the Frenchman seemed less real to her now than the knowing look in her husband's eyes. He was able to touch her thoughts as he did her helpless body.

"Will there ever be any peace for us together?" she asked him suddenly.

164

Stephen winced, but he answered, calmly, "Peace is not what I'm after, my dear, or I would never have married you." He took her hand to ease some of the sting from the remark.

Doña stared at the dark waters of the passing river, thinking, I do not know my husband at all.

She found in the days and nights that followed that Stephen's mysterious character was making him more and more attractive to her.

He did not mention Gerard and Torrance again and, as the steamboat drew nearer to the port of St. Louis, Doña was mystified that both men were so seldom seen. She remarked on this once to Stephen, who replied, "They probably gamble all day."

Although she accepted the truth of this—she had seen, through a half-open door, a crowd of hatted, frockcoated men surrounding other men at a table, watching them intently—Doña still wondered what game Torrance and Gerard were playing besides the games with cards.

The passengers of the *Princess* had a great deal of time on their hands. Watching the scenery was the most common way to pass the time, and some did a great deal of reading; the *Princess* boasted a library. Many liked to watch the crew's operations at landings, and there was sometimes dancing and impromptu singing by members of the crew or the passengers.

At one such concert, on a mild afternoon, Doña and Stephen were sitting lazily on the main deck, listening to a north-bound Irishman sing an old ballad about an Irish highwayman.

Stephen grinned at the words and gave Doña a look; she was wearing one of the "bandit hats" he had chosen in New Orleans, the black one with a swooping brim. It gave her prim gray traveling dress the look of a riding habit, and in its slanted shadow her dark eyes shone with mischief as she met his stare.

He leaned to her and whispered, "Let's go in. I feel the need of a nap."

She rose and laughed at him softly. "Surely no other

165

people spend so much time in their cabin," she said in a low voice.

"Do you wonder?" he retorted, and his ironic eyes surveyed the overdressed women around them. "If I had to wade through all that horsehair and iron, I'd get mighty discouraged."

Doña was framing a retort when she head a passerby speaking of a "race." She felt Stephen's arm stiffen.

"What's the matter?"

"I hoped there wouldn't be anything like that, this trip," he said, and his voice sounded worried.

"Like what?"

"A race."

"But it sounds very exciting," she protested.

"It's exciting, all right. So exciting that the boat can blow up, and we could land in the river." He glanced down at her. "I wouldn't mind seeing one, if you weren't along."

She could see that his concern was very real. Now, passengers were gathering at the rail, talking excitedly. The ballad singer had stopped his song and had joined the others.

"Yes, I'm afraid there is going to be a race."

Stephen put his arm around Doña and moved with her toward the rail.

Another boat, the *Queen of the East,* was sailing alongside the *Princess.*

"Why do they do this, if it's so dangerous?" Doña asked.

"Fast boats attract business, and the winner proves how fast he is. This will be a short one, thank God. We're almost at St. Louis."

Doña could feel a stronger vibration below their feet. "What's that?"

"They're feeding more fuel, to increase our power."

The race began, and as the boats headed upriver, Doña realized that the deck was getting hot below her feet. She held to her wide-brimmed hat against the rising wind of the speeding boats. There was an ever-stronger vibration, a whirring and shaking below their feet that she could

166

feel in her very hands and face. The flesh of her cheeks actually quivered with the increasing strain of the racing boat. She looked up and saw fires flickering from the smokestacks.

Stephen followed the direction of her look; his face was taut and pale, but he smiled at her. "It'll be all right," he said. "It's not too bad yet."

But soon the shaking of the whole vessel was jarring Doña; she opened her mouth to cry out over the incredible noise, but her teeth met suddenly, biting her tongue. She grasped Stephen's arm tightly as the boats labored up the river.

A woman screamed, and men were shouting.

"There it is, thank God!" Stephen said to Doña loudly, to make himself heard over the voices of the others. "St. Louis! I don't think she'd have made it much farther."

He was sweating, despite the rushing wind and the coolness of the air.

With one last burst of speed, shaking the passengers like helpless dolls, the *Princess* pulled into the port of St. Louis, a little ahead of the *Queen of the East*. The thick smoke from the stacks of many boats swept over the deck of the *Princess,* still hot under Doña's feet.

She coughed and felt the damp perspiration on her brow.

"All right?" Stephen asked, bending to her with concern.

She nodded, unable to speak for her relief.

"Let's get inside," he said, and led her toward their stateroom.

When she glanced down at the levee, Doña saw Philippe Gerard and Alfred Torrance stepping off the ramp onto the landing. Gerard raised his gray slouch hat to Doña. She was thankful Stephen had not seen. There had been enough excitement for one day.

Chapter Fourteen

Doña felt very much at home in the big, bustling town of Chicago. As Stephen said, it was still considered a frontier town by the older cities of the East, but he believed, like so many others, that someday it would be a great city.

More than half the country, Stephen had told her, lay to the west, and was still undeveloped. The timber for Western houses would have to pass through Chicago; manufactured goods from the East were channeled through the young port at the end of the lake waterway. And for years now the goods of the West, too, had been passing through Chicago.

At first Chicago had been a camping ground for gold-prospectors headed to the West, and business in covered wagons and guns still boomed.

With the growth of the city, the need for transportation had grown; and by now Stephen Raike's city stages had even outdone those of the famous Franklin Parmalee, who first introduced horse-drawn omnibuses on Wabash Avenue.

Proudly, Stephen hailed a Raike Stage as he and Doña stepped off their train. He pointed to its scarlet-painted door and a large initial "R" that imitated the Raike brand of Texas.

When the driver had stowed their luggage and was closing the door, he took a closer look at his passengers, and exclaimed, "Why, Mr. Raike!" He grinned with pleased surprise. "Heard you been away. Welcome home!"

"Thank you, Palmer."

The driver grinned even more broadly, and said, "Don't know how you remember us all." His gratification was plain.

"Like you to meet Mrs. Raike," said Stephen. Touching his hat, the driver said, "Pleased, ma'am. Sure hope you'll like our town."

"I'm sure I will," Doña replied, smiling at the dazzled Palmer.

As she looked out of the rather grimy windows of the coach—Chicago was a very grimy town—Doña realized that her comment had been more than polite. She did like Chicago, its streets crowded with motley and colorful traffic. Carriages drawn by handsome horses passed side by side with creaking wagons drawn by stolid oxen. Why, it was almost like Texas!

She saw a number of riders on horseback, frontier men with pistols in their holsters; here and there men had knives stuck in their belts. There were farmers in produce wagons, hunters with game bags over their shoulders.

Stephen opened his door a few inches and called, "Drive us up by the new courthouse, would you, Will?" He closed the door and smiled at Doña. "There's a nice view from there."

Doña saw a number of the red Raike coaches on the rutted streets. The ride was a bit rough; the streets were almost solid mud, yet the buildings that lined the streets were fairly tall, and there was a profusion of stores. She found it all very exciting.

"Oh, look!" she said to Stephen, and pointed to a passing coach. Painted on its panel was the picture of a young girl whose luxuriant hair covered half the side of the bus.

Stephen laughed. "That's one of old Parmalee's family coaches," he explained. "That's the picture of one of his daughters. When they're all drawn up together, you'll see Mr. Parmalee and all the little Parmalees. Shall I have 'em paint your picture on the Raike buses?"

Doña looked at him in consternation, until she saw that he was teasing her. His gray eyes were twinkling. He seemed different; the brisk, cold air and the bustle of Chicago was acting on him like a tonic.

Looking down on the city from the courthouse tower, Doña could see patches of browning green among the buildings. Churches and houses were set in the middle of wide lawns or under cottonwood, elm, ash and linden trees, which were now losing their leaves.

"See, over there," Stephen pointed. "We're right in the middle of a prairie."

The emptiness of the great expanse made a startling contrast to the hurly-burly of the town. "I like it," Doña said, and Stephen looked pleased. "I haven't seen many towns as big as this, you know."

"There's a lot more, and you'll see it all. But now maybe we'd better get to the hotel. You must be tired, and it's getting pretty cold."

It *was* cold, very cold, she thought. That was the only thing about Chicago that bothered her. But then, when she had heavier clothes—Stephen had been right about that.

In the carriage once again, Stephen consulted his pocket watch. "Good. It's about time for the dressmakers to come calling."

"Dressmakers calling?" she repeated, mystified.

"Oh, yes, it's a tradition here. When a new bride sets up house, or comes to town, the dressmakers are on her like a duck on a junebug, drumming up trade!" He grinned. "Very handy for us. We've got to get you some warmer things. I can go to the office while you're picking them out. No need for cash—they know me well enough."

Doña could not resist the feeling of childlike excitement that rose with his casual words. How freehanded he was with money, and how wonderful to think she could choose whatever she wanted. It was like Christmas every day. Nevertheless, she said a little hesitantly, "But you must tell me, you must give me some idea of how much I can spend. I just don't know. I've never—"

"I know you've never," he said in a soft, teasing voice, and took her hand, raising it to his lips. Then he named a sum that took her breath away. "Remember," he said, "most of that will go for some kind of fur thing. All the women have them in the winter here—well, the women with—" he stopped, and finished a little awkwardly: "rich husbands."

She had noticed before that he was shy of his own position sometimes, and attributed it to the proud blood of Louise Gerard.

"You see," he said then, rather suddenly, "It's all—nothing, any of this stuff, when you consider how I feel about you."

She looked into his gray eyes, seeing for the hundredth time that waiting look. What was it? she wondered, that he was waiting for?

She said quietly, "Whatever you say. I still think you are very good to me."

He looked strangely disappointed at her reply, but quickly, to hide what he was thinking, he said, "We're right here, just across the way from the courthouse."

As Palmer handed their luggage down to an attendant, Doña looked up at the facade of the six-story building.

"It's huge!" she said.

"The Sherman House," Stephen explained. "I had a smaller place here, but they've moved us into a larger suite of rooms." He followed Doña into the hotel and spoke to the man at the desk.

"Right away, Mr. Raike," the man said in a respectful manner, then looked admiringly at Doña. "My wife, Mr. Random," Stephen said, and Doña smiled at the man's courteous, eager greeting.

Mr. Random snapped his well-tended fingers and a porter came to take the luggage.

A young clerk bearing the key led Stephen and Doña to a door like a cage; through the grillework Doña could see heavy ropes made of metal. "What's this?" she asked Stephen.

"It's one of the new vertical railways. It carries us right up; no walking. But no luggage is allowed."

"That poor man will have to climb all the stairs?"

"I'm afraid so," Stephen said. The clerk, glancing admiringly at Doña for her expression of concern for the porter, banged on the cage with the key.

"Sometimes this gadget's so slow you have to fire a gun up the shaft," Stephen remarked. Sure that he was joking, Doña broke into laughter. "Oh, no, ma'am," the clerk said. "It's true!"

And as the strange open cage bore them to the third floor, Doña reflected how very much at home she was going to be in the wild, half-civilized city of Chicago.

Stephen had barely left for his office, and the hotel maid was still in the midst of unpacking, when a soft, firm knock summoned Doña to the door of their suite of rooms.

A big, deep-bosomed woman with suspiciously golden hair stood on the threshold; behind her were two young people. One was a pop-eyed young man laden with furs, the other a thin young woman carrying two great paper boxes.

"Miz Raike?" said the golden-haired woman in that harsh but friendly accent Doña was already beginning to associate with the town.

"Yes?"

"I'm Miz Dolly Bright, the dressmaker. Mr. Raike said you might be needing us."

Doña invited the trio in.

"Well, now," said Mrs. Dolly Bright, immediately at home, "we've brought along a few things for you to see. Of course, you know they're only suggestions."

Doña, feeling like royalty, hardly knew how to answer. She merely smiled, and watched Mrs. Bright's answering smile, which revealed a pristine row of porcelain teeth.

"Please," said Doña, "won't you sit down?"

"No time to sit down!" Mrs. Bright protested, with a whinnying laugh. "Got to get you outfitted. Mr. Raike— well, everybody in town knows Mr. Raike, and thinks the world of him! Mr. Ransom says, Mr. Raike told him don't spare the expense. Now I've brought along a *Godey's Lady's Book,* too, 'cause that's where we get our best things from."

172

Apparently Mrs. Bright was typical of the hurrying city, as unlike Madame Gautier as the town was to New Orleans, Doña thought, amused.

"Fine," she said briskly, taking a leaf from Mrs. Bright's book. "Perhaps first I'll look at the furs."

The next hour was a busy and pleasant one. Doña chose a long, luxurious fur cape that nearly reached the floor, glorying in its warmth and loveliness. She found that Mrs. Bright made many sensible suggestions, and the dressmaker agreed, when she was shown the New Orleans purchases, that not too many additional things would be needed.

Doña judged wryly that the price of the fur alone had satisfied Mrs. Bright's greed for sales.

Doña was unable to resist a beautiful cashmere shawl, a wonderful fur hat that matched the cape, and several pairs of half-length kid evening gloves, with backs embroidered in delicate silks, with a jewel sparkling now and then among the colors. She also chose several dresses of wool, and two more evening dresses, with the new paneled skirts which Mrs. Bright said would be "coming in" in January, one of plain silk and the other of embossed brocade.

At one point, when Mrs. Bright exclaimed, "But you haven't picked out your drawers!" Doña blushed furiously and glanced at the pop-eyed young man. "Oh, don't mind Herbert," she said, with her neighing laugh. "He's used to all this. I mean the street drawers. Here, Jenny, hand 'em here."

And Mrs. Bright displayed to Doña some loose trousers of opera flannel in pearl gray and ash color, embroidered in scarlet, blue or magenta, and buff and brown pairs with decorations in orange or bright green.

"It's freezing here in winter," Mrs. Bright declared. "The ladies wear these Turkish drawers under their dresses. You can't imagine how cozy they are till you put 'em on."

Doña took a pair of the trousers in each color.

"*Now,* then!" Mrs. Bright cried in her high voice, when the selection was completed. "I think that'll hold you for now, Miz Raike. Maybe later on you'll want some little suits. Those little suits are a mighty good idea in the cold weather."

Doña laughed and said lightly, "If I buy everything you suggest, my husband will be a pauper."

The three burst into loud laughter, even the sad-looking thin-faced Jenny.

"You like to joke, Miz Raike. I like a lady that can joke a little. It's a short life, I always say, so it's nice to have a little fun."

When they were gone, Doña thought about their reaction. Was Stephen so rich, then?

She wandered to the bedroom and contemplated the long, extravagant fur cape spread out in dark richness on the bed. She stroked it with her hand; it was soft as down.

"Furs and jewels and gold and gowns," she said idly, aloud. And she recalled what Tahre's mother had said, that it would be sweet revenge to take the old bear's only cub; her own triumphant thought, on the night she had accepted Stephen—that she would wear the name and property of Raike like a scalp of gold.

Why did she feel there was something missing? Maybe you'd rather be sleeping on buffalo hide, she ridiculed herself. And putting the foolish thought aside, she awaited Stephen's return.

There were numerous pleasures and distractions in the days that followed, yet Doña's strange feeling of rest-lessness persisted. She was haunted by a sense of some-thing lost—that driving urge that had sent her riding at the head of the robber band, an envy of Stephen's busy days, of the intensity with which he pursued his business.

Her yearnings could be shared with no one; certainly none of the women she had met—the wives of Stephen's acquaintances—could understand so unwomanly a desire as hers. They were dedicated, as proper ladies should be, to the care of their husbands and children and homes.

Doña had amusement enough, in the evenings: within the first week Stephen had taken her to two public balls, and to call on several families he knew who lived on the wealthy North Side in large frame houses set in spacious yards and lawns.

The theatrical season in Chicago was an unorthodox one—it began in spring and extended through the summer, with no performances in winter or fall.

But Doña's days were empty and long: her rare visits to the wives of Stephen's friends were stifling.

One evening in November, when a driving sleet discouraged their evening outing, Doña sat absently turning the pages of a novel in the parlor of their suite, while Stephen read his paper. She glanced at his face, intent on the news, his handsome gray eyes squinted against the wreath of smoke curling upward from his cigar.

She sighed, wishing she could find the news as fascinating as Stephen did. He looked up and smiled. "It's a bad night," he commented. She nodded, hearing the whispering impact of the sleet against the window, and returned to her book.

A moment later, she heard him exclaim, "Well, well! And what do you know about *that?*"

"What is it?"

"Do you remember my telling you about William Walker in New Orleans?"

"Yes."

"Well, it seems the federal marshals arrested him on the tenth. They've charged him with outfitting a steamship with arms and men to go back to Nicaragua. And it seems some of the arms were shipped from St. Louis." He had a speculative look.

Doña let her novel fall on her knees. "And Torrance had some business in St. Louis, didn't he? Do you think he and Gerard were in it?"

"I wouldn't be surprised at all. Torrance only got back yesterday. It's very, very interesting. Whenever there's something shady going on, that bastard's in it." Stephen laughed. "He's going to be mad as hell when he finds out I've bought up that parcel of land at Wells and Monroe. I think he wanted to put another free and easy there."

"Free and easy," Doña had learned, was Chicago's

175

name for a brothel. Stephen had pointed out, during a drive, a series of buildings with bright blue window shades. On all the shades, there was painted a large gilt question, "Why not?" This had been the subject of many indignant whispers among the ladies in the homes they had visited.

"Tell me about it," Doña urged Stephen, brightening. She spoke with such eagerness that he put down his paper and studied her.

"It's a dull subject," he said carelessly. "Much too dull for you to bother with." His eyes were warm, as he stared at her smooth hair, vivid in the lamplight, her dark eyes bright and sparkling in her tawny face. She was wearing a simple gown of wool almost the color of her hair.

He got up and went to her. Kneeling beside her chair, he touched the stuff of her gown along her slender thigh. "I want to warm myself on you," he said softly. "You look like fire."

He bent his head and kissed her knee. Through the thin wool and cambric, his breath felt hot upon her, and something deep in her stirred to resistance.

She did not respond, but he did not seem to notice. Suddenly his touch was rough and demanding, and there was no trace of the tenderness she had come to know. She felt that a stranger was touching her.

Her book fell with a thud to the carpet as his strong hands, grasping hers, drew her to her feet. He took her into his arms with a bruising motion, kissing her hair and cheeks and brow and lips with quick, rough kisses.

Doña felt the harshness of his thick mustache chafe her tender upper lip, and she struggled in his grasp. She made a moaning sound of protest but he paid no heed, only drawing her closer and closer to his hard, seeking body.

His hands, with swift and urgent skill, were unfastening the back of her gown. The garment fell soundlessly from her, forming a fiery pool on the dark carpet below their feet.

And all at once, the moment of resistance was gone. Trembling, she felt his touch upon her head; he was drawing the pins from her high-piled hair. Its silken weight struck her back and shoulders softly; then he unfastened her chemise, tugging at her petticoats until all of her garments had fallen away and she stood naked in the lamplight.

Her bright hair veiled her breasts, some of its vivid strands extending far below her thighs. Stephen, with a quick, excited breath, stroked her hair.

Uttering a hoarse, savage murmur, he kissed the trembling flesh veiled in the long, bright-colored hair.

Responding with an excitement akin to his, she felt her whole self go limp as he rose and lifted her into his arms, striding into the shadows of the neighboring room.

Doña lay against his hard, broad chest, listening to the slowing rhythm of his breath. A kind of sanity was coming back to her, and her thoughts were cool and clear.

It is always like this, a sharp little voice reminded her in silence. He makes a puppet of me with his body. But I will not be conquered, ever!

He must have felt her body stiffen, for his questioning hand was upon her, exploring, stroking, as if he could discover with his fingers what was in her mind.

"Doña?" he said. She was silent. He repeated her name and, raising himself gently, slid her tousled head onto the pillow. Leaning on one elbow, he stared down at her face in the dimness.

"What are you thinking?" he asked, a question, she reflected, that he had never asked before.

"I'm thinking," she said brusquely, "that if I don't have something—to do—to occupy myself—I cannot stay with you any longer."

He was transfixed; his face became stiff, as if it had received an actual blow.

He let out a long breath, then, propping a pillow against the headboard, lay back, staring straight ahead.

"That's the first honest thing you've said to me since—Texas," he remarked after a time. "Thank you for that."

She could not tell whether he was offended, for his calm face showed nothing.

"What is it you want to do?" he asked quietly. "I thought in the spring, when we started to build a house, that—"

"A house!" she said scornfully. "The only house I—"

"The only house you want," he finished for her, "is your father's house. Isn't.that right?" Now she could hear the raw anger and pain.

"No," she lied. "No, Stephen. I was only going to say that a house isn't—a house isn't what I'm talking about."

"I see." He turned to her and studied her face. "What *are* you talking about, then?"

"I'd like to help you in your business."

"What? Why, women don't—I can't imagine you—" She had never heard him at a loss for words before, and could not help laughing.

"What about the things I've done before?" she demanded. "How many women have done what I've done?"

After an instant of silence, he began to laugh, too.

"I guess I can't picture you pouring tea. But what do you want, Doña?" His deep voice was unreadable. She waited. "What do you want, to be my partner?"

"I just want something to do," she answered quietly.

"It doesn't make any difference to me," he said lightly, yet she could hear the lie in his words. "I don't give a damn what people say, but it may be difficult for you."

"What do you mean?"

"When the women start on you, and even the men, you won't like it." He leaned to the bed table and took up a match and cigar. By the match's flare, she saw a look of amusement on his face.

"Start on me?" she repeated.

"Doña, you're such a child." He put his arm around her, drawing her head to his chest. "Have you ever heard of a lady in business? Except for, well, dressmaking, or teaching music, or something like that? Don't you know these women? Can't you hear them when we go to visit?" He chuckled.

178

"I don't care!" she cried passionately. "I can't live like those women. I can't live without—"

"Raising hell, robbing trains and stages?" he finished drily. He laughed again. "Even I won't help you do that."

"You're making fun of me," she said angrily.

He put down his cigar and gathered her into his arms. "No, darling, I'm not. But you see, you'd be breaking all the rules, and you'd have to take the consequences. That's what I'm saying. I've been breaking the rules for years, and I know what I'm talking about."

She was silent, listening to the rumble of his slow, deep voice against her cheek. "I don't care," she repeated stubbornly. "I want something to—do."

He gave her a squeeze. "I'll think about it."

She raised herself in his arms and kissed him.

"You're a real *milo*," he said. "I'm always wondering what you'll think of next."

But under his teasing words, she heard something else, a note of rough desire, and a strange yearning.

She kissed him again, feeling his arms tighten about her and his breath quicken. There was an urgent tension rising in him. He held her to him tightly, kissing her with such savagery it took her breath away.

And in the swift, hot meeting of their bodies, she thought, What a fool I've been! Why, she had a hundred times more power over him than he had over her!

In the embrace, she pretended submission, but felt, for the first time, triumphant.

Chapter Fifteen

One morning, with an almost indulgent air, Stephen asked Doña if she would like to have a tour of some of his properties. She accepted eagerly, but he was surprised when she expressed more interest in his real-estate business than in Raike Stages. He had expected that her riding skill, her easiness with horses, and the colorful aspects of the stagecoach business would hold greater appeal for her than would his real-estate ventures.

But after he had shown her around the large sheds that housed the horses and city coaches, she said eagerly, "I'd like to see the land office."

Doña had heard the men talking at dinners at the Hamiltons' and the McCormicks' about land speculation, an activity that one ironic speaker compared to highway robbery.

"But you don't get arrested," he had added drily.

This scrap of talk had excited Doña beyond measure. When Stephen told her that he had bought a tract of land six years ago for ten thousand dollars and sold it recently for three million, she resolved to learn all she could about the acquisition of Chicago land.

If she could only get her hands on money like that— and Doña thought again of the night in New Orleans, when she had decided to run away.

In their conversations on the subject of land, Stephen was at first condescending and patient, then amazed to discover Doña's quick perception, her natural aptitude for business. It was a side of her that was totally unexpected.

The Raike land office was in a five-story building phen owned on Lake Street; for the time being, until land business grew, he was renting out the two upper floors to Keen and Lee, booksellers and publishers.

The male employees of Raike Lands, introduced to Doña, treated her with respectful admiration, half-expecting to hear some foolish, feminine questions. But when they saw her examine the maps on the wall in a sharp-eyed manner, and remark on a deed that Stephen picked up to study—they had hardly expected a woman to know what a deed was—they felt a strange uneasiness and resentment. What did this visit mean? It couldn't possibly be that she was interested in the business. Not a woman so young and beautiful!

Stephen looked on with a mixture of irritation and pride, impressed by the shrewdness of Doña's questions, as well as her ability to size up a situation without any questions at all.

"This is the property that Torrance was bidding for, isn't it?" she asked Stephen softly. She was standing near him at his desk, and her question could not be heard by the others.

He nodded, pleased that she had retained so much of their earlier conversation. "Yes. There's more here than meets the eye. It could be the beginning of something big, bigger than profits. See here," he pointed, "here this parcel borders Conley's Patch."

"Conley's Patch!" Doña stared at him. "But they say that's the worst, most tumbledown section of Chicago!"

"That's the point. If Torrance gets this land, he'll put up more free and easies—the lowest kind. They'll be the breeding grounds for more crime and disease. Long John Wentworth is hell-bent on tearing Conley's Patch down. If I take over this land, I'm going to talk old John and his friends into investing in some decent places for people to live. If they want to get rid of vice, let 'em put their money in." Stephen grinned. "You see, I've got a lot riding on this."

Doña nodded, looking at the map with new eyes.

They left the office and when they reached the street,

Stephen said, "So you see, it's not a very pleasant place to be cooped up in all day." Doña did not reply, so he added, "And there's another thing. If you were to do what I do, you'd have to drive around showing land to prospective customers. You can see how unsuitable that would be. And you couldn't drive in this mud."

Doña chafed to hear this, but she had to admit that the ever-present mud of Chicago's streets made it very difficult for her to drive alone; the wheels and horses' hooves moved so laboriously through the gluelike streets that once when she had tried driving, her arms and back had ached for hours.

The mud, as a matter of fact, was a common topic of conversation in Chicago. When ladies went visiting, they often had to gather up their fine skirts and huddle in the rear of a sturdy wagon whose wheels would not break in the mud. The streets were badly paved; sidewalks, raised high above street level, were made of rough wooden planks, the nails in the planks forever catching in women's skirts.

Doña blessed her narrower skirts, which escaped the nails. Stephen ridiculed crinolines, so she rarely wore them, except in the evenings. And the marvelous Turkish trousers she'd bought from Mrs. Bright protected her dress hems from the splattering muck, and were conveniently slipped off when she came indoors.

Various plans had been drawn up to conquer the mud, but none of them succeeded. So, it was decided to build an entirely new surface. Some of the streets were raised as much as ten feet. The process left Chicago with such uneven sidewalks that sometimes pedestrians had to walk from one level to another several times in only one block.

Stephen had once handed Doña a small visitor's guide from the lobby of the Sherman House, entitled "Tricks and Traps of Chicago." The booklet warned feminine tourists of "sidewalk oglers" who hung around the sidewalk stairs in hopes of seeing a lady's limb.

"As a matter of fact," Stephen had said, "Chicago women have wonderful legs. It's from climbing all those stairs." Doña had noticed early on an ache in her own calves; then the aching went away as she grew used to the climbing and her own long legs were shapelier than ever from the exercise, a fact that Stephen had commented on fervently.

Wearing the Turkish trousers, Doña climbed the stairs without trepidation.

It is a day for trousers today, Doña reflected one raw and chilly morning in December, seeing a mist of wet snow from their bedroom window in the hotel.

"I'm not taking you with me today," Stephen said, tying his cravat before the mirror.

"Why not?" she asked. "The weather's not that bad." Doña had adjusted more quickly than she had expected to the blustery climate of Chicago.

"It's not the weather." Stephen turned from the mirror, smiling down at her. "And you'll never believe it if I tell you. You'll have to see it. Tell you what, I'll pick you up before lunch, and show you."

Her curiosity was aroused, but he would say no more.

A little after noon, they drove to the block on Lake Street that housed the Raike Lands building. A large crowd had gathered along the block, despite the cold, staring at the line of buildings with their familiar signs— "Keen and Lee," "Raike Lands," "Printing," "Apothecary," "Clothiers."

A small army of men was doing something to the foundations of the buildings.

Stephen pulled at the reins and brought their buggy to a pause. "Now watch," he said, in a tone of amused excitement.

Suddenly there was a signal from a man who seemed to be in charge of the army of other men, and the buildings slowly rose, ever so slightly.

"What on earth?" Doña cried.

Stephen laughed at her expression. "They're raising the block," he explained. "A Yankee fellow, a cabinet-maker by the name of George Pullman, got the idea when they were widening the Erie Canal and some buildings had to be moved. See those things?" He pointed to a line

183

of metal gadgets under the buildings that the men were maneuvering. Doña nodded.

"Jackscrews," Stephen said. "Six thousand of them!" As the block rose slowly into the air, other workers shored it up with timbers. "The block'll be raised four feet," Stephen explained, "and when the new foundations are ready, the buildings will be lowered again. It'll be done so gradually it won't even interrupt business. All the same, I didn't want you in the building for a few days."

"But why are they raising the buildings?"

"Well, when the streets are built up, the buildings look as if they're sinking. That's why they put the new third story and tower on the courthouse, but most people can't afford that expense, so Pullman figured it would be cheaper to raise the buildings."

"You were right," Doña admitted, smiling. "I wouldn't have believed you if you'd told me. I thought you were just trying to keep me at the hotel."

As they drove on, Stephen was silent a moment. Then he said, "Business is not a game, Doña. It's a rough and tumble world, and no place for a woman."

She did not respond and he saw her assume that stubborn expression he was beginning to know well.

"Come on, Doña," he said easily. "Haven't you gotten over that idea? Spring will be here soon and there'll be a lot to amuse you. And what if—what if we have a child?"

Doña turned and stared at him. A child! What would happen if they had a child? She would be trapped.

She, who had been so careful to use the precautions she had learned almost accidently one day at a chemist's in New Orleans. A painted and overdressed woman had described to the chemist what she wanted, and when she was given the French contraption she'd requested, Doña boldly stepped forward and asked for one too. Using it, she hoped to remain independent. She still remembered vividly the play about the shrew named Kate, and she was determined never to become a household Doña.

She was so still that Stephen glanced at her thoughtfully. Her expression made him feel very uneasy.

Mrs. Burton Hamilton, lately of Kentucky, confided to Mrs. Leander McCormick that she hoped they could build a Southern society in Chicago. Mrs. Hamilton did not like the New England Yankees much, and she also thought that they ought to "let the Germans, Irish and French all alone."

When Mrs. Hamilton protested to her husband that the wife of Stephen Raike "didn't fit in," Mr. Burton Hamilton retorted that Stephen Raike's mother had been a Gerard of New Orleans, after all; he reminded his wife that when a young man was accepted in the business community in Chicago, it was the same as being accepted socially.

And so, this holiday, the Hamiltons' Christmas social included Stephen and Doña Raike, over Mrs. Hamilton's protests, and the up-and-coming Washington Brink of Vermont, whose business was delivering parcels of any value, as well as another new arrival from Massachusetts, Marshall Field. Field had bought out another Yankee, Potter Palmer, who had made his fortune in a dry-goods store before he was forty years of age.

Burton Hamilton liked Field and Brink; he put his elegantly shod foot down this Christmas, so that these two Yankees, and others who were their friends, had received invitations to the social, written in the hostess' own hand and delivered personally. .

Sending invitations by mail was a risky business in Chicago, because they were often lost. Usually, the hostess would drive to the houses of those she wished to invite and send in the invitations with her coachman while she waited in the carriage.

The Fields and Brinks had accepted—the men of the families were heartened by the prospect of madeira or eggnog which members of the Southern colony, living in the West Division, generally kept on their sideboards. In other neighborhoods the serving of wine was considered risqué.

The Hamiltons' red-wallpapered parlor, that cold December evening, was an inviting place, with a fire blazing in its white marble fireplace. A glittering crystal-laden chandelier hung from the white molded ceiling, lighting the women's silken gowns, reflecting itself in the gold-leafed mirror over the mantel. The windows' rich hangings—lace undercurtains, swagged gold brocade overcurtains—closed the guests cozily in, and illustrated Mrs. Hamilton's love for fussy furnishings. Here and there gaslight spheres, held by bronze figurines, added their white light to the brightness of the candles and chandelier.

Two of the men stood a little apart; one gestured slightly at the beautiful young woman sitting on a rose-wood settee.

Washington Brink savored his madeira and remarked to Field, "The women are in a flap about the Raike girl."

"She's something to look at, I'll admit," Field responded, "but what's this about her always talking business with the men? Never heard of anything like that." He studied Doña, who was seated with Stephen on the other side of the immense parlor. "A beautiful woman," Field repeated.

Doña's bright, heavy hair was arranged on the top of her head in thick braids, surmounted by a comb of gold and turquoise that matched her vivid gown with its paneled skirts.

"Looks like she's got a fortune on her back," Field commented.

"He's got it to spare," Brink returned. "No fear, young Raike has plenty of money invested in land."

The women of Chicago were cautious in adopting luxurious styles; their husbands' business reputations could be damaged if people thought their money was being spent for display rather than real estate.

"Yep, he's sound as a dollar, Raike is," Brink said. "And just as well for you, Marshall! What would happen to *your* business if people didn't spend?"

Field snorted. "Well, good God, he could have married a white!"

"What do you mean?"

"There's more than a drop of redskin in that one, Washington."

Brink sipped his wine. "You're kind of high and mighty, Marsh. Twenty-five years ago nearly every customer in Chicago stores was an Indian."

"You've got a point there. Well, anyway, merry Christmas."

And the dry-goods prince raised his glass to Brink.

Across the room, Stephen touched Doña's shoulder to say "Excuse me a moment" and stepped away for a word with Leander McCormick. Doña looked about the festive room, filled with chattering people, the men in dark evening dress, the women in rustling silks or somber satins.

A small four-piece orchestra had begun to play in the adjoining room. Doña looked in through the open, glass-paneled doors, watching as some of the guests formed themselves into the intricate patterns of a dance. She had danced with Stephen in New Orleans—a waltz and reel, a polka—but now they were doing a dance she did not know.

Mrs. Hamilton, addressing a group of men around the eggnog bowl at the sideboard, in her coy Southern manner, said, "All right, now, you naughty men! We're forming for the German cotillion! You've been at the punchbowl long enough!" And she made a shooing motion toward the adjoining room.

Stephen and McCormick shook their heads at her, smiling, and resumed their conversation. Doña murmured, "I do not know the dance, Mrs. Hamilton," and was rewarded with a surprised look from the hostess.

As she watched the dancers, Doña suddenly remembered the dances of the Indians, and she was assailed by a great wave of nostalgia, so overwhelming she feared she would be ill.

She could see again in her mind's eye the dances of the Festival of Love, the warriors dressed in their martial feathers, their heads covered with white down. They carried feathers of the same color in their hands or fastened to white scraped canes as scepters of power.

They danced in three circles, with wild and quick

187

sliding steps to keep time with the clay-pot drums covered with thin deerskins, beaten with a stick, singing *Meshi yo, meshi yo, meshi he, Meshi wah.*

Doña could almost hear their voices, keeping time with the clay-pot drums and the rattling calabashes; the music of the cotillion faded away. The warriors dancing, and the women, in their ceremonial robes made of the skin of deer and buffalo . . . Patche and Tahre, Easooba!

How did they fare? Patche! Doña cried silently, remembering the small, kind eyes of Tahre's mother.

"Mrs. Raike?"

Doña started and looked up. A short, plump woman in a gray velvet gown, her gray hair arranged in puffs and swirls, was smiling down at Doña. Except for her fair, smooth face the woman seemed all gray, for her shrewd, good-natured eyes were that color as well.

"I am Miranda Blair. I've been watching you, and you seemed very far away."

"Won't—won't you sit down, Mrs. Blair?" Doña said hesitantly, confused at this abrupt awakening from her daydream.

"With pleasure," said Mrs. Blair. Doña tried to place her speech; it was the accent she had come to know as "Yankee," as they called New Englanders in Chicago. "I see you do not dance the cotillion, either," Mrs. Blair added in a friendly way.

"No. I—I do not know it."

Mrs. Blair studied Doña with her keen eyes. "Forgive me, my dear, but I am a plainspoken woman, not like Mrs. Hamilton and the other ladies here." She smiled mischievously, and looked for a moment far younger than her years. "You are a beautiful and elegant young woman, but you seem like a fish out of water."

"I am," Doña replied with sudden frankness, thinking how delightful it was to say exactly what was in her mind.

"You're from Texas, they tell me."

"Yes." Again, the feeling of sharp homesickness struck Doña.

"My husband and I were there, in September."

188

September! The time of the Short Line raid, the month she'd met Stephen. Doña looked into the other woman's gray eyes, and the unreality of the present scene came to her once more.

"As a matter of fact," Mrs. Blair was saying, "I was scared to death."

"I—I beg your pardon?"

"I was terrified, my dear. Can you imagine? They actually robbed the train we were on! But after it was over —well, it's really the most exciting thing that ever happened to us."

Doña managed to murmur a reply. What on earth was the woman talking about?

"But you don't want to hear my stories," Mrs. Blair said, smiling. "Are you enjoying yourself in Chicago?"

"Oh, oh, yes," Doña said.

"I imagine you must have been quite a rider, in Texas. Most folks there are, they tell me. You must go to the races here in the spring. Have you been to the trotting races?"

"No. I *would* like to go," Doña said, warming to the little woman.

"You know, you look so *familiar* to me," Mrs. Blair commented, leaning toward Doña. "Did we meet in Texas? But surely not, for I'd remember. I'll tell you frankly, Mrs. Raike," she rushed on in a confidential way, "I wanted to get to know you. You're such an interesting-looking young lady! You're interested in your husband's business, I hear."

"Yes." Doña hoped fervently that the information would not put off Mrs. Blair, for she found herself liking the woman very much.

"Well, I congratulate you."

"Do you mean that?" Doña asked in amazement. "The —the other women are upset by it, I think."

"Nonsense! There are probably a dozen women here who were very different, years ago, when their husbands were starting out. Why, do you know, I kept my husband's books for him, when we were young? Now he's the biggest shipbuilder in Massachusetts!"

"You did?" Doña studied the well-dressed little woman, noting the excellent cut of her gown, the beautiful smoky topazes that glittered in her ears and on her neck.

"I certainly did, and I loved it. I had the time of my life! Of course, we never had any children. But I've kept myself busy, always, and I can see you're the kind of woman who likes to do the same."

"Yes, I am," Doña admitted, smiling. If she only knew my former occupation! she thought, and the thought made her smile even more widely.

Doña saw Stephen approaching. When he caught sight of the gray-gowned woman, his expression froze. In an instant, however, he wore his usual calm, unreadable look. After a quick glance at Doña, he smiled at Mrs. Blair and bowed to her.

"You know my husband, then, Mrs. Blair?"

The other woman looked up at Stephen and her round face mirrored her astonishment. "Why it's *you!*" she cried. "You're the young man on the train!"

"The train?" he repeated.

"The Short Line," she said. "The one that was robbed. My husband and I were in the next car. Don't you remember?"

Doña knew at once the import of the woman's earlier tale. Good God, she'd been on the Short Line that evening, Doña thought uneasily.

Stephen answered in a steady, friendly way. "Why, of course. So you were. Well, this is a coincidence, isn't it?" He took Mrs. Blair's hand, glancing at Doña.

"Stephen," Doña managed to keep her voice light.

"Yes, my dear?" He turned to her attentively.

"Could you get me a cup of toddy? I'm feeling a little cold."

"Of course. Mrs. Blair?" He turned to the older woman.

"No, thank you." She smiled up at him. Stephen went off on his errand.

"Do you think you've caught a chill?" Mrs. Blair asked Doña. "I've got my Turkish drawers on, right under my evening gown," she added, grinning. "I just cut the hems off."

"What a clever idea," Doña said, with forced enthusiasm. She was wondering if the Blairs could have seen her that evening. Surely not! It had been much too dark. Doña relaxed a little, and turned to listen to Mrs. Blair's comments on current fashions.

When Stephen returned with her toddy, the three chatted pleasantly for a time.

Then Doña, who imagined that Mrs. Blair was staring at her intensely, said to Stephen, "Please forgive me, but I'm not feeling much warmer."

He picked up his cue at once, saying, "I think we should be going now. I do have an early morning tomorrow."

"What a shame!" Mrs. Blair cried. "I've just begun to enjoy the party. May I call on you, my dear?"

Doña rose. "I'd love for you to. We're staying at the Sherman House."

"The Sherman House," Mrs. Blair repeated, smiling at them. Stephen left to get Doña's fur. When he returned, he said, "I've made our apologies to Mrs. Hamilton. It was delightful to meet you, Mrs. Blair." Stephen put Doña's cloak around her bare shoulders and they made their way to the entrance.

When the front door closed behind them, Doña asked Stephen softly, "Do you think she could have known me?"

"I don't think they could see you from their car."

Doña said, "Can you imagine what she would say if she knew the elegant Mrs. Raike had robbed a train?" Doña began to giggle a bit hysterically. The toddy must have gone to my head, she thought.

Stephen grinned in response, but then he said quietly, "Hush, darling, there's someone there by the steps."

Mrs. Blair was sorry to see the interesting young couple leave and, as her husband returned to sit beside her, she said, "Oh, what a shame you missed them, Ben."

"Missed who, my dear?" Benjamin Blair was a small,

thin man with graying hair; he had the same shrewd, friendly look as his wife, as if their long years of living together had made them resemble a brother and sister.

"That handsome young Raike man, the one on the train!"

"Good lord, do you mean on the Short Line train last September?"

"Yes, of course."

"So that's Stephen Raike. The Short Line's a Raike train, you know."

"Did you meet his wife?"

"The beautiful young woman with red hair? No, I didn't as a matter of fact."

"She is unusually lovely, but—" Mrs. Blair was interrupted in mid-sentence by the approach of their hostess, Mrs. Hamilton.

"Mrs. Blair, Mr. Blair," Mrs. Hamilton said as Blair got to his feet, "I'd like to present Mr. Philippe Gerard of New Orleans. It's so interesting—he's Mr. Raike's cousin." Mrs. Hamilton's social tone barely concealed her wonder—this elegant Southerner related to Stephen Raike and that wife of his! her look seemed to say.

Gerard bowed like a dancing master to Mrs. Blair and kissed her small ringed hand. "This is a great pleasure," he said effusively. "It atones for my disappointment at missing my cousins."

Mrs. Hamilton murmured a sweet insincerity and excused herself to attend to other guests.

"You are visiting Chicago, Mr. Gerard?" Blair asked.

"I had thought only to visit, but I may make Chicago my home. I have certain interests here, and then it will be pleasant to renew my acquaintance with my cousin—and his beautiful wife. She is a lady of mystery, is she not?"

Glancing up at the young man, Mrs. Blair wondered what he meant about Doña Raike, but he did not go on to explain, so she chattered on sociably.

As Mrs. Blair recalled aloud her first visit to Chicago, Philippe Gerard was trying to fathom the meaning of the conversation he had overheard on the stairs between Stephen Raike and his wife.

Chapter Sixteen

"Well, look who's here, the old bastard himself." Alfred Torrance put his well-laden fork back on his plate, glaring across the dining room of the New Tremont House.

"So that is the famous Long John," Philippe Gerard commented lazily. "He is hardly elegant; he has the face of a bulldog and the stomach of a pig. *Mon dieu!* Is all that food for him alone?"

Gerard's glittering black gaze took in the two hurrying waiters with laden trays. There were at least thirty dishes on the trays.

"It is not possible," Gerard protested, laughing.

"The hell it isn't," Torrance said. "Thirty to forty dishes every damn meal, and a pint of brandy. Old devil looks as mad as a wet hen; they're supposed to have the dishes *on* the table when he gets there. He marks the menu in his room every morning. Hope he chokes on it," the gambler added savagely.

Gerard chuckled. "You seem to have quite a grudge against the mayor."

The Frenchman looked again with interest at the colorful mayor of Chicago. Wentworth was a six-foot-six giant with a grim face, a barrel chest and portly body. Gerard had heard about Long John Wentworth, the outspoken anti-vice mayor. The man had walked into Chicago barefoot twenty years before; since then he had been a member of Congress and twice mayor of Chicago. But Gerard was not acquainted with the more recent activities of Long John and his "devils," as the gamblers called the mayor's police.

"Damn straight I've got a grudge," Torrance growled. "Don't you know what the bastard did last spring? Moved some of my girls right out on the street and pulled my buildings down with a team of horses."

"Good God! Where were you when all this happened?"

Torrance admitted sheepishly, "Out at the Brighton Racetrack with some of the boys. Dogfight between Dutch Frank's dog and Bill Galligher's hound, a five-hundred-dollar purse."

"I can see why he is not popular, this Long John."

"Well, come next election, he'll be out. Plenty of us to see to that, I'll tell you. But what about you, Phil? I didn't think you'd be hanging around this long. What's up?"

Gerard smiled and sipped his wine. Deliberately he took a cigar from a leather case in his frockcoat, and made a great business of cutting and lighting it. When it was drawing to his satisfaction, he drawled, "I find things to interest me here."

"Not going into business, are you?" Torrance studied the elegant Gerard with surprise.

"Hardly." The other laughed. "As long as the rice grows well, I am glad to say, I will not have to go into business. Though I must admit that that little transaction in St. Louis was helpful. And I thought it might be politic to stay away from New Orleans until things—die down."

"What are these interests here?" Torrance asked abruptly.

"My unfinished business with Mr. Stephen Raike."

Torrance waited until the waiters had removed their plates and set a large wedge of pie before him, coffee before Gerard. He said, "That business on the boat? That's nothing. What do you want to get all riled up for? You're a good shot, but Raike is better."

Gerard, repressing an angry reply, answered softly, "You might say I represent the Gerards, in a way."

Torrance speared his bite of pie and asked around a large mouthful of cherries, "What the hell does that mean?"

"My family never forgave Raike's father for taking

194

Louise Gerard away. I think it might be amusing for a Gerard to steal something from a Raike, for a change."

The gambler swallowed another mouthful of pie and took a swig of his coffee. "The woman, you mean?"

"The woman, yes, and whatever else I can take. It is amusing to encounter them socially at various homes." Gerard's tone was spiteful.

"Well, I've got to admit, you go a lot of places I couldn't get in." Torrance laughed a short, hard laugh. "What will your fine friends say if they see you with me? That's not too smart."

"I have never bothered being wise," Gerard retorted in an arrogant tone. "I leave discretion to duller men. And by the way, I learned something very interesting at the Hamiltons'."

"What's that?"

Philippe Gerard repeated to the gambler what he had overheard on the stairs between Doña and Stephen Raike.

"Well, well. What do you know about that?" Torrance's heavy face brightened and he smiled an unpleasant smile. "I'd like to get my own back, myself. Raike's done enough to me. Maybe I can help you find out more. I have some friends in Galveston, and New Orleans, and plenty of other places, who might know something."

"Splendid! I have a feeling it could be important. There is something about that woman; she has not had a conventional past, I will bet on it, my friend. There was talk at the Hamiltons' that she is interested in going into her husband's business. Now what kind of woman would do that?"

"Jesus Christ. Raike must have his hands full."

Gerard smiled, and there was a malicious light in his black eyes. "Indeed, I'm sure he has. I have a feeling, my friend, that Mr. Raike's troubles have just begun."

Before Mrs. Blair had the chance to call on Doña at the Sherman House, the two met each other at one of the city's skating rinks, where the younger members of

Chicago society came to waltz about the ice. The Blairs loved watching.

Stephen, of course, was skilled at the sport, having spent several winters in the North. Doña was less sure, but already she had mastered enough of the art to stay upright and move with him if Stephen skated slowly enough. But Doña's greatest pleasure was to watch him skate alone; he had the same lean grace on the ice as he had had on the horse at the rodeo.

One afternoon, a few days after the party at the Hamiltons' house, Doña was seated with Mrs. Blair at the edge of the rink, the two women admiring Stephen's figure-threes and figure-eights. Grinning at them, and obviously showing off, he executed something he called the double roll.

Doña, bright-cheeked in the brisk air and vivid in jade-green velvet and dark furs, clapped her gloved hands, and Mrs. Blair joined in. But Doña's smile faded when she saw Philippe Gerard walking toward them.

Looking resplendent in a heavy, furred greatcoat, Gerard swept off his hat and bowed, saying, "Mrs. Blair! Doña Raike! What an unexpected pleasure."

"Mr. Gerard," Mrs. Blair said pleasantly, but Doña did not speak, only nodded coldly. Stephen, who had skated off to the far side of the rink, had not yet seen Gerard.

"What a pity you missed each other at the Hamiltons'," Mrs. Blair said.

"You were at the Hamiltons'?" Doña commented. Her voice was not cordial.

Gerard, ignoring her tone, made a sound of regret. "I was, and I was desolated to miss my fair cousin." He bowed again. Just then Stephen skated up to them, and he gave Gerard a cold look.

"What is this about your fair cousin?" Stephen asked.

As Gerard explained, Mrs. Blair watched the three young people in a rather puzzled fashion. Stephen's enmity and Doña's discomfort were all too plain.

Doña could see in Stephen's eyes the same thought that was running through her own mind. It was going to be very unpleasant to encounter Gerard so often on social occasions.

Undismayed, the cool Gerard said to Stephen, "You are a paragon on the ice, as you seem to be elsewhere, cousin."

Stephen could hardly contain his dislike, but Doña said quickly, "Yes, he is." She smiled at Stephen, who gave her a tender look.

"You are not a skater, Mr. Gerard?" Mrs. Blair asked.

"Hardly, madame. Alas, a poor provincial from the South cannot compete in these matters." He emphasized the last two words in a significant way, meeting Stephen's look as if he were throwing down a challenge.

Doña felt increasingly uncomfortable. "Stephen," she said suddenly. "We mustn't forget our appointment."

"Our appointment? Oh, yes." Stephen responded. "I'll get rid of my skates. Be right back."

As they watched the tall, lean man move gracefully away, Gerard announced, "I will call on you soon, my dear Doña."

"And so shall I, my dear," said Mrs. Blair. "We mustn't let her keep running away from us," she added lightly to Gerard.

"Indeed, we must not," Gerard said, and gave Doña a long look from his gleaming dark eyes. "I have no intention of letting her escape."

When Stephen returned, he was doubly annoyed to see Gerard kissing Doña's gloved hand. That damn bastard is too attentive by far, Stephen thought, and the incident was to rankle for days.

Stephen watched Doña uneasily; she was standing at the window with her back to him, her whole demeanor mirroring her restlessness and discontent. He walked to the window and put his arms around her, kissing her hair. She did not turn.

"Doña," he said softly. When she did not reply, he repeated, "Doña."

"What is it?" she inquired coldly, still staring out the window at the misting snow.

"I'm sorry about all this, I really am. If I could trust anyone else, you know I'd send him. But I've got to do it myself, I've explained it to you. I've go to be the one to go to Springfield."

"I know."

"And you know the roads are bad now; I don't want to take you in this kind of weather. I won't be long."

"I know," she said in the same cool voice.

There was trouble in Springfield involving Stephen's westbound stage; reluctantly he had concluded that it was a matter he could not delegate. But he hadn't expected her to take it so to heart.

"Doña, look at me," he said, and gently turned her in his arms so she was facing him, but she did not look up.

He took her chin in his hand and lifted her face to his He saw the boredom and rebellion in her dark eyes, and gave a silent curse: damn Springfield and damn Gerard!

"This thing about Gerard and the Blairs," he said. "You've been very patient, I know, but lately they have been going everywhere together and—" Stephen thought, silently, I'll tangle with that bastard yet. "Come on, sit down a minute with me and let's talk. I have a few minutes before I must leave."

Hesitantly she followed him to the sofa and sat beside him.

"The truth is, I can't stand to watch the way Gerard makes up to you, darling. Don't you know what you mean to me? Just the way he looks at you and talks to you makes my blood boil."

Doña nodded wearily, as Stephen went on, "And socializing with the Blairs means that Gerard will be around. I know it's been hard for you, cooped up here," he added, taking her hand in his.

For the last four days, Doña had kept to the hotel, sending Mrs. Blair a note thanking her for her calls and flowers, but obeying Stephen and refusing to see her.

"How long will this go on?" she demanded.

"Just have a little patience."

"Patience!" she cried. "The way I've been patient with

your other evasions?" Doña turned on him with such an angry face he was astonished.

"What evasions?"

"You said you would think about my going into business with you," she said coldly. "But you have put me off, time and again. You think I am a child, that I don't know my own mind."

"That's exactly what I think," he retorted with sudden anger. "And I won't hear another word of it, not now. I've got a lot on my mind, and you damn well know it."

He had never sounded so angry before: Doña was intimidated into sullen silence.

"Doña, Doña, my darling," he said then. "I'm sorry." He kissed her, but she turned her face away. He rose and strode to the door, where his grip was packed for the journey, waiting.

"Goodbye, Doña," he said, pausing and looking at her with a wistful expression. "I'll see you in a few days."

"Goodbye," she said, but her voice was as cold as ever.

She heard the door shut, but did not move from her place on the sofa. She had no idea at all how long it was that she sat there, but finally, when the dusk was turning dark, she rose with a sigh and went to turn on the lamps.

Examining the small gold watch that hung on a chain at her waist, she saw that it was only five o'clock. Five o'clock! The evening stretched before her endlessly. She paced back and forth on the deep carpet. It would be hours before she could sleep.

Doña wandered to the window, thinking, This is the night of the Bachelors' Ball. Mrs. Blair, in one of her friendly notes, had expressed regret that Doña's illness would prevent her from attending.

"But I will attend!" Doña found she'd spoken aloud. She would send Mrs. Blair a note, and the Blairs would take her to the ball! How simple it was. And Stephen need never know.

It was foolish to hide like this; the Blairs would not remember her. How could they? Stephen himself had said they probably couldn't see her from their car. And even if Gerard were at the ball, she could handle him!

Going to a table by the window, Doña sat down and pulled out the drawer containing the notepaper of the Sherman House. She wrote a swift message and addressed an envelope to Mrs. Benjamin Blair, Tremont House.

Smiling with secret delight, Doña went to summon a maid who would have the message delivered to the Blairs. That done, she hurried to the bedroom to choose a gown for the ball.

The Bachelors' Assembly Balls at the Tremont House Hotel were among the few large social affairs of Chicago's winters. The town's young single men gave the dances to repay those families who had entertained them in their homes, the families who might have single daughters.

Single women in Chicago were so few in this year of 1857 that they could not make up a ball alone. Therefore women of all ages—mothers and aunts, even lively grandmothers, and married women accompanied by their husbands—were invited to the Bachelors' Ball.

Filled with pleasurable excitement, Doña entered the ballroom with the Blairs. She felt like a wild young mare released from its stall, and the sound of the orchestra quickened her excitement, bringing vivid color to her tawny face. She was a striking picture with her hair center-parted and drawn back severely into a heavy coil of braids in back; a small tiara of gold, with beads the colors of a peacock's wing—blue-green and bronze and russet—surmounted the rich coil.

Her low-cut gown was golden-bronze, with open sleeves revealing an inner fabric. But where most gowns of the time were inset with lace, Doña's was filled with golden chiffon. Her pretty arms were seen in all their perfection; she wore half-length evening gloves of kid that matched her gown, sparkling with beads like the ones in her tiara. In her neat ears were simple drops of warm red-gold.

"You look lovely, my dear," said Mrs. Blair, dressed in a rich gray gown with a bertha of pale mauve lace.

The older woman's jewels were a remarkable *parure* of pearls and amethysts. "Where did you find your dress?"

"In New Orleans." Doña smiled happily, delighted that she had come and forgetting the pang of guilt she had felt for a moment. She gave herself over to the pleasures of the present; her body felt light and free, ready to sway into the rhythms of the dance. She was glad now for those long-ago lessons she had so resented, when, at her mother's insistence, she had learned to dance in Galveston.

Noting her sparkling eyes and the almost visible response of her body to the music, Benjamin Blair said, "We must find you a livelier partner than I, Mrs. Raike."

"I am sure no one could be livelier than you, Mr. Blair. On the other hand, no one can be more eager than I."

All three turned at the sound of the smooth, arrogant voice. Philippe Gerard was regarding them, smiling. The Blairs greeted him with pleasure, but a cold dismay overtook Doña.

Yet she made herself smile as Gerard swept her into the waltz.

They danced for some moments in silence, until Gerard said, "You seem uneasy, my dear—cousin." She colored with resentment at the familiarity in his voice. "Now why is that?"

She did not reply, only looking up at him for an instant and then downwards again, reluctant for him to see the consternation that must have been plain in her look.

"I do not see your husband at the ball," Gerard said insistently.

"He is—away," Doña replied curtly.

"Away," Gerard said, tightening his hold on Doña's waist and whirling her off, out of the view of the Blairs. "Then he is even less wise than I thought. If I were your husband, I would not let you out of my sight. You are the most exciting woman I have ever known."

Her discomfort increased; there was something so threatening in the man, and yet she could not help being flattered by his ardent looks and bold words. Again she did not answer, but felt the quickening beat of her heart and her faster, shallow breath; she hoped that he would not notice.

Suddenly, to her bewilderment, he said in a cool, social tone, "You must have been to many balls such as this, in the fine homes of Texas."

She was so taken aback by his change of mood that she blurted unthinkingly, "I was not invited to fine homes in Texas."

Gerard stared down at her with interest. "That is hard to believe, a lovely creature like you. How, then, did you pass your time?"

Doña's dark eyes held his gaze, then looked away. She was certain now that there had been some sarcastic undertone in his light question. She felt her hands grow cold and one of them trembled in Gerard's grasp.

"I fear that you are tired," he said. "Shall we sit down?"

She nodded, unable to speak, and he led her to the edge of the floor toward the Blairs.

Gerard handed Doña into a chair and smiled brilliantly at Mrs. Blair.

"You dance well," the older woman said in her warm way.

"You are too kind. We have been discussing the festivities of Texas." Gerard glanced at Doña, who felt the same peculiar apprehension she had felt as they were dancing.

"It's a fascinating state," said Benjamin Blair. He cocked a humorous eye at his wife. "But don't get her started on the place. We'll have to hear the train-robbery story again."

"A train robbery!" Gerard exclaimed. "Such a story could only be fascinating. Tell me about it, Mrs. Blair." Again he glanced at Doña, and she moved uneasily in her chair.

"Unless it would upset you, my dear cousin," he added in a silken tone.

"No, no, of course not," Doña replied quickly, but she felt that the others were staring at her curiously. She tried to compose her expression. She was afraid her thoughts were being revealed to them all.

"I really don't think Mrs. Raike should have to hear it again," Mrs. Blair protested, and smiled.

Doña disagreed politely, but she wished fervently that she had never come.

To her disgust she felt her face grow hot.

"Why, you're quite flushed, my dear," said Mrs. Blair. "I hope you're not catching a cold."

"Maybe I am," Doña said.

"Do let me see you to your hotel," Gerard urged. "There's no need to inconvenience the Blairs."

Mrs. Blair looked at her husband uncertainly. But then, after all, the man was her husband's cousin! So she said, "That's very kind of you, but we would be happy to take her."

"Entirely unnecessary," Gerard declared. "I shall see my dear cousin safely home."

Doña rose and took his arm with reluctance. It was worse than she thought; there was no way on earth to explain her reluctance to the Blairs. Still, she thought, anything to get out of this place, and away from their curious eyes. She knew what they were thinking: how strange it was for her to shrink from her husband's relative.

"Please rest, my dear," said Mrs. Blair kindly. "I'll drop by tomorrow to see if there's anything I can do."

Mr. Blair interjected, "Maybe she should just rest; a visit might not be the thing right now."

Doña, hardly knowing what she said, but unwilling to hurt Mrs. Blair's feelings, blurted, "But I would love to see you."

As Gerard led Doña from the ballroom, Benjamin Blair said to his wife, "Now I wonder—I wonder why a woman would call her husband's cousin Mr. Gerard."

He looked after them thoughtfully.

"I'll see you to your door," Gerald declared, over Doña's protests. She had already been quite embarrassed by the inquisitive stare of Mr. Random in the lobby.

Surrendering to the inevitable, Doña waited silently at his side while the Otis contraption creaked downward to fetch them and then bore them slowly up to her suite.

"You must let me send for your maid," Gerard said, when they reached the door. Doña shook her head and started to speak. "I insist. Go in now and rest. I will have her sent up to you."

Back in the lobby, he presented himself to the manager. "My name in Gerard. I am Mrs. Raike's cousin by marriage." He was amused to see the look of relief on the manager's curious face. "Mrs. Raike is not feeling very well; could you send up her maid, please?"

"Of course, of course." The manager snapped his fingers for an attendant and as he was leaving, Gerard glanced back over his shoulder. The maid summoned to the manager was a small, thin woman with a wealth of untidy brown hair and a decided squint.

The maid is memorable enough, Gerard decided with satisfaction. Jean-Jean could never miss that squint!

And when later he described the woman to his body-servant, he handed the man several bills of large denomination.

"The first thing in the morning, Jean-Jean. Do not forget. Now tell me again what you will say."

The next day the maid was very late, Doña noticed. Doña had risen after noon, feeling logy and despondent; perhaps she was really ill, and felt more despondent than before.

Why, oh why, did I invite Mrs. Blair to visit? she raged in silence. And why hasn't Willamae come to do the rooms?

There was a light tap at the door, and Willamae appeared.

"I'm sorry I'm late, ma'am," the woman said in her querulous tone.

"It's all right," Doña replied distractedly. "Why don't you do this room first? I'm expecting a visitor. Then, while we visit, you can tidy the bedroom."

The maid nodded and set to work. Doña went into the bedroom to dress.

Studying herself in the mirror, Doña felt that she was looking a bit drab and decided to wear a bright green woolen dress, which she took from the great cupboard. It was such a gloomy day, perhaps the dress would raise her flagging spirits.

When Mrs. Blair arrived a few minutes later, Doña felt more composed.

"Why, you're up," Mrs. Blair said in surprise.

"Yes, yes." Doña's reply was awkward, hesitant. "I—I'm feeling better now."

"I'm so glad," Mrs. Blair said warmly.

"Please, let me take your things," Doña said.

And Mrs. Blair followed Doña into the bedroom, where she slipped off her fur cloak and removed her plumed hat before the glass.

The maid, very laboriously, was dusting the mantel. How slow she was today!

Doña's guest smiled pleasantly at the maid and they returned to the sitting room.

As Doña served the coffee, Mrs. Blair leaned back and glanced around the room. "How pleasant this is. I do regret that we must leave tomorrow. It would have been so nice to—know you better."

Repressing her sigh of relief, Doña managed to look regretful, and murmured, "I am sorry." Then with greater sincerity, for she truly liked the little woman, she said, "You're the first—friend I've made in Chicago. The others are so—" she stopped, chagrined. She had been about to criticize Mrs. Blair's friends.

"It's all right." The other woman looked at Doña with understanding and smiled. "I feel the same way. I told you that night at the Hamiltons' that you and I are different from the others. Just the way you *dress,* for instance." She laughed. "I am a frivolous old woman. But the gloves you were wearing last night were exquisite. Did you buy those in New Orleans, too?"

"No, from our local woman, Mrs. Bright. Please let me give you a pair," Doña said on a sudden impulse. She wanted very much to atone somehow for her lies to this warm-hearted woman.

"Oh, my dear, I *couldn't!*"

"Of course you can," Doña insisted, smiling. "Come, I think I have a pair that would look lovely with the dress you wore last night." And with the same impulsiveness, Doña took Mrs. Blair's plump hand and drew her upward from the couch.

Mrs. Blair laughed. "I feel as if I'm back in school."

When they entered the bedroom, the maid, looking strangely disconcerted, brushed past them toward the sitting room.

What ailed Willamae today? The thought passed swiftly through Doña's mind and then was dismissed.

"Here," Doña said gaily, opening a bureau drawer.

On top of Doña's gloves lay a bright blue silk scarf, and a Colt .44. Doña gasped: someone had been in the drawer—the maid? She was sure that the scarf and gun had been hidden at the bottom of the drawer.

Doña took out the gloves she'd been looking for and turned to Mrs. Blair, closing the drawer with haste.

The little woman accepted the beaded gloves and said softly, "Thank you. They are lovely."

As she led Mrs. Blair back into the sitting room, Doña saw that Willamae was still in the suite. Doña looked at her with surprise and the servant hurried from the sitting room without a word.

They sat on the couch and resumed their conversation, as Doña poured them each another cup of coffee. Mrs. Blair asked when Stephen would return and they discussed his business for a few moments.

"You know your husband loves you very much," Mrs. Blair said with a sigh. "The way he looks at you is enviable. You are a very fortunate young woman. Do you love him?"

Doña looked at the older woman for a moment and then answered frankly, "I don't know." Mrs. Blair seemed amazed.

Doña could not help laughing at the older woman's expression.

206

Miranda Blair asked thoughtfully, "And this Gerard, my dear? What about him?"

Doña told her of Daniel Raike and Louise Gerard and the meeting with Torrance and Philippe Gerard in New Orleans and on the boat.

"Be careful of him," Mrs. Blair said. "I don't trust the rogue at all, fine family or no."

Doña said, "I don't either. And I'm afraid there will be trouble between him and Stephen."

"You must try to prevent it," Mrs. Blair said firmly. "Your Stephen is one man in a thousand." She saw Doña's uneasy expression and said quickly, "Now, my dear Doña, I suggest you change your gown."

Doña looked at her questioningly.

"Change your gown," Mrs. Blair said again, "so we can take you out to dinner on our last night in Chicago. I don't know when we'll meet again, and it will be something to remember."

"You have such a nice way of saying things," Doña said as she hurried off to dress for dinner.

Later that evening, in Philippe Gerard's hotel room, the man named Jean-Jean stood before his master to report what Willamae had told him.

"Magnificent," Gerard said lazily, drawing on his cigar. He studied his bodyservant with glittering eyes, his narrow face amused and triumphant. "You have done very well. Bring me my pocketbook, Jean-Jean. I think you deserve a reward."

Stirring to wakefulness, Doña opened her eyes and thought, Stephen will be home today.

Guiltily she realized how much she had enjoyed her freedom while he was away. And she realized how much she would miss Miranda Blair. There had been no one in her life, since Patche and Easooba, to whom she could unburden her heart. How much there was now that she had to keep from Stephen!

She had disobeyed his orders, meeting the Blairs again. And Philippe Gerard had been seen escorting her to her room the other evening. That fact disturbed her most. She could not forget the look in Stephen's eyes whenever he saw Gerard.

Doña felt that she must prevent trouble between the two men. But how was she to do that?

It struck her, then, that she was worrying about Stephen. And in that act there was a kind of commitment, a commitment she had been avoiding in her heart until this moment. Mrs. Blair had called him a man in a thousand.

Yes, Doña reflected, that is just what he is.

Later, when she heard him enter the sitting room, and call her name, Doña rose and hurried to him, going into his arms with gladness. The recent coldness between them was forgotten, and she felt again that warm confusion, that half-unwilling excitement that she always felt when Stephen touched her.

"I must go soon." Stephen smiled, surveying his clothes that had been scattered about the room. "I can't laze here the whole day, as much as I'd like to." Gently he detached his arms from Doña's body and got up from the bed.

She stretched her arms and looked up at him, enjoying the familiar sight of his lean, muscular body, his fine head with its thick light-brown hair, and austere features softened now from their lovemaking.

She watched him move about the room as he dressed. Rising, she bent to retrieve the discarded garments from the floor and the chairs.

"Let the maid do that," he said indulgently, taking her in his arms and holding her tight against him.

She colored and laughed. "It's too—private a thing for that."

Stephen smiled at her and said, "Come into the sitting room. I want to talk with you a minute. I'll send for some coffee."

She tidied her hair and put on a full, lacy wrapper before she followed him into the sitting room.

He was sitting on the sofa when she entered, looking solemn. "There's something I want to ask you, Doña."

She started guiltily, trying to hide her consternation. Had he heard, then, of the visit of Gerard—or the Blairs?

"Sit down."

She obeyed. He moved closer to her on the sofa and took her hand. "There's something we've got to talk about." She waited, as he studied her. Then he asked bluntly, "Do you still want to go into the business?"

The question took her completely by surprise. It was the last thing she had expected.

"Why, why, yes," Doña said weakly, still struggling with her surprise.

"Are you sure?"

"Yes. Yes, I am sure. But what made you change your mind? You were so set against—"

He smiled. "I thought about it while I was away. I thought about *you*. There's never been another woman like you, Doña. And I realized I was crazy to think you could settle down like the others." He laughed. "I told you I couldn't picture you pouring tea."

"Then you're willing to teach me?" she asked eagerly.

"It's going to be hard."

"Things have been hard before."

"I know that." He touched her face gently. "That's why I thought for a while I'd like to make it easy. But you're not an easy lady—there's something in you that won't let you rest. But like I say, it's going to be hard. In the business you won't be my wife; you'll have to prove yourself."

"I've always had to prove myself." She thought of the day when she had had to prove her marksmanship to Tahre and the others, all the times she had had to forget that she was a woman. "Always," she repeated stubbornly.

"I know you have." Stephen looked at her, impressed anew with the proud, independent cast of her small chin and shapely mouth. "I'll try not to be too tough on you," he said. "But you're going to have plenty to fight, and I want to tell you about it now. It's only fair.

"First of all," he said, "the men will resent you. Sure, I'm the boss, but that won't stop them from resenting you. I've only got one female employee, and she's fifty if she's a day, and ugly as a mud fence. She'll resent you, too. And the customers will resent you. Our acquaintances will be shocked and disapproving." He gave a contemptuous, one-sided smile. "I don't give a hoot in hell about any of them. You know that. But you're going to have to contend with all that. Are you willing?"

"Yes," she said, grinning. "I don't give a hoot in hell about them either."

"All right, then. You know what you're in for. I've told you before, there's not another woman in Chicago in business, unless you count Irish Molly and her pals."

Doña smiled broadly at the mention of the notorious madam who was such a close friend of Torrance.

"You've got guts, Doña," he said quietly, and she could hear the admiration in his voice. "You've got guts and sense and brains. So I guess I don't have to tell you how to dress and how to act in an office."

"No, sir," she said quickly, with mock submission.

He laughed. "All right, then." He rose. She got up, too, and took his arm.

"Oh, Stephen, I—"

"Yes?" Something eager and expectant had come into his voice, and she saw his gray eyes gleam as he looked down at her. Again there was that sense of waiting that she had seen so many times before.

"I'm grateful to you. I am beholden."

The gleam faded, and he answered lightly, "We'll start you tomorrow. And I'll teach you everything there is to know about Raike Lands. And Raike Stages."

When the employees of Raike Lands learned that Doña was joining them, they were hard put to hide their dismay.

Miss Matilda Johnston, the aging clerk who was given tasks the men were unwilling to do, was coldly polite, and there were murmurs among the men about the craziness of the whole enterprise. All waited for the expected favoritism to emerge. And William Eaton, Stephen's manager, told the men privately to have patience, that young Mrs. Raike would soon tire of the routine. It was just a foolish indulgence on the part of a newly married man. "It'll pass, boys. It'll pass," Eaton said with a knowing smile.

But as the weeks went on, and as they all observed her quiet, friendly, businesslike demeanor, they were torn between amazement and acceptance. Gradually their respect for her increased in spite of the suspicious questions of the men's wives and their own masculine conviction that this was no place for a lady. Certainly not a lady who was so young and beautiful, and whose husband was rich —and alive. It was all right for a widow, maybe.

Even the cold Miss Matilda Johnston began to be won over. Young Mrs. Raike was industrious and willing, and respectfully aware of Miss Matilda's experience and knowledge. When Miss Matilda was convinced that her position was not in danger she began to relax. "After all," Miss Matilda said indignantly, answering one of the skeptical men, "Mr. Raike hired *me*." She was very proud of being one of the few female office employees in the whole city. "And it's his business, isn't it?"

The young male clerk was sheepishly silent.

Stephen himself delighted in Doña's discreet demeanor and in the conscientiousness with which she did the tasks assigned to her. Her magnificent hair was always plainly dressed; she wore elegant but sober-colored dresses of wool with warm jackets. She seemed to be as much at home in the office as most women were in their parlors.

And her interest in learning was insatiable: in a month she could speak as knowledgeably as any man of maps and deeds and plots. Quietly, quickly, she absorbed every scrap of information that she could.

Stephen had begun to enjoy talking things over with her in the evenings. Her quick intelligence and never-flagging interest made her a wonderful companion, and he delighted in the many-sided woman she had become.

He watched with satisfaction as she won over the others in the office.

There was still the matter of his business friends and their wives. But Stephen had a feeling she could meet that challenge, as well. A woman like Doña, he concluded, could handle just about anything.

Chapter Seventeen

Alfred Torrance's gambling house on Randolph Street was the most popular one of them all; its spittoons were more brightly polished, its rugs deeper, and its gilt-framed mirrors more numerous than those in other dens. The black, white-aproned waiters in Torrance's house moved a bit more quickly and the champagne glasses on their trays were filled with a better vintage.

Therefore his clients numbered fewer bounty-jumpers and drunken sailors; the soldiers on leave were generally officers and there were more top hats on view.

One early March afternoon, the eight men seated around Torrance's mahogany table all wore top hats of the highest luster; the well-brushed gleam shone in the light of the white-globed chandeliers.

"That's all for me," said Philippe Gerard, drawing the stack of chips toward himself.

"It's a hell of a time to cash in, you bastard." The man on Gerard's left surveyed the pile of chips and bit down on his thick cigar.

"Sorry, gentlemen, I have some business to attend to." Gerard rose, cocked his gleaming hat forward over his brow, and grinned. His white teeth contrasted strongly with his narrow, swarthy face.

"Monkey business," commented the man with the thick cigar, and the others laughed.

"Who is she today, Gerard?" someone asked.

Without replying, Gerard made his way across the smoke-filled room toward Alfred Torrance.

"Phil!" Torrance extended his heavy hand. "Haven't seen you for a few days. What's up?"

"I want to talk to you, my friend."

"All right. Come into my office." Torrance gestured to Gerard expansively, opening the door to a private room furnished even more splendidly than the main hall.

"Drink?" he asked, moving toward the table against the wall, where a row of brass-tabbed decanters stood in neat, military array.

"A little brandy, perhaps," Gerard murmured. Torrance poured brandy into two massive snifters and handed one to his companion.

"Thank you. I think you'd better close the door," Gerard said.

"Oh, it's like that, is it?" Torrance's rough voice mocked. Nevertheless, he shut the door. Returning to his desk, he sat down and confronted Gerard. "Well?"

"What are we waiting for?" Gerard demanded. "I've had the information for months, and we're not moving."

"Easy, friend. I wouldn't want to throw away good stuff like that on nothing. There's a certain little deal that Raike is cooking now—so it soon may be time to move. You know I've never played for small stakes."

"What deal?" Gerard asked impatiently.

"I'm not sure of the details yet, that's the problem. But he's pulling something off, I think, with an Eastern buyer. And we can't move until the right time. What's your hurry, anyway?" Torrance laughed coarsely. "Are you running out of women?"

Gerard had earned an enviable reputation for pleasing the ladies during his Chicago stay.

He grinned and pushed his tall hat back on his head. Then he leaned back in his chair and put his elegantly shod feet on a table. "Hardly. But I could use a little change."

"Jesus, Phil, with all the whores in Chicago, you're still set on that skinny little thief?"

Gerard frowned. "I would hardly call her that."

"Come on, don't get huffy. As soon as my New York

contact lets me know, we'll move. You can approach the woman. You know what to say."

"Indeed, I will have a lot to say to Mrs. Raike."

"I don't give a damn about you and your women, pal. I'm interested in land. Women are a dime a dozen, but the parcel Raike is holding out is what I need—if I get that, for the right price, I'll be on Easy Street for life. So will you. So have patience, my fine-feathered friend. Have a little patience."

"I can't wait to see her face when I tell her what we know." Gerard smiled.

"And *his* goddam face! It'll be good to pay him back for what he's done."

Gerard said, "He's bested you in more ways than one, hasn't he, Al?"

"Damned straight he has. And he made a monkey of me in New Orleans. I haven't forgotten that, either."

"This is going to be a very interesting game," Gerard remarked, "the best game we've ever played together." Taking off his top hat, he tossed it at the table lined with decanters; the hat landed on one of the heavy flagons and hung there rakishly.

"I take off my hat to you, Al," he joked, then asked lazily. "What's on the agenda this afternoon?"

"Oh, I don't know. Maybe I'll show you a little surprise."

"Surprise? By all means."

Torrance took up a brass bell on his desk and rang it loudly. An aproned black man appeared, cautiously opening the ornately carved door.

"Sir?"

"Ask Miss Molly to come downstairs, would you, Willie?"

"Yes, sir." The black hurried away.

"What's this?" Gerard asked curiously.

"I want Molly to tell you about her new merchandise," Torrance replied. "A late arrival, from New Orleans, as a matter of fact. She has a touch of the tarbrush, they tell me, and knows some tricks you wouldn't believe." At Gerard's skeptical look, Torrance laughed, and protested,

"Tricks even *you* wouldn't believe, my friend. They say this one will do anything. And I mean anything."

Gerard removed his shining boots from the table and sat up a little straighter in his chair, waiting eagerly for the arrival of Irish Molly and her new girl.

Just as Alfred Torrance was "top sawyer" among the gamesters of Chicago, his close friend Molly Dromore ran the most genteel of parlor houses, and her "boarders" were young women of beauty and quiet deportment.

Molly's rates were correspondingly · higher: whereas most parlor-house cards listed fees from five to ten dollars, Molly Dromore's charges ran from ten to twenty dollars. Her elegant, nicely printed calling cards, giving simply her name and address, at 2020 South Dearborn Street, advertised seven boarders of "unusual gifts." And the card continued, "Her house is full of interesting people with whom one may pass an evening of frolic. All who call at Miss Dromore's boarding house will be kindly and courteously received."

"Unusual gifts" had been the reason for hiring Josette, a beautiful mulatto from New Orleans with strangely weary eyes. The black, large eyes of Josette had seen too much. But even in the New Orleans "circus," a name given by the knowing to a house specializing in peculiar tastes—Josette had never met anyone quite like Philippe Gerard.

When he told her casually what he required, even the blasé Josette hesitated a moment before she awarded him her bland, professional smile and, taking the buggy whip from his hand, complied.

And he gave her a very large tip, indeed. After all, Josette concluded, if he wanted to humiliate himself, it didn't matter to her! However, when the other girl was called in, Josette had to grit her teeth. This, *parbleu,* was a bit too strange, even for her. Animals, yes, but other women?

Nevertheless, Josette performed to Gerard's satisfaction, and departed with the other girl—both had been tipped handsomely—leaving him sprawled half-asleep.

"Dear Jesus, I'm glad he only watched at the last, and didn't touch us—the way he was!" Josette's companion whispered. "How did you stand it?"

"It's a lot of money, Estelle. A lot."

And Josette smiled pleasantly at her employer's friend, Alfred Torrance, who was passing them in the corridor.

When Torrance was out of earshot, Josette poked Estelle in the ribs, and giggled. "Look, he's going in there." She pointed to the room they had just left.

"Christ in heaven, are you insane?" Torrance demanded, glaring at Gerard's bloody back.

"What I do in bed is my own business," Gerard answered coldly.

"But my God, two women at once? Did they both whip you?"

"No. Anyway, it's none of your goddam business. What do you want? I'm sleepy."

"I don't wonder. You ought to be dead, the way you go at it. Get dressed and come downstairs. I want to talk to you. It's time to move, right now, with Stephen Raike."

Gerard's languor disappeared at once, and his strange dark eyes grew sharp with excitement. "Ah! I'll be with you at once."

Without another word, Torrance turned on his heel and stalked off down the corridor toward the stairs.

The early spring thaw was flooding the low-lying areas in Chicago, making the streets almost impassable with mud. More streets were being raised, and the women found walking even more difficult than it had been in the winter.

But one day at noon, when Doña had climbed up into the new courthouse tower with Stephen, she saw a few patches of faint green between the buildings. In summer, Miss Matilda had said, the land at the edge of the city would be full of prairie flowers—golden yellow, after the white and blue flowers of spring.

Seeing the first sign of green, Doña felt the exultation of the new, hopeful season; it was the time of year the Indians took off their moccasins to walk, so as not to bruise the pregnant earth. And even her brief, sharp pain of homesickness was allayed by the fullness of her new life in Chicago, where every day now brought a fresh challenge and excitement.

Waving goodbye to Stephen that day in front of the land office on State Street, Doña watched him drive away toward the distant sheds that housed Raike Stages. Suddenly, she felt possessed of a deep content.

It is going to be fine from now on! she said to herself as she mounted the stairs to the office. There was nothing more to fear: Stephen had said nothing more about Philippe Gerard. Apparently he had never learned of her attendance at the ball. And the trouble that had threatened to brew between Stephen, Gerard and Torrance seemed to have evaporated, as quickly and easily as the winter snow.

Her relations with Stephen, these past months, were happy and calm. The restlessness that had tortured her so long was stilled at last. She moved with a new pride, pride in her own blooming beauty and in her accomplishments.

She had never known how full of complex things the wider world was, the world beyond Texas, but she was learning them every day. She had begun to read the newspapers and delighted in discussing the news of the day with Stephen. By day she was his companion, and by night she felt more than ever a woman, amazed that her familiarity with Stephen's body had not in any way diminished her strong desire.

Why, it's as if—as if I loved him, she reflected with wonder. The days of her vengefulness seemed very far away.

She entered the office, noticing as she did that most of the men were gone, on errands or at lunch. Only Miss Matilda and the shy young clerk were at their desks.

"How pretty you look today!" Matilda Johnston said to Doña. They had become good friends during the months of Doña's employment.

Doña thanked the other woman, and removing her veiled cap and brown velvet caped jacket, hung them in the recess for coats and hats. Then, following Miss Matilda's example, she put on the celluloid cuffs that would shield her cream-colored shirtwaist sleeves from ink and grime, and joined the other woman at a long table, where they were going over the books together.

They worked companionably for a time until they finished the previous month's accounts. Then Matilda said to Doña in a low voice, so the young clerk, Jeb, would not overhear, "I know you must be on tenterhooks about the Eastern matter."

Doña nodded. The Eastern matter was Matilda's discreet way of referring to Stephen's current negotiations with the New York buyers. He had warned Doña and other key employees that the negotiations must be a closely guarded secret; if the matter got out, prices of land might go so high through competitive bidding that the New York buyers could be scared away, and Raike Lands would suffer a staggering loss.

"Yes, I am nervous," she murmured to Matilda Johnston. "But I'm sure it will all go well."

"Of course it will!" the older woman said firmly in the same quiet voice, and glanced at the young clerk writing in the corner. Evidently he had heard nothing, for he worked on steadily, and when he paused, looked absently through the window as if his mind were very far away.

"I think Jeb must be in love," Matilda whispered, grinning. "He's so distracted."

"It seems so." Then Doña turned back to the books with Matilda, checking off the figures they had entered.

So intent was she on her task that at first she hardly noticed that someone had entered the office, and vaguely heard the young clerk Jeb say, "Mr. Raike is not in. He will return at four. Is there any message?"

Doña looked up, and to her dismay, saw Philippe Gerard standing by the counter.

He smiled brilliantly at her, his white teeth startling in his swarthy face, and Doña's first swift thought was: *Nassooba!* Instinctively, from the depths of her consciousness, the Comanche word for "wolf" had leapt to her mind.

"You misunderstand me, my young friend," Gerard said in that soft, almost threatening tone that Doña so disliked, "it is the beautiful *Mrs*. Raike I am seeking."

Doña felt her face grow hot with embarrassment and anger. How dare he come here? she raged silently. Jeb and Matilda were looking at her now, Jeb with undisguised curiosity, Matilda uneasily.

Doña rose and walked toward the counter. When she spoke she was relieved that her voice sounded so steady. "Miss Johnston, Jeb," she said, "this is—my husband's cousin, Mr. Philippe Gerard."

The others murmured greetings, and Gerard bowed to Matilda, saying, "This is *indeed* a pleasure, mademoiselle." Matilda Johnston's worn face colored, and she preened a little, to Doña's disgust.

But as she looked back at Philippe Gerard, Doña forgave the older woman, for she had to admit that Gerard looked unusually handsome today, for all his wolfish air. He was faultlessly dressed in a suit of pale pearl-gray, as if to mock the muddy streets outside. He held his matching grey top hat in his well-tended hand; his white shirt was ruffled, and on his maroon cravat was a beautiful old cameo stickpin. In his frockcoat's buttonhole was a flower, purchased, no doubt, at great expense from Chicago's only florist.

The boutonniere had been introduced recently to Chicago by an émigré from Maine, Johnathan Scammon.

Doña recalled that Stephen had scoffed at it, saying, "You won't find me wearing a Scammon-cabbage in my buttonhole."

Still, the dark red carnation which Gerard was wearing now gave him quite an air, Doña was forced to admit.

"And what did you want to see me about?" Doña asked Gerard, trying to hide the tension she felt. She was afraid that her voice had a nervous edge.

"Nothing much, my dear Doña," Gerard said casually. "I thought we might go out for a little coffee, unless your arduous schedule forbids it." The irony in his words was all too plain, as if her being in an office were a grotesquerie beyond his understanding.

"I'm afraid it does," she said, glad that she was managing to stay so calm, but hoping that neither of the others would notice how she avoided the use of his name. "Mr. Gerard" would sound too strange; "Philippe" she could not cope with!

"Ah, that is such a shame! Well, give Stephen my warm regards, dear cousin. And tell him—" he lowered his voice and stared at her meaningfully—"that I have some interesting information for him. About last year's Short Line robbery."

"The Short Line robbery," she repeated in a weak voice, looking into Gerard's glittering eyes. She thought she saw amusement in them.

Doña forced herself to answer easily, "Of course. I'll tell him." She enjoyed Gerard's look of surprise when he heard her even tone.

"Thank you." Gerard stared at her keenly. "I shall leave you to your—affairs, then." He bowed again in the direction of Matilda Johnston. The woman, for all her calm good sense, seemed flustered by Gerard's attentions.

Then Gerard was gone, and Doña was left to face the rest of the afternoon in great turmoil.

Young as Doña was, and inexperienced as she had been in the world of business, Stephen had come to rely on her opinions. She brought to the land business a freshness of viewpoint that he had in a certain measure lost, and he found it fascinating to measure her ideas against his own.

Doña had also made some very sound suggestions about the interiors and furnishings of the Raike Stages. She pointed out some minor but vital details in the arrangements of the seats and their upholstery which had never occurred to Stephen in all his years of managing stages—changes that made the coaches more comfortable for female passengers with their voluminous skirts and high-piled hair surmounted by plumed hats. It was a matter of inches here and there, but they were vital inches; when the seats had been adjusted, lower and farther back, and another kind of carpet had been laid on the coach's floors, the improvement was so vast that Parmalee's coaches were now being passed by, as the female travelers in particular ordered Raike Stages for their transportation. Besides, when it was time to repaint, Doña had suggested certain small changes in color that gave Raike Stages a new smartness and made Parmalee's look shabby and inferior.

Stephen fairly burst with pride when Doña's newly incorporated ideas showed such a handsome profit. As a result, late on the afternoon of Gerard's visit, Stephen asked Doña to drive with him to the sheds to take a look at some new designs for the drivers' uniform and new trappings for the horses.

"What's the matter?" he asked her, puzzled at her abstracted air and ill-disguised indifference to the project. "I thought you'd be bursting with notions for this new addition."

"Oh! I *am*," she answered stiffly. "I'm very glad you want to share this with me. It's just that I have a . . . slight headache, that's all."

"Maybe we'd better take you home."

"No! Oh, no, please!" Her dismay was evident, and he turned to look at her. She could not face the thought of going home just now; in the quiet and leisure, she would have too much time to brood about Gerard. "I—I need the activity!" Realizing how strange that sounded, she rushed on, "I mean, I'm not tired or sick at all, and I'm very anxious to see the new designs."

But Stephen kept giving her side glances; her usual self-possessed manner was absent.

He reined in the horse outside the great stage sheds and turned to her. "Something's wrong. What is it? Did something happen this afternoon?"

"Really, nothing is wrong at all. Honestly." She smiled at him and took his hand.

Reassured, he helped her down from the carriage and they went together to the stage office to look over the drawings, and soon Doña forgot her anxiety in the pleasure of the project.

Her nervousness did not return until they were driving

back to the hotel. Stephen avoided the block between State and Dearborn, known as Hairtrigger Block, because there were so many shootings there between feuding gamblers. But farther on, they saw the early evening promenade of gamesters. At this same hour, before the evening's games began, the gamblers, usually accompanied by their friends from the bordellos, strolled along to the parlors. The women wore their gaudiest hats, their brightest-colored gowns. But Doña caught sight of one dressed more quietly than the rest. Her hair was a brassy, spurious gold, but she had obviously chosen her clothes with care and wore them smartly. "How different that woman looks," Doña remarked idly.

"Which one?" Stephen followed the direction of her glance. "Oh, that. No wonder, that's Irish Molly, the richest madam in town."

"Torrance's—friend."

"Oh, yes. And speaking of the devil, there he is, himself. And Philippe Gerard."

Doña heard the hard anger in Stephen's voice and turned to look at his handsome face. His mouth was drawn in a grim line, and his gray eyes were like stone.

His eyes looked like that, she thought uneasily, the afternoon he fought with Lamb and Scurry. Once again, she feared that trouble was ahead. The confrontation between Gerard and Stephen was bound to come.

She moved closer to Stephen in the carriage and put her hand on his knee. It was not often that she made such gestures, and he reacted at once to her touch, making a sound of surprised delight. He looked lovingly at her, and Doña's senses stirred; she felt a stronger yearning for him than she had ever known.

When they reached the suite, the windows had been opened to the suddenly milder air. A dusky twilight shrouded the sitting room.

Doña heard herself say in a voice she barely recognized as her own, "Don't turn on the lamps, not yet." Stephen tossed his hat on the sofa and in a moment his arms were around her, holding her hard, drawing her so close to him that she felt his body's urgent seeking.

Something new and wild stirred in her, the feeling that had been awakened on the abandoned night in New Orleans returned. She moved out of his arms and began to remove her garments, snatching off the broad-brimmed hat, hastily unbuttoning the tight jacket and shirtwaist.

She stepped from her skirt and the last of her hidden laces and cambric. In a soft whisper, she said, "The day has been too long."

Dazed, he looked upon her naked body. He did not speak, but kissed her bare, satiny skin and caressed her passionately. The heavy fall of fiery hair, loosened now from its pins, streamed like a curtain of flame about her and she urged him, "Closer, come closer!"

Tearing off his clothes, he pulled her down to the carpet. At that moment, Doña felt there was nothing else in the world but this, their coming together. No more fears, no more worries and uncertainties, only her delight in her powers to excite him, and her own wonderful ache that was almost too great to bear. Suddenly, an explosive redness danced under her closed eyelids, and then there was an incredible peace.

Somewhere in that timeless interval she heard him cry out, too. Now as he held her closely at his side, she saw the dew of his sweat upon his softened, joy-distracted face.

Stephen planted swift, small kisses on her nose and brow and chin, still holding her tightly to his body's muscular length. He ran his hard hand down her curving side and she felt her skin vibrate to his touch.

She could not be close enough; she burrowed into him. He held her closer and closer. With a sense of disbelief, she felt a stirring of new lust within them both and realized, from the sounds he was making, that their bodies would meet again.

This time, to his delight, she fell upon him with a strong, relentless motion, and this encounter was a more excruciating pleasure than before; their outcry was a primitive thing, their shuddering flesh meeting in an emotion so powerful she feared the beating of her heart would cease.

224

As they lay against each other, spent, Stephen circled her still in his arms. Her bright hair curtained either side of his face, and she looked down on his peace-heavy eyes. Lazily he raised his hand and caught a glimmering tendril of her hair.

She made a sleepy sound and moved as if to free him of the light burden of her body. But his arms protested, clutching her; she stayed, drowsing on the edge of sleep.

"Doña, Doña," he whispered. Then he said, "You will be cold."

She murmured, "No." But very gently he moved her from him and reaching over her, took up his frockcoat from the floor and wrapped her in it.

They were sitting close together now, leaning against the sofa. She raised her head from his shoulder and kissed his neck.

He put his hand on the top of her shining head.

"I love for you to touch my head," she whispered; he slid his hand down her hair, caressing her ear. Bending his head, he kissed her again and again.

"I don't know what—came over me."

"I don't care what it was," he said, laughing shakily. "I am just so glad that it did." His hand stroked her slender neck, and then his caressing fingers moved from her neck to the soft breast exposed between the lapels of the too-large coat.

He said her name again, the sound of it muffled against her flesh as he lowered his mouth to her breasts. At the sighing sound of her breath, he rose again and gave her a long kiss on the mouth that made her tremble.

Stephen held her tightly once more, pressing her to his broad chest. She raised her mouth for his repeating kiss.

"Again, oh, please, again," he said, and his voice was so urgent that she let the coat fall back, and her quickening body replied to his. She felt a warmth so excellent and sweet that she could not contain the cries that were emerging from her; she heard them almost with wonder, as if they were the cries of someone other than herself.

When they could speak again, he said softly, "Just

when I think I know you, you always surprise me again." She looked up at him and saw that he was smiling.

Then he got up, saying, "Wait." In the gathering darkness she saw him go into the bedroom; there was the sound of the cupboard opening. Then he was returning with one of her soft, full wrappers.

"Put this on," he said quietly. "It's getting cold again."

She obeyed. He put on his dressing gown and lit one of the lamps.

Going to him, she raised her hands and took his face between them.

Hearing his sharp intake of breath, she asked, "What is it?"

"I dreamed about that once," he replied in a low voice, his sleepy gray eyes staring into hers. "I dreamed it, after the evening on the train." And he enfolded her into his arms.

"I—I have never felt so close to you before," she said softly against his chest.

Again she could feel the strange relaxation in his body, that release of the tension, the waiting in him, the thing that had happened so many times before.

She knew at last what he was always waiting for. He was waiting to hear her say that she loved him. Perhaps that time was at hand. Doña marveled at the knowledge within her, still hesitant, still reluctant.

If she admitted to him, to herself, this deep emotion that threatened to overpower her, then he would possess far more than her responsive body; he would own her outright.

And the past was still not dead. No, the past remained, no matter how dear he became to her.

The gray eyes that looked at her now, in his suddenly unreadable face, were still the eagle eyes of Daniel Raike. And, almost embarrassed, Stephen looked away from her as he spoke. "By the way, I'm going to New York for a little while."

Doña waited for him to ask her to go along, but to her surprise he did not.

Quickly, Stephen apologized. "It's going to be a hurried

226

business trip. I wouldn't have any time to show you the town. Next time I'll take you."

Doña was hurt, but she managed to ask calmly, "Will you be away long?"

"No, not long. Most of my time will be spent traveling. I'll stay in New York only two or three days. I think you'd find the trip dull and tiring. When I can spend more time there, we'll go together." He studied her again, hoping for a sign that she understood.

But she only said, "I'd better dress. It's time for dinner."

As she went into the bedroom to dress, Doña wondered where their magical closeness had gone so quickly.

When Stephen left the next morning for New York there was little warmth in their goodbye.

Chapter Eighteen

The Raike land office closed at noon on Saturdays. The Saturday that Stephen was away, Doña decided to distract herself with a visit to Colonel Wood's Museum, which had "150,000 Curiosities of every kind." But viewing the museum's ninety-six-foot fossil, its sea lion and hall of paintings did little to improve Doña's somber mood.

She was standing before the lighted panorama of the city of London, looking at it with indifferent eyes, when she heard an unwelcome greeting. Turning, she saw Philippe Gerard, his costly hat in his hand, smiling at her. With him was Mrs. Marilou Hamilton.

"Why, Mrs. Raike!" Marilou Hamilton cried in her sugary voice. The Southern woman was elaborately dressed, as always, with far too much splendor for the afternoon, and Doña's heart sank at the encounter. The woman always had some spiteful thing to say in her cloying manner.

"My dear Doña," said Gerard. Doña was even more dismayed to meet them both at once—her two least favorite people in the city.

She smiled at Mrs. Hamilton but only nodded coolly to Gerard. "Where is the handsome Mr. Raike?" Marilou asked.

"He's out of town," Doña replied bluntly.

"Ah! Then you must let me be your escort," Gerard said. Doña was silent.

"I was fortunate to encounter this lovely lady," Gerard continued unabashed, indicating the flirtatious Marilou, "and now I meet my beautiful cousin. How lucky I am today. Won't you join us for some refreshment?"

"Thank you, no," Doña answered, finding it very difficult to be civil to Gerard. "I am a little tired, and I think I'll be going home."

"Do let me take you, then," Gerard said eagerly.

"I wouldn't think of it," Doña replied curtly and walked away.

As she hurried from the museum, Doña thought she heard Gerard say to Marilou Hamilton, "Quite jealous, I'm afraid," followed by a tittering comment from Marilou.

What did it mean? Doña thought angrily. What the devil had he said to the gossipy Mrs. Hamilton?

Doña could not forget the unpleasant meetings with Philippe Gerard, nor his hint of dangerous knowledge about the Short Line train robbery.

On Monday, as she hurried along Lake Street toward the land office, she was hardly surprised to hear him call out from a private carriage that had pulled up beside her below the elevated walk.

"May I drive you somewhere?"

She turned and walked on quickly.

The carriage began to follow her slowly. When she reached one of the sidewalk stairways, she heard it pause, and Gerard intercepted her on the walkway.

He looked down at her with his piercing black eyes and said softly, "I think it would be to your advantage to talk with me. Now."

Doña was about to frame an indignant reply when she saw the threat in his eyes. "I do not think you want to make a scene," he said.

"What do you want?"

"I want to take you for a little drive, so we can discuss a very important matter."

"What makes you think I want to talk to you?" she asked coldly.

"Don't be difficult, my dear Doña. I know everything. And I want to help you."

Glancing fearfully up at the office windows, Doña saw with relief that no one was looking out. Her body felt cold in the spring sunlight, and her thoughts began to race: what if someone overheard? There was no way out of this. Surely the only thing to do was to go with Gerard.

Still, she was stubborn enough to hold her ground. "I don't know what you're talking about. I want you to leave me alone."

"Very well," he retorted in mock resignation. "You force me to discuss it here, in this public place. I am talking about the matter of certain robberies—in the state of Texas."

A passing woman paused to stare at them curiously, and Doña realized that it was Marilou Hamilton.

"Well, well." Marilou shook her head, and the pink ruffles of her large hat fluttered with the motion. "I've caught you two again, you naughty things!"

Doña started to protest, but seeing the look in Marilou's eyes, she remained silent. Whatever she said to the woman would be misinterpreted. So she asked calmly, "How are you, Mrs. Hamilton?"

Gerard meanwhile stood looking purposely sheepish, smiling like a mischievous boy caught at a forbidden pleasure. Doña wanted desperately to slap them both.

"I'm very well indeed," Marilou said. "And your handsome husband, is he still away?"

"Yes, he's still in New York." Doña was immediately annoyed at herself for confirming the fact.

"Oh, I see," Marilou smiled. "How nice that you have Philippe to console you in his absence."

Doña was too angry to reply.

"Well, I'll be running along." Marilou twinkled at them, wiggling her fingers roguishly at Philippe in farewell.

"I've been telling Marilou how close we are," Gerard said in his soft, insinuating voice. "And I believe she's mentioned it to the Bartletts—and the Palmers and Brinks —probably the Fields, too."

The smile on his face filled Doña with horror.

"What are you trying to do to us?" she demanded.

He took her arm saying, "Come, my dear cousin. We shouldn't discuss these matters on a public street."

He handed her down the sidewalk stairs and into the waiting carriage.

"They will wonder where I am," she protested weakly, as the carriage started off toward the edge of town.

"We will not be long." Gerard's reply was triumphant and calm. His thigh was pressed against hers in the narrow carriage; she drew a little away, and asked bluntly, "How did you know?"

She realized her question had given her away; he laughed, and said smugly, "I have my methods. I have learned of your rather—surprising—occupation in Texas. The bank, the stages, the train. And that your romantic husband forgave you to such an extent that he married you and brought you to Chicago. Which makes him an accessory to a crime."

She was speechless. Then, after the carriage had driven a few jouncing blocks over the muddy, rutted streets, she asked, in an almost inaudible voice, "What do you want?"

"My good friend Alfred Torrance and I—" Gerald grinned, "far from condemning you, greatly admire your enterprise." He leaned toward her.

Stiffly, looking straight ahead, she repeated, "What do you want?"

"You can be of great help to us in a business matter."

"Get to the point," she said savagely.

"You are not courteous," he reproached her. "Very well, I will: you can bring us the bids and correspondence relating to the New York negotiations."

"What?" She turned and frowned at him. "Do you think I would do that to my husband? You must be crazy!"

"Would it be better for the both of you to go to jail?" He was still smiling the smile Doña hated. "There is a certain marshal—what is his name, now? Ah, Bonner! Marshal Bonner would be most interested in the information I have."

He smiled at her expression.

"Listen to me, my dear Doña, and listen well. Torrance wants that information—but more than that, *I* want *you*. And I have always gotten what I wanted, always. No," he held up his hand, "let me finish.

"I would want you even if you were not the wife of a Raike, although I must admit that gives the situation added relish. If you do not help me, I shall continue until I destroy Stephen Raike."

"That's absurd! What can you do to Stephen?"

"It is what I can do to you *both* that is important—already, he shows his jealous dislike of me. And the co-operative Marilou Hamilton is spreading the story of our love affair all over town."

"Our *love* affair!" Doña repeated with disgust.

"Our love affair," Gerard continued calmly. I'm sure Stephen would be fascinated to learn what happened on the night of the Bachelors' Ball."

"That is even more ridiculous! You saw me to my door. The night clerk must have seen you leave the hotel a few minutes later."

"Ah, but the maid Willamae saw me return up the rear stairs, and leave early in the morning," he said triumphantly.

"She wouldn't tell such a lie!"

"My dear Doña, anyone will say anything if the pay is right."

"You—you are despicable," she gasped. "What do you think you'll gain by this?"

"A great deal. Even if he did not believe the stories, the upright Stephen would be so enraged by the gossip that he would be certain to try to shoot me. I have fought seven duels in Louisiana, my dear, and I have left seven men dead."

For a moment Doña wavered. It was hard to imagine a better shot than Stephen was reputed to be, yet Stephen himself had once remarked on Gerard's marksmanship. Even if Stephen were not killed, and he killed Gerard—this was not Texas, or Louisiana! The staid businessmen of the East would be outraged. Worse, Stephen might be imprisoned.

"You are finding every possible way you can to destroy my husband."

"How quick you are, Doña!" Gerard said with maddening smugness. "I am indeed; I am weaving a net with many strands to catch you in. But there *is* a way out for you."

"What do you mean?"

"If you would be—kinder to me," he said significantly, "I might be persuaded to forget the business information."

"If you mean what I think you mean," she retorted, "I would rather kill you first."

"Why, Doña! What a little savage you are. And you are not flattering." He laughed, not at all dismayed by her rough answer. "What do you say? If you become more of a—loving cousin, I will keep quiet about the Short Line, I will put a stop to the talk, I'll even make it right with Torrance about the papers." He moved near her and took her in his arms, his hands kneading her shoulders and her arms, moving toward her breasts.

She shook off his hold, and said coldly, "Take your hands off me." To her surprise, he obeyed.

What a stupid fool I've been, she thought. I should have told Stephen at once; Stephen would have known what to do. But it was too late now. Gerard would never wait for Stephen's return. Doña knew of no way now to hold him off. Well, she would have to do the best she could.

She turned away again and was silent for a long moment. When she spoke, it was with an effort. "And if I do get the information for you, how do you imagine I can get away with it?"

"Oh, come now." Gerard took her hand and she shrank from his touch, but he was holding her so tightly that she could not pull away. "If you are so determined to satisfy Torrance instead of me, surely anyone as enterprising as you can manage that. You could copy the information."

"I don't know," she said in a tight voice. "He's probably taken the papers with him to New York. And what guarantee have I that you'll leave us alone?"

"You have my word as a gentleman."

Doña laughed. "Thank you very much. And how am I to deliver this information to you?"

"Come to Torrance's house on Randolph Street."

"How can you ask that?" she cried. "I will be recognized. I can't. I can't."

"Lower your voice, my dear Doña. As I said before, any lady as enterprising as you will find a way to go *incognito*. I have a feeling you did that well enough, in your blue scarf, when you were robbing trains."

Willamae! So that was it. To her horror, Doña felt very near tears. But she'd be damned if she'd let Philippe Gerard see her cry.

Choking back her tears, she said, "All right. I'll do it."

The carriage had turned and was re-entering the populous section of town. "Stop here," Gerard said to the driver.

Disdaining Gerard's helping hand, Doña struggled down from the carriage, stepping directly into the deep mud, furious as she heard Gerard's mocking laughter.

Chapter Nineteen

At half-past five, when the others were getting ready to leave, Matilda Johnston saw Doña still at her desk. She did not remark on it, assuming Doña had nothing better to do while Stephen was away.

But Jeb, the junior clerk, the last to leave, paused at the door and asked shyly, "Will you be all right here, ma'am?"

"Of course," Doña replied sharply. Then, ashamed of her irritable reaction to the boy's concern, said more gently, "Yes, Jeb. Thank you."

He looked hesitant, but answered, "All right. Good night, Mrs. Raike."

"Good night."

Doña listened to his footsteps fade down the wooden stairs. With trembling hands she began to tidy up her desk. She walked to the window and looked up and down Lake Street. No sign of the boy. Expelling her breath in relief, she went into Stephen's office.

There was a cold, sick feeling in her stomach, the same apprehensive excitement she had so often experienced in the old days, before she had ridden on raids with Tahre and the other men.

She dared not think about the thing she must do, only that she must do it. There was no other way. And she set to work quickly, methodically, listening all the while for any sound of a footstep ascending the stairs.

She took a small key from under the blotter on Stephen's desk and went with it to a locked cabinet in the corner. She knew exactly where to look and what to take—if the papers were there. Stephen had gone over the Eastern matter with her several times. All the figures, the letters and deeds were in one neat folder in the bottom drawer.

A footfall sounded then outside on the stairs. Doña paused, transfixed before the confidential file, her heart fluttering in her ears. But the footsteps did not pause, continuing down, not up the stairs.

She drew a shuddering breath. Someone from Keen and Lee, upstairs, she thought. Her body was dizzy with panic; she leaned for a time against the file until she could control the shaking of her hands and knees.

Quickly she withdrew the file. The papers were there! Jeb must have made copies for Stephen to take to New York. She glanced at the file to see that all was in order and slammed the cabinet shut. The lock clicked. Too late, she saw that an edge of paper had gotten caught in the drawer and protruded.

Her fingers were quivering so that it was difficult to insert the key again into the lock, but she finally managed. Another sound reached her from the corridor.

She was breathing now almost in sobs, and the key was stuck in the lock. She tugged at it, breathing quickly and hoarsely.

At last it gave, and she straightened the offending paper in its folder, slamming the cabinet door again. The sound in the corridor had stopped. Now there was only silence.

Doña hurried to Stephen's desk, replaced the key, and hastily went into her own cubicle. Sitting at her desk, she began the laborious task of copying the file.

For two successive nights, she stayed late to finish the copying.

On the third night, she rose from her desk and stretched her arms, sighing with relief. Her eyes stung from the close scrutiny of the small figures, her head and neck and back ached. But she sat down once again to check her final copy with the original.

Then, stiffly, she replaced the original papers in the file and locked it again in the cabinet in Stephen's office.

236

As she emerged into the dusk of the street, she saw Philippe Gerard in a carriage in front of the office.

He called her name softly, and she went to the carriage on reluctant feet, frowning.

"What are you doing here?" she asked coldly. "Do you want us to be seen together?"

"My dear Doña," he said with his unpleasant smile, "it is always a pleasure to be seen with a woman so beautiful."

"What do you want?"

"Get in," he ordered curtly. She thought it would be wise to comply and got in the carriage. "I want to know if you have the information."

"Here it is," she said, thrusting it at him. "Take it."

"Oh, no, my dear lady."

She stared at him, puzzled. "Why not? It's what you wanted."

"I want you to come to Torrance's place tonight at midnight."

"But why? Why do you ask that of me?" she demanded, on the point of tears in her nervous exhaustion.

"Because it amuses me, my dear Doña. It will amuse me to see you among the gamesters and the whores."

She looked at him in disgust. But it was clear that she would have to play his cruel game, down to the last detail. "I suppose I have no choice," she said.

"No, you do not. Now, my dear Doña, let me drive you back to the hotel."

She was too tired to protest further and leaned back in the carriage, closing her eyes.

Neither of them noticed that someone was watching from another carriage, a tall, lean man with gray eyes.

When Stephen saw Philippe Gerard and Doña, he had felt his customary reaction. His blood boiled. Home from New York, at last, he had been on his way to the hotel, but, passing the land office, he had noticed the carriage in front and had the driver stop when he saw Gerard in it. Then, to his amazement, Doña came out of the office and after a short discussion, got into the carriage with Gerard.

Curiosity as much as anger made him follow them on

their odd little circular journey. He realized that they must have been making an assignation for later, when after only a few minutes Doña emerged from the carriage a full block from their hotel.

Pure rage made him gasp for breath and he called to the driver to move on. Even if he had known what to say to Doña, even if he had wanted to confront her now, it was well nigh impossible because the wagons and carriages and carts on both sides of the muddy street were jammed together.

What in the name of God did it mean? What had she been doing with Gerard? How long had that been going on?

The tortured questions were thundering in Stephen's brain. As the driver paused before the Green Room Tavern next to McVicker's Theater, Stephen decided to get out and have a drink. Drinking was not a usual solution for Stephen, but he felt he needed time to think. So he thanked the driver and headed toward the doorway where the white-aproned barkeep lounged beneath a huge sign that proclaimed "Sands Pale Cream Ale" was sold there.

Doña entered the suite and suddenly felt torn between anxiety and an overwhelming relief. Stephen was obviously not back from New York. Conscious suddenly of the heavy carryall containing the copied material, she threw it on the bed. She grabbed a handkerchief and began dabbing at her face, feeling the unpleasant moisture of perspiration in her clothes and at the edges of her hair. She had not realized until now how terrified she had been. Her whole body was clammy and chilled.

Taking off her hat and jacket, she called the maid to prepare her bath.

When Willamae entered the sitting room, Doña recalled all at once what the woman had done; the sick feeling in her stomach worsened, the chill on her flesh turned icy. But Willamae, again, did not meet her eyes; she prepared the bath and hurried away without her usual friendly goodbye.

Everything, everything has changed, Doña thought

sadly. There was nothing now but hostility and fear. She dared not look ahead, dared not think of what would happen when the New York project fell through. Stephen had told her he would take a staggering loss if the deal were not consummated.

What a fool she'd been! She should have thought of something, but she was so upset and confused. Now she was committed to follow through.

A cold sweat broke out again on her body, soaking her shirtwaist and underthings. Well, she could not think of it now. First there was this terrible night to get through, and that would be hard enough.

She hurried to the bathroom and undressed, sinking with relief into the steaming tub. When she emerged, she dried herself and slipped into a loose wrapper and sat on the bed worrying.

Doña ordered dinner to be sent up to the suite. She was so apprehensive she could barely swallow; after picking at the meal, she sent it away again.

For what seemed hours, she paced the suite. At intervals, she lay down on the bed, in a vain attempt to rest for the ordeal ahead.

Once, half-drowsing in her exhaustion, she relived in her mind the six months of her acquaintance with Stephen. Six months! It seemed like a lifetime.

Her body was warm suddenly with yearning, her heart heavy with regret. Perhaps, she thought, perhaps I should have waited and told him of Gerard's threats! But no, they would fight each other, and Stephen might be killed.

Killed. When the word repeated itself silently to Doña, she shivered. If Stephen died—if he died, she could not bear it.

I could not bear it! Doña thought. And she missed his strong presence then more than she ever had thought possible; she missed him deeply, achingly.

Where was the old hatred, the ancient desire for revenge? She did not know in that moment. She only knew she missed Stephen, needed him. How much had changed in these last months.

"No," she whispered aloud, lying on the wide bed and

staring out the window at the sky of spring. "No, I could not have told him. I brought this on myself, and only I can make it right."

He would sustain the financial loss; everything would work out. . . . Only *she* must face Gerard. She drifted into half-sleep.

The clock on the table by the bed indicated eleven when she woke. She raised herself slowly, listening. Faintly through the open door she heard the sound of heavy, even breathing from the sitting room.

Surprised, she rose without sound and tiptoed to the door. Stephen was asleep on the sofa, still wearing his boots. His hat lay on the floor.

Mystified, she moved softly toward him. Then the strong aroma of bourbon explained it all. He had gotten drunk! Stephen, drunk. And he rarely drank at all.

But she could not pause now to puzzle it out, to wonder what it meant. His returning now was a piece of bad luck, but if he did not wake—then she might keep her terrible appointment and return before he knew that she had gone.

Nevertheless, she could not resist pulling off his boots to make him a little more comfortable. He still did not wake, only turned, half-smiling, at the ease of being unburdened.

With desperate haste, Doña returned to the bedroom and began to dress. She chose a plain brown dress and threw a black cloak around herself. On her head a black lace mantilla that she had bought in Texas but had never worn.

She took up the brown carryall containing the file and tiptoed through the sitting room past Stephen. He seemed to be deeply asleep.

Doña held her breath until she was at the end of the corridor. She ran down the back stairs used by the servants. Once, when a maid passed her—she thanked her luck that it was not Willamae—Doña turned her head away and pulled her mantilla forward.

Behind her she heard the woman's footsteps pause, aware of her curiosity, but hurried on until she reached a rear exit from the Sherman House.

On the dark street, she was possessed of a new dismay: an unescorted woman, at this hour, could only be taken for a woman of the streets. She hesitated, fumbling below her cloak, glad that she had had the presence of mind to pin on her watch. She consulted the small golden timepiece and realized there was not much time left before her meeting with Torrance and Gerard.

She hailed a private coach, asking to be let off at Randolph Street. Doña read the coachman's amazement as he helped her in; such a pale, quietly dressed woman was a strange fare to Hairtrigger Block.

Stephen opened his eyes, his head pounding, his mouth dry, but cold sober.

His feet felt strangely light. He looked down. His boots were on the carpet beside the sofa.

Doña had taken off his boots.

"She took them off," he said aloud.

Why would a woman take off her husband's boots to make him comfortable, when she was going out to meet another man? Surely that was where she was headed: her stealth, the dark scarf concealing her hair and half her face. It could only mean that Gerard was her lover.

Slowly, to ease the pounding of his head, the queasiness of his stomach, Stephen raised himself from the sofa.

He padded to the bedroom in his stocking feet and changed his linens for fresh ones. He washed his face and combed his hair. Then he went back to the sitting room and put on his boots. Rising he went to a cabinet by the window and, opening one of its drawers, took a revolver from the drawer.

He loaded it quickly, and picked up his hat from the floor, settling it low over his brow.

When Stephen left the suite, his heart was sore and angry. But he was still puzzling over the matter of the boots.

Chapter Twenty

As the coach reached Randolph Street, Doña was not reassured by the sight of the rough pedestrian traffic. Mingling with the gamblers in expensive but gaudy clothes, were staggering sailors and soldiers, unshaven plainsmen and seedy-looking men, shabbily dressed, who cursed and shouted, elbowing their way among the others. There were almost no women; the few who were there were obviously prostitutes, smiling professionally and undismayed by the hurly-burly air of the block.

When Doña called out, "Here," the coachman reined in and descended to help her to the rough plank sidewalk.

As she was paying him, he asked hesitantly, "Are you sure this is the place you want, ma'am? This is no place for you."

"I want Mr. Torrance's house," Doña said curtly.

"Mr. Torrance's! But there are no women allowed there except—" The driver stopped, peering at Doña's unpainted face, the dark elegance of her clothes.

"I want Mr. Torrance's house. The rear entrance."

"Ohhh—" the man said, and his expression altered. Grinning, he said with indifference, "Right down there, girlie." And he turned away, remounting without a backward glance.

Doña took a deep breath and walked determinedly down the noisy sidewalk in the direction indicated by the coachman. She cursed herself for coming, regretting bitterly now that she had not waited to confide in Stephen.

I'm a bigger fool than I thought, she judged as she hurried along with bent head, pulling the sheltering black lace forward to hide her features. A tipsy man in clothes of dusty buckskin suddenly barred her way. He bowed unsteadily, removing his battered, broad-brimmed hat, and mumbled, "Can I buy you a glass of wine?"

For a brief moment, she paused and looked up into his bleary eyes. He exuded a strong smell of sweat and bourbon, and when he smiled at her, his teeth were broken and tobacco-stained.

Turning her head away, she rushed past him down the rough walk, hoping her small heels would not catch in the splintery planks to delay her, dreading the next encounter.

A soldier caught her by the arm. She cried out, shaking off his grasp with a strength that surprised her, and began to run the rest of the way.

After what seemed a nightmare of grabbing hands and leering faces, she reached a dark alleyway that was blessedly quiet and empty.

She reached a dimly lit door, but not before her foot had encountered a limp, trousered leg in the shadows. Doña screamed: the leg belonged to a ragged, sleeping man lying against a trash barrel. Again she was assailed with the strong odor of stale drink. She almost sobbed with relief, for the man had not moved or noticed her at all. Even her loud outcry had not disturbed his sodden sleep.

Doña rapped sharply on the door, feeling dizzy and sick with dread. At last the door opened, and a narrow bar of light pierced the darkness of the alley.

A black man wearing a white apron greeted her. He had sad eyes and a gentle face, and without surprise he listened as she asked in a trembling voice for Philippe Gerard. Standing aside, he signaled for her to enter.

The elevator was very slow, and Stephen Raike had no stomach for waiting. He walked rapidly down the three flights of stairs to the lobby of the Sherman House.

The surprised night clerk watched Stephen stride by, without a greeting, through the lobby to the street.

Trying to ignore the cold ache of anger within him,

Stephen concentrated on the grim task ahead. He walked quickly to the small stable adjoining the hotel and entered. The hostler was asleep on a cot near the door.

With the practiced ease of man long used to horses, Stephen led his horse from the stall, and hitched the animal to the trap, hardly knowing what his hands did, like a man moving in his sleep.

As he drove the trap away, he ignored the startled cry of the awakened hostler and headed for Randolph Street.

Driving alone on the quiet streets, Stephen was suddenly struck as if by a physical blow, with the remembered picture of Doña on their wedding night in Galveston. His heart began to pound in his ears, as it had that night, when he opened the bedroom door.

And vividly, he was with her again. The night had been a little cool, he recalled, and she was standing by the hearth. He could see through her thin nightgown her naked body with its slender roundness.

The memory brought a hard, bitter laugh to Stephen's throat. He was almost at Torrance's

Stephen had wanted only to make Doña love him. And he had done everything he knew to bring it about—given her everything he could, even taken her into his business, when he knew other men would laugh at him for spoiling her. None of it had mattered, none of it!

Her body had responded to his, with a passion equal to his own. Yet all these months she had never said what he was so anxious to hear. She had never said, "I love you." Never once had she said a word of love, even while she was being pleasured—as if he were a damned . . . fancy man.

Stephen Raike's anger flared anew, hotter than ever, and he felt again the terrible ache in himself, an ache he could not name. It was probably the hurt to his pride, he thought somberly, the famous Raike pride that had made the name a Texas legend, that had made the name of Stephen Raike a proud one in Chicago.

Well, his name would still mean something when he had taken care of Gerard. There was not a jury in the country that would condemn a man for protecting what was his.

Stephen tried to put out of his mind the memories that would weaken his resolve—the memory of a brave, red-haired young girl who had sworn to avenge the Olwens' murder; the childlike excitement she displayed when he had given her still another present or amusement; the sweetness of her in his arms—

No, he thought angrily, Gerard has known that, too! And that was why she had never told him she loved him. She loved Philippe Gerard.

All this time they had been lovers. Stephen felt for the gun in his pocket. Its cold, metallic presence was a great comfort now.

He knew where he would find them: around town it was pretty common knowledge that Gerard, the woman-izer, spent a great deal of time in rooms above the gambling chamber in Torrance's house.

Yes, when he found the two of them, he would put paid to his account with Philippe Gerard.

And Doña. What about her?

He could not think of her now, could not decide what he would do about her. But he had a feeling that he never wanted to look in her eyes again.

Stephen found himself in the noise and hurry of Hair-trigger Block and came to his senses with a start. Guiding the horse to an empty lot a little way from Torrance's, he reined in and tied the animal to a scrubby tree.

Crossing the muddy street, he leaped onto the plank sidewalk, scorning the stairs, and began to shoulder his way through the crowd toward Torrance's gambling house.

A streetwalker, noticing his lithe body and handsome face, accosted him. But his cold gray eyes looked right through her; he looked so strange she was almost glad he had not responded.

Alfred Torrance sat in his office, pouring two glasses of whiskey. He handed one to Philippe Gerard.

"So where are we meeting the redskin, Phil?"

Gerard frowned. More and more, Torrance's manners were becoming a source of annoyance to the elegant Creole. He sipped his whiskey and answered, "She's coming here, at midnight."

"Coming here!"

Torrance paused in the act of lighting his cigar to glare at his companion. "You damned game-playing fool. Why did you do that? Do you want them to connect this with us? They will, you know."

Gerard repressed his indignation. He was not fond of Torrance's name-calling. Nevertheless he managed to say casually, "No one will know her, I assure you. I told her to come here in disguise."

Torrance made a disgusted sound. "This isn't your goddamned Mardi Gras, Gerard. This is Chicago. And this is business—big business, not some kind of college prank."

This was not the first time Torrance had mocked Gerard's origins, sneered at his education, which, he considered, had made the Creole soft. Gerard at this moment was finding it increasingly hard not to lash out at the gambler.

And Torrance, in his turn, liked their association less and less. Gerard's arrogance was getting harder to take. If only the bastard didn't have entry into so many respectable houses, Torrance thought, I'd dump him like a shot.

But then there had been the St. Louis connection, too. And Gerard had been extremely helpful in conscripting men, with his slick line of talk.

Torrance bit down on his cigar. Remembering it was still unlit, he applied a match to it. His grim expression did not lighten.

"You are so irritable, my friend." Gerard's soft words made Torrance even angrier than before.

"I still don't like it, I tell you. What if Raike shows up? I don't want any trouble in my place. It's the only house on Hairtrigger Block that's had no trouble yet."

"I am not surprised. You pay the police enough. As for Raike, I don't think he'll show up. He isn't in town at the moment."

Torrance started to say something further but was interrupted by a quick knock on the door.

"What is it?" he asked sourly. A white-aproned black with sad eyes stuck his head tentatively through the crack of the opened door.

"Mr. Torrance, sir?"

"Well?"

"There's a lady—lady at the back, asking for you and Mr. Gerard."

"Well, don't just stand there, Henry. Bring her in, for Christ's sake."

The dark head disappeared and the door closed with little sound. In a short time the man returned with Doña Raike.

Gerard exclaimed. He had never seen her so pale and grim; in these few hours her young face seemed to have thinned. There were purple shadows under her eyes. And still the face concealed in part by the black mantilla was more beautiful, somehow.

Mon dieu! he said to himself. She is a prize for any man, and I am going to have her.

"My dear cousin," he said in his effusive way, coming toward her, bowing over her hand.

She seemed not to see him at all; her hard eyes gazed through him in a way that was disconcerting to a man accustomed to charming women. As if she were alone in the room with Torrance, Doña looked only at the gambler. She took the file from her carryall and held it out to Torrance, saying abruptly, "Here it is. I must go."

"Not so fast." Torrance took the folder from her and grabbed her narrow wrist with his other hand. She cried out in pain, and Gerard took a step forward.

"Sit down," Torrance ordered. "I'm going to look this over before I let you go. You don't think I'd trust a common little thief, do you?"

An indignant flush dyed her pale cheeks, and Gerard uttered a low curse, taking another step forward.

In a cold, controlled voice, Doña said, "I prefer to stand."

"Suit yourself." Torrance sat down at his desk and

began to scrutinize the papers in the folder. He studied every word with care; he ran his blunt finger down the columns of figures. Doña stirred restively. Now and then the gambler grunted, in question or pleasure; occasionally he betrayed surprise.

"Well," he said to himself. "Well, well." He turned to her then and demanded, "So this is the goods? If you've manufactured this, if you're stringing us along, I'll make you regret it, I guarantee you."

"Those are the figures, that is the information you need." Doña sounded on the verge of tears, and Gerard said uneasily, "Come now, Al."

"Shut up," Torrance said harshly. "What about this?" He addressed Doña. "Come here."

Doña did not move. Her look met the gambler's head-on.

"I said, come here." She glanced at Gerard as if in appeal, and the younger man cried out, "Need you use that tone?"

"I've told you, Gerard, your women don't interest me. This is business."

Doña turned to Gerard accusingly and demanded, "What does he mean, 'your women'? What lies have you told him about me?"

Torrance chuckled and said with a nasty inflection, "I wonder what your redskin here would think if she knew about your—private games."

Gerard's face was suffused with anger, and, too late, Torrance realized his mistake. "Forget it, Phil. Maybe I spoke out of turn." He was anxious to get back to the subject at hand. In a milder voice, he said to Doña, "There's some kind of mix-up here, it seems to me. You'd better explain it to me now." His voice hardened again. "Or you and your fine-feathered husband will end up in jail."

Reluctantly Doña came toward the desk and stood at Torrance's side.

"Here." The heavy finger indicated a group of figures. "What about that?"

Doña looked at the figures and replied brusquely, "The

bid was raised during negotiations. That's why this change was made."

Torrance put down the papers and looked up at the pallid woman standing by his elbow. "You're a regular little encyclopedia. I guess you were right, Phil, she knows her stuff all right."

"May I leave now?" Doña's question was stiff and cold.

"All right, girlie. You're pretty smart for an Indian, I must say." He laughed, noticing her clenched fists and angry eyes. "Bet you wish you had your gun right now, don't you?"

"That's enough, Al." Gerard's exclamation took the gambler by surprise.

"What's eating you, Gerard?" Torrance rose slowly from his chair, confronting the Creole.

"I said that's enough. Why are you baiting her? Our business is done, and now I am going to take her away."

Torrance laughed loudly. "Take her away! You won't have much luck with this little spitfire. Better stick to Molly's girls. They might put up with your nasty ways."

Then Torrance's laughter died; his face underwent a sudden and drastic change. Gerard's face was white as paper, as he reached into the pocket of his trousers.

"What the hell are you doing?" Torrance's voice turned into a croak of fear.

Doña was edging toward the door, but when she saw the object in Gerard's hand, she was hesitant to move. She had seen men shoot wildly before when anyone made too sudden a movement.

"I've had enough of your coarse mouth." Gerard aimed the pistol at Torrance. "And I've had enough of your jibes about my ancestry, my city, my education and manners and personal life." His smooth voice was almost unrecognizable; it was shrill with a rage of madness.

"Why don't you just simmer down, Phil?" Torrance retorted. Slowly, almost imperceptibly, the big man's heavy hand reached toward a drawer in his desk. With desperate calm, Torrance spoke again. "You don't want to do anything you'll regret, now, Phil. Why don't you just take the lady and go?"

Even in her horror, Doña was aware of all that was going on below the surface; Torrance was playing for time. Transfixed, she watched the two men—Torrance, outwardly cool, standing with his hand on his desk; Gerard with the look of a man who would soon be out of control.

"Don't move." Gerard's easy Creole manner was gone. His words were clipped and hard.

All at once behind her, through the closed door, Doña heard men shouting, heard someone cry out, "You can't go in there, sir! That's a private room! You can't go in there!"

There was a loud curse, a scuffle, and the door opened with such violent suddenness it slammed back against the wall, jarring Gerard's gun arm. His fingers jerked convulsively, the gun in his hand discharging with a deafening explosion.

With a dreadful look of pained surprise, Alfred Torrance crashed to the floor. Blood gushed from a terrible flower-shaped hole in his massive forehead.

Doña cried out and turned to the door.

Standing there with a gun in his hand was Stephen Raike.

Gerard recovered himself and jammed his gun into his pocket.

Amidst the confusion of voices, Doña heard another man bellow, "This man killed Torrance."

The black waiter and an elegantly dressed young man, who seemed to have come in right behind Stephen, stepped aside as Torrance's men rushed in. The elegant young man turned and slipped away.

Doña stood stunned for a moment, then screamed, "Stephen!" and moved toward him, but to her horror he would not look at her at all. He continued to stare with savage hatred at Gerard.

In the next few crowded, chaotic moments, Doña hardly knew what was happening. With dizzying rapidity, everything began to move at once: she was aware of gun barrels trained on Stephen. Without a struggle he let himself be led away.

In a swift, awful instant, she saw a look in his eyes she had never seen before—a stare of unseeing, angry resignation.

Once more she cried his name, but he gave no sign that he had heard.

Then Philippe Gerard grasped her arm, and said curtly, "Come! Come out of here!" She tried to protest, but his grip was unrelenting, so she screamed out to the sad-eyed black waiter, who was standing as if hypnotized in the open door, "I've got to be with my husband!"

One of the gamblers in the outer room turned when he heard her cry, but Gerard only laughed and said to the man, "Molly's girls are getting above themselves. He slept with her once and now he's her husband."

The listener gave a shrug and turned away.

Sobbing loudly now, Doña felt herself being dragged along in the iron grip of Gerard. "Now, Doña," he said soothingly, "Doña, come with me. We will go upstairs now and you can rest."

Suddenly, she began to fight him then with a tigerish strength. "Go upstairs!" she screamed. "Go upstairs with *you*? You must be mad!"

She felt mad herself with the intensity of her desperation, the fire of her overpowering anger. But the few who noticed her, in the milling crowd about Stephen and his captors, did not give her a second glance.

With a sinking heart, she knew no one would help her; they would assume that she was one of Gerard's whores. And the realization gave her new strength; she wrenched herself from Gerard's grasp, biting his reaching hand as savagely as a wild animal.

The brief moment of his instinctive recoil gave her the chance she needed, and she raced, running like a deer down the corridor, toward the rear door of Torrance's house.

When she reached the sheltering darkness of the alley, she concealed herself behind the large trash barrels there, to gain her breath and plan her next move.

And in the lonely dark, taking grateful gulps of air into her tortured lungs, Doña knew at last what she had feared

251

to admit from the first—when she had first looked into Stephen's eyes, above the barrel of her gun. She loved him. She loved him without doubt and without reservation, she loved him with all her heart and body. Now that it was too late.

3

Return

Chapter Twenty-One

"Take his gun," said the burly man who held Stephen's left arm. A thin man with a seamed face—one of the gamesters, if one judged by his clothes, took the Colt from Stephen's hand.

"Did anybody call the police?" the thin man asked.

"Long John's Devils?" the burly man scoffed. "Not likely. We've got to talk things over first. Bring him in here." He indicated a small room off the main salon.

Stephen did not resist: he had fought it out many a time with one or two men, even four. But now there were at least five guns pointing at him, more than twenty hostile men around him.

The burly man shoved him into the small room. Then he called out, "You—Marshall, Jackson, Pierce. Come in here. The rest of you wait out there, will you?"

"Who are you?" Stephen said bluntly to the burly fellow.

"Robert Dexter, if it's any of your business. Sit in that chair."

Robert Dexter. Stephen remembered hearing him called Torrance's "right hand." Stephen stayed where he was.

"I said sit down." Dexter made a significant motion with his Smith & Wesson. Shrugging, Stephen sat down in the straight, hard chair.

"Close the door, Pierce," Dexter ordered the thin man with the seamed face.

Stephen looked at the others. One was very small, with a hard-bitten face like a monkey; he looked like a jockey. The other was obscenely fat and he had very small, mean eyes. A fine crew, Stephen thought trying to shut out the picture of Doña cowering in Torrance's office. What in the hell had she been doing there?

The nasal voice of Dexter broke in on Stephen's thoughts. "Why did you shoot Al?"

"I didn't. It was an accident. Gerard did."

The small man with the monkey face cursed and shouted, "That's crazy! Phil Gerard was his partner."

"Shut up, Jackson," Dexter said.

"My gun wasn't fired," Stephen told Dexter calmly. "If you'll smell it, you'll know I'm telling the truth."

"Give me that Colt," Dexter said to the gaunt Pierce. Pierce handed him Stephen's Colt. Dexter raised the gun barrel to his broad nose and sniffed deeply.

"It hasn't been fired." Dexter looked at the others. "We're up the creek if they get this gun. The word'll get out—and they'll be here soon, you can bet."

"The gun hasn't been fired *yet*. That doesn't mean it can't be." Philippe Gerard had entered the room, and his voice was smooth again, insinuating. He was once more in command of himself, not a hair of his dark head was ruffled. He smiled at the four men.

Stephen made an impulsive movement forward, glaring at the Creole, but all too soon the fat man shoved Stephen back into the chair and was pinioning his arms behind him. The fat man's strength was prodigious, and Stephen at last gave in.

"You're right, Phil," Dexter said, and handed the Colt to Gerard. "Will you do the honors?"

"With more pleasure than you know." Gerard stared at Stephen, his dark eyes glittering with malicious triumph. He hurried from the room. They heard, from the direction of the alley, the sound of a pistol being fired.

In moments, Gerard was back with the smoking pistol in his hand. "Now, gentlemen," he said softly, "we're ready for all the devils Long John can send."

Angrily Stephen struggled in the fat man's grasp. But his eyes, cold with hatred, did not leave Philippe Gerard.

Even as Gerard broke into laughter, he read the gray eyes' message and his laugh rang hollow.

From her hiding place in the alley, Doña had waited in the shadows, praying that Gerard would not find her. At one point, she had nearly fainted with terror: there was a gunshot and a man's footsteps struck the rear stairs, and a thin blade of lamplight stabbed the friendly darkness.

She held her breath, crouching behind the trash barrels, and waited. Finally she heard an impatient curse, and then miraculously the footsteps receded, the door was shut and the sheltering blackness fell again.

Almost sobbing with relief, she listened a little while longer and, hearing no one, scrambled to her feet and ran into the night.

But she was weak with the aftermath of fear and horror; she knew she could not go much farther on foot. And she had reached a deserted block where no carriage would be passing by at this hour.

Desperate with indecision, she stood for a moment in the blackness, turning this way and that. She would be lost, surely, if she continued in this direction, and could imagine what perils lay in the deserted night. Better to face those she knew!

And reluctantly Doña turned and began to walk rapidly toward Hairtrigger Block; she could lose herself in the milling crowds and in the confusion find a carriage to take her back to the hotel. Already, as she neared the busy scene, the noise outside Torrance's house had reached a crescendo.

Stepping into a shadow, she saw that the police wagon had arrived. Escorted by an armed man on either side, Stephen was being herded into the wagon. She cried out involuntarily, then covered her mouth.

But in the babble of the street, her cry was no more than a whisper.

"Stephen," she called out, and then she realized that she had called his name without sound.

A curious coachman had pulled up his cab at the edge of the crowd and sat staring. Doña drew her mantilla over her face and hurried to the carriage, her small boots clinging to the ever-present mud, making her progress painful and awkward.

"Please," she said breathlessly to the coachman, and again realized that she could barely make herself heard. "Please," she said more loudly, with a great effort, knocking on the window of the carriage.

Attracted by the sharp sound, the coachman turned and got down obligingly to help her in.

"Just a minute, lady," he said through the window. "Want to see what's going on. Some excitement here."

She nodded helplessly and leaned back against the cushions of the carriage, trembling so that she could no longer hold the mantilla about her face. It slid away and fell onto the cushion. She felt the tears gathering in her eyes, blinding her, and convulsive sobs tearing at her body. In the noise, she knew that no one heard.

When the police wagon had jolted away, the coachman returned to the window and said excitedly, "Somebody killed in there, looks like. Seems they arrested the culprit."

Doña covered her face with her hand.

"Well," the man added, "they won't hold him long. These gamblers always get off. Where to?"

Doña summoned all her courage, almost too overcome to speak. At last she managed to say, "The Sherman House."

When the driver had delivered her to her destination, she stood before the entrance until he had gone, then hurried around to the rear. The door was locked.

Holding her scarf about her face, Doña retreated again to the shadows to wait. Now she was nearly dropping with exhaustion. Her eyelids felt leaden; she could not stay awake much longer.

Sitting down dejectedly, she leaned against a wall. Its protrusion would hide her for the moment.

Dawn was coming, and the sky was gray before she was jerked from her sleep by the sound of the unlocking door. It was almost time for the milk to be delivered, she judged. And finding the door open, she slipped through it and made her weary way up three flights of stairs to her suite, meeting no one on the way.

When she had reached the haven of her rooms, she locked the sitting-room door and leaned against it, weeping. She flung the mantilla from her aching head and stumbled into the bedroom. Without even removing her cloak, she flung herself on the bed, weak with fatigue, her heart pounding loudly.

She was so tired she ached in every bone and muscle. Yet sleep would not come. Trembling still, she made herself rise and undress. Then she unpinned her hair and shook it out over her shoulders. She took a deep, shuddering breath and lay down again, staring out at the arriving day.

Again and again her weary mind repeated, I love him, I love him. And he had not even looked at her with hate. She could have borne that, for everyone knew that hatred was akin to desire.

But he had not looked at her at all. If he saw her, he saw her as a woman in league with Torrance and Gerard.

Gerard! The name repeated itself loudly in her brain. That's why Stephen was there—that's why he was carrying a gun. He thinks that I was meeting Gerard!

Doña sat up in the bed, stricken with a new dismay. "But I must tell him!" she said aloud. Yes, she must go to Stephen and tell him that it wasn't true, that she loved him, only him, and never any other.

She would tell him why she had gone to Torrance's house. No matter how it angered him, it was better for him to know that, than to think that she was having an affair with Gerard.

With new hope, Doña rose again and went to wash herself in the cold water left over from the night before. And as she found fresh underthings and dressed herself, arranging her bright hair anew, she planned what she would say to Stephen.

It wouldn't be long now until she could see him. Surely the police would allow a visit from his wife!

And when I see him . . . when I tell him, Doña

thought with a high heart, everything will be all right again I know.

Suddenly her weariness was forgotten.

Josiah Bartlett, attorney, was a man Stephen Raike had always trusted. The soft-spoken Yankee, with his shrewd blue eyes and grizzled hair, had handled business affairs for Stephen since he had first arrived in Chicago.

Now, in the early morning light of the grim little room in the city jail, as Bartlett sat across the table from Stephen, a worried frown creased his lofty brow.

"I can take care of the business, Steve, as you know. But I'm no criminal lawyer."

"All we have to do is tell the truth," Stephen said again. He was grimy and exhausted; there were deep circles under his gray eyes, and an itchy stubble had appeared on his chin.

"It's not that easy, I'm afraid," Bartlett said patiently. "It all sounds too—unlikely. Making a jury believe they fired your gun."

Stephen started to protest, but Bartlett held up his hand, saying, "Wait a minute. I know, I know. But even men like Dexter and Pierce and Marshall have witnesses. You have only your wife. And she was there under—" Bartlett paused delicately. "Questionable circumstances, to say the least."

"Leave her out of this," Stephen said coldly. "I will have no more to do with her."

"I can understand your feelings, of course." Bartlett's tone was conciliatory. "But in case of real need, her testimony, biased as it might appear to a jury, may be needed."

"I will have nothing further to do with my wife." Stephen's words were hard and final. Bartlett shook his head. "You've already gotten my instructions on what to do about a—a provision for her. That's it."

Bartlett sighed. "Very well. Now I want to go over your instructions again."

He consulted his notes. "You want to rescind the partnership agreement drawn up just recently, allowing your wife a voice in the running of Raike Lands and Raike Stages."

Stephen nodded grimly.

"You want this lump sum—" in his cautious way Bartlett showed the figures to Stephen without stating them, but glanced at the guard "—paid to her account and this allowance paid regularly so long as she is not—" Bartlett cleared his throat "—cohabiting with another man?"

"Yes."

Bartlett repeated the other instructions relating to the trusteeship of the businesses.

"I hope such provisions won't have to be enacted, Steve, and that you'll be running things again very soon."

"It's all right, Jos. You don't have to say that. You admitted it looked bad. Well, I want the businesses in good hands, just in case."

"All right, just in case." Bartlett gathered up his papers and put them in a briefcase, preparing to leave.

The guard rattled at the barred door. "Somebody to see the prisoner," he called.

Bartlett got up and went to the door. "Who is it?"

"Mrs. Raike."

The attorney turned back to Stephen. Stephen shook his head.

"Stephen—" Bartlett began. He had met Doña Raike and liked her. "Don't you think you should at least talk with her?"

"I have nothing to say. You'll be in touch with her. And Jos, send my junior clerk to the hotel, would you, to pick up a few things I'll need?"

"Very well." To the guard Bartlett said, "The prisoner does not wish to see Mrs. Raike."

The guard stared at Stephen an instant, then opened the door for Bartlett, and gestured to Stephen. "I'll be back for you," he said.

As the guard and the attorney walked down the corridor, the guard exclaimed, "What's the matter with him? If I had a wife like that—" He shook his head.

"It's a long story," Josiah Bartlett said.

Tipping his hat to Doña as he passed her, Bartlett went out into the bright April morning with a sad heart.

The fact that the amiable Josiah Bartlett did not stop to speak with her was a shock to Doña. When they had met in the homes of mutual acquaintances, or briefly in the office, the attorney had always been the soul of friendliness.

But now, seeing his half-averted face, Doña concluded that he was embarrassed, but she didn't understand why.

The answer came to her when the uneasy guard approached her and said, "I'm sorry, ma'am. The fact is—"

"What is it?"

"Your, er—husband doesn't want to see you, ma'am." The guard looked miserably away from her stricken face.

Doña thanked him with all the calm she could muster and hurried out of the jail. Josiah Bartlett was standing indecisively on the street.

"Mr. Bartlett!" she cried, and, raising her silken skirts above the splintery planks, hurried toward him.

His hat was in his hand, and he flushed. "I am a coward, Mrs. Raike."

"A coward?"

"Forgive me. I should never have let the guard be the one to tell you what he did. But I—didn't have the heart," Bartlett said.

"Mr. Bartlett, you've got to help me!" she pleaded.

"Have you had any breakfast, child? You look very pale." The attorney stared at her anxious face below its broad-brimmed gray hat. She was wearing a dress and matching jacket of rich green silk. How pretty she is! Bartlett thought. And how terribly young.

"No," she admitted, "no, I haven't. Just a little coffee."

"Well, come with me. I'll get you something right away. After that, we'll talk."

A Raike coach approached them and stopped, Bartlett, placing a protective hand under her elbow, was touched by its fragile smallness. She had grown much thinner since he last saw her, he thought as he helped her into the coach.

He said no more until they were comfortably seated in the dining room of the Tremont House, and he had ordered a substantial breakfast for her.

"There now," Bartlett said in a fatherly way, "eat something, my dear. You look a bit peckish."

Doña could not help smiling at the peculiar word, but contemplated the food without appetite. Nevertheless she obediently began to eat.

At last she said, "That's about all I can do."

Bartlett looked at the still half-filled plate disapprovingly, but he smiled at her and said, "All right. More coffee?"

She nodded and he signaled to the waiter. When a fresh pot of coffee had been brought, the attorney said, "There are some practical matters we have to talk about. It might be better if we discuss them in a more private place. My office?"

"Tell me," she urged impatiently, "tell me why Stephen will not see me!"

"Lower your voice, my dear," he said with his lawyer's caution and Yankee reticence. He obviously found it distasteful to discuss the subject, but plunged on. "Stephen feels—injured by your association with this Gerard."

"I knew it, I knew it!" she said, and began to cry. "It's not true, Mr. Bartlett. It's just not true. I was there because—"

She stopped abruptly, suddenly realizing that she could not tell Bartlett—or anyone—why she had been at Torrance's house. To do so would be to involve herself and Stephen in still more trouble.

"Yes?" Bartlett's face was encouraging and kind.

"I—I can't tell you," she said in a low voice.

"My dear, I am your husband's attorney. And I want to help you—both."

"I'm sorry, Mr. Bartlett. I can't tell you. Not even you."

"Very well." The attorney's shrewd eyes reflected both impatience and disappointment. "Very well, Mrs. Raike." She heard a new coolness in his manner of address, and her heart sank.

There seemed to be nothing she could do, nothing to help Stephen. All that remained to her were the horrifying images of that night, the terrible mental picture of Stephen at the door of Torrance's office, the two men behind him—the *two* men!

Doña exclaimed.

"What is it?" Bartlett asked.

"There were two men behind Stephen at the door."

"*Two* men! Good God!" Bartlett's face reflected his excitement.

Doña nodded. "The black waiter, and another."

"Describe him," Bartlett urged her.

Doña closed her eyes, trying desperately to remember. She said in a low, discouraged voice, "I can't. Oh, God, I can't remember the other man at all. He was almost hidden by the waiter."

"You must try."

"I am trying, I am," Doña protested. "But you see, it all happened so fast."

"A white man? Young, old? How was he dressed? His hair color? Anything." Bartlett shot the questions at her.

Doña closed her eyes again. When she opened them, she looked sadly at Bartlett. "It's no use. He was a white man, young, one of the customers at Torrance's, maybe. It all happened too fast. And then he just—disappeared from the doorway, I think. I can't be sure of any of it, you see. His face just flashed before my eyes."

There was a moment of silence, and Bartlett said, "I see. Well, it's something. It's *something*." He tried to smile at her.

"Shall we go to my office, then, to discuss the other matters?"

"What other matters?"

Bartlett sounded cool again. "The question of financial provisions Stephen has made for you. And very generous ones, too, I might add."

"I want nothing!" she cried. "Nothing."

"Don't be a foolish child, my dear. You must live, you know. I advise you not to refuse these funds. But come, we cannot discuss it here. Come with me to my office now. I will have the papers drawn up while you are there."

Doña was too tired now to protest. When Bartlett had settled the bill, she allowed him to lead her away.

The news that Stephen Raike had shot Alfred Torrance rocked Chicago. One of the town's most respected businessmen. Newly married. A wealthy young man . . . had shot a notorious gambler in an unsavory brawl on Hairtrigger Block!

Some were sympathetic, others just curious. But everyone wanted to watch the scandalous trial. Few people, even the concerned would have recognized Raike's "poor wife," the beautiful and mysterious redhead, as the veiled and somberly dressed figure sitting in the middle of a crowded row, halfway back in the courtroom.

Doña had purposely chosen a rather inconspicuous place, hoping that from there she could see without being seen. Her conference with Josiah Bartlett had been a difficult one. She had obstinately refused all but a nominal sum of money, but in the end the insistent lawyer had persuaded her to leave the matter in abeyance until she had given it more thought.

Again, her dismay and exhaustion left her without the strength to argue, and she consented. Somehow accepting the money from Stephen symbolized to her the acceptance of the end of their marriage. And she could not face that. Surely, sometime, he would talk to her again; and when she made him understand, all would be right.

This hope sustained Doña through the blank, lonely days following her visit to Bartlett's office. To pass the time, and to seek friendly company, she had gone to the land office the morning after she had conferred with Bartlett.

There she received the sharpest blow of all: Stephen's manager told her, with a sheepish look, that her husband had left instructions with him to end her association with Raike Lands. Already, she noticed, a man sat at her small desk in the corner.

Shrinking from the compassionate glances of Matilda

and Jeb, Doña had hurried away from the familiar rooms and down the wooden stairs. Blinded by her tears, she walked back to the Sherman House, hoping she would tire herself enough to sleep.

Sleep had been eluding her, these nights, until she had become so pale and thin she hardly knew herself. The image regarding her from the pier glass was another woman—a woman older than her years, with a fragile, sad quality.

The only bright spot in her black days was Gerard's failure to appear. She had lived in dread of seeing him, and wondered why he had not pursued her. Doña knew that soon he was bound to seek her out, and decided to move to a small, respectable boarding house on the edge of town.

Overseeing the packing of her things, it occurred to her that there were many things she could not in conscience keep—the extravagant jewels Stephen had given her, for example. Keeping only her wedding and engagement ring, the gold bracelet that he had bought for her in Galveston, and the wonderful, barbaric necklace of red and yellow and green gold, she bundled up the rest of the precious pieces into silk scarves. She took them in a velvet carryall to Bartlett's office, and asked him to put them in the bank until Stephen could reclaim them.

"You are making a mistake," Bartlett said disapprovingly. "Stephen meant these things for you, and there may come a time, my dear, when you will want them badly."

Bartlett's earlier coldness had melted when he saw her thin face and sad eyes. It would do no harm, he thought, to try to protect her against her own naïveté.

"Stephen's a rich man," he added bluntly. "Keep the things, my dear. Or rather let me put them in the bank for *you*; I don't trust this boarding house you're moving into."

She had refused, and reluctantly the lawyer deferred to her.

Doña went about her business with an aching heart. Finally this morning, even though she knew it would pain her, she decided to come to the trial. She had chosen one of her quietest ensembles—a neat, somber suit of lavender-gray, and an uncharacteristic hat, narrow-brimmed, over which she wore a heavy gray veil to hide her face as much as possible.

There was a rustle and flurry in the courtroom, and people stood up: the judge entered, and then Stephen with his lawyers. Stephen, too, was thinner and his face was hard and grim. But as always its expression was cool and unreadable.

Everyone sat down again, and Doña sank gratefully on to the seat, her knees were shaky, and her heart thudding painfully at the sight of Stephen.

She hardly heard the opening words of the officials of the court, so intent was she on his face. There was no way to tell whether Stephen had seen her, for his handsome, lean face was inscrutable as his gray eyes swept the courtroom for a moment.

Then, to her consternation, she saw Philippe Gerard coming to sit beside her. Oblivious to the disturbance he was making, he bowed and whispered, "Excuse me," as he trod over the feet of the intervening spectators. Unfortunately there was an empty place beside her.

Stephen, who knew every inch of Doña with a long, familiar knowledge, had seen at once that she was the woman in the gray veil. Her vivid hair glimmered through it, and he recognized the proud set of her head on her shoulders.

And Gerard was coming toward her now. Even now, he thought savagely, even here. They are very brazen. He swallowed painfully and hoped no one could read his expression.

Then he forced his attention to the remarks of the prosecution and the men who would decide his fate.

Chapter Twenty-Two

Stephen watched as Gerard approached Doña, but then looked quickly away, so he did not see her stiffen. She moved as far as she could from the smiling Creole, but there was little room on the crowded bench.

Gerard moved nearer. His muscular thigh pressed urgently against her body. He leaned to her and whispered through her veil, "I see you are still incognito. Are you still trying to hide from me?"

Doña, in a cold fury, neither looked at him nor answered. She was trapped: even if she wanted to leave the courtroom now, her exit would attract attention. There were very few women in the court. And Gerard, of course, would follow. Resigning herself to the inevitable, she raised her head to watch the proceedings, trying to ignore the man beside her.

But his presence was strong, insistent; she was conscious of the mingled scents of immaculate linen and broadcloth, fine bourbon and a faint, fresh sweetness, like limes. And there was another emanation that disturbed her more—something she could not name, a musky scent of the hunter, like the killer's musk so frightening to the wild prairie animals.

Nassooba, her mind said, the Indian name that had sounded like an alarm that day in the Raike Lands office. And moving her head so slightly she was sure he would not know, Doña glanced at Gerard in bitter fascination. For the first time she noticed that his long-fingered, well-tended hands had coarse black hair below the knuckles. The hands were resting on his knees; the fine gray broadcloth strained over his muscular horseman's thighs. She felt an unpleasant coldness.

Alert as a wild animal, Gerard had seen her slight movement; when she looked up at his face, there was a smile on his lips, and his dark eyes glittered. "I have missed you, Doña," he said in a low voice. "But you must excuse me for now."

Still indifferent to the annoyance he was causing, Gerard rose and moved down the row of spectators toward the aisle. He was going to testify then, Doña thought, as she watched him approach a seat near the front, and caught the impatient frown of the prosecuting attorney, who had obviously been waiting for Gerard.

Stephen's sharp mind was trained to notice everything at once, a gift that had made survival possible in more tight places than he could name. He exercised it now, in the crowded court, listening to the testimony of Robert Dexter and thinking at the same time of the woman in the small gray hat and heavy veil.

When he had first caught sight of her, Stephen had been struck in spite of himself by the fragility of her body; in a quick glance he saw that the smart little jacket was no longer snug and trim upon her waist. She looked as thin as a child, and his anger fled; for a split second he was touched by compassion, thinking, What if Bartlett is right, and I am wrong?

He remembered the lawyer's quiet words, "I do not believe there is anything between her and this Gerard." Bartlett had held out an envelope. "She has sent you this letter and asks that you read it."

Stephen had not been able to bring himself to read the letter, but he carried it still, unopened, in his pocket. He shifted now uneasily in his chair and heard its slight crackle.

I would have read it, he thought bitterly to himself as he turned an impassive face toward the witness in the box, if I hadn't seen them together again.

"The prosecution calls Philippe Gerard."

Doña watched him take the stand, elegant and cool, hating him with renewed force.

She barely listened to the prosecution's preliminary questions, but then she heard the Creole say with mock reluctance, "I regret to say that I saw him shoot my friend and business partner, Alfred Torrance."

"By 'him,' of course, you mean the defendant, Stephen Austin Raike?"

"I do." Gerard's reply was loud and clear, carrying throughout the hushed courtroom. And yet he still managed to convey a mock-reluctance to reveal such damaging information, a tone that made Doña's anger flame hotter and hotter. She longed to rush forward, screaming, Liar, liar, and to scratch at his complacent face with her nails, like a raging wildcat.

As she sat listening to Gerard's testimony of lies, Doña had to restrain herself from crying out. And Bartlett had told her Stephen refused to let her testify! She could not believe that Stephen hated her so much.

Silently, she began to cry and fumbled in her small pouch for a handkerchief. She lifted her veil enough to wipe her cheeks with a small square of lace-edged cambric.

At last she was dimly aware that Gerard had stepped down and the people about her were rising. A recess had been called.

She watched Stephen walk away between two guards, disappearing into a mysterious hall behind the courtroom. As the other spectators began to file out, she sat on, helplessly, staring straight ahead, hardly knowing what to do.

Gerard walked down the aisle and stopped where she sat. Leaning toward her, he said softly, "May I offer you some refreshment? I believe we have time before the court reconvenes."

She turned and stared at him, hardly believing her senses. The man was speaking to her as if they were at some festive event, like the races, and were on the best of terms. She was made speechless by his effrontery.

But she found her voice, after a moment, and said clearly, knowing her reply would go unheard in the babble of voices, "If you do not leave me alone, I will kill you. I have a gun, and I will kill you if you ever speak to me again."

Gerard was unable to control a start of surprise. But all too soon he was his smooth, unruffled self again. And he laughed softly.

"Doña, Doña, you are a jewel. Surely there has never been anyone like you." His swarthy face was amused, indulgent. "Do you think you can scare me with your little tempers? My dear, when your fine husband goes to prison, you will need someone to look after you. And I will be there, Doña. I will be there, I assure you."

Rising, he bowed to her, donned his elegant hat, touched the brim mockingly, and strode on up the aisle.

The Yankee lawyer, Josiah Bartlett, and the amiable Southerner, Burton Hamilton, emerged from the courthouse into the sunny spring afternoon. A crisp wind stirred the branches of the mighty trees lining the courthouse yard—some so venerable and tall they reached almost to the third story of the imposing building—whipping the flag on the tower.

"Beautiful day," said Bartlett in his economical manner.

"Yes, indeed. But not so beautiful a day, I fear, for our friend Raike." Hamilton pushed back his mane of white hair and settled his beaver hat on his proud head. His kindly brown eyes were somber in his handsome face.

Bartlett assented. The two men stood for a time on the corner of LaSalle and Randolph Streets, each wrapped in his own thoughts, watching the busy traffic pass; a dray wagon burdened with a huge coil of metal wire nearly collided with a smart trap occupied by a well-dressed man and woman. Groups of frockcoated men were taking the air, and wide-skirted women hesitated at the corners before descending from the sidewalks over the slanting, narrow ramps of wood into the mud of LaSalle Street.

"Burt," said Josiah Bartlett, "by the time the mud dries, that boy'll be in prison."

"Good God! I hope not. But it doesn't look good, does it?"

"No." Bartlett added, "Let's not stand here. Want to go over to the Sherman House?"

"That place will do." Hamilton indicated a modest saloon across LaSalle whose sign advertised Cordials and Wines.

"All right." Waiting until a carriage had passed, the men plunged into the mud of LaSalle Street, its thick ooze rising above their polished Wellingtons and staining their trouser hems.

When they were seated in the saloon, and the waiter had gone to fill their orders, Burton Hamilton said, "I can't believe Raike did it, Jos. And yet the evidence is very damning."

"The lack of it, you mean." Bartlett looked gloomy. The waiter set their glasses of wine before them. "How is the joint of beef today?" he asked the man. He smiled at the waiter's enthusiastic reply. When he had once again left them, Bartlett remarked, "The joint is always at its best, sir—and never tastes very good." Then he sipped his sherry and repeated, "One damned eyewitness, Burt, that's all he needs. All the character witnesses in the world, even men with names like yours and Field's and Brink's and Palmer's—yes, even Long John himself— lack one great advantage, the advantage every one of those shady characters has."

"And that?"

"They were *there,* Burt. The character witnesses weren't."

"My God, what kind of character do those men have, men like Marshall and Dexter?" Hamilton's question was scornful.

"Torrance was careful," Bartlett said in a weary voice. "He was always just on the right side of the law, and he took care to hire men with no actual record. Only a convicted felon is dismissed as a witness, you see." He paused, and said again, "Damn it, no eyewitness. Except—"

271

He paused, thinking of Doña. Stephen had asked him not to mention her presence to anyone.

"Except—?" Hamilton prompted.

"A black waiter," Bartlett said, shrugging, "to whom no one would listen. And a man we cannot find, a white man."

"I see." Hamilton frowned. "How do you think the revenge argument is going, Jos? That Gerard was vengeful against Stephen and is trying to pin it on him?"

"I don't know, Burt, I really can't tell at this point." Bartlett smiled grimly. "But I'll tell you one thing: the prosecution's contention that Raike was firing at Gerard and hit Torrance by mistake is going to get the prosecutor laughed out of court. If Stephen Raike aimed at a man, he'd get him!"

Hamilton nodded. The judge himself had gone target-shooting with Stephen, and knew first-hand.

"What they'll do now, Burt," Bartlett added, "is build on the business rivalry between Steve and Torrance. And keep hitting again and again at the eyewitnesses' testimony. We've got to find that missing man."

Hamilton shrugged without hope. "And if you don't? What about the wife?"

"Doña?" Bartlett looked away. "The testimony of a wife would be as useless as the black waiter's. Any jury would assume she'd lie in behalf of her husband. Besides, Stephen's forbidden her being called."

"Good for him! The man's a gentleman." Bartlett did not reply; he had no intention of talking about the young couple's estrangement. "I hope it goes his way," Hamilton continued earnestly. "He's one of the finest men around."

"I agree." Bartlett's Yankee answer was spare. "Torrance was no loss. Raike is."

A glowing tribute, Hamilton thought, by the standards of the reticent Josiah Bartlett. They finished their indifferent meal in silence. As they were crossing the muddy intersection of LaSalle and Randolph again, Bartlett said with sudden anger, "It's a damned shame, that's what it is, Burt. The boy is a credit to Chicago."

The two men made their way back to Stephen's trial

while the fresh April wind stirred the venerable branches of the courthouse trees.

"Has the jury reached a verdict?"

"We have, Your Honor." There was an agonizing silence as the juror passed the folded piece of paper to the judge.

Doña, in a crowded row near the back of the room, bowed her head, almost unable to take a breath.

She looked up and saw the judge scrutinize the folded bit of paper with an impassive face and pass it back to the juror.

"We find the defendant, Stephen Austin Raike, guilty of manslaughter."

Doña took a loud, sobbing breath that emerged in a groan, but the sound was lost in the uproar of other voices about her.

The judge frowned and pounded with his gavel. "Order!" he cried sternly. "The bench has not passed sentence."

Doña waited for the next terrible words, her head bowed in her hands.

"The defendant," the judge said, "has been found guilty, with a recommendation for clemency because of his probity and community standing, and because it is judged that there had been provocation to an extreme degree. Therefore the defendant, Stephen Austin Raike, will be sentenced to imprisonment at the State Penitentiary in Joliet for the term of twenty-five years."

There was another uproar from the spectators. Doña sat stricken, her face still hidden in her hands, the tears gushing from her eyes and wetting her heavy veil.

At last she forced herself to look at Stephen: he was standing straight and tall, scorning the attorney's gesture toward a chair. Then his proud head turned and he scanned the court. Doña imagined that he caught sight of her. But his handsome face was without expression as they led him away.

Doña did not know how long she sat there, with bowed head, dimly hearing the loud, confused voices about her, the shuffling of many feet as the spectators left the court.

She was conscious then of a great quiet, and she raised her head. Everyone had gone.

Then she head a single pair of footsteps behind her. Someone was walking down the aisle toward her.

Doña turned, recognizing Josiah Bartlett. He did not smile, nor did he greet her, but the face below his grizzled hair was kind. He turned in at her row and walked to her. "Come," he said with the blunt gentleness that characterized him. "Come, you can't stay here, you know." Bartlett held out his hand, and Doña took it, slowly rising.

He led her to the aisle and gestured her to precede him. When they emerged into the bright sun that seemed to mock her grief, the old lawyer said, "We'll go this way. Avoid the crowds." He gently urged her toward the rear of the building and out through the grilled gate onto the sidewalk.

A newsboy cried to them, waving his paper, "Mormons make war on the United States!" Doña looked at the great black headline: there was something about President Buchanan. Such things seemed very far away and unreal to her.

Bartlett glanced at her uneasily; she seemed in a state of shock. "I think you need a restorative," he said. "You are coming home to my wife and me."

She swayed dizzily, and he grasped her arm as he signaled for a carriage. When one arrived, Bartlett settled her in it and gave the driver a North Side address.

She was grateful to Bartlett for his silence; he made no attempt to soothe her with falsely consoling words as the carriage rattled toward the river, climbing to the entrance of the Rush Street Bridge.

The sun was dazzling on the water; with blurred, absent eyes she saw a sailing ship anchored on the other bank, a steamboat, with the name of *Comet,* chugging along. On the other side of the river she could see fashionable carriages passing, a few top-hatted men strolling in the sun. The men were laughing, and one raised his hat to an elaborately dressed lady in a shining trap.

As the carriage reached the middle of the bridge, Doña recalled Stephen's remarks about the North Side.

"We won't build there," he had said. For to reach the fashionable North Side, one had to cross the Rush Street Bridge, manned by very unreliable bridge-tenders. The Chicago River was thick with marine traffic, and the passage of the ships made the bridge tender an important man. The city had no control over these unruly employees; once a drunken tender had opened the bridge to let a whistling tugboat pass, dumping a man in a buggy, and his horses all into the river. "I wouldn't want you crossing that bridge every day," Stephen had told her.

She could hear his voice so clearly in her imagination that she began to weep. She wept without sound, to spare the feelings of Josiah Bartlett, but the old lawyer, seeing her fragile body shaking with the force of her silent weeping, leaned over and patted her hand.

However, he still did not speak as the carriage crossed the hazardous bridge and reached the North Side. Again Doña felt a warm gratitude; she feared he would try to distract her, and she knew if that happened she would scream.

Vaguely Doña was aware of a great house in the midst of huge grounds, with rustic bridges, man-made ponds, and even greenhouses.

She hoped this intimidating place was not the house Bartlett was taking her to; but the carriage passed on, and she saw an even finer house, the only one on the block. Soon, she found that the sight of the beautiful houses and lawns were soothing her in spite of her pain.

One home looked over another square block area of trees and grass, and a broad piazza extended across the front of the house. She glimpsed stables, a conservatory bright with spring flowers, and a glass house filled with fruit trees.

Watching her take notice, Bartlett commented, "Bill Ogden's place." Doña wondered at Bartlett's familiar address of Ogden; Ogden was a millionaire twice over and had been Chicago's first mayor.

"All kinds of interesting folks have stopped at his

place," Bartlett went on, with uncharacteristic talkativeness. He was encouraged that Doña's attention had turned outward. "Daniel Webster and Emerson, and that Bryant fellow. But I think he's a lunatic," the old lawyer added in his salty manner.

Doña spoke for the first time, in an unsteady voice. "Do you have a house like this?"

Bartlett chuckled. "Hardly. But I think you'll find it pretty comfortable."

The "comfortable" house before which the carriage paused seemed huge to Doña. It was set far nearer the road than the imposing mansions she had seen before, but the grounds were spacious enough, and its broad front yard was planted with a dozen beautiful old trees. There must be at least thirty rooms, she thought, accepting Bartlett's helping hand to step down from the cab.

He unlatched the grilled gate and they walked up a short path toward the entrance. The house had a modest porch, Doña noticed as she glanced up at its graceful facade, ornate with a central tower room over the roof and surrounding cupolas. There was a roofed balcony over the entranceway, and the windows on either side of the tall, two-story structure were pointed, like the windows of a cathedral.

Its ornament, strangely, gave it a comfortable and friendly look, Doña thought. Bartlett tapped the brass door knocker and instantly the door was opened by a smiling black man.

"We are going to have a guest, Isaiah," Bartlett said. "Mrs. Raike. Is Mrs. Bartlett home?"

The man bowed to Doña and replied, "No, sir. She said she be back about dinner."

"All right, Isaiah. You tell Cook to fix us some coffee and something to eat. Bring it to my study."

The smiling Isaiah left them and Bartlett led Doña into a wonderful room just off the entrance hall, a richly carved and painted room of paneled bookcase walls. There was a high, beamed ceiling, and the room was furnished with a beautiful old table-desk standing on fluted columns. The writing surface was inlaid with green

276

leather and the edge was bordered in ebony. The gas fixture above the table had three frosted glass lampshades and three upright gas jets of brass.

Great, softly upholstered chairs were scattered about. The room looked very old and very comfortable.

"You sit down there," Bartlett said to Doña, as if he were speaking to a child, and obediently she sank into a big chair of tufted brocade; its arm-ends were winged cherubs' heads. Her sudden relief was so great, the peace of the house such a contrast to the uproar of the day, that Doña felt quite exhausted.

"Take off your hat, my dear." Bartlett went to a side table and poured them both small glasses of sherry. She took off her veil and her hat, and he placed them on the side table.

"Drink this. And when you're rested a bit, I'll show you to your room upstairs."

"My room?" Doña said. "Oh, but I can't stay."

"Well, we'll talk about it," Bartlett said easily. "But drink this first."

She sipped the delicious, nutty-tasting wine and soon felt a measure of calm return. Her eyelids were heavy with exhaustion and she was very hungry.

When Isaiah entered with a tray containing a coffeepot and cups, and plates of small sandwiches. Doña ate several of the sandwiches and drank the strong black coffee gratefully.

"Now," said Bartlett kindly, "I think you'll be able to make it up the stairs. You've been looking so peaked lately you seem like a little ghost."

She was so warmed by his concern, so overwhelmed with gratitude that she was afraid she would start crying again. But she restrained her tears and smiled at Bartlett.

"Thank you so much. You have been so good. I think I *would* like to go upstairs."

Bartlett went with her to the corridor and called out, "Annie?"

An amiable-looking, plump woman of middle age appeared.

"This is our guest, Mrs. Raike. Would you show her the guest room, please?"

The woman nodded, and led Doña up the curving stairs to the prettiest room Doña had ever seen. Its shining floors were uncarpeted except for random scatter rugs of white, and the postered bed had a striped canopy of pale orange and white. There were cheerful matching curtains and the wallpaper was patterned in a small design of green and orange flowers. There was a handsome little chest by the bed and another larger chest by the window.

Before the white-painted fireplace, filled with yellow flowers for the spring, was a shining round wooden table with a bowl of yellow and white flowers in its polished center. Two graceful chairs were placed at the table.

Doña exclaimed with pleasure at the room's cheerfulness. When the plump Annie had left her alone, Doña put her hat and veil in one of the drawers of the chest and went to the window. There was a pleasant view, through the long French panes, of the wooded side lawns of the Bartlett house.

Suddenly so tired she could hardly stand, Doña undressed and poured water from the pitcher to wash. She took down her hair and shook it out. Clad in her underthings, she turned back the white spread under the cheerful canopy and lay down.

She knew that she would soon be asleep, for she could hardly keep her eyes open. But as she drifted off, a series of questions drifted into her weary consciousness: if she had not planned to stay, why had she put her hat and veil in the drawer?

Doña smiled to herself.

And the other question was, What would Mrs. Bartlett be like? As kind as her husband?

The horrors of the afternoon were fading, mercifully, in this serene moment, at least. And Doña, almost drugged with fatigue, after a last dim look around the pretty, shining room, was surrounded by the dark of peaceful sleep.

Chapter Twenty-Three

"A *daughter!*" Marilou Hamilton repeated shrilly. "Why, Hannah Bartlett, I do believe you've lost your mind!"

"Please, Marilou, lower your voice. Doña might hear you." Hannah Bartlett was a slender, handsome New Englander; her thick, vital hair was frankly gray-threaded, her brown eyes velvety, with a look of settled sadness. She said to the woman facing her over the tea things, "You know it has been the sorrow of my life, never having children. I'd like to welcome Doña as a daughter, and so would Jos."

Mrs. Burton Hamilton looked at her hostess with a kind of wonder. "But Hannah," she said, in her small, coquettish voice, "why, no one knows where the woman came from, or anything about her. Except that she entrapped that poor Stephen Raike into marrying her."

Hannah Bartlett studied Marilou Hamilton before replying; Hannah knew she must keep a hold on her temper! It was also an unexpressed sorrow of her life that her husband was such a close friend to the pleasant Southern banker, Burton Hamilton. For that meant that she herself must befriend his silly wife.

Hannah, who had been something of a bluestocking in her youth, nourished on serious books of the great writers, and on beautiful, stately music, had very little in common with Mrs. Hamilton.

She disapproved of the Southern woman's tinted hair and slightly rouged cheeks, disapproved of her flirtatious manner, a little absurd in one of her age. And most of all, Hannah Bartlett was irritated by Marilou Hamilton's elaborate dresses. This afternoon she was wearing one that, in Hannah's estimation, was far too grand for a simple call—a skirt thick with flounces, a bodice cut too low, the whole a rather kittenish shade of pink.

Hannah had often wondered how Marilou's ever-present flounces would fare in Chicago's ever-present mud.

But now, gathering her wits and repressing an angry retort, she said to Marilou Hamilton, "I know all I need to know—that Doña is a lovely and intelligent girl, that her own parents are dead and she has no one in the world now that Stephen has—left her."

"Left her!" Marilou Hamilton gave an indignant snort. "I don't doubt for a minute she was responsible for the whole thing. They say that—"

"Please don't tell me what *they* are saying." Hannah's quiet, crisp tone was quite offensive to the Southern woman.

"Well, anyway, its mighty funny that she's so rude to her husband's cousin—that charming, charming Philippe. She certainly saw enough of him before!" Mrs. Hamilton simpered. "He's been asking for her everywhere. And I've been told she will not receive him. Surely he only has her best interests at heart. I don't think she can afford to look down at her nose at a family like the Gerards. Alone in the world as she *appears* to be." Mrs. Hamilton's honeyed voice emphasized the word with malice. "It seems to me, she needs the protection of a family like the Gerards."

Hannah Bartlett smiled grimly. "His interest in her is not so cousinly as he would like it to appear. At least that's what she told me."

Marilou scoffed, "I don't believe it. Why, there's no one in Chicago as utterly—delightful as Philippe." She made a sweeping gesture with her arm, as if to illustrate Gerard's place in the wide society, and her sleeve, heavily ruffled, too, nearly swept her teacup from the table.

"Really, Hannah." She went on. "I think you're making a terrible, terrible mistake."

"Thank you very much for your concern, Marilou," Hannah replied drily.

"But you'll do what you please, anyway. I know you stubborn New England Yankees!" Marilou Hamilton said with that labored little-girl air that so irritated Hannah, the air that Marilou seemed confident would excuse her rudest utterance.

"Yes, I will," Hannah Bartlett replied in a matter-of-fact tone. Her whole heritage, austere and common-sensical, seemed to echo in those few ironic words. Marilou Hamilton studied Hannah's unpainted face and neat, uncolored hair. Her simple but costly day dress was the color of heavy cream; the shade was most becoming to Hannah's fresh cheeks, brown eyes and shining gray-threaded locks.

She has that same—plain way of dressing as that damned little Indian whore! thought the Southern woman. And still they always look so—smart, so ahead of the styles! It was maddening.

Marilou said with sudden spite, "And really, Hannah, you know that girl isn't even *white*."

"What on earth do you mean?"

"Well, she's part Indian." Marilou lowered her shrill voice and her small, hard, blue eyes darted sideways as if to make sure they were not overheard. The glance gave her an unpleasant look, reflected Hannah, rather like a cornered rodent.

"I am not concerned with such matters," Hannah said firmly, and now Marilou was furious. The slavery question, and the matter of color, were subjects Hannah and Marilou could not even discuss without tempers flaring. Marilou's family, of course, owned slaves by the hundreds; Hannah's minister-father in Massachusetts preached thundering condemnations of slavery from his pulpit. All of the Bartlett's servants were free men and women.

Marilou rose precipitately, her rouged cheeks redder with her anger. "Well, I see you won't listen to any sense. I don't know what else I could have expected from such a—Ni—Nigra-lover."

Hannah noticed with amusement that Marilou's flounces were dribbling into the tea-things, and a brown stain appeared on the pink ruffles.

"Now, looka there!" Marilou cried. Her less elegant accent, as always, appeared in her excitement. "Look what you made me do, Hannah! It'll serve you right if that little—halfbreed carries off all the silver in the house!"

Mrs. Hamilton snatched up her pink purse and stormed from the library, her flounces quivering.

At the door she all but collided with Doña Raike.

Hannah Bartlett was shocked into speechlessness. Good heavens! she thought. What if the poor child heard?

Doña had heard Mrs. Hamilton clearly, and all through dinner that evening she could see that the kind-hearted Hannah Bartlett was worrying about it.

But Doña, because of her warm concern for Hannah, had pretended that she had not heard, and during the meal made an attempt to present the Bartletts with a smiling face.

In the week since Josiah Bartlett had first brought her to the house, Doña had come to love both Bartletts. She marveled that the visit had lasted so long: she had intended to leave the first evening, but her exhausted sleep had lasted the whole night and into the early afternoon of the next day.

With the resilience of her twenty years, Doña had awakened so refreshed that she felt she could face the world again—even her separation from Stephen.

Doña's first conscious thought was of him. After a brief pang of grief, she thought in incorrigible hope, We will find a way. A witness will be found, and he will be cleared! And then, when I see him again—her uncompleted thought trailed away into a vague but rosy hope for the future, and by the time she got up and dressed she was almost cheerful again.

Doña was further heartened by her meeting with the dignified and gentle Hannah Bartlett. With quiet insistence Mrs. Bartlett persuaded her to stay "another day or two," and with Doña's permission, sent to the boarding house for a few of her things.

The younger woman was touched by Mrs. Bartlett's need to mother someone, although she did so in an offhand and inoffensive way; Doña herself could not resist being pleased by the older woman's attentions.

And the second day somehow extended into a third, a fourth, a fifth. Now a week had passed since the beginning of her visit. When Mrs. Bartlett hinted that Doña might move the rest of her things to the house for a protracted stay, Doña could see the way things were heading.

Then, when she had overheard the conversation between Hannah Bartlett and Mrs. Hamilton, she knew that her earlier supposition had been the correct one: the Bartletts wanted to take her into their home.

Doña was filled with gratitude at the knowledge, yet something restless and wild in her—the same unease and nameless urge that had driven her to ask Stephen for "something to do"—told her that the arrangement would be impossible.

For even in the kindly Bartlett's pleasant house—now that her tired body was rested and renewed—Doña felt stifled. She could not imagine a life in Chicago society, as a well-behaved young woman. Even if Hannah Bartlett was an intelligent and unusual woman, her life was not unlike those of the other society matrons from whom Doña felt so estranged. And Hannah would suffer, sheltering her.

That evening, after dinner, when she had gone to the library to look for a book to read, Doña caught sight of a late newspaper on the table. Idly she picked it up. A small item on the front page caught her eye: it was the story of a battle between a band of Comanches and federal troops on the border of Texas and Oklahoma. The Comanches had been routed and banished to a spot farther north.

Doña held the paper in her hands, staring at the news item.

Tahre! she cried out in silence. Tahre and Patche and Easooba. All her friends. Were they the banished Indians? Suddenly Doña longed for them unendurably, ached for the wide, dusty plains and the rugged hills and the feel of a horse beneath her. How long it had been since she had even been on a horse!

And like a distant, enticing perfume, she smelled again the odor of the sage and the dusty wind, the snug leather of her vest and trousers, the oily smell of her gun.

She had not known until now how she missed these things, how she missed the freedom of the old, wild life. And the Indians! How she missed the Indians.

Doña remembered what the hateful Mrs. Hamilton had said, that she "wasn't even white."

No, Doña thought angrily, I am not white. And even the Bartletts, kind as they had been, were in the last analysis enemies of her friends. Their skin, too, was white, and hers was almost coppery red, like her mother's, the woman murdered by Daniel Raike.

And the son of Daniel Raike scorned her now! He would not even look at her during the trial or accept her help. A long-repressed feeling of anger swept Doña as she stood in the shining library with the newspaper in her hands.

She would go back. Yes, she would go back where she belonged. Not to Texas; that was no longer safe, but somewhere in the West, where there would be people she could understand. She had been a fool to imagine that Stephen would ever be free; that she could ever win him back—or even want to.

Chapter Twenty-Four

The beautiful young woman on the middle deck of the luxurious steamboat *John Simonds* was looking so intently at the St. Louis levee that she appeared not to notice the curious glances trained on her. Her fashionable gown of tawny autumn-colored stripes—russet, dark green and cream—with its soft cream-colored coat, three-quarter length, trimmed in dark green with dashing mousquetaire sleeves would have been enough to call attention to her, even without her air of mystery.

On her head she wore a neat little cream-colored hat with a concealing veil; through the veil could be seen a glistening coil of jet-black hair, in a soft chignon at the back of her slender neck. A soft ringlet lay on either side of her collar, below the veil.

She was obviously preparing to disembark, for there were several valises at her feet; she carried in one gloved hand a russet carryall, holding it in an almost protective fashion against her side, rather than letting it swing from its straps.

Two men standing near her, also waiting to land, were staring. "The mystery lady," one remarked in a low voice, grinning. His white teeth glistened below his luxuriant black mustache; he was dressed in the clothes of the river gambler.

The other man, taller and more quietly dressed than his companion, was as fair as the gambler was dark. He wore an elegant suit of blue-gray broadcloth that matched (though he would not have noticed such a thing) his clear, alert eyes. His blond hair was concealed by a dark-gray beaver hat. "She is beautiful," he said to the gambler.

His accents were those of an educated man, whereas the river gambler's voice was rough and his speech careless. The way the quiet man spoke of the dark-haired woman differed from the insinuating manner of his companion. His face was earnest, serious.

"Does anyone know who she is?" he asked the dark man at his side.

"Why, I believe you're smitten, Bill!" the gambler twitted his fair companion.

The blond man laughed in a rather self-conscious way and said casually, "Not at all. But who can resist a mystery woman?"

"Not I, my friend. But wait. Listen."

A steward was approaching the beautiful dark woman. "May I take these, Mrs. Hamilton? We are about to land."

The woman thanked the attendant and slipped a coin in his hand. The two watching men caught a glimpse of very white teeth through the light veil, as she smiled at the thought of how angry it would make the unpleasant Marilou if she were ever to discover that Doña was using her name.

The dark man said, "Well, there's part of your answer, Bill. Now you know her name, at least."

The tall fair man looked embarrassed; the gambler laughed at his expression. Apparently glad to change the subject, the man named Bill asked, "You're not coming ashore?"

"Not this round, friend. I didn't do too well on this run, and they'll pick up some new marks in St. Louis."

The other man laughed good-naturedly and said, "Maybe I'll run into you again some time, Jeff."

"We'll have a game."

"Not likely! Have a good trip." And the tall blond man moved toward the stairs to the lower deck, carrying only a small valise.

As the *John Simonds,* St. Louis' pride, was pulling into the busy landing, William Hackman, vice president of St.

Louis' largest bank, continued to stare at the veiled woman, the light, neat little hat over shining jet-black hair.

Doña Raike studied the St. Louis landing with eager eyes: through her cream-colored veil, she thought, everything looked very white and clean, much nicer than Chicago. But it was a very busy-looking city all the same; she was exhilarated, as always, by new sights and sounds, and began to count the smokestacks of the steamboats, lined up along the waterfront. There were so many she gave up.

Beyond the smokestacks were a number of light-colored buildings, many five and six stories high, crowded together. On the levee she looked back at the other shore and saw a train chugging busily along close to the river bank.

The obliging steward hailed a public carriage for her and helped her in; a burly roustabout stowed her trunks and valises in the space beside the driver.

"Please take me to the best hotel," Doña said firmly to the teamster.

He touched his battered hat and the carriage rattled off. Doña examined the traffic of the streets, noticing a large-wheeled vehicle that looked like an omnibus, set higher than the street-stages of Chicago.

"What kind of omnibus is that?" she called to the driver.

The man, with a look of surprise at such a question from a lady, replied, "A Stephenson bus, ma'am. They make them in New York." He laughed then. "Some say pretty soon there'll be cars on rails, right in town. But I don't think we'll live to see it."

The driver, encouraged by Doña's question, began to point out the sights to her as they drove along.

"There's our courthouse, ma'am," he said proudly, indicating a three-story cross-shaped building occupying a whole square on what she saw was North Fourth Street. The other signs said Broadway, Market, Chestnut. The great building had a gloomy cast-iron dome and was supported by enormous columns.

Doña felt a pang at this grim reminder of the last weeks in Chicago and fervently hoped that the hotel would not overlook the courthouse.

"Farther down there," the driver said, pointing, "on South Broadway, that's the Home of the Friendless."

She wondered what the driver would say if he knew how friendless she herself was, and something about the name caused a shadow to fall over the day.

"Here we are," the driver said a little while later as they drew up before the hotel. It was hardly the Sherman House, she reflected, but it would do until she found another place to live.

She paid the coachman and followed the porters as her baggage was being carried toward the stairs. The man behind the desk looked at her curiously.

She lifted her veil and smiled at him. At once he reacted to the sight of her glowing face with its tilted dark eyes framed in the soft waves of black hair.

"Yes?" he said in a friendly voice.

"I will be staying for a good while," she said in the firm new voice she had lately acquired. "My name is Mrs. Issa Hamilton, of Cincinnati."

"Yes, Mrs. Hamilton. If you will just sign here. Is your —husband joining you?" the desk clerk asked delicately.

"I am a widow," she said, letting her voice tremble ever so slightly.

"Oh, forgive me! I am *so* sorry," the chagrined clerk said effusively.

She gave him another brilliant smile. "There is no need to apologize. I have been a widow for—some time."

The desk clerk came out from behind the desk and personally handed young Mrs. Hamilton up the stairs to her rooms on the second floor. "I'm sure we will do everything possible to make your stay pleasant," he panted, trying to keep up with her light, quick ascent.

At the top of the stairs, she smiled again and said, "I'm sure you will, Mr.—"

"Yancy. Delbert Yancy," he replied eagerly, red-faced.

"Mr. Yancy," she said warmly.

288

And the dazzled Mr. Yancy showed Mrs. Hamilton to her rooms.

When the cloying Mr. Yancy, and his train of laden attendants, had disappeared, Doña sighed with relief.

She closed and locked the door, glorying in the quiet and aloneness. She had asked Mr. Yancy to have the maid wait for a while before unpacking her trunks, explaining that she was very tired from her journey and would doubtless sleep.

Doña removed her veil and took the narrow-brimmed hat from her shining black hair. She looked at herself in the glass and smiled. Surely no one would recognize this dark-haired woman as Doña Raike!

Leisurely moving about the room, taking off her coat and dress, tossing them casually onto a chair, Doña leaned down and unfastened her narrow boots. Then she continued her tour of the room, wriggling her stockinged feet with pleasure as she trod the soft carpet.

Her statement to Mr. Yancy had not been far from the truth: she was bone-weary, tired out from the whirlwind days before her departure from Chicago, her almost-chance settling on St. Louis as her new city of residence.

Doña loosened the soft knot of hair at the back of her neck, shook her hair loose about her shoulders and threw herself full-length upon the bed with a sigh of content.

She began to review in her mind the quick succession of events that preceded her hasty boarding of the *John Simonds* in Chicago.

The morning after she had read of the Comanches' banishment in the Bartletts' newspaper, Doña had asked Hannah Bartlett if Isaiah could drive her into the city in the buggy.

"I must see to some business," Doña explained.

Mrs. Bartlett agreed at once, saying that in any case she and Jos were visiting that afternoon and she was glad Doña would not be left alone. Feeling a stab of guilt for the deception, Doña wrote a note to Hannah Bartlett and left it on the shining table of her room. In it she expressed her gratitude for their kindness but her need to go away. Doña then packed her small valise with the few things she had brought to the Bartletts' and joined Isaiah in the buggy. The discreet black man glanced at the valise but did not refer to it.

When they had crossed the perilous Rush Street Bridge, and Isaiah asked her where she wished to be taken, Doña suddenly thought of how little money she had. Impulsively she gave the servant the name of one of Stephen's banks, the branch where there was an account in her name.

She bade Isaiah a warm goodbye and pressed a coin in his hand. Almost indignantly he refused, and she felt another guilty pang, as if he were telling her that he could not take money from someone who was deceiving the Bartletts in this fashion.

Doña watched him drive away a little sadly. Then she squared her shoulders and marched into the bank. She had decided, in that quick moment, to do as Bartlett had suggested—to take the money Stephen offered. I'll need it, she thought defiantly. And Stephen had so much!

When she silently pronounced his name, Doña almost cried aloud in her pain. Stephen—in that prison, alone. She forced the image from her mind and determinedly sought out a vice-president of the bank. She wrote out a withdrawal slip for the staggering lump sum in cash.

The spluttering manager, sure that a woman—and one so young!—could not know her own mind, tried to dissuade her. But she stood her ground and, at last, left the bank, her valise stuffed with greenbacks and gold.

Catching sight of a hairdresser's shop, Doña had a sudden inspiration. She entered and told the proprietress what she wanted. The woman almost groaned, saying, "But, madam! Your beautiful hair." Again Doña was persistent, and when she left the shop several hours later, her hair was jet-black.

The only things that remained to be done were packing her clothes at the boarding house and booking passage from Chicago. But where?

West, Doña said to herself urgently. I will go back to the West. And in the packet office she heard a man say,

"St. Louis is the coming town. The Panic hasn't affected the river traffic, you know, or the stages."

The stages! Doña made another swift decision, and bought a passage on the luxurious three-decker, the *John Simonds*.

Now in the St. Louis hotel, she was at journey's end. Safe from Gerard, free of all the past! A new life awaited her here in this bustling river city. And Doña could almost forget her pain and aloneness, in her new hope for tomorrow.

Chapter Twenty-Five

In his cell, Stephen Raike opened the letter from the criminal lawyer first: the one from Josiah Bartlett would be more personal, therefore more pleasurable. And as a man whose pleasures were few, Stephen was careful to prolong his anticipation of them. His adaptability to prison amazed the guards, who were unaware how much his life had toughened him.

The first letter did not impress him, even though it referred to his appeal, and said, "I still feel the missing witness will appear."

"Hogwash," Stephen muttered and opened the letter from Jos Bartlett. It was very thick; inside were several folded pages and a small sealed envelope. The envelope looked worn. On it was written his name in Doña's hand. The letter he had left behind! Stephen hesitated, then lay the envelope gently on his cot, reading the letter from Bartlett.

The admirable Yankee, Stephen noted, had used no evasions. He had written, without preamble, "I thought it proper to send you the enclosed, which you may find now you want to read. Your wife, a lovely and brave young lady, stayed for a time with me and my wife and, I may say, captured Hannah's heart. However, Doña has now gone quite away, and it appears she has left Chicago. The bank has informed me that she withdrew in cash the generous sum you had deposited to her account; she left no forwarding address for the receipt of the allowance."

The letter closed with Bartlett's characteristically blunt and awkward expressions of friendship.

So Doña was gone, Stephen thought. There was a knot of pain in his throat that made it hard for him to swallow. He took up the letter from Doña and apprehensively, tore it open. His sharp gray eyes flew along its gracefully written lines; he took a quick excited breath.

That bastard, Gerard, always Gerard! That was his "hold" over her. And they had not been lovers at all. She loved *him*, Stephen Raike. After all the months of watching and waiting and hoping, Doña had said that she loved him.

Stephen was overtaken by a wild exultation that mingled strangely with his despair.

But *was* it despair? No, by God, it wasn't! Nothing had ever defeated him, and nothing would now.

The worst part was the waiting: Stephen Raike had never waited for anything. He had seen what he wanted, gone after it and taken it. Well, I can wait too, Stephen said to himself grimly. As long as I know she loves me, I can wait for anything.

Waking from her second sleep, Doña saw that it was morning. The sun streamed across the foot of her bed.

"I will not think of him today," she whispered to herself, consequently recalling Stephen.

Sharply she remembered waking in his arms, feeling his kiss upon her face and hair. And determinedly she threw back the coverlet and got up to face the day. She would not go on mourning a man who had rejected her.

Doña dressed herself in a cheerful ensemble of yellow, because the day appeared warm and sunny. The color looked even more becoming with her black hair than it had with her red hair.

The first order of business would be to deposit the money in a bank: all through the journey from Chicago she had been uneasy, carrying such an outrageous amount of cash. It was far more than she and Tahre had ever carried even after they had raided a stage, a train or bank.

Her visit today, it occurred to her, would be quite different from some visits she had paid to banks. And the thought made her smile.

The impressionable Mr. Yancy, on duty downstairs, was so enchanted by the lingering smile that he personally found her a public coach to deliver her to the bank.

William Hackman, wearing a suit of sober dark gray and a black cravat appropriate to a banker, looked up from his desk as the beautiful black-haired woman came in.

He exclaimed softly. It was the woman from the boat. Appearing to consult a paper in his hands, Hackman watched from the corner of his eye as she approached a teller, who pointed out the desk next to Hackman's.

The officer who occupied that desk had stepped away. Hackman made a gesture to the teller, meaning that he would speak with the client.

And the woman came toward him, in her jonquil-hued clothes. Unveiled, her face was more beautiful than he had thought; there was a tawny color to her silken skin, and her dark eyes had a smoldering quality that made his clothes feel warm and tight.

However, he stood composedly and pulled out a chair for her. She was carrying a huge carryall of black cut-velvet; she placed it carefully at her feet when she sat down.

His clear gaze dropped to her left hand—she had removed her gloves—and his heart sank. She was wearing a wedding band and engagement ring. Did widows—

"Mrs. Hamilton!" he said impulsively, but was annoyed at himself when a cold and watchful look came to her warm dark eyes.

"How did you know my name?" Her voice was both soft and forceful. William Hackman's admiration soared.

"I beg your pardon," he said smilingly, once more in command of himself. "I happened to overhear the steward call you that. I was on the *John Simonds* when it landed."

She stared at him, not commenting on his statement.

He said hastily, "But what can I do for you?"

"I would like to open an account." She smiled at him.

"You plan to stay in our city, then?" His question was eager.

"Yes. I think I will make this my home."

294

His exhilaration knew no bounds. "I will be happy to take care of it. If you will just complete this paper—" He took a form from his desk and handed it to her with a pen. Their fingers met and his hand tingled from the contact. Good God, he thought, this is an overpowering woman.

Quickly and neatly, she filled in the necessary information, Doña handed him the paper. His eyebrows rose when he saw the amount of the initial deposit.

"But you have listed this as cash," he said. "Surely such an amount will be transferred from another bank in your former city."

"No," she said bluntly. "I have it here, in cash." She negligently indicated the valise at her feet.

"What!" He stared at her, appalled. Then he smiled in an indulgent manner.

At once she realized her mistake. Assuming a rather coy, shamefaced manner, she laughed lightly, and said, "I suppose it was naughty of me." Then sobering, she added in a soft voice, "You see, I was so—anxious to get away. Chi-Cincinnati had such sad memories for me, since my husband—died." For good measure, Doña felt in her small pouch for a dainty handkerchief and pressed it to her eyes.

William Hackman reacted as she knew he would, "Oh, my dear lady," he said gently. "I am sorry. But I'm afraid you ladies do not always do the—wisest thing."

Having observed Marilou Hamilton many times, Doña knew just what to do next. She let her hand rest on the desktop near William Hackman's fingers; he moved his hand ever so slightly nearer hers.

He could have sworn she had boarded the boat at Chicago; but no matter. Poor little thing. She needed someone to look after her. "You must let me advise you in every way I can," he said gallantly.

"You are too kind." She gave him a grateful look from under her half-lowered lashes.

"Now," he said briskly, rising and taking the carryall, "I will see that your, er, resources are safely deposited at

295

once. In a few days your checks will be delivered to your hotel, and the account will be operative."

Accepting her soft-voiced thanks, William Hackman stood and watched as she left the bank, resolving that he would deliver the checks to her himself.

Then, seeing an amused teller observing him, Hackman gave the man an oppressive look and growled, "If you have nothing to do, Jensen, I can find something."

Hackman entered a cage, thinking of the beautiful Mrs. Hamilton.

Doña, who had kept a good deal of cash for immediate spending, left the bank with a holiday feeling. She thought of Mr. Hackman with amusement, and reflected how good it was to be in a city where she knew no one at all. It was very exciting, and her spirits lifted higher and higher.

She would, she resolved, take a few days for sheer frivolity, before she investigated the purchase of a business. That would be the only thing that could bring her a measure of security and content. Something of her own —never again to depend on the bounty of a man.

But first, the more feminine matters: it had been so long since she'd bought new clothes. A length of rose-red material in a dry-goods window attracted her. She had never been able to wear that color with her red hair. She went in and bought it, with several other things, and then a jeweler's, farther on down the street, caught her eye.

She casually purchased a bracelet of heavy gold, set with leaf-green peridots and another ornamented with rose amethysts. The young assistant was flabbergasted at the offhand manner with which she took the greenbacks from her bag. Perhaps such conspicuous wealth was not too wise for a woman alone. She resolved to be a little more discreet in future, for she thought she saw a dark man look at her with special interest as she emerged from the jewelers'.

But the next sign she saw drove other concerns from her mind: it was a stage office, and not a western branch of Raike Stages, either, she thought drily; that office was in St. Joseph. She decided to go in.

A gloomy-looking man was seated at a desk behind the counter.

"Is the owner in?" she asked him.

The man surveyed her hungrily, taking in her jaunty hat and elegant dress. "The owner, ma'am? Not now. Is there something I can do?"

She smiled to soften her answer, "No. I was in the stage business in another part of the country. I just wanted to compare notes and see how things are in St. Louis."

Her statement was not untrue. Before the troubles had begun, she had learned the Raike Stages business thoroughly.

"*You*—ran a business?" The man's incredulity was most annoying. "Well, ma'am, in St. Louis, women don't run businesses." His nasal voice was heavy with resentment.

"I see." She met his eyes levelly. "Well, thank you very much."

Doña left the stage office, closing the door softly. When she glanced back over her shoulder, the sullen man was staring after her. She almost laughed aloud.

Then she realized that the man she had dimly noticed outside the jewelry store was following her. It was not her imagination, for when she stopped before another store window, his tall, lithe form was reflected in the sideglass. But she could not see his face, for he kept to the shadowy recesses along the sidewalk. Uneasily she wondered if she were about to be robbed.

Nonsense, she thought. It was broad daylight and the streets were crowded with pedestrians. She moved along in the sun; the man was gone.

Doña was not unduly surprised a day or two later when Mr. Yancy sent up an attendant to announce that Mr. William Hackman of the Merchants Bank was waiting to see her.

"Please have him come up," she said.

He had come personally to deliver her checks.

"Why, Mr. Hackman!" she exclaimed with mock innocence. "Surely an officer of the bank doesn't concern himself with such petty matters."

Hackman colored and replied, "I was in the neighborhood, Mrs. Hamilton." He looked as sheepish as if she'd caught him stealing.

She said kindly, "Please stay and have some tea or coffee."

He brightened at once, and she gestured at the sofa in her sitting room.

"I'm glad you came, as a matter of fact," she said after she had rung for a servant.

His pleasure was so evident that she said hastily, "I wanted to discuss some business with you."

"I see." His clear blue eyes met her dark ones.

"I'm sure you can help me. I want to buy—or buy into—a business in St. Louis."

He looked shocked. When the maid had been dispatched with an order for coffee, Hackman protested, "I can hardly believe that you are interested in such matters."

Doña reflected that Hackman's disapproval was only a politer version of the clerk's ridiculing manner at the stage office.

But she held on to her patience, replying calmly, "I am very much interested. And I'm confident you can tell me which ones would be available for purchase."

Stubbornly he said, "A lady like you, Mrs. Hamilton —well, you will marry again, certainly."

"I will certainly not ever marry again, Mr. Hackman." His eyes widened curiously at her cold reply, and again he studied her lovely, vital face between its smooth wings of gleaming black hair.

He smiled that indulgent smile, then, which Doña had learned to expect from all men when a woman made a serious statement. "I can hardly believe that, Mrs. Hamilton."

She thought if he used the expression "A lady like you" again, she would brain him with the coffeepot that the maid was now bringing in on a tray.

"I do not care to debate with you, Mr. Hackman," she

said softly, pouring his coffee. "Do you take cream and sugar?" She delicately indicated the cream pitcher and sugar bowl.

He was very disconcerted, she could see. "Well, Mr. Hackman?" she demanded. "Can you advise me, or should I seek advice elsewhere?"

Her question was so businesslike that he recalled himself to his position and answered in a like tone, "Of course, Mrs. Hamilton. I will be happy to. Do you have any—special interests?"

"The stage line," she said bluntly.

Again he almost winced at her unfeminine directness, and she smothered a smile behind her ringed hand.

"I would strongly advise against it," he said, "without even examining their account sheets. The competition from Wells Fargo and from Raike Stages in St. Joseph is very strong."

"I am not at all afraid of competition," she said boldly. "I'm only interested in finding out if the owner cares to sell. Apparently when a woman broaches such a matter, it is an occasion for a joke."

He stared at her keenly, hearing the bitter edge to her words. "You are quite serious, aren't you, Mrs. Hamilton?"

"Quite serious, Mr. Hackman. I did not keep you here to flirt with you."

He colored brightly; nettled, he got to his feet. He bowed coldly, saying, "Very well, Mrs. Hamilton. I will undertake to advise you."

"Thank you, Mr. Hackman. Just send me the bill for your services." Smiling, she held out her hand.

He did not take it, but said curtly, "There will be no charge, Mrs. Hamilton. Consider it a service for our client."

When the door shut firmly and quietly behind him, Doña began to laugh.

"Isse-Loa, Isse-Loa." The mocking voice, coming from the direction of her bedroom, startled Doña almost out of her wits.

She whirled about and saw Tahre standing on the threshold of the sitting room.

"Isse-Loa," he said again, warmly, hurrying to her across the carpet.

"Tahre!" she cried out and threw herself into his arms. His tall, lithe body felt strong and comforting, and she stood for a long moment in his embrace, without speaking, the hot tears coursing down her cheeks. He kissed her hair.

"Isse-Neennak, Night-Deer you are now, with your black hair," he murmured. "More than ever you look akin to me."

She leaned back in his arms to look at him. "How different you are! And yet how much the same."

He had cut his hair, and wore the rough clothes of a roustabout. But the fierce pride of his warrior's face was unaltered, his dark eyes still had the power to inspire fear unless they were gentle as they were now, looking at her.

"Why, you are the man outside the jeweler's!"

Tahre laughed. "None other."

"But how did you come here?"

"By stealth, as always, Isse-Neennak. An Indian is not announced and sent up by the maid in St. Louis." He spoke matter-of-factly, but Doña flared with anger.

"The others," she said. "Tell me about them—Patche, Easooba, the children. Were you, were they—harmed in the raid? That was our tribe, wasn't it?"

She took him by the hand and urged him down beside her on the sofa. "You say *our* tribe still, in spite of all your fine clothes and your fine husband." Tahre's voice was full of affection.

"But tell me!" she urged him. "Tell me how everyone is."

"Patche is dead," he answered bluntly, "and three of the children."

A great wave of nausea swept her as she whispered, "The *children*."

Tahre nodded; there were grim lines about his mouth. With trembling hands, Doña poured him a cup of coffee, handing it to him.

"Thank you, Isse-Loa." Seeing her stricken face, he said, "Let us talk no more of that time. It was more terrible than anything we ever endured, but it is over. The tribe is scattered. Some went into Oklahoma with our kinsmen, the Kiowa."

"But you, Tahre. How did you come here?"

He shrugged. "Much by accident. I heard that there were many jobs that I could do. And I was tired of being a fugitive on the plains." He smiled. "I suddenly had a hunger for the cities, and to find a way to beat the white man at his games."

She looked thoughtful. The memory of the old days was very clear. Tahre, half-willing, yet skilled and brave at the exploits they had experienced together.

"And you, Isse-Loa. You are here alone, in a new guise, without your husband. What does it mean?"

Doña set down her cup and leaned back against the sofa. Haltingly, she began to tell him of all that happened in the intervening months, the meeting with Gerard and Torrance, the business in Chicago, Stephen's trial and imprisonment.

There was a long silence after she had finished. At last Tahre said, touching her dark hair with his sinewy hand, "You have known a great deal, and suffered. You are now a woman, Isse-Loa, and no longer the wild girl I knew on the plains." His voice had a sad sound.

"I am still the one you knew, Tahre." And she told him then of the many times she had ached with homesickness for their old days together.

"Yes," she said, "I am very much the same. But I have learned something," she added with bitterness. "I've learned how powerful money can be."

Tahre raised his brows and gave her an ironic smile.

"You don't believe me," she said. "But I have brought a great deal of money to St. Louis. And I intend to buy into a business, to have something of my own—*our* own," she amended. "I would like to share it with you, my dear cousin. You are my only friend, all that remains of my heritage."

"Do you really think," he asked gently, "that a warrior

would be beholden to a woman?" His tone and the smile with which he said the words took the sting from them, but Doña sensed the seriousness behind the question.

"You rode with me once," she retorted, "and even took my direction." Then sobering she added, "There is no being beholden between us, Tahre. We are beloved kinsmen."

Something stirred on his proud, impassive face, she noticed. He had almost the look he had that day on the meadow below the Olwen house, when he told her she would be happier with Stephen Raike.

But he asked calmly, "What is this thing you want to do in St. Louis?"

She told him about the stage line, and her work with Raike Stages.

"I see." His black eyes glinted with new interest. "You know, Isse-Loa, there is no cleverer disguise than owning a stage line."

"Disguise?"

"Surely you have not forgotten how we used to fool the buffalo," Tahre grinned. "Throwing another buffalo's skin over our heads and shoulders to confuse the beasts. Creeping, creeping forward—then, the arrows!" He made a wide, tossing motion with his powerful arm. "In the disguise of a respectable business, more than one bandit had robbed other stages to the south of here." His eyes glittered and he smiled widely.

"Tahre! I never heard you talk like this. There were so many times when you told me we should give up stealing, that you saw death coming."

"Ah, but I have changed since then. I have changed a great deal, Isse." His voice became dreamy, and he said softly, "I have heard there are cities to the East where a man's skin does not matter; all that matters is his gold. The old life will soon be dying, and the old ways. I have a great desire now for gold, to help Easooba and the others—gold of my own," he said, glancing at her, "so you will not sleep on buffalo skins in the future."

The meaning in his last words struck her suddenly. "What is it you are saying, Tahre?"

He slid to the carpet, kneeling before her, and took her hands in his. "I am saying that I've always loved you, Isse-Loa, as you have always known. Perhaps there will be a life for us together now."

Doña did not know how to answer; she looked down at him, at his lithe body, his powerful shoulders, the tendons of his horseman's legs straining the seams of his rough trousers. Her gaze returned to his regal face with its stern mouth, relaxed now into softness, the fierce black eyes that could be so gentle.

And her body's long hunger betrayed her. Crying out his name, she leaned forward and took his face between her narrow hands, lowering her mouth to his. His hard arms reached out for her and drew her toward him with such savagery that she nearly toppled. He kissed her again and again, with long, hungry caresses, and before she could protest, had risen to his feet, towering above her.

He looked down at her now with blazing eyes, breathing quickly, and held out his hand. She put her hand into his and felt him urging her upward. He took her body into his arms, his hold relentless, and she felt herself melting, melting to his lean body's demand.

Quite suddenly he had swept her up in his cradling arms, was carrying her into the bedroom of her suite, stilling her breathless protests with his mouth.

Her body, long denied, was ceasing to protest: she felt herself relaxing in his firm hold, warming to the familiar feel and sound and smell of him.

His body was a remembered home, and the hands that now released her gently for a moment as he lay her on the bed were the hands she had held when they played as children.

She heard him say her name again and again in a hushed, excited voice that sounded unbelieving, jubilant; through her half-closed eyes she saw him taking off the rough clothes from his magnificent body. His skin gleamed like copper in the fast-failing light.

Doña closed her eyes, giving up her protests, giving herself to the feverish moment. She felt him near her on the bed and put out her arms. As her hands met the hot,

303

smooth copper of his back and shoulders, stroking, she felt his flesh answer in a quick, savage, electric reaction.

Tahre's mouth was bending over hers, and she felt a hot wave of weakness when he kissed the hollow in her throat and his full, excited lips began to wander downward, zigzagging in small nibbles from her neck to her breasts. His fingers trembled, and a little awkwardly began to undo the buttons of her dress.

"Tear it," she said softly, smiling. He hesitated. "Tear it," she repeated, "tear it all away."

His strong hands obeyed, and her body felt the harshness of the tearing clothes; it excited her even more. Then she was lying on the shell of her gown and the thin undergarments; she felt herself being lifted; with closed eyes, perceived that he had swept the clothes from under her.

"Isse, Isse," he said hoarsely. Opening her eyes a little, she looked up at him, saw his dark look blazing down at her nakedness, darting to the long wings of black hair spread out on either side of her body.

His mouth fell on her flesh again, moving, moving ever downward over her soft convexities, finding the copper-shadowed core.

And Doña felt, like a sweet, sudden burn, Tahre's strong caress, and gave herself to lapping waves of overpowering pleasure that spread in increasing circles like circles upon water, upward and outward; there was a throbbing fever that pulsed and pulsed again until she cried out, shuddering throughout, until she felt another kind of sensation, a great fullness, and they were together, the pulsing within her throbbing more hotly.

"Stephen!" Doña cried out the name in a kind of frenzy. She felt the man in her arms wince, grow strangely still.

She opened her eyes and looked on the desolate face of her childhood friend.

Chapter Twenty-Six

A miserable neighborhood known as Conley's Patch lined a section of Chicago's waterfront. The vice-hating Mayor, Long John Wentworth, was as eager to tear down Conley's Patch as he was the districts of vice.

And on this summer night, Henry Lee, tossing on his grimy cot in one of the Patch's shanties, would have fervently agreed, if he could have read the papers. But there had been a law in Arkansas, where Henry was born, that said blacks were not allowed to learn to read. Henry's family had taken their name from their owners, cousins of the big Virginia people. When Henry ran away, a kindly Yankee in Ohio had given Henry some false papers that said he was free.

Henry had made his way to the city of Chicago, where he heard there were many places that a man could work for wages, and had been overjoyed to find a job in Alfred Torrance's house on Randolph Street. Henry, who had worked in the fields, was dazzled by the softness of his tasks; it was good to walk about in a clean apron under the bright chandeliers, like a house slave did at home.

Everything was fine until the night that dandy Gerard had killed Mr. Torrance, and the other white man, the nice-looking fellow they called Raike, was held to blame.

Henry Lee opened his eyes to the stuffy dark, the sweat running into them, and remembered. He remembered standing there, still as could be, looking at Gerard. Henry had always hated the man, hated and feared his smooth, uppity ways and soft hands and fine clothes. He was just like the masters back home. They said he had beaten his slaves back in Louisiana, and done worse.

When Gerard had put his gun in his pocket, and Mr. Pierce and the others had come in and taken hold of the man Raike, Gerard saw Henry staring at him, and made a kind of motion to the little fellow, the one that looked like a monkey, Mr. Douglas, he was called.

"Take care of him," Gerard said, and disappeared.

Later Mr. Pierce and the little fellow threatened Henry. They said if he told what he had seen they would kill him. Henry had been so scared he had run right out of the house as soon as they stopped watching him, leaving his things upstairs in his room and what little money he had saved.

Henry had not known where to go, but finally he thought he'd better hide out in one of the patches on the waterfront. Pierce and the others would not come there. Luckily Henry had his papers in his pants pocket—he was never without them, because you never knew what would happen—and the next morning early he had gone around to the boats to see if they wanted a man to help with the loading and unloading.

The dock boss had looked at him suspiciously, but it seemed all right when he looked at Henry's papers. And Henry was hired. He bought a hat to pull over his eyes and when he'd see a strange white man near the boats, he'd bow his head to hide his face, in case. But no one from Torrances ever came, thank the Lord, and Henry began to feel all right again, even if he hated the stinking shanty where he was forced to live.

A few days after he was hired on the docks, one of the white men, a big, rough fellow with a lot of hair on his face, who Henry kind of liked—because he was friendly to Henry and some of the other blacks and even talked nice to an Indian working with them—was sitting on the pier with a newspaper in his hands. Henry had looked at the paper, wishing he could read it.

The big, hairy man started to talk about something he was reading in the paper, about the Texas fellow by the name of Raike. Raike was on trial for killing Alfred Torrance.

Henry thought of how he had seen Gerard shoot Mr. Torrance, and the hate turned his stomach so sour that he put down his sandwich and couldn't eat another bite. He was glad the other men didn't pay much attention. But Henry Lee couldn't get it out of his mind. The big man told them the paper said there was nobody to speak up for this Raike.

I'm not the only one, Henry thought to himself, as he lifted the heavy crates through the afternoon. He wondered what had happened to the rich young white. Maybe he was too scared to tell, too.

Then one day, the man with the newspaper said that Raike had been sent to jail.

Henry Lee turned again in the squeaky cot, feeling his rancid sweat trickle down his body. And he remembered what his daddy had told him, when Henry was just a little boy: "There's only two ways to do things, Henry—right and wrong. Don't you ever be afraid to do things right. Because then you'll be a man in the sight of God."

Henry smiled in the close darkness, thinking of his daddy, who had talked almost as good as a preacher. There was something about the way he said things that made you remember.

And the Raike man was in jail—they said he'd be there the most of his life. While all the time Gerard was walking around, rich, free, laughing up his sleeve at all the rest of them. Henry Lee felt sick thinking about it. It had been worrying him so long! Why didn't that rich boy speak up? People would listen to him.

Henry didn't know the boy's name, but he'd seen him at Torrance's before. Henry remembered him especially because the young man had a diamond-studded watch fob, shaped like a four-leaf clover, which the boy'd rubbed for luck.

Maybe I ought to tell, Henry thought. Maybe if I told them they would take care of me so Pierce and the other men wouldn't hurt me.

Henry gave up the idea of sleep and got up from the

cot. He started to walk up and down the little shack. Dear Lord, help me do the right thing! he prayed.

Tomorrow, he thought, maybe when he was moving the boxes, he'd ask one of the other men what to do.

There was one man, a black man from Alabama who knew how to read; he'd ask him. The bearded white man had moved on, and the Indian had, too. But maybe the man from Alabama would tell him how to find out the name of the people he should go to see.

And for the first time in weeks, Henry Lee lay down on his narrow cot and slept at once, sweetly.

While Henry Lee was falling to sleep again that last hot night in June, Judson Palmer and Harry Kinsley followed their young ladies from the music hall in the Tremont House. The night before, Ole Bull, the famous Norwegian violinist, had given his "one farewell concert"; tonight had been his "positive farewell."

Neither Kinsley nor Palmer had attended much to the music, and now after a laughing remark about the indecisive Norwegian's appearance, Kinsley said to Palmer in a low voice, "After we take them home, would you like to go down for a game?"

Palmer thought again of that night at Torrance's. "Not I, my friend. I've got to go a little easy for a while."

As the young ladies moved away to the women's dressing room Kinsley asked, "What's the matter? Your old man kicking up again?"

Uneasily, Palmer answered, "Listen, Harry, I'm in up to my eyes. My father said he'd cut me off without a dime if I run up any more debts."

Kinsley laughed. "You ran up plenty at Torrance's. Say, weren't you there the night that Raike fellow shot old Al?"

"Me?" Palmer laughed uneasily. "Not me. Why, they'd have called me as a witness at the trial if I'd been there."

"That would have fixed you up just fine with the old man, wouldn't it?" Kinsley laughed again. "Damned lucky for you you weren't."

"Damned lucky," Palmer agreed rather weakly. He

began to sweat, and the sweat was not wholly due to the weight of his evening clothes. To calm himself, he ran his thumb over the diamond-studded watch fob that he always carried for luck.

Doña dreamed of Stephen: he was dressed in the robes of a judge, and she was the prisoner being tried. He stared at her coldly with his sharp gray eyes, the eyes that had once been so warm with love, and intoned, "I find the prisoner guilty of robbery in the first degree; she is condemned to spend her life alone. She has robbed me of everything."

She tossed restlessly in the bed, moaning, feeling a vague warm presence at her side. She heard a low voice murmur soothing words, words in the Comanche tongue.

"Stephen! Stephen!" she cried out, whether in her dream or waking, she could not tell.

When she opened her eyes, it was to semi-darkness: one of the lamps was lit. Doña turned. Tahre was sitting in a chair by the bed, dressed in his rough clothes, looking at her with sad tenderness.

"Isse-Loa." He smiled slightly, neither moving nearer nor touching her. "It is best that I go. Soon I must go to the river again, to my work. And I must not be seen here."

She sat up in the bed and the coverlet fell away from her breasts. She realized she was wearing nothing; he kept his eyes averted as she covered herself.

And then she was painfully aware of what the night had been—for her, only an appeasement of her body's hunger; for him, the hope of a fulfilment of a long dream. But she could see in his eyes that his dream was lost. He had heard her, she was sure, crying out for Stephen.

She was horrified at what she had done; to give herself to Tahre had been almost like giving herself to a brother.

Now she feared he could see her dismay on her face—he knew her so well.

But his proud face revealed nothing but a remote sorrow. He rose and touched her hair gently. "You have given me the greatest happiness I ever knew," he said.

309

"But it was wrong. You still belong to Stephen Raike."

"Tahre—"

'We will never speak of this time again."

"Please," she began.

"I must go, Isse-Loa." He strode from the room, and she heard the rustle of paper, the scratching of a pen, in the sitting room. In a moment he came back, holding a piece of paper out to her.

"This is the place where I live. When you need me, you will send for me there. We still have other business together." He smiled, and she recalled what he had said about wanting gold.

Soundlessly then he was gone, moving as softly on his booted feet as he had in his moccasins. The outer door closed quietly.

Doña's head began to ache. She rose and dressed, then looked for her gun. She weighed it in her hands, reflecting how long it had been since she had fired a gun. Loading it, she placed the Colt in her handbag and went to the window.

Dawn was coming to the city. She knew now what it was she wanted to do. Going lightly down the stairs, she asked the sleepy man at the desk to direct her to a public stable.

Riding through the waking streets to the edge of town, Doña found the place she needed, where she could get in target practice unobserved. And until the sun was high, she fired the Colt again and again. She still was far from being as sharp as she wanted when she stopped firing.

Dusty and weary, aching with discouragement and from the unaccustomed exercise of riding, Doña returned to the hotel about eleven.

Delbert Yancy greeted her with surprised pleasure. "Why, Mrs. Hamilton, you look like you've gone a far way this morning."

"I have decided to take up riding again, Mr. Yancy."

"I see, I see," he said, staring at her dusty clothes and tired face. "Oh, Mrs. Hamilton, I have a letter for you. A messenger brought it about an hour ago."

"A letter? Thank you." She took the envelope from

his eager hands and glanced at it as she mounted the stairs. It was from William Hackman.

When she had reached her rooms, thrown off her riding hat and washed her hands and face, Doña took the letter to the sofa. "Would you do me the honor," it said, "of accompanying me to dinner tonight at Tower Grove, one of the great homes of our city, where the other guests will be outstanding citizens, fitting company for a lady such as yourself."

Doña grinned. "A lady!" The whole letter read like an after-dinner speech. Stephen had always made such fun of flowery talk. *Stephen.*

She felt like crying. But she must forget Stephen, must try to get on with living. It would be wise to accept the banker's invitation, to see what St. Louis' "outstanding" people were like, to see what she could learn of the city's business. No doubt some of the guests would be businessmen.

The flowery letter concluded that if she were kind enough to accept, William Hackman would call for her at seven.

She sent a note to the bank, accepting.

William Hackman, in faultless evening clothes, dismissed his carriage and gave his arm to Doña. They walked up the long front walk to the villa called Tower Grove; on either side of them lay an enormous velvety green lawn.

The house was finer than many millionaires' houses in Chicago, Doña judged. It was a graceful two-story building of painted brick and stone. Its third floor was a simple rectangular tower; it reminded her of the great villas of France and Italy she had seen in pictures.

Noticing her upward glance, William Hackman said, "I see you admire the house. You have good taste!" He smiled. "The exterior design is so restrained. See how plain the lintels are over the windows. And there are so few of the columns and arches so dear to architects' hearts."

She murmured in an agreeable way, thinking that he

311

talked very much like his letters. In person it sounded even stranger.

"You must know a great deal about these things."

"Oh, not really," he said modestly. "I wanted to be an architect once, and studied in the East. I looked at many buildings in Europe, too."

So that was why he seemed such an unlikely banker! Doña thought and felt a little sorry for him. She glanced about her at a great grove of sassafras trees and wonderful lawns and flowerbeds surrounding the house.

"There's so much land!" she said wistfully.

"It's a wonderful place," Hackman agreed. "Henry— Mr. Shaw, our host—decided to build this place when he saw the Crystal Palace in England seven years ago."

A dignified black butler answered Hackman's ring. Behind him stood a portly, smiling man in his late fifties, elegantly dressed. The man came forward smiling and took Hackman's extended hand.

Doña handed her light wrap to the servant, and their smiling host bowed to her. "Mrs. Hamilton, I am Henry Shaw. Welcome to Tower Grove." He had a British accent; she learned later that he had been born in England.

"Come, the others are in the parlor."

Shaw led them through the high-ceilinged entrance hall, with its great pier mirror, to a room full of gilt-framed mirrors, crystal chandeliers and marble busts.

Doña was surprised to see that there was only one other woman, a grim-looking matron. Four men rose when Doña and Hackman entered. She was introduced to Mr. and Mrs. Robert Campbell and their two sons; the other man was a Mr. John Marshall.

"Robert," said Henry Shaw, "is an emigrant, too. He came to this country from Ireland. But he has led a far more adventurous life. He was an explorer and fur trader in his youth."

Doña looked at the weathered, middle-aged man with interest.

He smiled back at her as they all sat down again, saying, "Those were the grand old days. I have become a mere merchant now."

"A merchant!" Mr. Marshall scoffed, smiling.

"I would hardly call you a merchant, sir," said William Hackman. "Your business interests are so wide. Mr. Marshall here," Hackman said to Doña, "is president of our rival bank."

Doña liked these people—they were more open and matter-of-fact about themselves than the people she had met in Chicago. And the men made no polite attempt to discuss topics interesting to the women; they spoke of business freely, and Doña listened with all her attention.

St. Louis was evidently recovering well from the panic of 1857, and land values were rising. But, as the men in Chicago had said, the most dependable sources of high revenue had to do with stage lines and river traffic.

She was glad to be able to learn all this, so easily, and relieved that she did not have to talk with the grim-looking Mrs. Campbell.

Doña was irritated when Henry Shaw said, "Please, boys! Enough of the dull world of trade! We are boring the ladies. And besides, I had enough of it when I turned in my business twenty years ago!"

"You must admit, Henry, you made your pile quicker than other fellows," the plain-speaking Campbell said. "That was some business you had—import-exports, I mean, let alone the land. It's quite a feather in your cap, retiring at thirty-nine."

"But I *have* retired," Shaw said firmly, "and have devoted myself to travel and the acquisition of beautiful things."

"In that you have succeeded as well as you did in business," William Hackman said, looking about the room with admiration.

The butler announced dinner, and Henry Shaw offered Mrs. Campbell his arm. Doña was pleased that the elder Campbell was quick to offer his arm to her. She looked forward very much to talking with him.

Shaw's dining room was one of the grandest rooms she had ever seen; over the damask-covered oval table hung a brass chandelier, brilliant with candles that reflected themselves in the mirror over the hearth. The silken curtains were a wonderful bronze-green, the wallpaper printed in a pineapple design of the same bronzed green, russet-red and somber gold. A tall centerpiece of russet and gold flowers echoed the other colors, and the glasses set at the diners' places were the color of fine sherry.

"I am sorry," said Robert Campbell with heavy gallantry, "that we talked so much of business. Maybe we were rude."

"You weren't at all," Doña said with warm frankness. "Nothing interests me more. I am hoping to buy a business here myself."

Campbell raised his shaggy brows and said good-naturedly, "That is very enterprising of you, Mrs. Hamilton."

She judged that his rough, adventuresome life had left him with few of the prejudices of more conventional men. Across the table, William Hackman looked a little uncomfortable. She gave him a brilliant smile.

His blue eyes admired her; she was beautiful this evening in a gown of peach, with simple lines and a modestly low neck that set off to perfection her necklace of red, green and yellow gold; plain red-gold drops were in her shapely ears, shining below the smooth wings of glistening black hair.

She noticed that the two Campbell sons—presentable and slender, but with none of the force and vigor of their father—were also looking at her with admiration.

"You interest me greatly, Mrs. Hamilton," Robert Campbell said in his frank, loud voice. He took a healthy swig of his wine, saying, "Ah!" in appreciation. "Maybe I can be of help to you, in the line of advice."

"I would be most grateful," she said. But catching Hackman's eye, she added politely, "Mr. Hackman has also said he would help."

"You couldn't do better," Campbell remarked kindly. "But I was meaning from the point of view of a simple businessman."

Henry Shaw laughed at the man's description of himself. "Simple!" he repeated. "Robert has his finger on the pulse of business as no one else has, Mrs. Hamilton."

She turned to Campbell eagerly. "What do you think of the stage business in Missouri, Mr. Campbell?"

"A veritable gold mine," he declared. "But you need some really stalwart men—men like the ones I used to fight with in the old days." He grinned. "For more and more stages are being robbed these days, both Wells Fargo and St. Louis Stages. Very frankly, I don't think much of the manager of St. Louis Stages."

Doña listened to him intently, and asked, "Why not?"

"He hasn't the kind of men a proper stage line needs, and doesn't seem to know how to get them."

Doña thought of the men she had known, Tahre and Frank and their companions. *She* could find the right men, she was sure.

"Raike Stages' St. Joseph Line seems to do better," said Campbell. "Now there was a fellow I could understand."

"Who do you mean?" Hackman asked. "Stephen Raike, the young tycoon from Texas?"

"Yes. What a pity he got mixed up in that shooting in Chicago. Why they sent him to jail I'll never know; he performed a public service, as far as I can tell."

"Robert!" Mrs. Campbell's scandalized voice was heard for the first time at the table.

"Well, it's the truth I'm saying, Jane. That Torrance was one of the worst scoundrels in Chicago."

Doña's hand, raising her wine glass to her lips, jerked involuntarily, and the red wine made a great stain on the white linen cloth.

"Oh, dear!" she said. "I have—ruined your lovely cloth."

"It is nothing at all," Henry Shaw assured her, although his shrewd eyes studied her with great interest. He made a deft motion to the butler who placed a fresh napkin under Doña's plate so swiftly that he hardly disturbed her.

"Yes," Campbell went on—this was apparently a favorite subject of his, and the less forceful members of the dinner party seemed to be content to hear him. "The Raike Line hasn't done too badly. Maybe they're robbing the others!" He laughed a hearty laugh.

Mrs. Campbell said again, "Robert!" in her reproachful fashion, but he ignored her.

"I think St. Louis Stages needs a shot in the arm—some new blood, you might say." Campbell's twinkling eyes met Doña's, and she smiled at him, oblivious of the puzzled Shaw, the disapproving bankers, and the fascinated Campbell sons.

When the evening was over and Hackman had delivered her to her hotel, he said hesitantly, "I hope you were not bored this evening. It did-not—turn out as I expected."

"I was never bored for a minute," she protested warmly, and thanked him for the evening.

In her rooms, she reviewed the hours past, thinking with satisfaction, It turned out better than I could have dreamed!

In the morning she wrote a note to Tahre and had it delivered to the address he had given her.

Then she dressed in her new brown riding habit, with its narrow, practical skirt. She donned boots of saddle-brown leather and set a wide-brimmed tan hat on her head.

She rode from the stable to her secret spot on the edge of town and relentlessly, for the next three hours, fired the Colt again and again and again.

She fired from a standing position, kneeling and prone. She fired while at a canter and at a gallop.

This time she hit her chosen targets' centers nine times out of ten.

It was not good enough. Sweating, she reloaded the Colt and started all over again. By the end of five hours, she was hitting her target ten times out of ten.

With a feeling of great elation, she galloped toward the sycamore that she had been using. Straining to reach the lowest branch, she examined the particular leaf; there was a great torn hole, dead center.

The woman who called upon William Hackman that afternoon at the Merchants' Bank did not look like a woman who had spent the morning at target-practice.

Washed, brushed and changed, she presented a pretty picture: her cream-colored gown and matching veiled hat were the height of feminine stylishness.

Hackman rose from his desk, his aristocratic face bright with pleasure, and settled her into a chair.

She patiently suffered his polite inquiries and effusions before she said quietly, "I would like to make an offer to the owner of St. Louis Stages."

"Do you mean you wish to buy into that business, Mrs. Hamilton, after all that Mr. Campbell said last night?"

She thought wryly that she had decided *because* of what Campbell had said last night, but restrained her expression and replied, "I wish to buy outright."

"Outright!" Hackman looked scandalized. He was obviously used to more conservative buyers.

"Outright," Doña repeated, smiling at the young banker.

Reluctantly, he said, "Very well, then. I will begin checking out the possibilities."

As she left the bank, delicate and beautiful in her light, floating gown, Hackman thought that he had never met such an incorrigible woman—or wanted one so much.

Chapter Twenty-Seven

The summer sun beat down on Henry Lee's bare back and shoulders while he and Willie bent down to pick up the crate of guns.

Willie Jones grunted. "Wish we could get us a cargo of feathers." Together they bore their burden up the ramp to the boat.

Henry, who always laughed at the things Willie said, did not smile now. He was still thinking of his problem. After the night he had resolved to tell about what he'd witnessed, he had asked the men at work what to do. And all of them had told him to keep quiet.

"You take care of yourself, Henry Lee," one man had said. "No white man goin' to stick his neck out for *you,* or believe you. Let that rich boy do it."

But Henry thought of the man in Ohio that had given him the paper, and the man by the name of Bartlett whom Willie's cousin Isaiah worked for. Even Willie, who did not like white men at all, said Mr. Bartlett wasn't a bad man.

Following Willie Jones down the ramp for another load, Henry was still thinking about it. A whole month had gone by, and he still hadn't done anything.

Before she went in, Doña paused to read the notice posted on the door of the stage office:

OFFICE OF THE ST. LOUIS STAGES,
St. Louis, July 9th, 1858.
NOTICE IS HEREBY Given, that the St. Louis

Stages have sold their line of stages between St. Louis and Leavenworth, Kansas, to MRS. ISSA HAMILTON, the sale to take effect from the 30th day of June, 1858. Said MRS. HAMILTON assumes all liabilities of said line created since that date, and the Company ceases to be responsible from that date.

BRADFORD SCOTT Sup't. S.L.S.

Doña entered the office. She was wearing a simple cotton dress of apple-green; her face was sheltered from the blistering sun by a wide-brimmed hat.

Richard Krause, the sullen man who had received her on her first visit to the office, stood up when she entered. Krause was unsmiling. Doña knew that he was about to say something she would not welcome.

"Mrs. Hamilton," he said bluntly, in his rough voice, "I'd like to give you my notice."

Without interest or surprise, she answered, "Very well, Mr. Krause. When will you be leaving?"

"This week." He seemed a little disappointed in her reaction.

"All right," she replied calmly. "Meanwhile, perhaps you'll show me where everything is, so I can teach the next clerk what to do." She took off her hat and hung it on a hook behind her desk.

"Sure." Krause gathered up the ledgers from his desk and pulled up a chair by hers.

Scanning the accounts, Doña was appalled at the slipshod way that things had been managed. But she kept her own counsel, her quick brain already busy planning improvements.

There were eight coaches belonging to St. Louis Stages, only two fitted out for passengers. And they looked, Doña had said indignantly to Tahre, like wagons that hauled pigs. One of her first projects was to scrap the two coaches in the worst condition and to replace them with larger and newer ones. She would advertise the new coaches as having "every comfort" for passengers.

Meanwhile the other coaches were being repainted,

reupholstered and fitted out for rougher duty. She had not told Hackman yet—or Robert Campbell, who had taken a lively interest in her enterprise and had been of great help, though she had so far declined his offer of an investment—but she planned to extend the stages' run beyond Leavenworth and farther west along the California Trail.

One thing at a time, she thought now with satisfaction. It had been bad enough for St. Louis to learn that a woman was buying the stage line—worse that she had an Indian for a partner. If they learned that she was getting in over her head, their amusement would be unbounded, and their smug assessment confirmed.

She would have to prove herself all over again, just as she had in Texas. Recalling Texas, Doña grinned. There was one way to be sure she'd win out over the other stagelines. All at once the old excitement, the craving for danger began to pull at her again. She wanted to ride again at the head of a band, to feel the exhilaration of risk, of escape, of adventure.

A week later, when the Wells Fargo stage was robbed just outside Independence, Doña summoned Tahre.

"I want to hire the ones who robbed that stage."

Tahre looked at her. "Why? Why risk your neck now? You have money. You're beholden to nobody."

She grinned. "You know why. Do you think I can give all that up so easily? I dream about it at night sometimes. There's something in me, Tahre, something that makes me want the old days again."

"And you think I know who the men are."

"I *know* you know," she said. "The Indians always know everything. I want them to go to work for me. Can you get them?"

"It will take a lot of money, Isee-Loa."

"We have it."

"Then I will see the man I know, and talk to him. He is a Kiowa," Tahre said.

"I thought so. Go, please, Tahre, and see the Kiowa."

After her cousin had left, Doña reflected with wonder

how smooth things were between them again. It was as if the night in the hotel had never happened. She marveled at Tahre's impassive demeanor. Perhaps it was truly over, and they could be friends again, and companions, as it had been in the other days on the Texas plains.

"What is it, Isaiah?" Jos Bartlett looked up from his newspaper.

"It's about my cousin, Willie Jones, Mr. Bartlett."

"Yes."

"Well, sir, he works by the boats, you know. And there's a fellow named Henry Lee."

Bartlett waited. Isaiah, he knew, would get to the point in his own good time.

"This man named Henry Lee used to work for Alfred Torrance."

The old lawyer's expression grew alert.

"Well, he told Willie he was there the night Torrance was shot."

"What!" Jos Bartlett's newspaper slid to the floor, forgotten. He got to his feet.

"Yes, sir. This Henry Lee says he's afraid to tell because of what they would do to him."

"They? Pierce and Marshall and the others at the house?"

"Yes, sir, I reckon so."

"Thank you very much, Isaiah. You don't know how much this means to me. Where can I find this Henry Lee?"

"Oh, sir," Isaiah protested. "He lives in a shack in Conley's Patch. You don't figure to go down there."

Jos Bartlett laughed. "Try and stop me," he said, hurrying from the library for the hall, where the hat stand was.

But as Jos Bartlett's carriage took him over the Rush Street Bridge into the city, and he sighted the tumbledown shanties of Conley's Patch at the other end of the river, he wondered if his errand couldn't have waited for morning. The place, even at this distance, was not a reassuring sight in the gathering dark.

Isaiah, who was driving him, grumbled, "You better let me come in with you, Mr. Bartlett. You might run into the Bengal Tigress."

Bartlett laughed. The Bengal Tigress was a powerful procuress who ruled Conley's Patch. The Tigress was reputed to love a fight, and when she was in a boisterous mood, even the men in the Patch barred their doors and windows and stayed out of sight.

"I'd fight her myself, Isaiah, to help Steve Raike."

"Yes, sir," Isaiah murmured, unconvinced. "All the same, the Patch is bad enough by day."

They were arriving now at the edge of Conley's Patch, a collection of what Long John Wentworth called the "dirtiest, vilest, most propped-up, fall-down, miserable shanties" in Chicago.

"That's Henry's place," said Isaiah. When he stopped the carriage, he asked, "You want me to come in with you, or watch the horse?"

"Better watch the horse, Isaiah. I'll get Henry, and we'll drive out of here a ways and talk."

To Isaiah's relief, Josiah Bartlett emerged from the shanty in record time, the surprised Henry Lee in his wake.

The two black men greeted each other, smiling, and Bartlett said, "Get in, Henry. We'll drive on a little way and talk all this out."

As they drove away, Bartlett listened intently to Henry Lee's story. When he had concluded Henry said "So you see, we're the only ones. Me and that rich boy."

"*What* rich boy?" Bartlett exclaimed.

"Don't know his name, Mr. Bartlett, but he's rich all right. Dresses fine, with them finicky ways." Henry grinned.

"Tell me how he looked, Henry. Tell me everything you can about him." Bartlett's voice shook with excitement.

Henry described the elegant young man haltingly but accurately, and added that the young man had an unusual four-leaf clover watch fob with diamonds in it.

"Judson Palmer," Bartlett said softly. "Well, I'll be

damned. And he was standing right behind you. He saw Gerard shoot Torrance?"

"Don't see how he could have missed it, Mr. Bartlett. But then I guess he just ran away."

"That's right; he wasn't listed among those present. He wasn't called as a witness." Bartlett's voice was grim. "Well, he's not going to run away from me, Henry. Isaiah," he called out "let's take Henry Lee with us for now. He can bunk with you. First we're going to call on the Palmers. That all right with you, Henry?"

"All *right?*" Henry Lee repeated, grinning. "Lord, sir, I reckon it *is!*" Willie Jones had told him that Isaiah had a mighty fine set-up at the Bartletts'. "I just reckon it is, and I thank you."

To his relief, Bartlett caught Judson Palmer on his very doorstep, preparing to go out. The elder Palmer was not at home. Bartlett was glad, for he knew of the boy's uneasy relations with the stern old man, and he was convinced this matter would take his most delicate handling. Bartlett could get far more out of Jud in Caleb Palmer's absence.

But it was only after an hour's earnest argument that Judson Palmer consented to drive to Bartlett's office and sign an affidavit. The lawyer himself drew it up. His clerks had long departed.

When Bartlett's carriage dropped Palmer in the city's heart, before heading again for home, Palmer said ruefully, "I never thought I'd have the nerve to tell that story. Now, I'm ashamed I waited. When my father finds out I didn't tell before—"

"You've told it now, Jud," Bartlett said. "Let's count on that to cool him down."

Palmer looked skeptical. "At least it's out," he said. "It's been eating at me for a long time."

"I can well imagine." Bartlett's voice was dry. He watched the young man about town disappear into the crowd before McVickers' Theater.

"Let's go, Isaiah," Bartlett called out. "I've got a lot of work to do. The night has just begun."

And as the carriage moved away toward the bridge, Bartlett was thinking, First a writ of *corum nobis,* to the governor, to get Steve released. From there it's going to go like a hot knife through butter.

The second court appearance of Stephen Raike was nothing like the first: Stephen sat with the spectators, and not at the defense table. He was tougher and leaner than ever, after his prison stay. As always he was immaculately turned out, his face relaxed now, his gray eyes bright with anticipation.

He glanced at the sullen Gerard, seated at the table where he himself had sat, the table of the accused. With bitter satisfaction, Stephen saw plainly, on Gerard's handsome face, the man's fear and bewilderment.

Stephen smiled. The warrant for Gerard's arrest had given nothing away: neither Gerard nor his lawyer knew who the mystery witness was, only that one had been produced. At that moment Gerard, glancing about the courtroom, caught Stephen's steady gray look, and the Creole's face reddened. In his black eyes was a glare of sheer hatred.

When the prosecution called Judson Palmer to the stand, Stephen leaned forward with expectation. It was a delight to see Gerard's expression of puzzlement, then stupefaction, as Judson Palmer testified to the Creole's guilt.

Torrance's henchmen—Marshall, Dexter, and the others, including the monkeylike, illiterate little Douglas —were seated a few rows behind Stephen. As Palmer's testimony unfolded Stephen could not resist turning for a quick backward look. Torrance's employees were stunned, as if they had been struck across their unpleasant faces. Stephen could not restrain a grin.

They were called, one by one, to the stand, and stumbling over their testimonies, managed to make their various stories contradictory and conflicting.

But the greatest pleasure, for Stephen, was still ahead —to see the arrogant Gerard on the witness stand.

Gerard, dressed in a suit of fine gray broadcloth and a

ruffled shirt of paler gray, a costly stickpin in his maroon cravat, walked to the stand and was sworn in. Stephen thought he saw a crack in that facade of coolness as he peered at the Creole's face; it was damp with nervous sweat.

Throughout the prosecution's battery of hard questions, Gerard repeated his stubborn denials. But then the prosecuting attorney called out, "If you did not shoot Alfred Torrance, Mr. Gerard, and if, as you now admit, neither did Stephen Raike, who *did?*"

"Dexter!" Gerard cried out desperately. "Dexter!"

"Why, you lying bastard!" Robert Dexter rose from his bench, shouting, his hard eyes gleaming with anger and his heavy face flushed dark red. "You know damned well you did it, and I'm not lying for you any longer!"

Pandemonium broke out in the court, and over the pounding of the judge's gavel, Stephen heard the prosecuting attorney raise his voice to his associate, catching the words "adjournment," "judge's chambers."

When the court reconvened an hour later, the friends of Torrance were recalled. This time their testimonies completely contradicted what had gone before.

The jury had been out for less than a half-hour, when it delivered its verdict of guilty.

When Gerard was sentenced to twenty-five years imprisonment, the courtroom broke out again into wild applause. The judge, with something like a smile on his stern face, rapped his gavel with a kind of good-natured inattention. Chicago, it seemed, loved Stephen Raike.

Grinning, Stephen grasped Bartlett's hand and said over the uproar, "One more thing, Jos."

"Whatever you say."

Stephen made his request. "It's a bit irregular," Bartlett said, smiling, "but I'll see what I can do."

Bartlett was successful: Stephen Raike was admitted to the corridor where Philippe Gerard would pass on his way to his first detention site.

At last he saw the handsome Creole coming down the hall between two officers.

Stephen said nothing, but stood smiling as Gerard approached.

As he got near, enough to Stephen to recognize him, Gerard cried out, "What are you doing here?"

Silently, Stephen took in the sight of Gerard's sweaty face and rumpled hair, the expensive cravat awry on the sweat-stained shirtfront, the stickpin crooked now. Gerard looked pathetic.

"Say it, Raike!" Gerard cried out with hatred. His full mouth was slack, with moisture gathered at the corners.

"Say it, goddam you!" Gerard shouted. "You've won, the Raikes have won, again."

Still silent, Stephen looked steadily at Gerard, and watched as he was led away.

Chapter Twenty-Eight

The release of Stephen Raike in August, 1858 was reported in newspapers from Texas to New York, because Raike financial interests affected businesses from West to East.

The arrest and conviction of Philippe Gerard was noted and discussed in some of the same articles.

Stephen's whole Land Office staff was gathered to welcome him when he entered the Lake Street office on a late summer day.

The faithful Matilda Johnston and Jeb had obtained, at their own expense, flowers from Chicago's florist, and had placed them in vases around the room, setting one huge vase on Stephen's desk in his private office.

He was deeply touched by this evidence of affection, and grinned at them all, saying, "It's good to see you."

Matilda was overcome with emotion and dabbed at her eyes with a handkerchief. Stephen patted her shoulder and murmured a quiet greeting.

"All right," he said then in a brisker tone, "we've got a lot of work to do. Matilda, I want you first. And then later, Jeb, I'll want you to write out a number of letters. Take this now." He handed the boy a sheet of paper. "And start copying out the envelopes."

Jeb eagerly obeyed. As he began addressing the envelopes, he realized the list contained names and addresses of detective bureaus in Boston, Cincinnati, St. Louis, and New York.

Stephen Raike's business connections in St. Joseph,

Missouri, made his release a newsworthy item in Missouri papers, too.

Doña read the article with mingled joy and disbelief. It was like a miracle, the witness appearing as if from nowhere. And Gerard—he would be the one, now, to be imprisoned, shut away, unable to harm her, or Stephen.

When she said Stephen's name silently to herself, Doña felt all the old pain and yearning once more. Stephen, with his lean body and gray eyes, his strong, deep voice and skilled, caressing hands. Doña took a shuddering breath, seeing him clearly again in her inner eye.

When Tahre entered the office later, he glanced at the paper in Doña's hands and said quietly, "You will write to Stephen now and go to him?"

"Never." Doña turned a cold, determined face to the Indian. "All that is over, Tahre. Please do not speak of it again."

"It's a big country, Steve," Josiah Bartlett said mildly, sipping his coffee. They were lunching together in the dining room of the Tremont House.

"That's right, Jos, but there are ways to find her."

"Where will you start?"

"With the banks," Stephen answered simply. "I have a feeling she's gone to one of the larger cities. And the banks will have to have a record of such a woman making a deposit like that. People always remember Doña."

Bartlett heard the wistful yearning in the younger man's voice and was stirred to pity.

"And what have the results been, so far?" he asked Stephen quietly.

"Nothing from the East," Stephen said. "It's been two weeks now. But I'm waiting to hear from Cincinnati and St. Louis."

"I hope you find her." Bartlett smiled at Stephen.

"I've got to, Jos. I've got to." The younger man stared for a moment into the distance, then he asked, "And Henry Lee? What have you done with him?" He made an effort to smile at Bartlett.

"Henry's safely stashed away at the moment with Isaiah in my servants' quarters." Bartlett grinned.

"Send him downtown to see me," Stephen said. "I'd like to thank the man."

Henry Lee sat across from Stephen in the Raike Land Office, waiting with anticipation for what the other man would say. He liked the man Raike more than ever, liked the courteous way he had risen when Henry came into the office, something no white men, in his experience, had ever done before.

"Well, Mr. Lee," Stephen Raike said. "Thanks for coming in. It looks like I owe you quite a bit." His smile was wide and dazzling in his tanned face. "Tell me how the job is, down on the docks."

"Mighty hard, Mr. Raike. My back like to break."

"I'll bet it does. Do you know anything about horses? How's your driving?"

Henry Lee answered with pride. "My driving's good. And I had a good bit to do with horses, down South."

"Well, what about a job with Raike Stages? I'd sure like to try you out." Stephen said. "The pay's good." He named a wage that made Henry Lee's face light up. "That suit you?"

"Suit me! I'll say so!"

"Just take this over to Raike Stages." Stephen scribbled a note and handed it to Henry. Henry thanked Stephen and left the office.

He was feeling mighty good as he hurried down the wooden stairs into the sunlight of Lake Street.

The Wells Fargo stage had left St. Louis in the early evening with eight passengers and the usual shipments of express and mail.

At a point one mile beyond the Baptist Cemetery and down a gentle slope, two masked men sprang up from the side of the road and ran toward the coach's horses. One grabbed the nigh leader by the neck and yelled, "Hold up, there! Put down that brake!"

Quick as lightning, the driver reined in, but the man

329

riding shotgun in the rear opened fire on the two bandits. The first bandit whirled and with incredible swiftness, shot the rifle from the guard's hand.

The second man ran up to the wheel horse and said to the driver, "Throw out the treasure boxes. Keep the horses quiet. Have that other fellow throw out the express, and we won't have any trouble at all."

The masked man had a strange, hoarse voice, and the skin of his upper face was coppery. He pointed his Colt at the driver, repeating, "Hurry up the express."

The driver threw out the boxes. "The treasure boxes," the bandit said. "And be quick about it. Now."

The other boxes came tumbling from the coach and settled in the dust of the road.

"Now get to the back of the stage." The driver obeyed. The second bandit had already retrieved the guard's rifle.

Two other masked men came out from the underbrush and picked up the boxes. They disappeared again with their treasure.

A third figure emerged now from the underbrush and the first man, who had a rough voice and coppery skin, gave a low curse at the sight of the newcomer.

So small and slim was he that he looked like a boy, the newcomer was wearing an oversized shirt and baggy trousers tucked into scuffed boots and his hat was pulled down over his eyes so that no one could see his eyes or hair.

The small newcomer made a gesture with his gloved hand, in which there was a Colt .44, and the rough-voiced man approached the passengers. "Empty your purses and pockets," he said. There were two women on the stage. The terrified passengers obeyed.

With split-second timing, the bandits scooped up their booty and moved out of sight.

The cursing Wells Fargo driver and his disarmed shotgun-man heard the sound of retreating horses' hooves.

Riding hard, the five bandits reached a spot three miles away where another stagecoach was waiting. Two leaped from their horses and slapped the animals on their rumps.

The horses ran off in the direction of a wooded grove a mile farther on.

The first two mounted the stage. And the other three, in feverish haste, dismounted and began to empty the express and treasure boxes into the opened boxes on the stage.

The small, slender bandit kept the bag of passengers' valuables attached to his saddle.

"That's it," the rough-voiced man said.

And the small bandit called out, "Get going. We've got to stay on schedule." The voice was that of a woman.

The driver laughed and slapped the reins against the necks of the team. The St. Louis Stage, carrying only express and mail this trip, took off in the direction of Leavenworth.

The driver would have to use some of the gold in the boxes to bribe certain people who could help insure their safety.

When the other three had reached the sheltered grove a mile along, Doña slid down from her horse and tore the hot, constricting handkerchief from her excited face.

She detached the sack from her saddle and emptied it on the mossy ground.

There were a gold watch, a beautiful crystal oval, some fine gold jewelry, a Derringer, a first-rate revolver, and cash in the amount of $2,571.

"Very nice," Tahre said, grinning.

When dusk fell, Tahre rode away with the Kiowa, leading the extra horses. But Mrs. Issa Hamilton stuffed her sweat-stained clothes into the bole of a tree and took out a thin dress from her saddlebag.

She put on the dress, dumped the treasures in the empty saddlebag and, mounting her horse, cantered leisurely back in the direction of town.

Stephen hurried into his Lake Street office and snatched up the letter Matilda had placed on the center of his desk.

It was from Cincinnati: the report said, "No one resembling the person you seek has deposited large amounts in Cincinnati banks, nor has such a person checked into likely boarding houses or hotels."

Swearing, Stephen scanned the rest of the letter, which proved unimportant. He threw it down on the desk and sank into his chair.

Doña, Doña! His mind cried out to her in silence. He stared, without seeing them, at the documents and vital papers in a high neat pile on the side of his desk. Nothing mattered now, nothing mattered but finding her. He would go down on his knees, if need be, to ask her forgiveness. Why in the name of God had he been such a blind, stubborn fool?

All of a sudden, out of nowhere, in the midst of the bustling office—perhaps it was the sound of rustling papers from the other room; he did not know—Stephen's memory took him back to the wild, wonderful night in New Orleans when he had won such a bundle from Torrance.

He could almost feel the slight, pleasant drunkenness he had known that night; he could almost see Doña's slender, naked body on the bed—

"Do you need me further this evening?"

Stephen winced, startled.

It was the voice of Matilda Johnston.

Stephen looked up into her nearsighted, curious eyes. He wondered if she had asked the same question before, for her words had the sound of repetition.

"I'm sorry, Matilda. My mind was very far away." He was astonished at the calmness of his voice. "No, I don't need you any more tonight. Go home."

He watched her leave the office. His body felt tired and spent, as if the memory of that night with Doña were an actual frenzy that had just emptied him of all his strength—as if it had happened just moments before.

Stephen shook his head to clear it, thinking, I was alone too long in the jail. It has been too long since I have been with a woman.

He smiled grimly and sighed. Maybe tomorrow. He didn't have the stomach for it, somehow, tonight.

Chapter Twenty-Nine

Doña riffled impatiently through the needlework designs in *Godey's Lady's Book*. It was beyond her comprehension that anyone would have the patience to follow these intricate directions to make such things as penwipers and sweet baskets and postal-card cases.

On the other hand she carefully studied the picture of a broad-brimmed summer hat of white split straw; it had a narrow blond fall and a wreath of daisies circling the crown. She went on to look closely at a pheasant fan and some new corsets—now that there was no one to criticize her underthings and she could wear what she pleased, she might try one. Some of her new dresses seemed to require different underpinnings.

But the item that most took her fancy was a Saragossa cape, like a burnoose, that could be made up in pineapple cloth, mohair or heavy silk. The cape featured the new, graceful quilling and was ornamented in back by two silken tassels enhancing the pointed shape of its rear hem.

The cape would be wonderful, she thought, in shades of bronze and claret red.

Doña stretched luxuriously and lay back in her bed. The peace of Sunday morning surrounded her. There was a soft knock and Doña said, "Come in."

The maid entered with a breakfast tray which she set on the table by the bed. There was a heavy white envelope on the tray.

Thanking the maid, who withdrew at once, Doña picked up the envelope curiously and examined it. There was no return address, only her name written in a careful, angular hand. She tore it open and found a note from William Hackman.

In it he asked, in his customary stilted way, if she would allow him to take her for a drive.

She tossed the note on the floor and smiled. However stiff and conventional he was, he certainly had persistence, and she almost admired him for it. There was a certain stubborn strength to a man who simply would not give up, despite repeated refusals. Ever since the spring, Doña had been saying no to his invitations.

Perhaps she had not been wise; it was through Hackman that she had met the invaluable Robert Campbell, after all.

Yes, she thought coolly, perhaps he could be of use.

And she rose to pen a note of acceptance to William Hackman, summoning the maid to have it relayed.

That afternoon, dressed in a cool, pale yellow gown and a wide-brimmed leghorn hat, carrying a yellow parasol, Doña joined William Hackman who was waiting for her in her hotel lobby. Despite the heat of the day, he was dressed with great formality in a light gray suit, a ruffled shirt and a wide black cravat with a stickpin headed by a giant pearl. He held his beaver hat in his hands.

Hackman's shy, handsome face lit up at the sight of her; his clear blue eyes gleamed. When she moved toward him with a pleasant smile, he said, "You are lovelier than I remembered."

She noticed then that he had been keeping one of his hands behind his back. He held it forward; in it was a small bouquet of white roses. She could not imagine a flower less appropriate to herself, but nevertheless accepted it, thanking him with sufficient warmth to bring a deep color to this thin-skinned face.

She could not help recalling Stephen's tanned face, his sharp gray eyes and the strong, impassive look he always wore.

William Hackman offered her his arm, and Doña

334

placed her fingers on his sleeve. She was irritated by the additional burden of the anemic-looking roses; she was already carrying a parasol and a small netted purse in her other hand.

When they reached his carriage, Hackman seemed to realize how awkward the bouquet was for her; apologizing, he took her parasol and the bouquet and placed them in the carriage, before handing her in.

To her amusement the parasol and bouquet now formed a barrier to her sitting down. Calmly, she put the bouquet aside and leaned her parasol against the other door, arranging her voluminous skirts about her.

As he got in beside her and took the reins, Hackman's ruddy color deepened another shade; he was so uneasy about the burdensome flowers and parasol.

The sudden memory of the clothes she had worn for the Wells Fargo job, and her hard, sweaty riding, in contrast to the ones she wore today, struck her so forcibly that she had to cough to cover her bubbling laugh.

"I beg your pardon?" he said, turning to her.

At his anxious inquiry, Doña could not prevent a wide grin from spreading across her face. Apparently he mistook her smile for pleasure in his company, for he swallowed and said in a halting way, "I cannot tell you how —how honored I am by your enjoyment."

She could not reply, for she realized with pity that he had misread her again. From his admiring expression Doña gathered that he had taken her silence for modesty.

He said in a stronger voice, as if her very withdrawal had made him feel bolder and more manly, "I have arranged to take you to tea at Tower Grove, if that meets your approval."

"Of course," she said politely, pleased at the opportunity to revisit the famous mansion. She had not been there since the dinner party in the spring.

Hackman opened his mouth to speak, but then seemed to think better of it, because he remained silent. She wondered what he had been about to say.

The villa of Tower Grove wore a different face in this hotter season; as they walked up the path between the dazzling green lawns Doña noticed that the flowers in the surrounding gardens were different colors and remarked on it.

"Henry will be pleased that you noticed that," Hackman said, smiling. "He says that the blue and purple flowers make him feel cooler in the summer. England is a much cooler country in the summer, you know."

Doña was aware of the cooling effect of the high-ceilinged entrance hall, as well, a blessing in the blazing heat of St. Louis. Henry Shaw met them at the door of his sitting room, where they were shown by the dignified butler.

Shaw smiled his welcome to Doña, and beckoned them into the dimness of the room, a smaller and more intimate one than the great library. Because of the brightness of the sun, the sitting room was unlit; Doña caught sight of flesh-pink papered walls, splashed with lozenges of claret-color, rosy velvet chairs and an upright piano against the wall.

The piano's face was ornamented with a pleated expanse of olive-green silk framed by rich wood. Two heavy busts of carved wood on pedestals stood on either side of the piano; one was the image of a bald, bearded man, the other of a younger man of great handsomeness, with thick, curly hair. The younger man reminded her a little bit of Stephen, and she felt a nostalgic pang.

"I see your are admiring our sweet singers," Shaw said, "my dear friends Will and George."

Doña did not have the slightest notion who the singers named Will and George could be, though she knew of Jenny Lind. Nevertheless, she smiled at Shaw, nodding toward the busts of Shakespeare and Byron.

Their host gestured to a tea table on the other side of the room. When they sat down, Doña saw that the great silver teapot was beaded with moisture; Shaw explained that it was far too hot for tea, and he had had lemonade prepared.

Gratefully Doña sipped the icy lemonade and listened to the men talk. They tried to draw her into their conversation, but she was mystified and a little bored by the

336

chatter about books and buildings and answered only in monosyllables, content to look around the graceful room and think her own thoughts.

When Shaw mentioned Shakespeare, however, Doña began to pay attention. Her interest caught his eye. "Ah! I see you are an admirer of Will, the sweet singer!" Shaw said.

So that's who he meant! she thought, and answered quickly, "Oh, yes! At least what I know of him," she added with frankness. "My father was always reading his plays."

"Do you have a favorite?"

"The Taming of the Shrew." Her quick answer caused Shaw to look at her with keen interest. For the first time, Doña felt part of the conversation and, in her enthusiasm, began to talk about the production she had seen in New Orleans, telling him about her disappointment in the play's ending. She forgot for a moment the inhibiting presence of William Hackman.

Shaw looked at her, fascinated, and commented, "I believe you have some of the qualities of the charming Kate, Mrs. Hamilton. If you don't mind my saying so," he added.

She looked into Shaw's intelligent eyes and the thought struck her: that is what Stephen said.

Misinterpreting the look on her face, the courteous Shaw said, "I *am* sorry. I have offended you."

"No, no, not at all." Doña's answer was sincere, but her thoughts drifted away again.

Henry Shaw glanced at William Hackman. His young friend looked disconcerted. The lad is serious, thought Shaw with a sinking feeling. And he is keen enough to know that I am right—this woman is very like the intractable Kate; he has bitten off more than he can chew.

He had had such hopes that their friendship would come to something more, something of which Shaw himself had hardly dared dream. William had always been so hesitant about women, eluding all the fond mammas' plans. Shaw turned from the handsome young face to look at Doña.

Doña in her turn had not even noticed William Hackman; she was reflecting sadly on all that she had lost when she lost Stephen—a man who was so many men. A man who had conquered the world of business and the wild, dangerous world of the West, and yet who knew so much of the mysterious world she did not know. Stephen had the same quick insights of a Henry Shaw, though Shaw was an even more traveled and lettered man. He was studying her now with the sharp, quick eyes of a fox, and suddenly she dreaded the next day's plan.

When the westbound Raike Stage was about three miles out of Independence, it came to a sharp turn in the road.

Just a few yards ahead, the way was blocked by a grain wagon; a man and a boy, seated on top of the wagon, both were tied and blindfolded. The horses had been unhitched and were tied to a tree.

As the stage pulled up a man, masked in black, stepped from behind a tree and pointed his Smith & Wesson at the driver of the stage. "Hold-up!" the masked man called out in a hoarse voice. "Throw down the boxes and nobody will be hurt."

The driver obeyed. The man with the Smith & Wesson whistled like an owl, and two more masked men came out of the underbrush. They picked up the boxes and disappeared.

The stage driver waited uneasily, wondering what more they wanted; the driver's face was slick with nervous sweat. And then the first armed man began to take a quantity of black scarves—the same kind that had been used as blindfolds for the boy and the man on the grain wagon—from his pockets.

He strode to the driver and, pointing his revolver at the man's chest, said, "Put it on."

The driver again obeyed. The man with the Smith & Wesson opened the doors of the stage and handed the other scarves to the terrified passengers, saying curtly, "Put them on." The passengers complied.

The whip was allowed to stay on the box to hold his six-in-hand under control, but the bandit ordered the passengers out of the stage and told them to sit down beside the road.

Stumbling, they came from the stage. With curious gallantry, the bandit helped the one woman passenger to the ground. With his victims completely blinded by the black scarves that fell below their shoulders, the bandit began to loot the woman's purse, the passengers' baggage, and express boxes at his leisure. He went back to the woman, noticing the glitter on her finger, and forcibly removed her diamond rings.

After he had completed his task, he put the smaller loot into a sack hanging from his belt, and whistled again.

Two men and a woman, dressed in dusty trousers and shirt and a broad-brimmed hat, all of them masked, emerged from the underbrush, took up the larger pieces, and disappeared once more into the trees.

The first bandit strolled back to the driver.

"What time is the eastbound stage coming through?"

"A half an hour, or thereabouts." The man's answer was muffled.

"We'll wait." The bandit's astounding answer reached the passengers huddled by the side of the road. One of the male passengers said, "I'll be damned."

The woman passenger turned in the direction of the oath, and cried out, "Be careful what you say."

It was not long before they heard the rattling of the eastbound Wells Fargo stage. All at once, the other bandits emerged from the woods, and all five ran around the grain wagon, drawing their guns.

When, at last, they rode away, they were laden with the boxes and treasures of the Wells Fargo stage. And four more passengers sat on the edge of the road with heavy scarves draped over their astonished faces.

Dismounting inside the sheltering grove with its familiar, mossy floor, the bandits took off their hot masks.

Tahre glanced at Doña; she was moist with exertion, trembling with fatigue.

"Your quarrel with the Raikes is not settled?" he asked.

She turned away, answering, "These are not the old

times. Raike or Wells Fargo, it is all the same to me. A Raike stage happened to be passing."

When they had left her so she could change her clothes, Tahre agreed in silent bitterness: it was not the old times anymore. It was not a happy thing, after all, to be working only for gold.

"Another one, damn it to hell." Stephen Raike slammed the letter, postmarked St. Joseph, on top of the other papers on his desk.

With the letter the writer had enclosed an item from a local newspaper.

Stephen scanned the clipping:

Another daring daylight robbery occurred on Wednesday, August 10, just two days after the spectacular double robbery of the Raike and Wells Fargo Stages, during which the passengers were forced to put on blindfolds and sit by the side of the road while their possessions were rifled.

He read on:

George Richman, the Wells Fargo driver, had lost a very fine gold watch which had been presented to him by the stage company, to the robbers in Wednesday's incident—whose description matched that of the malefactors in the double robbery.

A lady passenger on the stage was unmolested, but she commented that the bandits' spokesman had a peculiarly hoarse voice and that she believed one of the miscreants was a woman.

Stephen leaned back, holding the clipping in his hand. His eyes were thoughtful. A hoarse-voiced man, a woman. Even another gold watch.

"Jeb!" he shouted. "Has the late mail come?"

The young clerk came hurrying in with a pile of letters in his hand. "Just now, sir, but they haven't been sorted yet."

"Never mind. I'll just take a look." He took the mail from Jeb; glancing swiftly at each envelope, he tossed one letter after the other on his desk. Next to the last was a letter postmarked St. Louis, Missouri.

Stephen tore it open with eager fingers. The letter ran:

A woman of the approximate description of the one you seek, known as Issa Hamilton, became a resident of this city in May. She deposited a large amount of cash, approximately the sum you mentioned, in the Merchants Bank. In July, Mrs. Hamilton bought St. Louis Stages. However, she has black, not Titian hair. This of course could be an alteration of nature.

Stephen smiled at the dry, pedantic tone of the detective bureau's report. It had to be Doña. Even "Issa"— Isse-Loa.

"Jeb!" he shouted again, and as always the boy appeared with startling promptness. "Take this away." Stephen waved at the letters scattered on his desk. "I am going to see Mr. Bartlett." Then he remembered, with an impatient exclamation that Josiah Bartlett was away. "I'm going out," Stephen amended. He'd have to get out to walk or ride. Anything. But he couldn't sit here, with this news on his mind.

Robert Campbell's plain brick house, set on a small plot of land on St. Louis' populous Locust Street, was a far cry from Henry Shaw's Tower Grove.

And yet the elegant English bachelor admired the house very much. The delicate motifs of the iron balcony and fence lent just the right decorative touches to the building's plain, three-story facade, he thought. There was something honest and solid about the house, which reminded Shaw of its owner.

Shaw also greatly enjoyed his monthly invitation to the Sunday meal given by Campbell. It was exclusively for men—the austere Mrs. Campbell was never in evidence.

The guests were served by a manservant on those occasions, so not even a maid intruded on their masculine privacy.

William Hackman did not quite share Shaw's hearty pleasure in those gatherings; he, too, admired the plain grace of the house and appreciated the excellent food and wine afforded by his host. But the conversation at table, unvaryingly of business, money and women, lacked the aesthetic tone Hackman preferred. Even Hackman's cultured friend Henry Shaw seemed to become another man on these occasions—a hail-fellow-well-met type that never felt quite real to William Hackman. But he liked Robert Campbell a great deal and usually accepted his invitations.

However, this particular afternoon, as August neared its end, Hackman felt a restless annoyance as he sat over port with the other men.

Hackman's attempt to discuss *Ten Nights on a Barroom Floor,* the popular temperance play that had just opened at the National Theatre in New York City, had met with little success. In any case, Shaw had remarked a little acidly, it seemed sacrilegious to mention temperance when they were drinking such fine port.

And Shaw's own pungent comments on the last Lincoln-Douglas debate had done no better: Hackman was not convinced that the slaves should be freed, and the Campbells were just as certain that they should.

After the flurry of disagreement had subsided, the men turned as always to the topic of local business. And Robert Campbell brought up the subject of Mrs. Hamilton.

"She's a brave little woman," Campbell said. "And the stage line's doing damned well." He laughed his hearty laugh. "Right in your eye to the skeptics who said she'd never make it."

"It interests me," said Henry Shaw, the misogynist, "that the St. Louis Stage is the only line that hasn't been robbed lately."

"What do you mean by that, Henry?" the sensitive Hackman inquired.

"*Mean*, William?" Shaw asked with mock innocence.

Robert Campbell noticed Hackman's disturbed expression and, waving aside Shaw's comments, said not unkindly, "Come now, Henry, I think our young friend here has a special interest in that quarter."

Hackman looked more uncomfortable than ever.

"Isn't that right, William?" Campbell pursued.

"Mrs. Hamilton wishes to remain a widow," Hackman said impulsively. Then, realizing he had given himself away, he changed color, a habit that so amused the bluff and weatherbeaten Campbell.

"Ah, my boy!" the host said teasingly. "Then you have asked her?"

"Not exactly," Hackman admitted, feeling very foolish.

"It is far better that you do not," Henry Shaw interjected bluntly.

The Campbell sons, who were very silent young men and apparently overpowered by their father's vitality, looked at Shaw in surprise.

"But she is a very beautiful lady," said the elder.

"As to that," Shaw shrugged. "But you remember, my dear boy," he asked Hackman, "that afternoon at my house? When she expressed such admiration for the Shrew?"

Hackman nodded, looking annoyed.

"I think she is a Kate herself, and something of a wildcat. And my dear William, you are no Petruchio, if I may be so blunt as to mention it."

The Campbells looked uncomfortable at Shaw's malice. But Robert Campbell admitted privately that William Hackman wasn't the man for the unusual Mrs. Hamilton. Campbell had been prodding his sons to make overtures in that quarter; she would be a very rich woman one of these days, and was pretty and smart as a whip, to boot.

But the young popinjays, Campbell thought sourly, were put off by her air of independence. Too bad he himself was tied up; otherwise he'd have a go in that direction.

William Hackman, with stiff politeness, rose and said

to Campbell, "I really must be going. Thank you very much for the dinner."

He gave a bow in the direction of the two younger Campbells and, ignoring Shaw, strode out of the room.

"Ah, Henry, you've done it now." Robert Campbell did not trouble to hide his irritation.

"I gave him the best advice that could be given," Shaw retorted calmly. "There are women who are not suited to marriage, as there are men who are not, either," he smiled. "But my objection to Mrs. Hamilton, I'm afraid, is deeper than that."

"What do you mean?"

"Come now, Robert," Shaw answered impatiently. "She came out of nowhere, telling William that she had come from Cincinnati, though he remembers her boarding the *John Simonds* at Chicago. First, she deposits an outrageous sum of cash in the Merchants Bank with the weakest of explanations. Then she buys the stage line, hiring the roughest-looking men she can find, not to speak of that Indian, who seems to be on almost equal footing with her. And for the first time in six months there is a spate of robberies—but her own line is untouched."

"I don't know what you're getting at, Henry, but it sounds slanderous to me," Robert Campbell said hotly.

"Why, Dad, what's the matter with you?" The younger son stared at his father.

"I ask the same question, Robert," Shaw said coolly. "I believe you're as enamored of the woman as our poor William is."

"Poor William is right!" the older Campbell replied in a rough voice. "He makes a mighty poor showing as a lover."

For the first time in their acquaintance Robert Campbell had openly criticized William Hackman and had quarreled with Henry Shaw—causing Shaw to reflect that the woman was a troublemaker of the worst kind, and he was still convinced that there was something not quite right about her.

On the other side of the massive table, the former adventurer silently resolved that he would have a talk with Mrs. Hamilton soon. She ought to know what people were saying about her.

As Campbell raised his glass of port to his lips, Henry Shaw and Campbell's uneasy sons were wondering just what ailed him.

Chapter Thirty

The following afternoon at dusk, Doña closed the ledger with a sudden, impatient movement. The heavy covers banged together, and she leaned forward, putting her elbows on the big gray book, resting her chin on her hands.

She was possessed of an irritable, empty feeling that she had rarely had before, and it bewildered her. All was as it should be: the stage line—thanks to their extra income—was prospering; their secret was safe. Missouri, like many other states, was not zealous in the pursuit of stage bandits, allowing that the security of the coaches was, in the main, the responsibility of the lines. The local Wells Fargo investigations were little better than useless. But Doña was not so sure about Raike Stages.

Stephen Raike was not a man to be taken advantage of—would he wonder who was robbing him? Would he guess?

Determinedly, Doña put him out of her mind. Life was good now, and she was free, free to be herself and beholden to no one!

And there was always the amusement of William Hackman's uncertain courtship. Doña smiled mischievously, a childlike smile that lit her sleepy dark eyes. She straightened and stretched her slender arms, feeling a new buoyance and content.

Yes, it was good to be free, splendid to have pretty clothes and jewels, and still be in command.

A tap on the frosted glass of her office door brought Doña out of her revery. She called out permission to enter. The young clerk stuck his head through the parted door and said, "Mr. Robert Campbell is asking for you."

"Ask him to come in."

As always Doña welcomed the sight of the hearty Campbell. He is a real man, she thought, as she watched him enter. His big, powerful body was clothed with a kind of rough elegance; he held a soft hat in his large, capable-looking hands. His weatherbeaten face, with its glittering hazel eyes, brightened at the sight of her.

"This is a pleasure," she said sincerely. "Sit down."

Campbell obeyed, taking the chair by her desk. He tossed his hat with an easy motion onto one of the cabinets by the wall and stared at her with undisguised admiration.

Doña looked into Campbell's strange-colored eyes, stirred in spite of herself by his overpowering masculinity. To Campbell, she knew, she was primarily a female body; her brains were incidental. This bland assumption of his, while it nettled her, aroused something primitive and lost in her, something she had nearly forgotten in the loneliness of her new nights and days.

However, she kept her expression cool, and asked him calmly, "What can I do for you?"

He hesitated for a long moment. It was clear that he had changed his mind about what he was going to say, because he smiled a little ruefully before he answered, "It is what I can do for you that brings me here today."

She waited, and Campbell went on: "I was in the company of Henry Shaw and William Hackman last evening."

He studied her keenly; her vivid face showed no reaction. He chuckled, and continued, "Henry Shaw had some very interesting things to say about the recent stage robberies."

"Oh?" Her tone was one of rather bored politeness.

Campbell's eyes gleamed with amusement. "Yes. I think he suspects St. Louis Stages of certain—dishonest practices. And I came here to warn you," he concluded bluntly.

"Your warning is unnecessary, Mr. Campbell," she said softly. "My stage line has never been guilty of any dishonest practices. Why don't you come right out and say what you mean?" Her voice was challenging and he grinned broadly.

"Henry appears to think your people are robbing the other stages." Again he studied her closely with his bright eyes.

"Why, Mr. Campbell, what an outrageous suggestion!" She smiled.

"You don't seem very angry, Mrs. Hamilton. Just amused."

"I am amused, Mr. Campbell," she retorted. "How could Mr. Shaw imagine that a helpless woman could manage such a thing?"

Campbell got up, laughing, and stared down at her, his look sweeping downward from her gleaming hair and smooth face, lingering frankly on the swell of her shapely breasts and the curving slenderness of her body. "That your are a woman would be obvious to a blind man," he said roughly, "but as to helplessness—you are about as helpless as an Apache, Mrs. Hamilton."

The big man laughed again. "I think that is why I admire you so very much. And just between you and me, my dear, I don't give a tinker's dam what you do; I've done enough shady things in my own time. Just be careful."

"I really don't know what you mean," she replied, shrugging. She looked up at him from under half-lowered lids, her eyes shining through her heavy lashes.

Campbell retrieved his hat from the cabinet and gave her another look that brought the quick color to her cheeks.

"Well, I'd better be getting along," he said casually. "I've got to get down to the Sherman House on Lake Street."

"The Sherman House!" she repeated. "But that's in—" she stopped, her color deepening.

"In Chicago, you were about to say? That's where you come from. Isn't it, my dear, and not from Cincinnati, as you told our hesitating young friend, Hackman?"

She had recaptured her poise, and managed to respond,

"I've visited Chicago, of course. Many times. But I am from Cincinnati, Mr. Campbell."

"You're a cool one, Mrs. Hamilton, I'll say that for you. I told you I don't care what you've done, or what you do now. And I'll tell you something else, while we're at it. What I didn't say before when you asked me what you could do for me." He said with sudden vehemence, "You can become my mistress, and give up all this nonsense. Because I want you more than I've ever wanted anyone. And I'm not that old a man, so don't look at me like that!"

She rose from her chair and said, "Get out of this office, you—you—" Doña spluttered, too angry to find the word she was seeking.

"Perhaps I was a little blunt. But think about it. I'll be back." Campbell grinned and placed his soft hat on his head at a rakish angle.

"Get out!" she repeated. He touched his hat and opening the door softly, left the office. The door was still standing ajar.

Doña walked to the door and slammed it; the frosted glass rang from the impact.

Give up this nonsense indeed! She was fuming. Give up all that she had worked for, sweated for, risked her neck for—to be the mistress of that—

Suddenly she began smiling. It was not Campbell's suggestion that had angered her: it was the idea that she give up all that was her own. Doña laughed aloud at her own stubborn desire for independence.

He had aroused not only her anger, she admitted to herself, but something very near to the excitement of desire. Her body had gone so long unappeased.

But she would not trade her freedom for anyone or anything; not now. Better to endure her body's hunger and the long nights' loneliness than to belong, ever again, to any man. Doña knew that at last she was truly free. She would never give herself to anyone again.

Not even Stephen? she wondered.

No, she replied, not even Stephen. Though the memory

of him and his lean body and gray eyes and gentle caressing, could still leave her breathless and aching.

"I'm free," she whispered.

At least, she concluded, she could thank Campbell for something—his warning. The time was right to rob a St. Louis stage.

When Bartlett's clerk told Stephen on Monday morning that the lawyer had not come back to the office, Stephen rushed off to find a public carriage. He was restless and impatient; two precious days had already been lost. He was determined to start for St. Louis that night.

Reaching the familiar Bartlett house, Stephen paid the coachman and strode up the short walk to the entranceway.

Isaiah opened the door, and when he saw it was Stephen, grinned so broadly it seemed his face would split. "Why, Mr. Raike! This is a real pleasure, sir!"

Stephen smiled at him but asked curtly, "Mr. Bartlett in? I'm in an awful hurry."

"Yes, sir, right there in his study."

Stephen nodded and went down the hall. Bartlett met him at the study door. "Stephen! What is it? You look all het up. Come in and have a drink."

Stephen went into the rich room with its paneled bookcase walls.

"Sit down," Bartlett said.

"No, I'll stand," Stephen replied. Bartlett thought he looked like a nervous, spirited horse about to start a race. The attorney went to a side table and poured a brandy for Stephen.

"Thanks, Jos." To Bartlett's amusement, Stephen put the glass of brandy down on another table as if he had not really seen it.

"Sit down, Stephen. I can't think when you're prancing around the room."

Stephen sat on one of the big brocade chairs, tentatively, as if he were ready to rise again at any moment.

"Look at this, Jos." He handed the St. Louis report to the attorney.

"The robberies?" Bartlett asked. Stephen shook his head impatiently. Bartlett's keen glance raced over the letter. He looked up at Stephen and asked, "Well?"

"Good God, Jos, is that all you have to say? 'Well?' When I've finally gotten the news I've been waiting for?"

"What is all the fuss about?" The calm, dry voice from the doorway made Stephen turn. Hannah Bartlett was standing on the threshold. There was a look of welcome in her velvety brown eyes. Stephen got to his feet, smiling, and went to her, bending to kiss her cheek.

"What are you doing to Stephen, Jos?" Hannah Bartlett asked. She came in to the room and took a chair near Stephen's.

"May I?" Bartlett asked.

"Of course."

Bartlett handed the letter to his wife. She read it quickly and looked up at Stephen. Her face was uneasy.

"What's the matter, Hannah?" Stephen demanded. They were both reacting very strangely to his news.

Hannah Bartlett examined her young friend's eager face. The months in prison had toughened Stephen, honed his face to harder, even more fine-boned, lines. The already firm lines of his mouth were firmer. He was as indestructible, Hannah Bartlett thought, as a fine, thin sword that could bend to incredible lengths without breaking.

She glanced at her husband and raised her brows. He nodded, and she said, "She's not an ordinary woman, Stephen. I'm not at all sure that she can ever—settle down with you, the way a man is entitled to expect a wife to do."

"Settling down has never been my highest ambition," Stephen retorted. "Besides, I thought you liked her, both of you."

"We did, and do, very much," Hannah protested. "But when she was staying here—Stephen, it was like watching a wild thing in a cage. I don't think she's made for the domestic life. You're young now, and maybe you think you don't want peace. But in a few years, believe me, you might change your mind." Hannah looked affectionately at her husband.

Stephen got up and moved about the room, restlessly, looking at some of the books on the shelves with an absent eye. Hannah Bartlett saw a stubborn tightness around Stephen's mouth, a look she knew well. The set of that mouth meant that nothing she or Josiah could say would make the slightest difference.

Josiah Bartlett remarked, "I always reckoned that if Romeo and Juliet hadn't died when they did, they would have had a cat-and-dog life together."

Stephen's gray eyes were impenetrable; his face wore the look of a man resolved. Hannah Bartlett frowned and shook her head at her husband, knowing Stephen was unreachable.

"You'll go to St. Louis," she said resignedly.

But her husband persisted. "All right, Stephen. I can't let you go without trying one more time. There was a time when this news would have made me very happy. But now that I've read the report, I think it's obvious she doesn't want to be found. Why else would she have dyed her hair, taken another name? She doesn't want to be Mrs. Stephen Raike anymore."

Hannah frowned at his bluntness, but the lawyer ignored her. "Why didn't she try to get in touch with you?" Bartlett demanded. "Your release must have been in every paper in the country, especially in Missouri, with all the interests you have there."

Stephen realized then that neither Josiah nor Hannah knew that Doña was a fugitive eager to keep her identity hidden in the West.

He smiled forgivingly at them. "I think she may still be angry at me," he said, although he knew it sounded weak. "I've got to change her mind. And I've got to get to the bank before it closes, Jos. Would you take a look at these, and tell me what my liability is in the robberies? Is it similar to Wells Fargo's?"

Bartlett, with his knowledge of the laws of the various states, was able to answer after a few minutes spent studying the papers.

Stephen took back the papers and got to his feet. "Thanks, Jos, Hannah. I'm leaving tonight. I'll let you know what happens."

The Bartletts watched him walk away; in every line of his body, from his straight, broad shoulders to the ramrod erectness of his back, there was an overpowering vitality and confidence.

"You know, Hannah," Josiah Bartlett said slowly after he had gone, "we may be all wrong." He chuckled. "Stephen's never failed to get what he went after."

"I hope we are," Hannah Bartlett said. "Good luck to him."

Stephen was alone in the hushed emptiness of the vault, examining the open metal box on the table. He took out the jewels Doña had left behind her.

Ignoring the more valuable pieces, he held in his hands the long chain of plaited gold and its accompanying medallions of topaz, of bright blue and orange opals. He recalled with a spasm of longing how the jewels had looked on her ripe, coppery skin.

Then he put the chain down and handled some of the other pieces—decorated combs that made him remember the fiery splendor of her hair; bracelets and necklaces that had once been warmed by her slender wrists and the soft flesh of her half-covered breasts.

Stephens fist closed around an emerald bracelet and he felt a tight throbbing inside him, thinking of her.

"A guard, Mr. Raike?"

"What?" Stephen's head turned quickly. The officious teller stood at the entrance to the vault.

"I was asking, sir, if you'd like a guard. These are very valuable items you're taking."

"A guard!" Stephen smiled and replied with amused, contemptuous courtesy, "No, thanks, I don't believe I'll need a guard."

Casually, he took the jewels from the box and put them in the small valise that he had lifted to the table. He shut the valise with a neat snap and left the box gaping.

"Thanks," he said perfunctorily, and, already intent on the journey ahead, brushed past the teller.

Leaving the bank, Stephen ignored a cruising coach and moved with long, quick strides down the crowded thoroughfare. He had never been so full of energy and determination.

By God, he resolved, I'll spread all these things right over her naked body, just as the way I showered her with money!

Doña felt the crisp sun of early autumn through her shirt of fringed buckskin: it was a wonderful day. She had found a secluded place for target practice, a place where she felt very safe. Mrs. Issa Hamilton was well known in St. Louis by now, and one afternoon, riding to her old practice spot, she had been a little disconcerted to encounter the small son of her chief clerk with some other children, playing in the woods.

What if they had seen her shooting? She had promptly sought out another site, deeper in the woods, too rough to attract the children, too dark to be a cheerful playground.

Now as the sun filtered through the heavy branches, her horse cantered easily to the spot. The reins were tied over the pommel of her saddle, but her tractable mount responded well to the pressure of her knees. "All right, boy," she cooed, soothing the horse to alert him to the coming percussion.

And she raised her Colt in both hands to fire at a specified peel of bark on the tall pine thirty yards away. The trained horse did not rear at the explosion; he only raised his fine head, neighing a little and cutting his great eyes at Doña. The peeling bark fell from the pine, and Doña's satisfaction was complete.

"Good boy, good boy," she said, patting the horse's sleek neck. Then she reached into the pocket of her buckskin shirt and produced a lump of sugar, leaning forward. The horse turned his head and took the sugar from her gloved hand.

"Bull's eye!" The rough shout, emerging from the

354

shaded light and darkness, was so startling that Doña winced, and the horse neighed with an uneasy tossing motion of its head.

"All right, boy," she said, stroking the animal's neck, but she could hear her voice trembling.

A crashing sound of heavy hooves through the underbrush followed. Doña thrust her Colt under the shirt into the waistband of her buckskin trousers and untied the reins, drawing them back to control the nervous mount.

Turning the horse she saw Robert Campbell, on a great stallion, riding toward her.

"Bull's eye!" he said again, genially, as he rode toward her. His stallion was a magnificent roan, and Campbell looked huge to Doña, erect and easy in the saddle, dressed in worn suede trousers and a rough wool coat, his soft hat set at the usual rakish angle on his big head.

"You are an excellent shot," Campbell said, laughing at her dismayed expression. "Did you think I didn't know?"

"What are you talking about?" she retorted coldly. "This is my—hobby."

"Hobby, is it?" Campbell roared with laughter, edging the stallion nearer Doña's smaller gray with a movement of his powerful hands.

Doña looked at the hands and felt a swift, cold fearfulness. It was so lonely here.

"Hobby, my dear," Campbell repeated. "It is an interesting hobby for a lady. When I think of poor William, sitting with you at tea, while you pick off the teacups with your Colt, it is wonderful!" The big man laughed again. "I'm glad you took my advice," he added in a more serious tone, his strange eyes gleaming. He examined her frankly, savoring the sight of her curving body in the tapering shirt and snug trousers, the dark eyes shadowed by the brim of her wide tan hat.

"Advice?" she repeated, amazed that her voice sounded so calm.

"Come now, Issa Hamilton, you know damned well what I mean. The St. Louis Stage robbery. It was very well done, my dear."

"Mr. Campbell, you are always saying things to me that I don't understand at all."

"Never mind that. Tell me. Have you accepted Hackman?" Campbell's mount was so near now to Doña's horse that she felt the big man's leg brush her own.

"What business is it of yours, Mr. Campbell?" she demanded.

"It is this, Mrs. Hamilton," he said roughly and, leaning from his saddle, took her face in his hard hands and kissed her with a brutal violence.

When he let her go, she gasped with indignation and fright. His strength was terrible, and they were alone here, so far from everyone. There was no one to hear if she cried out.

Campbell's weatherbeaten face was flushed, and his breath came in quick, ragged rhythm. He was down from his saddle almost before she knew what had happened, and pulled her from her own saddle to the ground.

He grabbed her to his body, holding her so tightly she could barely breathe; his embrace was overpowering, like the embrace of a huge bear.

Campbell bent his head to hers and kissed her lingeringly; there was a smell of sweat and leather and bourbon from him that made her dizzy, and the pressure of his full, sensual mouth was hot and bruising.

Whatever attraction she might have felt for him once was forgotten: she shrank from the hot, moist kiss, feeling sick with an impotent anger.

At last, after what seemed an age of the hard, whiskey-tasting vise of his cruel mouth, Campbell let Doña's mouth go, still holding her body close to his.

She looked up with hatred into his glittering hazel eyes, and he drew back a trifle in the force of her hate.

"A man is what you need," he said hoarsely, "a real man, Mrs. Hamilton."

His weatherbeaten face, at so close an angle, looked grotesquely rough and ugly.

"I do not need an old man like you, Mr. Campbell," she said cruelly, looking straight into his beseeching eyes.

"Old man," he said. "I'll show you who's an old man!"

And, horrified, she felt his hands tearing at her shirt. In the struggle, her gun slipped from her belt to the ground.

Summoning all her courage, Doña called up a mocking laugh from her own tight throat. The laughter grew in strength, and she thought, sometimes it rattles a man, to laugh at him. At least it will give me time. Her heart was thudding so loudly she thought it would leap from her very body.

She had calculated correctly: her laughter, so scornful and unafraid, seemed to have unmanned Campbell. His big hands fell from the collar of her shirt and hung by his sides.

Without another word or touch, Campbell mounted his stallion and wheeled its head away, crashing out of the shadowy woods.

Doña leaned for a moment against the warm body of her gray, and began to sob with relief.

Mounting her horse slowly, she waited for a long moment and then rode out of the woods, in the direction opposite to the one Campbell had taken.

Chapter Thirty-One

Stephen's single-minded passion, his formidable concentration that blinded him to all except his goal, made the river journey from Chicago to St. Louis pass by in a kind of blur. And so, it was almost with a start that he found himself walking down the ramp to the St. Louis levee, his valise swinging easily in his hand. Only the sound of a name, a familiar name, brought him back to the present: He heard a man's lazy, drawling voice say, "Did you make any time with the mysterious Mrs. Hamilton?"

With characteristic coolness Stephen hardly turned his head. But his sidelong glance pinned the likely owner of the drawling voice—a dark, shifty-looking customer with a luxuriant mustache, wearing the clothes of a river gambler.

Stephen saw that he had guessed right, for the man's companion, fair and quietly dressed, had a red face, as if the question were an embarrassing one. Stephen wondered what such a respectable type was doing with a river gambler.

Stephen moved a little nearer the two men, keeping an indifferent expression on his face, as if he were examining the river bank, staring out over the water.

"What are you doing here, Bill?" the drawling voice asked.

"I've come to meet a client," the other replied stiffly.

"So what about Mrs. Hamilton?" the gambler twitted. "Anything doing there?"

Stephen's look returned to the fair man. The latter's

delicate face was redder than ever. "Please do not talk like that about her. I have asked the lady to marry me."

Stephen controlled himself with effort. His dearest wish was to take the fair man's throat in his hands, throttle him and toss him into the river. He clenched his fists and turned away again. He had memorized the features of the man with the precise voice and elegant clothes.

"Marry!" The gambler was laughing. "That's not like you, Bill."

The tall, fair man stalked away without another word to his dark companion.

Stephen marched down the ramp. Waving away two public carriages seeking his patronage, he walked along on the river bank to cool off. He knew St. Louis well, and moved in the direction of the business area and the hotels, still raging inwardly at what he had heard on the boat.

Goddam her! he said to himself. No matter where she was, she was more trouble than a stampede of wild horses, than a tribe of wild Indians.

The fast walk and the refreshing breeze from the river calmed him a little, then, and he had to smile at his own irrational anger. Why should the men leave her alone? Could he?

And that prissy-looking bastard had said he'd *asked* her, not that she'd accepted.

Besides, Stephen had told the Bartletts that he wasn't looking for peace, and here he was, riled at the first sign of disturbance.

In command of himself once more, Stephen lifted his hand, signaling to a passing coach. He asked the man to take him to the hotel where Doña was supposed to be living.

Stephen heard none of the voluble driver's constant stream of remarks, and when he dismounted, he showed such an indifferent face that the driver did not expect much of a tip. Absently Stephen gave him a great deal extra, and, without answering the driver's thanks, entered the hotel.

The hotel clerk looked at the tall man approaching him, unable to classify the guest at all. And Delbert

Yancy's profession made the classification of men and women a necessity. This man, he thought, in spite of his very fine clothes and trim look, was a mighty hard-looking man.

Yancy judged he'd hate to cross the gray-eyed man who asked him for Mrs. Issa Hamilton.

"Well, I'm sorry, Mr. er—" Yancy paused politely, but Stephen did not enlighten him. "Mrs. Hamilton's away—won't be back for a couple of days."

The man glared, as if it were Yancy's fault, and snapped, "Where is she?"

Annoyed at the man's attitude and the shocking bluntness of the question, Yancy replied with dignity, "We do not question our patrons' private lives, sir. I could not tell you."

"You *would* not tell me, you mean," Stephen retorted, as he turned and walked out of the hotel.

Angry again, Stephen sought out the offices of the St. Louis Stages. From the head clerk there he received a similar answer.

The clerk, like Delbert Yancy, found the tall man's intense, passionate face a little intimidating.

"Is there any message, Mr.—?"

"No. And the name is Raike. Stephen Raike."

The illustrious name of the owner of that great fleet of stages threw the clerk into confusion. "Why, Mr. Raike, this is an honor, sir! Are you sure there's nothing I can do?"

Stephen thanked him, shook his head, and started out in the direction of the livery stable.

All of a sudden he hungered for a horse. He would ride to St. Joe, two days' hard ride, but one he looked forward to with eagerness. Sometimes he felt he'd almost lost his riding hands, it had been so long.

And he'd damned well have to get to St. Joe. The richest shipment they'd ever carried was leaving in three days; and Stephen had a strong feeling Doña knew it, too. That's where he would find her.

He hired a horse and cantered out of town, his possessions in a rented saddlebag, his valise left behind. The fine animal moved in a questioning manner, waiting for Stephen to establish their relationship. It pricked tentative ears and turned its head a little to the right, as if listening for a voice.

In a little while they had found each other's rhythms; Stephen's hands were firm but easy on the reins, his knees commanding without strain. The horse recognized a man born to the saddle. Reassured, it neighed softly and settled into a smooth gallop.

"That's right, fellow," Stephen said. "We've got a long way to go together."

His lean body felt right again, and he knew that whatever came, he could meet it with ease.

The Raike "up" stage, which would soon set out from St. Joseph toward San Francisco on the California Trail, would be loaded with valuable mails, and shipments of gold for Cheyenne, in Wyoming, for the banks of Salt Lake City and Sacramento. This vital stage would go more heavily armed than any of the others; some institutions trusted Wells Fargo, but the new Butterfield Overland Mail, which would begin its run on September 15, was an untried line. Raike Stages had been tried and never found wanting.

Northwest from St. Joseph, the stage would follow the regular trail used by travelers across the arid land; but then, in Nebraska, would follow the path of the Platte River and its tributary into Cheyenne. Horses could travel only a little distance without water, so most of the courses were river routes.

From Cheyenne the stage would head, with the payroll, for Ft. Bridger, then on to Salt Lake City, and across the desert to Nevada. Following another river, then across the burning desert again, the stage would come to Sacramento, and at last to the distant town of San Francisco.

For several years the California mail service had been run on a hit-or-miss basis; subsidies were increased each time a contractor went bankrupt.

Raike's rivals had to depend on government subsidies,

but Stephen, with his huge personal fortune, was ready to gamble heavily.

In 1857, when gold was discovered in Colorado, Stephen had been convinced that Denver would boom the way San Francisco had, and invested in another line from Missouri along the Santa Fe Trail. He made a huge investment in coaches, horses and equipment, building twenty new relay stations between Missouri and Colorado. And his gamble paid off.

With the profits from his Santa Fe Line, Stephen had added more and more improvements to the line that ran along the California Trail, and now in September of 1858 the Raike Stage Line outdid even its closest rival.

The fresh supply of cash resulting from the Denver operation was used for additional coaches and horses, establishing camps to keep the mountain roads open in winter and cut the running time between St. Joseph and San Francisco to twenty-five days or less. Where other lines failed from lack of funds, and lack of courage, Raike Lines was backed by an enormous fortune. And Raike employees were the highest paid of all; so his stages were manned by willing, tough, dependable men.

Losses from robberies were almost unheard of for Raike Stages.

Which is why, Stephen ruminated now, going at a swift but easy gallop over the Missouri trail, there has to be something special about those robberies at St. Joe.

The same stealthy approach, the suddenness of a rattler-strike, that was used when a handful of bandits took the Short Line that evening.

She is riding again, he thought. But her next attempt wouldn't be robbing a little stage carrying a handful of mail and a few thousand dollars; this payroll shipment was the biggest of them all. And the men manning the stage would be the best men Stephen Raike employed—quick, ruthless and determined, alert as eagles—and ready to gun her down before she had a chance to draw.

Stephen could not let that happen: he would accompany the stage: ride alongside it in a maneuverable position. If he were there, then she would have a chance.

They had chosen a campsite between Leavenworth and St. Joseph, in a spot between two hills surrounded by a heavy growth of trees. It reminded Doña of the Texas hideout they had used after they took the bank in that little town, she no longer remembered the name.

This time, too, they had a settled range to ride over, scattered houses where curious farmers might notice a strange group of mounted men. As before, they had come to the grove in a wagon, the others following two by two, a less threatening number to the isolated settlers between the neighboring towns.

Tahre had insisted that they make their camp two days early, to give the horses plenty of rest and to familiarize themselves with every inch of the territory. They did their reconnaissance in the early mornings and by night, when the moonlight permitted.

They were sleeping on the ground in sleeping bags; Doña slept apart from the rest, but Tahre and the Kiowa slept nearer to her, as if they did not wholly trust the white men in the band.

The group was tense with expectation, taut as a finely drawn wire with the thought of the morning. Some of the men were playing cards around a low fire, a fire that Tahre had taught them to make in a shallow bowl of the earth, surrounded by upright stones to keep the light from signaling to the world beyond the grove.

Doña lay on the outside of her sleeping bag, staring up into the still branches above her, hearing the far-away sound of the men's voices. One was grumbling loudly about the lack of whiskey. Doña had a rule about that. When they had work to do, she insisted that they not drink until afterwards. And evidently this deprivation was working a hardship on more than one.

Well, there's no help for it, she thought. This was going to be the biggest and most dangerous thing that they had ever done, bigger than anything in Texas.

Doña moved restlessly, thankful that the night had grown cooler. Yet her buckskin clothes were constricting, and the air about her too still. The trees hardly moved. A bad omen, she felt.

Tahre approached her, his feet soundless on the dry grass; he was wearing moccasins.

She sat up and greeted him.

"Isse-Loa," he said softly, squatting onto the ground beside her. "I have come to tell you something."

She waited, trying to make out his features in the dimness, but he was almost faceless in the gathering dark. She could only read his voice, and his words had something fateful in the sad sound of them.

"What is it, Tahre?" she asked gently, feeling for the hundredth time the guilt she always felt now in his presence, her remorse for that impulsive act in the hotel room.

"I had meant to keep it until tomorrow," he said, "but I cannot close my eyes this night, with its weighing on me. We all know that tomorrow we must have open eyes, and be wakeful and alert as the buzzard when it dives for its prey."

"What is it you want to tell me?"

"After tomorrow, Isse-Loa, I am going away." His voice sounded far and muffled, as if his throat were closing with pain.

"Going away! But why, Tahre? Why?" she cried out.

"Softly," he cautioned, and he turned his head to listen to the voices of the men. Their talk had not ceased. Tahre went on: "For many reasons, Isse-Loa. First of all, because of the one night I held my happiness in my arms, the night that will not come again. You must know I cannot be with you like this—yet not with you, watching you play with the hearts of other men; men like that poor squaw Hackman. And that other man with the eyes of a wolf, that Campbell."

She was silent, not knowing how to answer.

"And there is an even deeper reason. I had thought I would find my freedom, pursuing the white man's gold, no longer eating the meat of buffalo, and lying on their skins." There was a long, awkward stillness, and then a slight breeze began to stir the branches above them.

"I am glad that the leaves are moving," Tahre said. "I feel death in the stillness of branches."

Doña shivered.

He spoke again: "But the purpose of our old life seems to exist no longer. Once you robbed the Raikes in vengeance, for your mother and father. There was honor in that; I thought I did not care why we did these things. I thought the gold would be enough. It is not. And you are changing, Isse-Loa; you are changing. You are no longer warm and loving; sometimes now you look like a little painted doll fashioned of wood, with eyes that have no light, no purpose. And I think you still belong to Stephen Raike but go on arguing with your own heart."

"That's not true," she answered coldly. "I told you what happened: he turned from me, completely. And you are wrong about my vengeance: at this very moment I remember that the eyes of Stephen Raike were just like those of his father, the eyes of a man who knows nothing of loving, only owning." Her voice was scornful.

"They are all our enemies," she said, "enemies of our people."

"Isse-Loa," he said sadly. "You are no longer of my people."

"Tahre," she protested. His words filled her with unendurable pain. She had never felt so alone, not even in the terrible days in Chicago after Stephen had gone away. "But you are the only family I have," she said, in a childish way, woebegone, aching.

"Stephen Raike is your family, and always was."

"No, no, Tahre."

"Yes. And I must go away, after tomorrow. I cannot go on being your tame Indian." His voice was bitter. She could not see his face at all; full dark had fallen, but now she heard the slight sound of his rising, and his voice, when he broke the silence, came from above her.

"But I love you," he said. "I always will."

"Tahre," she said softly. "Wait."

She reached out her hand, but he was gone.

Doña lay down again on her sleeping bag, thinking of

what he had said; her throat hurt with unshed tears and with the aching of a loneliness too great to bear.

She had never been so lonely, or so afraid. Maybe they were taking on too much, to take on this heavily guarded stage. Doña remembered what Tahre had said about it: "Raike security is so strong they make other shotguns look as harmless as doves."

Would it be enough? she wondered now, tossing in the darkness. Their numbers, their stealth—their marksmanship and speed, that hawklike speed of attack that she had learned so long ago from the Indians?

"You are no longer of our people. Your family is Stephen Raike." Tahre's phrases haunted Doña, and sleep eluded her.

Moist and winded from his long, rough ride, Stephen was overjoyed to see the St. Joseph relay station for Raike Stages. This station was a special one, a neat and comfortable inn on the outskirts of the town.

Stephen trotted right into the stable; the good-natured, dependable horse would have to be seen to first. Stephen dismounted and watched the stablehand unsaddle the animal and rub it down, waiting until it had been examined, watered and fed.

"You've come a long way, sir, but you paced yourself right good. This horse is fine." The stableboy grinned at Stephen, patting the creature on its flank.

"That's good. I'll need a change of horse for tomorrow. Take care of that for me, will you?"

He nodded to the boy and entered the relay inn by the rear, glancing around the kitchen as he walked through to the lobby, his sharp eyes approving its clean, well-organized look. Stephen sometimes liked to take his people by surprise, so they rarely failed him.

But he was tired now and in no mood for the royal welcome the desk clerk gave him. He was civil but short, anxious to get to his room and a bath and meal.

"Mr. Raike!" The clerk, flustered a little by the appearance of the boss of bosses, came after Stephen as he

366

was mounting the stairs. "A letter for you, sir, from Texas."

Texas. Stephen wondered. He hadn't heard from Vard for quite a while. Then he asked the clerk, "Is Cyrus Lang in the station?"

"No, sir, but he'll be here in about an hour."

"Send him up to me, will you?" Stephen continued up the stairs, examining the envelope on his hands. It was postmarked Galveston. Now how in the hell did anyone know he was here?

After he had bathed and eaten, and an attendant had cleaned and brushed his clothes, Stephen sat down and lit a thin cigar. He was ready now for whatever the letter would tell him.

Vard's letter was an answer to his own written a short time before.

I wrote you in Chicago,

Stephen read.

but I'm writing you in St. Joe as well. If I know you, you like to be where there's trouble.

Stephen grinned. For sure nobody knew him like Vard.

Your pa,

the letter continued abruptly,

don't have much time. When you clear up the business there, maybe you want to get back here. He's changed a lot, Steve. It's like he knows what's coming. I sit with him a lot, and sometimes when he's in a fever, he asks for you. And he talks about Hugh Olwen. I think he's sorry now for what he done.

Stephen let the letter fall on his knee, aching with sadness for the lonely old man and his change of heart.

Maybe now, if he got there in time, they could make it right somehow.

He retrieved the letter and read the next lines:

> He even said once he'd like to give the Short Line to the Olwen girl, but I didn't rightly know what to do. He was feverishlike and it didn't seem right to take a man at his word at a time like that. I need you here, boy, to help me. You got an idea of these legal things. I wasn't about to send for a lawyer while you're gone. And I didn't tell him you was married, figured you ought to do that.

The Short Line, for Doña! So his father wanted to make good, at long last. Stephen felt comforted.

In answer to a knock at the door, he rose and opened it for Cyrus Lang, his lead driver on tomorrow's up stage to the West.

"Steve." Lang put out his hard hand, grasping Stephen's.

"Good to see you, Cyrus. Come in. Want a drink?"

"Not tonight. Tomorrow's a big day. I'll sit down, though, get a load off my feet."

Stephen eyed the laconic Lang, impressed as always by his air of command. Lang's leathery face was deeply burned by the sun, with pale squint lines around his clear, observant eyes. There was not a spare ounce of flesh on the man; he looked as neat and hard as a well-worn saddle.

"Wish you'd been around St. Louis." Stephen smiled slightly.

"Well—" Lang drawled. "We'll see that everything goes all right tomorrow. And after that, 'til Frisco," he added with a grin.

"I know the setup, but let's go over it one more time."

"Sure. We've got eight shotguns, instead of six, with your permission."

Stephen whistled. "You don't need my permission. So it's going to be like that. Who are they?"

Lang reeled off the names. Stephen knew the first six.

"Who are Walker and Josephs?" he asked. "Where did they come from?"

"We hired Walker away from Fargo; he's one of the few that never took a loss. And Josephs—" Lang paused, looking a little embarrassed.

"Well?"

"Got a dishonorable from the Army," Lang admitted. "Always fighting. Got the temper of a coyote. But he can pick off a cactus-needle at two hundred yards."

"That's good enough. I don't give a damn about the other."

Lang looked relieved. "We've got the best there are. Anybody comes near that stage tomorrow that's not an old woman in skirts, is dead."

There'll be a young woman in trousers, Stephen thought, his body clammy with cold, quick sweat. The woman I love.

But he said casually to Lang, "That's fine, Cy. You're handling it just right." He rose, indicating that the interview was ended. "It's late. We'd all better get some sleep."

Lang got up, too, replying, "I won't say no to that. See you at seven."

"Seven," Stephen repeated.

When Lang had gone, Stephen knew all at once what he had to do. He had to find her; he didn't know how, but he had to find her tonight and head her off before tomorrow.

The shooting would be too fast to be selective, he thought with a dark, bitter humor. They wouldn't stop to see that one of the bandits was a woman.

A beautiful woman with a body like a deer, and sleepy dark eyes. Stephen's insides roiled with desire and apprehension—the biggest, coldest fear he had ever known in all his life.

Quietly he left his room, ran down the stairs and went through the deserted kitchen and out to the stable.

The stablehand, as Stephen always ordered when he traveled, had tagged one of the stalls with Stephen's name; in it stood his replacement horse. There might have to be another one for tomorrow. "We're going to take a little ride, boy," he said to the beautiful white stallion.

Saddling him, Stephen headed out into the night. One chance in ten thousand that he'd find her, but he had to take it.

Chapter Thirty-Two

The air was cooler, the night sky clear. Stephen thanked the cloudless moon casting its white fire on the empty plains. Without the moon, his chances would lessen.

Looking west, he saw the dark green, sealike expanse of prairie, stretching in swells beyond to the horizon. They couldn't be far off: couldn't risk delay and the tiring of horses. Probably camped in a ravine, or between hills. Stephen knew this country; within a ten-mile radius of Leavenworth and St. Joseph, there were at least three such places.

He took a southerly direction.

"Miz Hamilton!"

Doña woke abruptly from sleep, alert at the sound of her name. She slid with a lithe motion from her sleeping bag, her hand on her holstered Colt. "What is it, Buford?"

"Don't need that," Buford answered, low. "But we got to talk."

Doña saw Tahre and the Kiowa approach, heard the sounds of the others stirring. They were good men, she thought gratefully, awake at the noise of a snapped twig.

"Its all right," she called out softly to Tahre. "Build up the fire."

Tahre squatted to feed the sheltered blaze. By its dim light Doña saw the others coming, hands on holstered hips.

"No sweat, boys," Buford said. "But I got something to tell all of you." He glanced at Doña, licking his lips. "Jack was down to the saloon near Leavenworth." He held up his hand to stem her indignant protest. "Never mind that now, Miz Hamilton. The liquor won't spoil his aim too bad; that's tomorrow. Anyway I followed him down to the saloon and brought him back. They were saying down to the saloon there's going to be eight guns on the stage. Hand-picked men. Fellow by the name of Josephs."

"Ray Josephs!" the man called Holder said. He cursed. "Nobody's better than Josephs, except that stage-boss Raike."

The unexpected sound of his name jolted Doña, but she said calmly, "Go on, Buford."

"Well, this fellow Josephs—got a temper like a snake— was trying to pick a fight, bragging nobody dast touch the stage. Said anybody wasn't an old lady in a dress, comes near, they'd be dead."

"An old lady in a dress," Doña said. Her voice was thoughtful. "Buford, Tahre—Holder. I've got an idea." She spoke to the nearest men. "We've got to scrap the whole plan; we can't do this by daylight. That was for five guns. Now the positions will be wrong. Tahre, bring me the maps and a pencil and paper."

When the Indian had brought her what she asked for, Doña made quick marks on the map and swiftly drew a diagram on the piece of paper.

"All right, everybody, look here." She held the sketch and map nearer to the firelight.

"We'll ride out an hour ahead of them in the morning. We'll take this route. Four of you will be in the wagon. You'll be here." She pointed to the map. "It's a long way to the next relay station." No one questioned her information: her knowledge of Raike routes and methods had always impressed them. "When the stage comes through, it'll stop for the wagon. We'll ride in on them down this hill."

"Why would they stop?" Buford asked, skeptical.

She told them the whole plan, why the stage would stop, what the men in the wagon would be wearing.

"Me?" Holder protested, and there was a grumbling

among the men. "Jesus, Miz Hamilton. Where'd we get anything like that, first off?"

"Tahre and I will get it tonight. There are plenty of farms between here and St. Joe. This is washday. And if that doesn't pan out, there's a house in Leavenworth where money will buy anything." She grinned, and Holder looked embarrassed at her frankness.

"I don't know," he said doubtfully.

"No, I think it'll work," Buford insisted. "It's a lot of money, boys. Ray Josephs let drop there's ten bags of gold with fifty thousand dollars in every damned one of 'em."

"That's better than we figured," one of the others said.

"Ten bags split eleven ways is—"

"Split ten ways," Doña said curtly. She could feel their surprise.

"You're cuttin' yourself out, Miz Hamilton?" It was Hanley, Buford's eighteen-year-old brother.

"Yes, Hanley." She smiled, thinking that if the men took that kind of money from this job, they would always follow her lead, from there on in.

"Are you with me?" she asked, looking around the fire at the circle of faces. She could see them considering the money.

"Yeah," Buford said firmly. "Hanley? Holder?" He called out the others' names and after a slight hesitation, they began to answer Yes.

"Fine," Doña said, "let's give it a try. We'll go over it again now."

Later she said to Tahre, "We'd better get going and get what we need or nothing will work out." He nodded without replying and they went to saddle their horses.

Stephen tethered his stallion about a half-mile away and crept up the side of the hill with the silent grace he had learned from the Comanches. At the summit, he crawled forward on his belly, looking down. Where the moon pierced the branches of the grove, he made out the forms of eight men. One, an Indian dressed like a white man, was sitting guard. Stephen held his breath; he knew

373

the Indian's sharp ears would catch the lightest noise. The man had a rifle on his knees.

Another man lay in heavy sleep; he looked drunk. Two others slept near him, but more lightly. Their bodies were not relaxed. The remaining two sat at a fire, sheltered Indian-style, drinking coffee. Stephen could see from the pile of ashes they had been here for a while.

There was no sign anywhere of Doña or Tahre. Stephen wondered if he'd been wrong; were they not in this, after all? He peered about the grove, and waited a long, tense interval. Still Doña and Tahre did not appear. Stiff and gritty-eyed with exhaustion, Stephen at last crept down the hill and stole away, carrying his boots in his hand. The dawn was coming. He was far from easy in his mind.

The sun was sinking when the Raike up stage rounded the last bend in the river road, its rosy redness shining in the driver's eyes and the eyes of the shotgun at his side. They held up hands to shade their eyes from the glare. Then the shotgun said to the lead driver, "Hold up, Clarence."

Clarence Ware's horny hands pulled at the six-horse lead and he shouted to the animals. The stage drew up. At once seven shotguns in the coach were at the ready; Stephen, riding his stallion behind, walked it forward, drawing his gun.

A wagon was stuck in the mud, half across the road, barring their way. But its four passengers were very unusual: there were three hefty-looking farmwomen, judging by the drabness of their dresses and bonnets. And they were bending over another woman who was half-lying in the wagon, surprisingly dressed in the bright satin and glitter of a bordello girl. The girl was young and slender, the men in the stage could see, although the wagon was several hundred yards ahead.

"Lord, it's only women!" Clarence said with relief.

"I'll go see." Ray Josephs, the lead shotgun, said, and got down from the stage.

Stephen called out, "Be careful, Ray." He didn't trust the look of it. Cynically, he reflected that farmwives seldom came to the aid of fallen women, no matter what the distress. He kept his Colt at the ready, irritated at the bright sun in his eyes.

As Ray Josephs neared the wagon, his rifle lowered casually, one of the farmwomen said in a strangely deep voice, "Lay your rifle in the wagon and don't turn around." Stunned, Ray Josephs saw that the woman had a rough, weatherbeaten face and chin stubble, and she was pointing a Smith & Wesson at his heart. "Smile," the gruff voice said. "Lay down the rifle, turn around and smile at your pals. And you won't die. Now wave at them and ask for two to come and help you with the wagon."

The trigger-happy Josephs, who had never met with such a situation before, found himself obeying. Two other unarmed men came toward them casually from the stage.

The rest of it happened so quickly that the shotguns hardly had time to cock their rifles. They heard the tall woman in the wagon bellow in the voice of a man: "Hold your fire or these men will die!" He and the other "women" in the wagon were now pointing guns at the three men from the stage.

"Hold fire!" Stephen shouted, his eyes darting to the seven riders now surrounding them. One of the masked riders was Doña and another was Tahre. They were covering the shotguns in the stage, but were so frantic with haste they had not seen Stephen, who was behind the great chassis of the coach.

In seconds, the ten heavy bags were thrown out of the stage and had been snatched up and carried away on the saddles of the riders.

At that moment there was a shout and a scuffle in the wagon, and Josephs and his two companions had turned the tables on the dress-clad bandits.

Meanwhile, the other seven had taken off over the hill and were galloping like the wind in four directions. The shotguns in the stage blasted away, but three of the riders, those headed east, slid down from their saddles, riding suspended from one stirrup so their bodies were protected from the guns.

"Lang! Heller, Robinson!" Stephen bellowed. "Unhitch the team and ride west, north and south. We're going to get them. I'll go after those!" He pointed east, already headed over the hill.

By God, Stephen thought with a crazy exultation, it worked out just right. They didn't get her.

And he urged the stallion to heart-bursting speed, as he caught sight of Tahre and the Kiowa, flying like great mounted birds over the vastness of the prairie about a half-mile ahead. They had a pretty good start, but he'd be damned if he'd lose them now.

Or Doña—ever again. And the stallion moved now with such incredible swiftness he wondered that its hoofs touched the plain.

When the distance closed between his white stallion and Tahre's black mare and the Kiowa's paint, Stephen Raike rode in on them with empty hands. Stephen decided he'd take the gamble.

And just as he had thought would happen, he heard Tahre shout to the Kiowa, "Hold fire!"

Stephen came closing in until their mounts were neck and neck; he let go the reins, leaning over to tackle Tahre by the middle, pulling him with a mighty lunge from the saddle, and they both fell to the ground, rolling over and over in a wrestler's hold.

The stunned Kiowa reined in, jumped off his paint and ran toward them. "Stay away!" Tahre bellowed at his cousin hoarsely, his breath nearly failing as he grappled with Stephen.

At last Stephen overpowered him, gasping for breath, holding his arm in a grip hard enough to snap his bones.

"Enough?" Stephen gasped at Tahre. The Kiowa stood by, his eyes protruding with amazement, his lips parted in wonder.

"Enough, Stephen Raike." Tahre's answer came in a wheeze from his spent, convulsive lungs.

"All right, Tahre." Stephen rose, releasing the Indian. "Give me the bags. And tell me where she's gone."

Tahre raised his bruised body from the ground and looked up at Stephen. He managed a wry smile. "You knew I wouldn't shoot you, Stephen Raike."

"Yes, Tahre. Where is she?"

"You'll find her at the Stone Gap on the road to Independence."

"I know where it is. The bags, Tahre." Stephen stared at the Indian, breathing heavily.

Slowly Tahre moved to his horse and began to untie the bags. "Wait," Stephen said. "Four bags are too heavy for my horse. Leave them where they are; I'll take your horse."

Tahre hesitated. "You'll get her back," Stephen promised.

"You have always kept your word." Tahre walked with Stephen to the Kiowa's paint and untied the two bags from the saddle, tying them to the saddle on Stephen's horse.

The Kiowa still stood by silent, transfixed with amazement, looking from one man to the other.

"She will be there until dark," Tahre said. "We had arranged it between us."

"Thank you, Tahre. Now please, get out of here, fast, you and your kinsman. Get out of Missouri."

"I am grateful to you, Stephen. Even if you yourself are the thief."

Stephen stared at him. Then he understood. He had taken Doña, the Indian's greatest treasure.

He held out his hand, and Tahre shook it.

"Maybe we will meet again some day," Stephen said.

"I do not think so, Stephen Raike," Tahre answered sadly. And he turned and walked away toward the paint horse, where his kinsman was waiting.

Stephen gave the winded stallion a brief respite and some water; the exhausted beast was wet and foaming, and Stephen hated to drive him onward, but for now there was no choice. After he saw to the stallion, he tended the Indian's sleek black mare. Then, tying her reins to his pommel, Stephen set off at an easier gallop toward the rocky rise known as Stone Gap, where Doña would be hiding.

Doña's gray was spent by the time she reined in at the foot of Stone Gap, a sharp ravine surrounded by stone elevations full of overhanging rocks that formed small caves. It was a perfect hiding place, and she would climb high, as the Indians always did, to give herself a view of the surrounding country.

She led the faithful gray into a shady place under the overhanging rocks of the ravine. He must have a little rest and water, she decided, before she left him in the shadows for the stiff climb upward.

She leaned against his side as he took the cool, clear water of the stream below the rocks, remembering with gratitude the stream Tahre had described to her on Stone Gap's steep side. She yearned to wash her dusty face and hands. Kneeling down by the horse's head, she scooped the cool water thirstily into her mouth, splashing it over her moist face, rinsing her hands. She would do a more careful job later.

At last she felt restored enough to begin the long, hard climb and, with a soft word to the horse, she grasped a little bush to give herself leverage and started to climb upward, secure in the knowledge that her tan buckskins and matching hat would make her hard to see against the dun, arid earth of the hill where the stubborn scrub pine was clinging.

Stephen sighted Stone Gap, and his heart beat faster. He thought he saw a movement of something up the side of the rise, but it was hard to tell; the dusk had gathered at the foot, although the red sun still shone faintly at the top.

With his knees he told the horse to hurry; the rested stallion took new heart and began to gallop forward.

Doña had barely reached the cavelike rock by the

stream when she heard the hoofbeats of two horses. Relieved, she crawled out of the cavelike shelter expecting to see Tahre and the Kiowa riding back from where they'd hid the gold.

But in the gathering dusk upon the plain, what she saw was a lean white man dressed in dusty gray, riding a snowy stallion; his face was shaded by his broad-brimmed hat, yet Doña knew at once, from the way he sat his horse, who the white man was. Not even Tahre had ridden with such ease and pride. But where was Tahre?

Then she recognized the riderless black mare being led by the man on the stallion.

Dear God, it was Tahre's horse! Stephen Raike had killed Tahre.

Killed Tahre.

As the harsh, desolate words echoed in Doña's exhausted brain, all the old anger and resentment, the old hatred for the name of the man who had murdered her mother and father, swept over Doña in a wide, hot wave. She trembled with grief and anger.

Stephen Raike, the man who had tried to own her, who had bound her to his body through the power of her unwilling desire, had killed Tahre. Killed her childhood's dearest companion, the only link between herself and all that was so dearly lost.

Doña reloaded her Colt with shaking hands.

This time she would make no mistake. He had killed her kinsman, was bearing now the hard-won bags on the horses' saddles, all that she had sweated and ridden for, risked her neck for. Well, he wouldn't take her. This time she would shoot him in the heart.

And Doña lay waiting for him to come.

She saw him disappear into the ravine and waited, calculating how long it would take for him to water the horses and climb up the rise before her. He would emerge in the center of her sights. And that would be the end of Stephen Raike.

Doña recalled with self-contempt the long nights and days she had dreamed of him, wanting him, aching and longing. Well, she didn't need him any longer. Or any man—she had waited too long, worked too hard, for her freedom. And now she was where she wanted to be. At the head of things, independent and respected, good as any man and better than many, at shooting and riding, taking what she wanted, when she wanted it.

But somehow in the silence, as she waited, the brave thoughts could not sustain her. He was taking too long: what was the matter?

Then behind her she heard the slightest sound, a soft footfall, and whirled, aiming the Colt.

He was standing on the other summit, outlined against the sinking sun. And his hands, unlike hers, were empty. She could see only his silhouette against the sunset; he looked big and forbidding for all his leanness, and he stood easily on the dangerous precipice, with that air of arrogance and command that had always half-angered her and yet had drawn her to him as if she were a creature pulled by invisible strings.

"Doña," he called. In spite of herself the sound of his deep voice, after so many months of silence, shook her. But she steeled herself and aimed the Colt at the center of his broad chest.

"Doña," he called out. "You can shoot me if you want—I'm wide enough. You can't miss at this range."

She felt a new annoyance at this aspersion on her skill.

"Shoot me if you want," he repeated, "but I would like one kiss before I go."

"How dare you?" she screamed at him, losing all control. "You killed Tahre! You killed him!"

He was moving down now from the summit, striding toward her without fear. Nearer, he said, "I didn't kill him, Doña. I let them go, Tahre and the Kiowa."

"Let them go?" She was so taken aback that she involuntarily lowered the Colt a trifle.

"I let them go." He was coming closer now, and she could make out his face more clearly.

The time in prison, she saw now, and the intervening months had made him tougher than ever—the fine bones of his handsome face were etched with a new hardness and beauty; his gray eyes were cool as ever, but deep with

380

ant and loneliness and a new wisdom. Her gaze took in the firm lines of his mouth below the thick, light brown mustache, and unbidden she remembered the touch of that mouth upon her mouth and face and body.

A thin hot thread of excitement was drawn, all of a sudden, throughout her veins. But she would not surrender, asking coldly, "Have you come for another bag of gold?"

"You know better than that. I have come for you, Doña."

She was at a loss to answer, and then he came to her, saying, "Throw down the gun, Doña. Throw it down."

Ignoring the lethal instrument she pointed at his heart, Stephen grabbed her by the arms and bent his head to take her mouth. He kissed her with such starving lips, such urgent pressure, that she moaned at his almost-bruising caress.

And then she felt her hand relaxing, felt the Colt fall from her grasp. Her trembling arms raised themselves, of their own volition, and she put them around his hot, hard, sunburned neck, letting her body move close to his, scenting the clean aroma of his powerful body, that smell of sun-warmed pines, that ocean-scent that was so truly his; the odor that had always confounded her half-willing sense and made her helpless at the touch of his hands.

"Doña, Doña," he was saying, his firm hands touching her back, lowering to the narrowness of her soft waist, pulling her closer, closer until it was all warmth again, and melting.

She could remember nothing of her anger, her wildness; the months apart might never have been at all, and Doña was responding to his body's demand, weak and warm and flowing as he kissed her again and again, with a caress that seemed unending and sweeter than anything her life had ever brought her.

Gently at last he released her, and they sat down on the ground together, as Stephen drew her tired head onto his shoulder, sending her wide-brimmed hat tumbling to the scanty grass. And she listened while he spoke of their separation, and his hunger; heard him telling her about Vard Williams' letter.

"You will come with me, Doña." She nodded and he smiled with pleased surprise.

"It is over," she said softly.

"Over? It has only begun." She looked up at him again and saw in his look, his long, intimate knowledge of her and her wild heart.

"No," she said, insisting softly. "It is really over." Astonished, she knew that she meant it with all her heart; she had come to a kind of certainty and peace.

"Then," he said calmly, "after I have taken care of certain matters—" he indicated the bag of gold under the rock—"I will take you to the inn in St. Joseph. We'll go to St. Louis from there, tomorrow. And then we'll go home."

"Home," she repeated with wonder and delight.

"Home to your father's house . . . and mine."

From the ravine below, they heard the whinnying of their horses, which were patiently waiting.

Well, they could wait a little longer, Stephen thought. Once again his arm went around Doña and his mouth found hers. There was no hurry now. Not anymore.

FREE
Fawcett Books Listing

There is Romance, Mystery, Suspense, and Adventure waiting for you inside the Fawcett Books Order Form. And it's yours to browse through and use to get all the books you've been wanting . . . but possibly couldn't find in your bookstore.

This easy-to-use order form is divided into categories and contains over 1500 titles by your favorite authors.

So don't delay—take advantage of this special opportunity to increase your reading pleasure. Just send us your name and address and 35¢ (to help defray postage and handling costs).

FAWCETT BOOKS GROUP
P.O. Box C730, 524 Myrtle Ave., Pratt Station, Brooklyn, N.Y. 11205

Name_____
(please print)

Address_____
City_____State_____Zip_____

Do you know someone who enjoys books? Just give us their names and addresses and we'll send them an order form too!

_____
Name_____
Address_____
City_____State_____Zip_____

Name_____
Address_____
City_____State_____Zip_____